Scandalous Lovers

Belongs
To

Mar Gella
Williams

"Gennie"

Also by Robin Schone

The Lady's Tutor

Awaken, My Love

Gabriel's Woman

The Lover

"A Lady's Pleasure"
in the anthology *Captivated*

"A Man and a Woman"
in the anthology *Fascinated*

ROBIN SCHONE

Scandalous Lovers

BRAVA

KENSINGTON PUBLISHING CORP.

http://www.kensingtonbooks.com

BRAVA BOOKS are published by

Kensington Publishing Corp.
850 Third Avenue
New York, NY 10022

All Kensington titles, imprints and distributed lines are available at special quantity discounts for bulk purchases for sales promotion, premiums, fund-raising, educational or institutional use.

Special book excerpts or customized printings can also be created to fit specific needs. For details, write or phone the office of the Kensington Special Sales Manager: Kensington Publishing Corp., 850 Third Avenue, New York, NY 10022. Attn. Special Sales Department. Phone: 1-800-221-2647.

Brava and the B logo Reg. U.S. Pat. & TM Off.

ISBN-13: 978-1-57566-699-0
ISBN-10: 1-57566-699-5

First Kensington Trade Paperback Printing: February 2007
10 9 8 7 6 5 4 3 2 1

Printed in the United States of America

I dedicate this book to women—all women—and to you men who are strong enough to love us for who we are, and not for what you want us to be.

Acknowledgments

Special thanks goes to Jean Wenger, Foreign and International Law Librarian at the Cook County Law Library. No question I asked was too trivial. She provided invaluable resources to Victorian law in England. Special thanks also goes to Melvyn Harrison of the Crystal Palace Foundation Organization. His love and knowledge of the Crystal Palace—the greatest theme park to have ever been built—is astounding.

I would also like to thank posthumously Mrs. Georgina Weldon, dubbed the "lunacy lawyer in petticoats," who in 1884 challenged the law and won. And of course, the members of the Men and Women's Club (1885–1889), who inspired my own club.

I take full responsibility for any inaccuracies in my portrayal of late Victorian law and lifestyles. I assure you, I worked very hard to paint as true a portrait of the times as I possibly could.

Love and appreciation goes to my husband, Don, whose unflagging encouragement and support kept me going when the going got rough, and to my mother, who gave me the supreme compliment of asking to read the loose-leaf manuscript because, she said, she was desperate to read a good book. Wow. That is high praise, indeed.

I have no words to express my gratitude to all my fans who have patiently—and sometimes, not so patiently!—waited for this book. You have not forgotten me, and that is the greatest gift of all. As for my playmates at Robin's Retreat, my net home . . . hugs and kisses all around! You kept me sane at a very insane time in my life.

Last but not least . . . Nancy, David . . . thank you.

Author's Notes

The Men and Women's Club did indeed exist. It was a London club formed in 1885 and survived four years, finally disbanding in 1889 because, sadly, of sexist hierarchy. The members—consisting of both men and women—met in order to discuss the social, moral, and philosophical issues between the two sexes, as well as lofty topics such as sexual relations in Periclean Athens and the role of Buddhist nuns. The founder of the club married the secretary, which inspired me to create my own "romantic" version of the Men and Women's Club. All of the members in *my* club—while reflecting some of the attitudes of actual, historical members—are strictly fictional.

Long before Disney World came the Crystal Palace in Sydenham, England, located seven miles outside of London. This "illustrated encyclopedia" theme park covered two hundred acres and represented historical as well as contemporary cultures from all over the world through statuary, gardens, artificial lakes, etc. Opened in 1854, the actual Palace unfortunately burned down in 1936. But some of the dinosaurs remain. For more information, please visit the Crystal Palace Foundation at *www.crystalpalacefoundation.org.uk*.

I took a small liberty which I hope you will forgive. Cherries Jubilee was indeed created for Queen Victoria for her Jubilee Anniversary (the Queen loved cherries). However, Frances partakes of this delicious dessert a month prior to the actual Jubilee Anniversary. Hmmm . . . Who knows? Maybe the chef engaged in a little culinary espionage?

I hope you enjoy Frances and James. Out of all the characters I've created, they resonate within me the most. Sometimes, when writing their story, I was completely stunned by their honesty with one another. I think, had they been members of the real Men and Women's Club, that they would have had an impact on each and every member, just as they do in *Scandalous Lovers*.

"Only the united beat of sex and heart together can create ecstasy."
—Anaïs Nin

Chapter
1

He saw through the eyes of a woman.

The five-globe gas chandelier. The twenty-foot-long mahogany table.

The twelve members of the Men and Women's Club.

Doctor. Banker. Publicist. Teacher. Student. Professor. Suffragette. Architect. Philanthropist. Journalist. Accountant. . . .

Unerringly he focused on the barrister who sat at the head of the conference table.

Silver frosted the crisp chestnut hair at his temples; uncompromising lines radiated outward from cold hazel eyes.

The truth forcibly struck him.

During twenty-four years of marriage, his wife had been the perfect hostess and mother. And then she had died.

Alone.

Pinned underneath the wheels of a carriage.

He had not known the woman who bore his name, and who had borne his two children. He had not known her fears, her dreams, her needs.

Staring at the man with the silver-frosted hair and the cold hazel eyes, he realized that *this* was the man she had seen over breakfast each morning: she had seen a stranger. James Whitcox. Husband. Father. Barrister, *Queen's Counsel*.

Recognition erupted into an explosion of sound. The mahogany door slamming into a burgundy-papered wall snapped James back into his own masculine perspective.

The woman whose pale green eyes he had for one infinitesimal moment stared through stood frozen in the doorway, hand extended to recapture the brass doorknob that had escaped it. Her face beneath a round straw hat was gently marked by maturity. Vibrant red hair framed her temples. Her green-checkered velvet coat with matching walking skirt and green silk polonaise were unapologetically feminine.

She was a woman who did not hide from her sexuality. Clearly she did not belong to the Men and Women's Club.

The squeak of a chair sliced through the quiver of vibrating wood. Even as he watched, the mahogany door rebounded off the wall.

She had a small hand. It was covered in a tan, kid-leather glove.

Any second now that hand would grasp the doorknob, and the woman would walk away. A stranger. As his wife had been a stranger. And he would never know. . . .

James snared her gaze. "What does a woman desire?"

The harsh words ricocheted off the gas chandelier.

His voice was not that of the gentleman he had been raised to be: in public; in court; in bed. It was the voice of a man: commanding; demanding.

The chagrin in the woman's eyes blossomed into surprise. At the same time, her gloved hand wrapped around the brass doorknob. "I beg your pardon?"

Her voice was clear, the clip of gentility softened by a faint country dialect.

She wasn't from London.

Her origins were of no consequence. James didn't want a socialite's pardon: he wanted a woman's honesty.

"Does a woman desire the touch of a man?"

His wife had in the past spoken of the latest *on dits*, charitable activities, and of their children. The members of the Men and Women's Club had in past meetings discussed the biology, the history, the philosophy, and the sociology of sex. Not once had they acknowledged the existence of simple human need.

But James did need. Did this woman?

He raked her face with prosecutorial eyes. "Does a woman desire to touch a man?"

Shock stunned the members of the Men and Women's Club—

men and women who had yet to understand the difference between sexology and sexuality.

"Are women repulsed by a man's sex?"

Passing carriage wheels shrilled. The faint blare of a German polka wafted up from the street below.

Inside the burgundy-papered meeting room, the silence was absolute.

"Exactly what is it," James pressed, "that a woman desires from a man?"

Something flickered inside her eyes—something James had never before seen.

"Pray accept our apologies, madam"—masculine censure shuttered her face—"on behalf of Mr. Whitcox. We are in a private meeting, as you see. If I may direct you. . . ."

Immediately her gaze skittered away from James and found Joseph Manning, founder and president of the Men and Women's Club.

She opened her mouth—

To accept the apology on James's behalf, perhaps. Or to ask directions to the room she had all along intended to visit, a museum exhibition where men would not inflict unwanted masculine needs upon her.

"Pray accept *my* apologies, madam," James ruthlessly intercepted, "on behalf of Mr. Manning. He forgets that the purpose of the Men and Women's Club is to discuss sexual relations."

The woman's gaze snapped back to his.

"Doctor Burns"—James indicated the woman who sat to his left with a short thrust of his head—"is a firm believer in Darwin's theory of sexual selection; whereas, Mr. Addimore"—he indicated the accountant who sat to his right—"is more interested in Malthus's thesis for population control. Mrs. Clarring"—he indicated the philanthropist who sat on the right side of the accountant—"is an expert on erotic composition in still-life paintings."

"Mr. Whitcox, this is highly irregular—"

"If you had not interrupted when you had," James ignored the publicist's sharp reprimand; she was a beautiful woman, but her beauty did not touch him, "I would even now be delivering a lecture on English law and divorce. Are you interested in English law and divorce?"

The woman's small, gloved hand clenched. "No, thank you—"

"Are you interested in Mr. Darwin's theory of sexual selection?"

"I'm not familiar with Mr. Darwin's theories." Dark rose tinted her cheeks. "I really must—"

Go.

But James couldn't let her go—not until he knew whether that brief flicker inside her eyes had been a result of feminine need and not the effect of flickering gaslight.

"Are you interested in erotic art?"

He knew her answer before she opened her mouth—the only answer any respectable woman could rightfully claim.

"I have never seen any works of erotic art—"

"Would you like to?"

The woman's head snapped back. Simultaneously, a volley of "Mr. Whitcox!" rang out.

"Miss Palmer." James turned to the thin, anemic teacher who underlined flowery prose in archaic French novels and labeled them erotic metaphors. "Have you ever seen a French postcard?"

Her pinched nostrils turned purple. "Sir!"

James glanced one by one at the men and women who sat stiffly upright, ten in medallion-backed armchairs, the journalist in a lattice-backed wheelchair. He had investigated each member before joining their circle of five bachelors, five spinsters, and one wife whose husband preferred the oblivion of alcohol over the comfort of feminine arms.

"We have discussed sexual symbolism in art"—his gaze slid past the young men in their dark, tailored wool suits that resembled his own, lingered on the young women in their conservative dresses and dark bonnets—"but how many of you ladies have ever seen a painting or photograph whose sole purpose is to arouse and titillate?"

Angry red blotching their faces, the women gazed past James's shoulder . . . or at the notes on English law and divorce neatly stacked by his left hand . . . or at the mahogany table . . . anywhere but into his eyes.

They knew how to respond to a sexless gentleman. They did not know how to respond to a sexual man.

"We are here to discuss sexology, sir," Jane Fredericks curtly rallied; the white feather in her black bonnet pointed to the ceiling like a signpost to heaven, "not pornography."

He studied the twenty-seven-year-old suffragette who idolized Josephine Butler, a clergyman's wife who had successfully campaigned to repeal the Contagious Diseases Acts on the basis that it enabled men to enjoy sex without suffering. Not once in the seven months that James had been a member of the Men and Women's Club had he seen inside her eyes a spark of warmth, of need, of curiosity.

"Have you never wanted to see what it is that excites a man, Miss Fredericks?" he dispassionately queried.

Frigid green eyes stared at the wall behind him. "No."

She believed her lie.

Seven months earlier James, too, would have believed it.

He sought out the woman with the pale green eyes. "What of you, madam? Do you desire to see a French postcard?" James remembered the gold with which he had paid his mistresses, and the jewelry with which he had gifted his wife. Compensations, both, for enduring his touch. "Or do you think that women are naturally repulsed by objects that incite lust in a man?"

Red-gold lashes shadowed her cheeks. She had elegant cheekbones.

Her gaze seared James's left hand. She stared at his wedding band, a badge of respectability.

Marriage had paved the way to political appointments.

What had marriage brought his wife? he wondered. Social position? Daughter of the First Lord of the Treasury, she had possessed a privileged place in society before marrying James.

What had marriage brought to the fashionably dressed woman who now stared at the lie that circled his finger? She shone with the confidence of knowing a man's protection, but did she enjoy satisfying a man's desire?

"I suggest, sir," the woman said finally, calmly; eyelashes slowly rising, her gaze pinned his, "that your wife would best be able to answer your questions."

Straw hat screening her face, she stepped back.

"My wife is dead."

The words ripped through the chill spring air.

She paused, head snapping upward.

James's gaze was waiting for hers. "I will never know which of my touches excited her, or which ones repulsed her. I will never know how I failed her, or even *if* I failed her. I will never know what she needed, because I never asked."

"Why not?"

The rejoinder was swift. The woman's body remained poised for flight.

"Because I was afraid," James said.

Feminine gasps greeted his admission: a man could do or say many things as long as he didn't admit fear.

"I am still afraid."

A masculine protest overrode the feminine gasps. "I say, there—"

James ignored the accountant's objection.

"I am forty-seven years old, and I have never experienced a woman's passion."

"Mr. Whitcox, sir!" the suffragette sputtered over the hiss of the gas chandelier.

"I need to know that it's not too late."

The woman with the vivid red hair remained motionless, her expression arrested.

"I need to know that men and women share the same needs."

A shudder vibrated the wooden table; a door slamming below.

"I need to know that there can be honesty between men and women."

A short, urgent shout sounded from the street outside.

The solitude that dogged his every waking moment stretched out before James. "I need to know that a man and a woman can live in the same house, and lie in the same bed, and be more than two strangers."

Low murmurs bounced around the mahogany table, feminine

whispers recoiling off of masculine rumbles: "I *never*—" "—does he—" "—not himself—" "—grief—"

"Mr. Whitcox, really, sir," Joseph Manning cut through the jumbled voices, "there's no need for this melodrama."

"I am being honest, Mr. Manning," James riposted, every fiber in his body concentrated on the woman who stood on the threshold. "Are you offended by honesty, madam?"

He had no difficulty reading what lurked inside her eyes: uncertainty.

"I try not to be."

"Are you frightened by your sexuality, or is it a man's sexuality that frightens you?"

"Sir, I cannot answer for all women."

"I don't expect you to answer for all women."

He only wanted her to answer for herself, one woman to one man.

"I'm not certain what it is that you're asking," she evaded.

James leaned forward, daring her to be a woman of flesh and blood, and not a paragon of feminine virtue. "I am asking if you want to be touched by a man."

Crackling paper underscored his challenge.

"I am asking if you are repelled by the thought of a man who needs the touch of a woman."

Her pupils dilated, darkness swallowing light.

James did not relent. "I am asking if you lie awake at night aching for the satisfaction that men are told respectable women do not desire."

Desire reverberated inside the room.

Sighing wool slid over squeaking leather. Six women leaned forward, waiting to hear a member of their sex acknowledge what they themselves were afraid to admit.

"I do not indiscriminately desire a man's touch"—the gently accented voice was quiet, resolute; the woman's chin firmed—"but yes, I do desire to be touched."

Emotion squeezed his chest. James recognized it as hope.

"Do you desire to touch a man?" he asked. "To give pleasure, as well as to receive it?"

The wooden table groaned as five men leaned forward to better hear her answer.

She took a deep breath, green-checkered coat rising and falling over her full breasts. "I do not believe that all men want to be given pleasure."

It was not the answer James had expected.

The question she had earlier asked shot out of his mouth: "Why not?"

Memory clouded her face. "If it were so, surely a man would not apologize to a woman when he touches her."

Pain slashed through James. He had apologized to his wife every time he had come to her bed.

He had apologized through his restraint, that he not overwhelm her with his masculinity. He had apologized through his silence, that he not repulse her with labored breathing or an animalistic grunt of completion.

Their sexes had touched, but they themselves had not.

Every release James had gained had been weighted with the knowledge that his wife did not share it. It had been her duty to submit. It had been his duty to procreate. Their duty had made them strangers.

"You are concerned that you did not satisfy your wife," a feminine voice unexpectedly charged.

James focused on pale green eyes instead of the past.

"There is no need for a woman to lie awake at night, aching with need. Women have hands and fingers." She notched her chin, daring him to judge her. "We do not need a man to give us satisfaction. We are quite capable of satisfying ourselves."

A shocked intake of breath shot down his spine.

"You said you wanted to know if women have the same needs as men," she continued, "I believe they do."

A distant Big Ben bonged the half hour.

"I believe there are women who may want more out of marriage than what their husbands are capable of giving to them, just as I believe there are men who may desire more than what their wives are capable of giving. I do not believe either are at fault."

The pain James had earlier felt briefly shone in her eyes. "You said you needed to know if there can be honesty between men and women. I believe we have both just now proven that it is, indeed, possible. Good day, ladies"—she curtly bobbed her head—"gentlemen."

Having opened the door on feminine desire, she now closed it.

"You *are* afraid of your sexuality," he goaded.

The closing door halted; her head snapped upward.

"I am forty-nine years old"—laughter abruptly illuminated her face; the soft skin at the corners of her eyes crinkled—"and have been married for thirty-four of those years. I have five children, and eight grandchildren. I assure you, sir, there has been no time to fear my sexuality."

Nor had she possessed the opportunity to explore it, she did not need to add.

James did not share the laughter she so generously offered.

She had married at the age of fifteen; he would have been thirteen, studying at Eton.

Silver glinted out of the corner of his right eye, a flash of metal spectacles.

Marie Hoppleworth, a perennial student at the age of thirty-six, focused on the enigma that stood in the doorway.

What was it that compelled one woman to speak honestly before twelve strangers, when the members of the Men and Women's Club could not speak honestly among themselves?

"You are not from London," he said shortly.

One second the woman's eyes were alight with laughter; the next second they clouded with wariness. "No."

James had been a barrister too long not to recognize the look in her gaze: she was hiding—but from what?

Deliberately he used the provocative term for the metropolis that lured like a flame both the young and the old, the poor and the wealthy. "Why did you come to the City of Dreadful Delights?"

"I wished to experience a season of entertainment," she said with sudden reserve, "and amusement."

James's voice was pistol sharp. "Without your husband?"

Had she come to London to find a man who would not apologize for touching her?

How could he blame her if she had?

She visibly recoiled. "I am a widow, sir."

A widow who did not dress in mourning black.

His youth had been filled with ambition. Her youth had been filled with children. Did she yearn to experience all the things as a woman of forty-nine that she had not experienced as a girl of fifteen?

Had she heard of the Men and Women's Club, and—as he had seven months earlier—hoped to learn about passion?

"You answered my questions," James said, intently searching her face. "What would you have a man answer?"

Her top lip—slightly fuller than her bottom one—quivered, firmed. "I would like to ask one question, if I may."

No woman had ever shared her sexuality with him, or asked him to share his sexuality with her.

He wanted her to question him. He wanted to be more to a woman than a *stranger*.

"What is it?" James asked softly.

The dusky rose circling her cheeks bridged a short nose, spilled over a rounded chin. "Where is the water closet, please?"

Chapter
2

Frances pushed open the lavatory door.

Stark hazel eyes riveted her gaze.

For one paralyzing second, she couldn't breathe for the yearning that swelled her breasts: the desire to be young; the desire to be beautiful.

The desire to be the woman that this man from the Men and Women's Club so obviously needed.

Following an all too familiar pattern, the door loudly bounced off the wall. She clutched the doorknob in one hand and her reticule in the other.

Biting her lip to stop the cycle from repeating itself—her pardon, his questions—she blurted out, "The tap won't shut off."

Light illuminated his sharp cheekbones. Stepping forward, he held out his umbrella. "Allow me."

Frances hesitated. He was an attractive man. Did he think—because of her honesty—that she flirted with him?

Had he heard her *relieve* herself?

Releasing the doorknob, she gingerly took the umbrella, gloved fingers brushing bare, masculine skin.

Heat penetrated kid leather; it rocketed up her arm.

He did not release the umbrella grip.

Startled, Frances glanced up.

She was seven inches over five feet; she was not used to men who were half a head taller than she. Standing this close, his mouth was only inches away from hers. His top lip was clipped, his bottom lip full—both looked petal soft.

Abruptly she realized that she blocked his entrance; at the same time he released the curved wooden grip.

Frances stepped aside, the umbrella a heavy anchor.

He disappeared through the doorway, only to reappear a second later, his black leather satchel gently swinging back and forth.

Frances involuntarily glanced downward. Tailored black wool trousers hugged long, muscular legs.

"The hot cock has a habit of sticking," he said over the low roar of blood that suddenly pulsed inside her eardrums.

"Yes." Frances jerked her head up. The silk scarf clinging to his wool coat was painfully white. What did a woman say to a stranger after telling him she desired to be touched, but that she did not need a man in order to gain satisfaction? Stiffly she proffered the umbrella. "Thank you."

Nodding politely, she turned away. Too late, she realized she walked in the wrong direction.

Two sets of footsteps clicked hollowly on the wooden floor.

The man followed her. . . . The man caught up with her.

The heat of his body scorched her right side.

Closed doors silently witnessed her dilemma.

Frances stopped. The man beside her also stopped.

She pivoted, bustle swinging. "Mr. Whitcox."

Whitcox echoed down the door-lined hallway.

His voice was as uncompromising as his gaze. "Yes?"

His breath smelled of caramel.

They were only thirty feet away from a staircase. The curator below—*someone* below, or perhaps someone behind one of those closed doors—would surely hear her if the need for help arose. There was absolutely no need for her heart to hammer against her corset as if it were trying to break through the whaleboned inserts.

"Mr. Whitcox." She lowered her voice. "I have already apologized for interrupting your lecture."

"There's no need to apologize," he said indifferently. There was nothing indifferent about his gaze: it was sharp and focused. "I'm not interested in English law and divorce, either."

Her request for directions had incited a spate of nervous laughter. But this man had not laughed.

"Sir, I have answered far more of your questions than a lady should."

The shadow-darkened eyes narrowed. "You *are* offended by honesty."

"Not at all," she quickly denied. And did not know if she lied or not. "It is merely that I have never before told a man that I—" The words *satisfied myself* caught in her throat; she squared her shoulders. "You will forgive me, sir, but I am not used to this degree of honesty."

"Neither am I."

"You, however, are a man," she reasoned.

Men were allowed far more latitude than women.

"Who also has hands and fingers," he replied.

Hot and cold chills raced down her spine.

"You are not alleviating my embarrassment, Mr. Whitcox."

Once again the chiseled face underneath the black silk top hat lit up as if it were equipped with an independent light source. "Then I will share it by admitting that I, too, satisfy myself."

The shock that such an admission should elicit did not come.

He had elegant hands; his fingers were long and tapered. One of which was encircled with a gold band not unlike the one that encircled her own ring finger.

"I am not your wife, sir," she said gently.

Frances had stepped off a train at Victoria Station three weeks earlier, and witnessed her first London miracle: electricity. A glass globe had one moment been lit, and then it had been dark. There had been no warning sputter, no gradual dimming.

She now recognized what it was that had previously lit up this man's face: it had been laughter. And now it was gone, vanishing as quickly as had the electric light inside the Victoria Station.

"Is that why you think I questioned you, because you remind me of my wife?" he asked flatly.

Contrarily—knowing that she was the source of his amusement— she wanted to see his face light up again. "Isn't it?"

"Do I remind you of your husband?"

"No," Frances said truthfully, "you do not."

Her husband would have been shocked to the very core of his being at her confession of self-abuse; whereas, the man before her had not blinked a single eyelash.

"Then, why did you respond to me?"

The scent of caramel overpowered the musty smell of the museum; underneath the tantalizing sweetness was the faint whiff of benzene.

His coat had recently been cleaned.

"Perhaps," she said impulsively, "because where I come from, a man does not ask a woman what it is that she desires."

"Where do you come from?" he unexpectedly asked.

Kerring, Sussex.

Inexperienced though she was, Frances knew that a woman did not give out her whereabouts to a stranger.

"A small village in the southeast," she evaded.

A distant laugh feathered her spine, more vibration than noise.

"And you think that men who live in small, southeasterly villages"—his gaze was too intense, his body too hot—"have different needs than men who live in London?"

"I think," she said, heart tripping, "that there is little land to farm in London."

The men in Frances's life had been gentlemen farmers—her father, her husband, and now her two sons—who stoically bore their pain.

Unlike this man.

"So yes"—she self-consciously tilted her chin—"perhaps men in the country are different from men in the city."

"What do men in your village ask a woman?" he probed.

"They ask for her hand in marriage." A smile washed over Frances in memory of her shy, gentle husband whose needs had been as simple as the land he toiled. "Nothing else is required or expected of them."

"Yet you required more."

"No," she said quietly, emphatically denying any neglect on the part of her husband. "I did not require more."

Muted applause drifted down the hallway.

There were, indeed, people occupying at least one of the rooms that lined the corridor.

"It's your eyes," he said abruptly.

Frances blinked. "I beg your pardon?"

"You have clear eyes, like the eyes of a child." There was nothing clear about his eyes—they were dark and stark. "There's no pretense in them."

It was the closest a man had come to complimenting her eyes—or any other part of her person—in more years than she cared to remember.

She opened her mouth—to thank him, to correct him, *my eyes are pale, not clear*—

"You smell of caramel," she said instead.

Her mouth snapped shut, too late to contain the personal observation.

"Court sessions can be long." His expression was enigmatic. "Caramels help relieve the tedium. It's a habit I've acquired."

The intimate revelation that he sneaked caramels inside court was superseded by dawning realization.

"Only two types of men frequent courtrooms: criminals and their victims," Frances heard herself say, and did not know if she said it in jest or in all seriousness. He had said his wife died. Had he *killed* her? She did not know London or its people. Exactly what kind of men and women joined a club for the express purpose of discussing sexual relations? "Which are you?"

Light illuminated his face. His voice was neutral.

"Barristers are sometimes mistaken for criminals."

Frances had never before met a barrister.

The spurt of pleasure she felt at putting the light back into his face promptly evaporated. While he might be neither a criminal nor a victim, one woman had died. Obviously he felt her loss very much.

"Please accept my condolences."

The darkness inside his eyes swallowed her sympathy.

"Why didn't you require a man to do more than ask for your hand in marriage?"

Why didn't a fifteen-year-old girl have the wisdom of a forty-nine-year-old woman? Why didn't a forty-nine-year-old woman have the body of a fifteen-year-old girl?

"Perhaps one does not require more from others, Mr. Whitcox, until one requires more from oneself."

Shadow engulfed his face. "You said you came to London for entertainment."

"Yes," she replied, gripping her reticule more tightly. *What did this man want from her?* "That is what I said."

"Have you found it entertaining?"

"Yes." Frances did not lie. She had visited dozens of parks and museums and curiosities—there were hundreds more waiting to be explored.

"Did you find the Men and Women's Club entertaining?"

"I found it"—*invigorating, terrifying*—"interesting," she said.

"Then you will find it interesting to join."

A dull thud hollowly rang out; it was followed by another. Footsteps. They were accompanied by a telltale click.

Someone climbed up the wooden stairs—someone who used a cane.

"Mr. Whitcox." Her heart fluttered. "Are you suggesting that I join your club?"

Short, black lashes shielded his eyes. "Yes."

Frances's pupils dilated in shock. "Why?"

He was a sophisticated barrister. She was a simple grandmother. They had nothing whatsoever in common.

"Because you are the only woman I have ever met who has the courage to admit the need for sexual satisfaction."

The shocked faces of five men and six women flitted before Frances's eyes.

"I do not think"—she swallowed, acutely conscious of the heat and moisture that permeated her kid-leather gloves, and the flesh between her thighs that would never be moist again—"that the members of the Men and Women's Club are prepared to engage in the type of honesty that you are proposing."

"*Au contraire.*" Frances recognized the phrase as French, a language with which all educated Londoners larded their speech. "Miss Hoppleworth found your honesty quite stimulating."

Surprise suffused Frances. "Who is Miss Hoppleworth?"

"The secretary."

Frances remembered the thin, dark woman who had worn silver-framed spectacles, and who had clutched a thick silver pen as if it were a lifeline. "How do you know she found my honesty stimulating?"

"She said so."

Frances sucked in air warmed by his breath. "You *discussed* me?"

There was no apology in his eyes. "Yes."

The halting footsteps on the stairs reverberated in her ears.

The thought of being discussed—and found "stimulating"—was both thrilling and dismaying.

"What of . . ." Frances momentarily drew a blank. Citified men did *not* invite countrified women to join private clubs in order to discuss their sexuality. ". . . of Mr. Manning? And the other members?"

"*I* want you." The barrister's dark gaze was impenetrable. "That is all that is necessary."

Her pale face reflected in the black pupils that were only inches away from her own.

No wrinkles marred the reflection. The heaviness of her breasts decried the youthful image.

"I'm from the country, Mr. Whitcox. I did not have a governess, or attend a proper school." Frances had been educated in a one-room school by an underpaid vicar and his overworked wife. Darwin and Malthus's theories had not been a part of their curriculum. She had learned to read, write, and do simple arithmetic—all that a country girl was required to learn in order to manage a comfortable household. "I have nothing to offer the Men and Women's Club."

"Education doesn't matter," he said. Staring up into his dark gaze, she could almost believe him: Frances knew differently. Education separated men and women as surely as did age, wealth and experience. "We none of us learn about passion in school."

Passion.

Regret sliced through Frances, for the youth that was no longer hers, and the pleasure the barrister had denied himself.

"You want to learn about passion from a woman," she said, voice barely above a whisper.

"Yes."

An image of her husband flashed before her eyes.

He had quietly passed away in his sleep, as unobtrusive in death as he had been in life. The heat of his body had slipped through her fingers like dusk into night.

"I had my first child when I was sixteen," she said, suddenly wanting him to understand why she visited his city.

For thirty-four years her laughter and her tears had been generated by the joys and the heartbreaks of her loved ones.

"I can't tell you about passion"—she searched his shadowed face, willing him to comprehend what she herself did not fully fathom—"because I have never experienced it. I know how to be a wife . . . a mother . . . a grandmother . . . but I don't know how to be a woman."

Understanding slashed through his eyes.

"But you *want* to be a woman," he murmured, his breath a dry rasp.

The tone of the halting footsteps altered, traversing a wooden floor instead of wooden stairs.

An inexplicable lump choked Frances.

"Yes," she said. "I want to be a woman."

She wanted to laugh her own laughter. Cry her own tears. Live her own life. Just this once.

"You asked if you reminded me of my wife," he said abruptly, eyes so dark Frances wanted to turn away.

"Yes." But suddenly she didn't want to hear his answer.

Strangers shared polite conversation. What they engaged in was neither polite nor a conversation: they shared the intimate confidences between a man and a woman.

"I was married for twenty-four years."

The cold starkness in his eyes wouldn't let her turn away.

"She died in a carriage accident while I read a brief before the House of Commons."

Approaching footsteps thundered inside Frances's ears.

"I knew she was going shopping, but I didn't know for what," he continued flatly. "I wanted to mourn her, but when I gazed down at her, all I saw was a stranger."

Frances wanted to comfort the barrister, but the words wouldn't come.

"Perhaps she satisfied herself, perhaps she didn't. I will never know. She bore me two children. I thought that was what being a man was all about: taking a wife, giving her children, being a successful provider."

An invisible fist squeezed Frances's heart, anticipating his next words.

"It isn't," he said brutally.

Tears pricked her eyes.

"I thought my ambition was for my family." He stared at the past. "It wasn't."

The bleakness in his voice clogged her throat.

"I thought I was a man."

The corridor closed around them.

"I was a husband; I was a father; I was a barrister—"

Frances didn't want to feel the pain that blossomed inside her chest, or the knowledge that tightened her skin.

"—but I wasn't a man," he concluded.

"But you want to be a man," she said unevenly.

Chapter
3

"Mrs. Hart."

Shock bolted through Frances, hearing her name: it was reflected in the barrister's eyes. Immediately she became aware of the corridor surrounding them, and the privacy that was an illusion.

She whirled around, bustle swinging, heart thumping.

The museum curator—a short, thin man with receding gray hair and a face lined with suffering—leaned on an ebony cane. It had been he who had laboriously climbed the stairs.

"Mr. Whitcox." He nodded pleasantly to the man at Frances's side. His voice was overly loud in the dim corridor. "How do you do, sir, madam."

"Mr. Harmon."

The barrister's voice was coolly composed, as if he had not just rocked the entire foundation of Frances's life.

Had the curator overheard them?

Her entire body had been leaning toward the barrister. What would have happened if he had not interrupted?

Frances forced a smile for the shorter man. "Good day, Mr. Harmon."

The curator was one of the few Londoners whom she was able to acknowledge by name. He was an educated man, yet not once had he patronized her because of her lack of education.

"Mrs. Hart." He frowned up at her. "I hoped I might find you. Pray accept my apologies, madam. I'm afraid Professor Pearson's discourse on prehistoric fossils has been canceled."

There was no leer inside the older man's pain-sharpened eyes. No sneer on his drawn lips. No condemnation in his cultured voice.

"I'm sorry to hear that," Frances managed.

"I will substitute with a lecture on my trip to Rome," the older man said. "I should be honored if you would attend."

"Thank you, but I believe I will have a quiet evening at home."

She felt both hot and cold, like a young girl on the threshold of womanhood.

Desirable. Desiring.

Or perhaps she was merely feeling the effects of the change.

"Of course," the curator returned distractedly. "If you will forgive me, I must see to the setting up of the magic lantern. I have picture slides, you see. Good day, madam. Sir."

"Good day, Mr. Harmon," Frances said. But he was already walking past her, heels clicking on wood, cane a sharper tap.

The barrister's body beside hers burned and throbbed.

"Mrs. Hart."

He now knew her name.

It shouldn't make a difference, but it did. Anonymous women shared their private needs with strangers, not forty-nine-year-old widows who bore the name of *Mrs*. Hart.

"Yes, Mr. Whitcox?" Frances asked stiffly.

Heat permeated her side. Warm breath tickled her ear, her cheek . . .

The barrister stepped in front of her. His white silk scarf glowed in the dim light.

"You are interested in prehistoric fossils."

The curator's footsteps receded.

Click. *Tap.*

No.

"Yes." Frances jerked her head up to meet the barrister's gaze, daring him to ridicule her. "I am."

The barrister silently weighed her words.

She bristled with unwanted sensitivity. "A woman is entitled to interests outside of her family and home."

"Yes," the barrister said softly, "you are."

She could not read his expression underneath the brim of his hat. Was his face filled with understanding? Or pity? Did he think—because she had lost one man—that she craved attention from another?

"I am not flirting with you, sir," Frances swiftly asserted.

She swallowed, too late to take back the words.

"I'm not interested in a flirtation," he returned imperturbably.

A closing door hollowly echoed in the distance.

No, men were not interested in women who were past their prime. They wanted young women, inexperienced women. Women who could give them children, not mothers who had grandchildren.

Frances had understood her husband's simple needs; she did not understand this sophisticated barrister.

Honesty forced her to admit the truth.

Life as he had known it had ended with death. He needed to make a new life.

"I didn't know it was possible for men and women to talk to one another in this manner," she murmured over the pounding of her heart.

Emotion flitted across his face; it was swallowed by dark shadow. "Neither did I."

A pulse inside Frances's left temple pounded a relentless rhythm. Trepidation. *Temptation.*

"Is there a difference between sexology and pornography?" she asked uncertainly.

"Yes."

There was no hesitation in his voice, no doubt in his gaze.

Frances had never before encountered the term sexology, nor had she ever seen an object of pornography. How would she know if—or when—the barrier separating the two was crossed?

A muffled groan of wood scraping wood grated her skin.

Just exactly how honest could a man and a woman be with one another?

"You asked a question," she volunteered, voice ringing in the empty corridor.

"I asked many questions." The dark eyes staring down at her were suddenly guarded. "To which one are you referring?"

The muscles inside her throat tightened. "You asked if I was repelled by the thought of a man who needs the touch of a woman."

"Are you?" he asked coolly.

The hair on the nape of her neck prickled. "No, Mr. Whitcox, I am not."

Frances found nothing repulsive about the man who stood before her.

"And would you like to see a French postcard?" he riposted.

She remembered the utter lack of expression in his eyes when asking Miss Fredericks if she had ever wanted to see what excited a man. She remembered the cold hostility in the younger woman's gaze when she had answered *no*.

Frances remembered his face, oddly vulnerable, when he had asked her if she was repulsed by objects that incited lust in a man.

Noise spilled over into the corridor—masculine guffaws, feminine titters.

Their time together was running out.

"Yes." She gripped her reticule, the heel-taps of approaching bodies pending, the scent of caramel enticing. "I would very much like to see a French postcard."

The barrister's face lit up; there was no laughter in his eyes. "Next Saturday, Mrs. Hart."

A cane nipped Frances's right heel. Stark dark eyes pinned her feet to the floor.

"Two o'clock," he said, words a muted murmur over the cresting cacophony.

An elbow slammed into her side. The whalebone lining her corset did not protect Frances from the painful jab.

She jerked away from the barrister's riveting intensity, and was instantly lost in a pushing, crushing wave of men and women.

Men and women who were young. Men and women who were educated.

Men and women who had yet to experience the uncertainties of middle age.

The conflicting emotions coiling inside her peaked.

He wanted to be a man. She wanted to be a woman.

Why did she resist his invitation?

Frances turned to confront her desires.

Chapter
4

The barrister was nowhere in sight.

One moment Frances was overwhelmed by the cloying scents of perfume and macassar oil; the next moment see stood alone, surrounded by chill, musky air and deepening shadows while an army of shoes—feminine heels sharp, masculine heels more solid—clicked and clattered down wooden stairs.

She wondered which set of tapping heels belonged to the barrister.

Frances licked her lips. For a fleeting moment she tasted caramel. Then the ringing echo of footsteps was swallowed by silence.

Loneliness fisted inside her chest.

She had told the barrister that she found London entertaining. She had not told him she had never before felt as alone as she did in London, surrounded by strangers.

She had not told him that every day she remained in London, she became more of a stranger to herself.

Slowly, steps measured—as if walking on fragile dreams instead of substantial wood—Frances closed the distance that separated her and the protective bar of wood that was the balustrade. It was hard and dry. The leather surrounding her flesh was soft and moist.

With each step . . . with each gliding descent of her hand . . . Frances thought of the barrister and the confidences they had exchanged.

He had been a widower for seven months. Why hadn't he asked how long she had been widowed?

He had admitted that he sought satisfaction from his own hands.

How exactly, she wondered, did a man manipulate his flesh to produce satisfaction?

A tawny head reared over her.

Stepping backward, Frances paused on the marble landing and looked up at a long, orange-blotched neck that tapered into sensitive, triangular-shaped ears.

Prior to her trip to London, she had never imagined that there existed a species of animal that was larger or more exotic-looking than the elephant which annually performed in the Sussex county fair. Yet here stood such an animal, three times taller than she.

Frances felt a sudden affinity with the towering giraffe, dead though it might be. It, too, was a long way from home. Perhaps, even, it had nursed babies and left behind grandbabies to mourn its departure.

She leaned forward to determine the giraffe's sex.

There was no evidence of either male of female genitalia.

Frances's brows snapped together. Surely these majestic animals must breed. The elephant in Sussex, gelded though he was, certainly retained evidence of his gender.

She leaned closer . . .

The hot boring of staring eyes interrupted her examination.

Abruptly recalled to where she was—*inside a public museum*—and to exactly what she was doing—peering underneath the belly of a seventeen-foot-tall giraffe—Frances sprang upright.

A slender man who wore a dark gray wool coat and felt bowler hat pointedly stared up at her . . . first as Frances gracelessly descended the remaining stairs . . . then down at her, as Frances stepped off onto the marble floor.

Her heart fluttered.

He had beautiful eyes. They glittered like blue and purple ice.

His face in-between bristling red-brown side-whiskers was expressionless. The burgundy leather satchel hanging from his right hand was motionless.

Acutely aware of his three-inch advantage and of her thirty pound, some-odd years disadvantage, Frances opened her mouth . . . to say what?

In the country, men and women were comfortable with an animal's sex, even if they weren't comfortable with their own. In the city, men and women referred to a chicken breast as a chicken "bosom" and a leg of lamb as a "limb" of lamb.

There was nothing that she—a country-bred woman—could say which would justify her actions in the eyes of the gentleman—a city-bred man.

Frances shut her mouth and walked away.

Muted murmurs rode the hollow ring of her retreating footsteps. She strode past a dented suit of armor, a chipped Roman sarcophagus, and a peat-blackened prehistoric fossil.

A glass and brass door loomed ahead of her.

A red-haired woman who wore a round straw hat and a green-checkered velvet coat with matching walking skirt materialized inside the thick glass door. Frances stopped, gloved hand outstretched, and stared beyond her reflection.

Men, women and children streamed by the museum, a river of dark bowler hats, feathered bonnets, and whipped hoops. Even as she watched through brass-framed glass, an omnibus covered with advertising bills pulled up to the curb and disgorged more busy Londoners.

No one waved at her in greeting. No one pointed at her in censure. Not one man . . . not one woman . . . not one single child knew her.

There was loneliness in anonymity, but there was also freedom. No one cares about the actions of a middle-aged woman.

She stiffened her spine and squared her shoulders.

The barrister had called London the City of Dreadful Delights.

Frances refused to find one single delight dreadful.

Chapter
5

Mary Bartle.

James knew her age: thirty-one years. James knew her place of birth: Oxford, England. James knew that she—along with twenty-six-year-old Evan Keaton, a chemist—was accused of poisoning her husband.

James didn't know the woman—her dreams, her desires—but he knew the law.

Her life lay not in the hands of justice, but in the hands of two men. The Attorney General would prove her guilty, or James would prove her innocent. Like directors of a theatrical play, they would command the emotions of every man and woman—laborers sitting side by side with the middle class in the gallery overlooking the dock; gentry sitting in the privileged seats to the left of the bench—who attended the trial.

Under cover of a semicircular table, James idly shifted on the hard, wooden bench reserved for counselors, and slid his hand inside the leather satchel that leaned against a spindly leg. Immediately his fingers found a familiar ruche of twisted paper.

The sweet-stuff maker—a man with a sardonic wit who kept a stall outside the courthouse—individually wrapped James's caramels inside unbound Acts of Parliament papers.

An odd pang pierced his chest.

The surprise on the widow Hart's face when he had informed her that he was a barrister had been chased by pleasure. James's profession had throughout the years evoked many responses: delight was not one of them.

He straightened, caramel in hand. And wondered if she had toured the Old Bailey. Built on the site of the old Newgate Prison,

the courthouse was quite a popular tourist attraction. Countless flog-
gings, mutilations, pressings—throwbacks to a time when a recalci-
trant defendant could legally be persuaded to plead guilty—burnings
at the stake, and hangings marked its history.

Unbidden, James remembered the words of a lawyer identified
only as Mr. Jones who, in 1871, wrote in his book *London Characters
and the Humourous Side of London Life*:

> *The Old Bailey, although extremely inconvenient, is beautifully
> compact. You can be detained there between the time of your committal
> and your trial—you can be tried there, sentenced there, condemned-
> celled there, and comfortably hanged and buried there, without having
> to leave the building, except for the purpose of going on to the scaffold.
> Indeed, recent legislation has removed even this exception, and now
> there is no occasion to go outside the four walls of the building at all—
> the thing is done in the paved yard that separates the court-house from
> the prison. It is as though you were tried in the drawing-room, con-
> fined in the scullery, and hanged in the back garden.*

It occurred to James that the last public hanging had taken place
outside Old Bailey. The trial, he recalled, watching the junior barrister who represented Evan Keaton anxiously thumb through a sheaf
of papers, had occurred in the very courtroom where he now sat.
James had been eighteen. His father had successfully prosecuted
one Michael Barrett, a Fenian charged with causing an explosion
at the Clerkenwell Prison in order to liberate two fellow Fenians.
The accused had been hanged on the twenty-sixth of May in
1868.

Calcraft had been the official public hangman of the day. He had
been an old man with a white beard who wore a black skull cap, and
a broadcloth surtout.

The accused, a twenty-seven-year-old Irishman, had insisted he
was innocent even while standing—pale but composed—on the
scaffold with a rope knotted around his neck. Two thousand men,
women and children had booed, jeered and sang "Rule Britannia"
and "Champagne Charlie" as his body dropped.

James's father had believed in the Irishman's innocence. But his job had been to prosecute, not to defend.

His father, James reflected as he lightly fingered the wrapped caramel, had been very good at his job. Almost as good as James.

A dry cough shot through the overcrowded courtroom.

Cursorily reminded that he was keeping the judge waiting, the junior barrister yanked a single page out of the stack of papers he had been rifling through.

"My lord. Before the Court proceeds to arraign the p-prisoners," he stumbled, face a mottled red, voice vibrating with nervousness, "I appear before your lordship in order to make an application on behalf of Mr. . . . that is, on behalf of the . . . the prisoner Keaton. Your lordship is aware of the depositions of the prisoner . . . as are my"—he gulped air, Adam's apple slipping up and out of his starched white shirt collar—"my l-learned friends Mr. Lodoun, the Counsel for the Crown, and, and Mr. Whitcox, the Counsel for Mrs. . . . for the prisoner Mrs. Bartle. For reasons apparent, and of course, k-keeping in mind that I have no intention of complicating and or, or delaying the proceedings today, I make an application on behalf of my client, that the two p-prisoners be tried separately."

Clothing rustled; wooden benches groaned a futile protest at the added burden of restlessly shifting bodies. Neither the laborers, nor the middle class, nor the gentry wanted to hear about applications; they wanted to hear about sex and crime, murder and mayhem.

"I quite understand and anticipate your reasons, Mr. Lockwood," the judge said dryly. Austere face framed by a white wig neatly layered in twenty-three rows of curls, he looked like a beardless pharaoh. "They are evident to anyone who has read the depositions."

James, too, quite understood and anticipated the dismissal of Evan Keaton: Mary Bartle's lover would make a far better witness than an accomplice.

Inside the reporters' box, sticks of charcoal slashed across paper. On the following day, London newspapers would sport many faces from the courtroom theater.

Would the widow Hart read about his role in the Bartle trial?

James wondered. Would the expression on her face be one of pleasure when they next met? Would she understand the fine line between truth and trickery?

Had she been disappointed to find that he had not waited for her?

"My lord," James said with feigned indifference, "I concur with
my learned friend's application for the reasons which your lordship
has anticipated."

Hostile blue eyes captured James's gaze.

He was momentarily arrested.

Jack Lodoun, the Attorney General, a Member of Parliament as
well as the Queen's Counsel, sported a short white periwig—much
like the periwig that James and the junior barrister wore—and reddish-brown Dundreary whiskers.

James had several times stood up against him before the bench.
Never before had the man—three years younger than James—dis-
played anything other than the cool cordiality that befitted a prosecutor of the Crown.

Immediately the Attorney General's gaze slid away from James.
His voice was cold and clipped: "It is unnecessary, my lord, for the
Court to consider the application. After anxious and careful consideration by my learned friends and myself, we resolved that there is
not sufficient evidence to be submitted with which we could ask the
jury to convict, and have already decided to try the prisoners separately. Following his arraignment, we do not propose to offer any evidence against Mr. Keaton."

James dismissed the glimpse of hostility he had witnessed in the
younger man's eyes. Whatever its reason, the anger was now gone.

They both knew there was no room for outside emotion inside a
court of law.

The judge's response was a muted buzz: he would reserve judgment until the case against Mary Bartle was adjudicated.

Out of the corner of his eye, James glanced up at the dock. Mary
Bartle, chalk-white face starkly revealed by the propitious place-
ment of gaslights, stood with her eyes downcast. A black bonnet
covered her hair; a black dress-collar choked her throat.

The sum of her life was crammed into the file that her solicitor had prepared, and which now lay in a small pile on top of the mahogany table before James.

Her marriage to a wealthy grocer had been arranged by a dominating father. No monies had been settled upon her, although the father had certainly prospered through the arrangement. Now the father turned his back on his daughter.

Where would Mary Bartle be now if she had been allowed to choose her own husband? James had never before questioned his value on the marriage mart: he had been young; he had been wealthy. Had his wife, James now wondered, preferred another man's suit?

An unfamiliar voice interrupted his thoughts.

". . . inform your lordship, as to Mr. Keaton, that I am a personal friend of his."

Instantly alert, James's gaze snapped toward the jury box. He focused upon the juror who had spoken.

"That is certainly no disqualification," the judge reprimanded the juror.

"If the Crown expresses no opinion upon the question," the Attorney General intervened, "I will be so bold as to say that Mr. Keaton may certainly be called as a witness. There can be no desire that any personal friend of his should be on the jury. I will, therefore, on behalf of the Crown, ask the gentleman to stand down."

James studied the juror in question. His bewhiskered face was pale; sweat beaded a broad forehead.

Perhaps he was a friend of Evan Keaton, perhaps he was not. One thing was certain: he didn't want to sit in the jurors' box.

What man wanted to think that a woman contemplated and planned the murder of her husband even as he exercised his conjugal rights?

"I have no objections, Your Honor," James said.

"Very well," the judge dourly announced, another actor in the drama that was about to commence. "You may retire, sir."

Clumsily the juror rose to his feet. Another man replaced him in the box.

"How do the prisoners plead?" the judge asked.

He did not have to glance up at Mary Bartle to know what her expression would be: she was frightened.

Tremulously she ascertained: "Not guilty, your lordship."

He did not have to glance up at Evan Keaton's face to know what his expression would be: he was relieved. It would not be he who was *tried in the drawing-room, confined in the scullery,* and quite possibly, *hanged in the back garden.*

Evan Keaton stolidly answered: "Not guilty, your lordship."

James remembered the condemnation that had greeted his questions in the Men and Women's Club. As if he could be affected by their censure when the lives of men and women daily balanced upon his ability to remove himself from the influence of either approval or disapproval.

Yet the forty-nine-year-old widow had affected him.

The jury were sworn.

Her need to be a woman rather than a wife and a mother had affected him.

Sternly the judge reminded the jurors that the accused "have, for trial, put themselves upon the country; which country you, the jurors, are."

Her determination to cultivate interests outside of the narrow boundaries of her family had affected him.

The two prisoners were given in charge on the indictment.

Her complete and total acceptance of his need to experience passion had profoundly affected him.

Sweat crawled like hungry ants down James's scalp underneath his periwig.

The junior barrister, less timorous now that the Attorney General had expressed a lack of interest in prosecuting his client, instructed the jury to say that Evan Keaton—Mary Bartle's lover—was not guilty in the murder of the man who had been her husband.

The foreman of the jury promptly stood up. "We find Mr. Keaton not guilty, sir."

The combined smells of beeswax, macassar oil, perfume, unwashed bodies, and decades-old despair hung over the courtroom like a noxious London fog.

There had been no despair in the widow Hart's scent: she had smelled of sweet vanilla and spicy femininity.

She thought passion was something to be learned.

Seven months ago James would have agreed with her.

Passion, he had thought, was simply another word for experience. The more experienced a woman, the more passionate her coupling.

Sex, James now knew, had little to do with passion.

He had wanted to be satisfied. He had never wanted to satisfy.

"Will your lordship take it upon yourself to discharge Mr. Keaton?" the junior barrister boldly asked, the flush on his face betraying excitement now rather than embarrassment. His youthful enthusiasm swirled through the courtroom like fresh water spilling into the sewer that was the Thames.

James tried to remember when he had become so completely divorced from feeling. Had it been before he had witnessed the public hanging of an innocent man?

"The grand jury are not sitting," the judge assented. "I will discharge Mr. Keaton."

Or had it been after a jury failed to convict a cold-blooded killer because James—knowing full well the accused was guilty—had convinced them that the murderer was innocent?

A swirl of black wool jerked him out of the past.

The junior barrister stuffed a batch of dog-eared papers into a brown leather satchel. Victory shone in his face. It was time for him to walk off stage.

The Attorney General stood, black silk robe swishing.

A wave of anticipation swelled over the courtroom. *Now* the play would begin.

No one loved a love story more than one that ended in murder.

"My lord, and gentlemen of the jury"—the Attorney General methodically proceeded with the opening speech for the Crown; James methodically proceeded to untwist the Acts of Parliament wrapper—"it now becomes my duty to lay before you the facts of this case in support of the indictment you have just heard read, and for which the prisoner at the bar is now arraigned. I will reveal to you that Mrs. Bartle feloniously, willfully, and with malice aforethought, killed and murdered Thomas Edwards Bartle. Lusting for the immoral embraces of a comely young man—for no other reason than to satiate her illicit carnal appetites—she did poison her kind and caring husband whom she had pledged before God to love and to honor. But before I enter upon these facts, I owe you a word of explanation as to the course which has just been taken in reference to Mr. Keaton. . . ."

The unwrapped caramel was warm and soft between James's fingers, like the skin of a loving woman.

Sitting back with his feet firmly planted on the floor to prevent the slick silk of his gown and the smooth wood of the bench from taking their natural course, he popped the sweet, creamy indulgence into his mouth.

The jurors watched the Attorney General. James watched the jurors.

While the members of the Men and Women's Club strove in theory if not practice to equally represent women, the English law made no such pretense: Mary Bartle, one woman, would be judged by twelve men. Men who had already been instructed by the Attorney General to condemn—not her crime—but her sexuality.

The widow Hart had asked if there was a difference between sexology and pornography.

James did not believe that feminine need was a moral weakness. Nor, he suspected, did the Attorney General.

He watched the shadow of emotion play across the jurors' faces. But *they* believed that sexuality in a woman was sinful, those twelve men whose only stature came from within the family hierarchy.

Jurors two, three, five, six, eight, nine, ten and twelve had swallowed whole the Attorney General's impassioned cries of "immoral embraces" and "illicit carnal appetites," and leaned forward in their hunger for more.

The widow Hart had been afraid of joining a society dedicated to discussing sexual relations between men and women.

Rightfully so.

James reflexively crushed the Acts of Parliament wrapper inside his fist.

Sexual honesty in the Men and Women's Club could engender a disparaging remark. Sexual honesty in a court of law would condemn a woman to a fine, imprisonment, or—in the case of Mary Bartle—death by hanging.

Chapter
6

A short, sharp *thunk* of the gavel ricocheted off the mahogany table. "This meeting is called to order."

Frances recognized the speaker from the Saturday before. His black hair and pencil thin mustache were ruthlessly controlled by a liberal application of macassar oil. "You may proceed, Mr. Whitcox."

The barrister did not use macassar oil: his hair shone like gold and bronze sprinkled with silver.

Laughter bubbled up inside her throat.

The need to understand passion had brought him to the club; Frances could claim no more noble reason than the need to relieve herself.

"Ladies and gentlemen, may I introduce to you"—the gas chandelier ominously hissed and popped over the barrister's clipped introduction—"Mrs. Hart."

Twelve pairs of eyes frankly appraised Frances.

The bubble of laughter dissipated.

For every Miss Hoppleworth who had found her honesty refreshing, there were a half dozen who had not.

Frances politely inclined her head. "How do you do."

A pair of startlingly blue-green eyes nodded out of view. In their place Frances stared at a strip of white scalp that neatly divided twin fields of pomaded black hair.

"Mrs. Hart."

Frances's head snapped to her right.

Her gaze was pinned by hazel eyes.

Awareness feathered her skin.

"Allow me to introduce you to the members of the Men and Women's Club." Harsh light illuminated the creases etched above the barrister's sharp cheekbones; Frances had no doubt that her every wrinkle was equally visible. "Miss Marie Hoppleworth."

Warmth welled up inside Frances, meeting the woman who had approved of her honesty; it was dammed by the cool reserve shining through the younger woman's silver-framed glasses.

"How do you do, Mrs. Hart. I am the secretary." Marie Hoppleworth held a silver pen over a leather-bound ledger. "Please state your full name for our records."

Frances's stomach knotted.

She belonged to a quilting committee, but the vicar's wife did not keep a record of members. Nor, she reflected, had the meetings been called to order with a gavel.

Frances gave her name.

A black tear quivered on the tip of the secretary's pen. "Spell your surname, please."

The last of Frances's anonymity slipped away. "H-A-R-T."

Marie Hoppleworth bowed her head, egret feathers a clawed shadow on mahogany wood. The steel nib scraped a black trail across unlined white paper. In Frances's mind's eye she saw a white silk scarf and black wool coat.

. . . *I, too, satisfy myself.*

"Mrs. Hart."

Heat trickling down her neck, Frances's gaze shot toward the barrister.

Briefly he nodded toward the woman to the right of the secretary. "Miss Jane Fredericks."

"I am a suffragette, Mrs. Hart." Hostility glittered in her murky green eyes; glossy brown hair curled riotously underneath a forest green bonnet. "I believe in the emancipation of women."

Frances's heart fluttered. Jane Fredericks could not be much older than Frances's youngest daughter, recently turned twenty-six. Clearly it did not occur to her that a woman who was both a mother and a grandmother might also yearn for emancipation.

"I would not be here, Miss Fredericks," Frances said truthfully, "if I did not believe in a woman's right to pursue happiness."

Instinctively she glanced at the barrister.

Passion was not politics. Did he support a woman's suffrage?

Face enigmatic, he nodded toward the man to the right of Jane Fredericks. "Mr. Louis Stiles."

Frances stared at a line of white scalp that bisected pomaded black hair.

"How do you do, Mrs. Hart." Louis Stiles doodled on paper, gaze focused on a picture Frances could not see. "You were very courageous last Saturday."

Frances smiled with genuine warmth. "Thank you, Mr. Stiles."

Leather crackled, the shifting of a body in a leather-padded chair.

The barrister nodded toward the woman to the right of the doodling young man. "Mrs. Rose Clarring."

The expert on erotic composition in still life art.

"How do you do, Mrs. Hart." The attractive young woman smiled; it did not alleviate the sadness inside her cornflower blue eyes. Gold hair shone under a black round hat. Frances estimated her age to be in her early thirties. "You are new to London, you said. I would enjoy showing you some of our sights. Hyde Park is a favorite of mine."

"Thank you, Mrs. Clarring." Tears pricked Frances's eyes at the unexpected kindness. She wondered if the young woman was also a widow. "I would enjoy that."

"Mr. John Nickols," the barrister introduced.

Black hair and black eyes jumped into focus, the first too long and the second too bleak.

John Nickols was older than Louis Stiles, but younger than the barrister.

"I do not see pity in your eyes, Mrs. Hart," he barked.

The attack momentarily paralyzed Frances. Slowly she inhaled to the count of ten. "Why should I pity you, Mr. Nickols?"

"I'm a cripple," he returned brutally.

Frances's heart constricted, gazing into his black eyes. It was not prejudice that fired his antagonism, she saw, but the expectation of condemnation.

He had known contempt. He had known derision. He had known rejection.

Each one had left an indelible mark upon his soul.

"I believe there are some here, sir, who think of a woman's age as being crippling." Struggling to control the pounding of her heart, she steadily held his gaze. "I am a forty-nine-year-old grandmother; I see no reason why you, a man in his prime, should not also be interested in sexual relations."

Tension fisted inside her chest, waiting for him to rebuke her.

John Nickols's dark, rugged face twisted in an unexpected smile. "*Touché*, Mrs. Hart."

He spoke French; the approval in his eyes did not need interpretation.

A thrill of excitement shot through her.

He was a young man. A handsome man.

Hazel eyes snared her attention. The barrister's sharp, perceptive face did not smile. Holding her gaze, he introduced: "Miss Ardelle Dennison."

"I am the publicist for the London Museum, Mrs. Hart." Frances guessed the young woman's age to be twenty-nine or thirty. She was breathtakingly beautiful; there was nothing beautiful about the sneer on her lips. "It is because of my position that we are allowed use of this boardroom."

"You are very fortunate in your position, Miss Dennison," Frances said sincerely. "Out of all the London sites I have visited, this museum is my favorite."

Ardelle Dennison did not acknowledge the compliment.

The rumbling passage of carriage wheels underscored the blatant snub.

The barrister's voice cut through the discord. "Mr. Joseph Manning."

Frances's fingers tightened around her leather reticule. The gunmetal-gray eyes that captured her gaze were no warmer than those of Ardelle Dennison.

"I pride myself on the quality of our empirical discussions, Mrs. Hart," Joseph Manning said with a curl of his lips. "Men learn through reason, not emotion."

Frances did not know what constituted an empirical discussion, but she knew that he did not expect her to be able to engage in one.

She stared for long seconds at the younger man's smug condescension.

All her life she had been shielded from men who would hurt her. Yet here she was, confronted by just such a man.

"What of women, Mr. Manning?" she asked finally. Quietly.

The smile did not leave his lips. "What of them, Mrs. Hart?"

"You said 'men' learn through reason," she carefully enunciated. "Do not women also learn through reason?"

"Reason is a masculine process," Joseph Manning indulgently explained. "In my experience, there are very few women capable of empirical thought."

"Yet, Mr. Manning, you are a member of a club that is comprised of both men and women."

The smile slowly slid off his face.

Emotion coiled inside the meeting room: discomfort, anger, and something else—

Frances turned her head.

Approval gleamed inside Marie Hoppleworth's silver-framed eyes.

The barrister's introduction broke over the secretary's favor: "Mr. Thomas Pierce."

The young man had wavy blond hair, baby-blue eyes, round cheeks, and could not be more than thirty years of age.

Frances bit back a smile: he looked like a cherub.

"I do not approve of shopping dolls, Mrs. Hart."

For one charged second she was rendered speechless.

The impulse to walk away from his contempt overcame her. The need to be more than a mother and a grandmother held her back.

"I am not familiar with the term 'shopping doll,' Mr. Pierce," Frances said courteously. "Forgive me, but my three daughters were not much interested in playing with such things."

Bright red suffused Thomas Pierce's cheeks. "A shopping doll, Mrs. Hart, is a girl who frivols away her money and her time on shopping for clothes and gewgaws."

His gaze contemptuously underscored Frances's emerald green velvet walking dress, and the peacock feather that wound around the crown of her straw hat.

"Thank you, Mr. Pierce." Frances held on to her hurt. "It has been quite some time since I was referred to as a 'girl.' I will take that as a compliment to my hairdresser and my seamstress, since I am obviously well past the age of girlhood."

Outside the window, a passing vendor hawked his wares, an unintelligible jangle of vowels.

"I am Miss Esther Palmer," a thin woman claimed; purple tinted her nose. "I teach mathematics at an academy where we instruct our girls to behave with decorum."

Implying, Frances deducted, that *she* was not behaving with decorum.

Esther Palmer was the fifth member to disapprove of her—only two more introductions remained.

"I taught my daughters decorum, Miss Palmer"—Frances's hands were clammy; she fisted her fingers to prevent herself from drying them on her skirt—"and sent them to school to learn mathematics."

A distant bong announced the quarter hour. Or perhaps it was the half hour that Big Ben announced.

Just how long did these meetings last?

"Quite right, Mrs. Hart."

Frances glanced at the gentleman to the right of the mathematics teacher.

Side-whiskers framed his long, gaunt face; a lock of reddish-brown hair unsuccessfully camouflaged a patch of pink scalp. He bowed his head. "George Addimore at your service, ma'am."

Relief swept through Frances at his courtesy.

His name struck a chord of familiarity. She racked her thoughts, remembering the barrister's voice, remembering . . . *Mr. Addimore espouses Malthus's thesis for population control.*

"How do you do, sir." Frances respectfully returned his civility. "I am not familiar with Mr. Malthus's theories. How does he propose to control our population?"

Gray eyes slanted away from hers. "Prophylactics, Mrs. Hart."

Another new word.

She took a deep breath. "What are prophylactics, Mr. Addimore?"

George Addimore's long, bony face turned a bright red. The color exactly matched the red that glinted in his bristly side-whiskers.

"He is speaking of preventive checks, Mrs. Hart," Marie Hopple-worth offered.

Frances glanced at the secretary. Her narrow cheeks were speckled with crimson.

The young woman did not expound.

"A prophylactic, Mrs. Hart"—the barrister captured Frances's gaze—"is a device that men . . . or women . . . use to prevent conception."

A shrill whistle penetrated brick and glass, the warning of a bobby.

"I have heard that nursing is beneficial in preventing conception, but I—" She could not continue; her mouth was too dry. Involuntarily she licked her lips to moisten them. "But I am not familiar with any . . . devices . . . that do so."

"There are machines," he said enigmatically.

Prophylactics. Preventive checks. Devices. *Machines?*

"I hope these machines are not equipped with cogs and wheels," Frances said dryly.

A strangled cough rang out. John Nickols's shoulders bowed forward.

"The machine in question is a thin sheath of rubber." The barrister's explanation snared Frances's attention. She wasn't fooled by his neutral voice: his face glowed with laughter. "What is vulgarly called a condom."

"This condom—" Frances tasted the word; it sounded far more pleasant than machine. "Where does it fit?"

The amusement lighting up the barrister's eyes abruptly died. "Over a man's penis."

Before her marriage, when investigating her parents' attic one rainy day, Frances had found a three-volume set of books bearing the weighty title of *Encyclopedia Britannica, or, A Dictionary of Arts and Sciences.* The first volume, dated 1768, had contained a one-hundred-and-sixty-five-page lesson in human anatomy.

Staring at the barrister, she felt the same excitement now that she had felt at fifteen when staring at the illustration of a man's penis.

"There is a rubber cap that fits inside a woman."

Determinedly latching on to the idea of a rubber cap—and not the mental image of a rubber sheath sliding over the barrister's penis—Frances searched for the woman who had spoken.

"Mrs. Hart"—deliberately the barrister drew Frances's attention back to him—"may I introduce Dr. Sarah Burns."

Frances had never before met a woman physician.

The doctor's greeting was coolly polite: it did not encourage questions. "Mrs. Hart."

Heart drumming inside her ears, Frances wondered what she should next say or do.

Or perhaps she had already said and done quite enough.

A black blur of motion caught her gaze. The barrister leaned down—his wool coat outlined surprisingly well-muscled shoulders—and straightened back up. He gripped what looked to be a stack of postcards in his long, elegant fingers.

Anticipation shot up between her thighs.

"Instead of lecturing on English law and divorce—" The barrister looked directly at Frances; he spoke at large, one card raised. "I took the liberty of bringing French postcards to stimulate a discussion."

"Mr. Whitcox"—condemnation radiated in Joseph Manning's voice—"we decided last Saturday that such things are not fit for a woman's viewing."

"Surely, Mr. Manning, it is up to we women to judge what is suitable for our viewing, and what is not." Tension banding her chest, she extended her hand; she would not allow the barrister to be blamed for an action for which she was responsible. "I would enjoy seeing the postcards, Mr. Whitcox."

The barrister's lips unexpectedly hitched upward. "Bravo, Mrs. Hart."

Frances stared.

He smiled.

He had not smiled the week before. The smile transformed an austere barrister into a seductive man.

She tore her gaze away from the barrister and glanced down at the sepia-tinted picture he had deposited between her fingers.

Her gaze widened.

Chapter
7

A dark-haired woman stared up from the French postcard. All she wore was a flirtatious smile.

Frances had never before seen what she now saw.

Sitting back in a wing-backed chair with outspread legs hooked over its thickly padded arms, there was no charm that the naked woman did not display. Breasts . . . navel . . . Frances skimmed over the dark vee of hair at the base of her stomach, and froze.

The woman held her sex open with slender fingers.

The one-hundred-and-sixty-five-page anatomy lesson had described female genitalia, but it had not included even the most sketchy of illustrations.

Frances fixedly stared at a small, tiny bud that protruded from soft, fleshy lips.

Recognition surged through her—a blast of heat that dove straight down to her toes—upon seeing what in the past she had only touched.

The bud looked soft; it wasn't. The woman's clitoris was hard—as hard as Frances's clitoris.

It throbbed.

A muffled shout drifted up through the window.

She felt the weight of twelve pairs of eyes. Appraising. Judging. Calculating the effect of erotic art on a forty-nine-year-old grandmother.

Quickly she glanced up.

Over his drawing pad, Louis Stiles avidly studied her.

Her gaze caught his. Immediately his pale skin flamed as hotly as her own.

"I would like to see the postcard, Mrs. Hart." Out of the corner of her eye, Frances saw Marie Hoppleworth's ink-stained hand determinedly reach across the table. Directly in front of her, Louis Stiles's electrifying blue-green gaze darted away. "If you are finished with it, that is."

"I am—" Frances cleared her throat; had the doodling young man noticed her involuntary arousal? "I am quite finished with it, thank you."

Purposefully avoiding the barrister's gaze, she gratefully surrendered the postcard to the secretary.

Hard, hot, masculine fingers scraped hers.

Squeezing her thighs together to offset any more unexpected thrills of sensation, Frances glanced down.

Only to be riveted by the sight of the barrister.

His fingers were longer than her own. Stronger. Tendons lightly veined the back of his hand. Surprisingly dark hair peeped out from under the stiff white cuff that hugged his wrist.

It took Frances several seconds to comprehend what it was that she saw in the postcard he offered.

A woman knelt on hands and knees, cotton drawers draped back over plump, sepia-tinted buttocks. Another woman—hardly more than a girl, really—knelt upright on the wooden floor, small round breasts nubbed, raised hand ascending . . . or descending.

Shock rocketed through Frances. "You find a woman punishing another woman titillating?"

Hazel eyes gauged her response. "I find the mental imagery of a woman spanking another woman's bare buttocks titillating, yes."

Bare buttocks resonated in her ears.

"If you are finished, Mrs. Hart," Dr. Burns interrupted.

The physician's square face was flushed with more than embarrassment: she was excited at the thought of a woman spanking a woman. Or perhaps it was the thought of a man spanking a woman that excited her.

Or perhaps—Frances's breath came more rapidly at the jolt of insight—it was the thought of spanking a man which excited the doctor.

"I'll have a look at your postcard, Miss Hoppleworth," nervously piped in a woman at the opposite end of the mahogany table.

Rose Clarring extended a pale, slender hand; her face under her black bonnet was flushed with anticipation.

Frances stared in surprise at the three women who a week earlier had not been able to look the barrister in the eyes when asked if they would like to view erotic art, but who now openly exchanged his French postcards.

There was no condemnation pruning their faces when they gazed at the pictures.

The barrister caught Frances's gaze. In his eyes was a question: was *she* repulsed by what she had seen?

Shocked, yes. Surprised, undoubtedly. But repulsed?

She held out her hand for the third postcard.

A dark-haired woman offered a sepia-tinted breast, as if to feed a hungry infant.

Frances had nursed five children. Her breasts were full and heavy.

As were the breasts of the woman in the postcard.

She stared in unwitting fascination at the woman's dark nipple.

It was hard and swollen. Ripe for a baby's mouth.

Or the mouth of a man.

Her vagina clenched.

"Miss Hoppleworth." Hurriedly she passed the postcard across the table to the secretary, arm reaching, corset cupping, breast lifting.

A shy glint of conspiracy shone in Marie Hoppleworth's eyes: sexual curiosity had breached the double barrier of age and education.

Painfully aware of the two women and six men who watched—as if she were a potentially dangerous animal—Frances accepted a fourth postcard.

A woman sprawled on a cushioned bed, shapely legs widely splayed; a long, thick object shadowed her right thigh.

"What"—ignoring the heat that scorched her face, Frances notched her chin toward the man who sat to her right—"is it that the woman is holding?"

Faint color tinted the barrister's sharp cheekbones. "A widow's comforter."

Realization speared through Frances: *she* was a widow.

"And what does this"—she forced herself to hold the barrister's gaze—"this *widow's* comforter do?"

"It fills a woman," he said bluntly, "in the same manner that a man fills her."

A distant peal rang out, the chime of a church bell.

Frances irresistibly glanced down at the postcard.

The long, thick object shadowing the woman's thigh was suddenly, glaringly obvious: it was fashioned in the likeness of a man's penis.

It was far, far larger than the illustrated member in the encyclopedia.

Longer. Thicker.

It was poised to enter a slash of pouting lips and gaping darkness.

The longing to fill her empty body was a sudden, physical ache.

Quickly she thrust the postcard toward the secretary. The barrister promptly filled her empty fingers.

The fifth postcard presented two women, one with elegantly coifed dark hair, and one with flowing blond hair. The dark-haired woman's face was buried between plump thighs, obviously kissing the blond-haired woman's genitals. The blond-haired woman's head was thrown back in ecstasy. Clearly she enjoyed having her genitals kissed.

Electric heat licked Frances's clitoris at the visions that raced before her eyes. Images of a gold-and-bronze-haired man buried between a woman's thighs. Images of a gold-and-bronze-haired man kissing a woman's exposed sex.

The pleasure derived from such a kiss, she realized with an odd lurch, would not be dependent upon a woman's ability to produce moisture.

Her head snapped up. The barrister watched her every reaction, waiting for . . . what?

Silently he extended a sixth postcard . . . a seventh . . . an eighth . . . a ninth . . . a tenth . . .

Frances stared up in expectation of the eleventh postcard.

The barrister's long, elegant fingers were empty.

Seven heads shadowed the mahogany table: three masculine, four feminine. They perused woman in all her glory. Thin. Plump.

Small breasted. Large breasted. With narrow hips. With ample hips. Each one unashamedly exposing her naked body, confident in her sexuality.

The barrister had said the purpose of the cards was to stimulate a discussion. If Frances did not do something, *now*, this second, she would burst from the heat that throbbed and pulsated inside her.

"There are no men in the postcards," she volunteered. "Why not?"

"Because, Mrs. Hart"—hazel eyes snagged her gaze—"the sight of men does not titillate me."

But the sight of naked women did. Women who offered their breasts and their buttocks. Women who stuffed themselves with widow's comforters.

"So these . . . postcards"—desperately Frances searched for words to form a coherent sentence—"are manufactured purely for a man's titillation."

"Yes," he said.

One by one the postcards made their way back to the barrister, passing from masculine hand to feminine hand to masculine hand.

"But surely"—she would *not* glance away from him—"if men and women are to share these postcards, would it not be best if they were created to titillate both sexes?"

Green and gold flecks glittered inside his hazel eyes. "Would you enjoy gazing at French postcards with a man, Mrs. Hart?"

Yes.

"I would think—" She floundered. "Would you not gain more enjoyment by viewing them with a woman, Mr. Whitcox?"

"French postcards are not meant to be viewed with women, Mrs. Hart."

The dry, masculine observation grated Frances's nerves. Gratefully she turned toward the man in the wheelchair. "But surely a man would—"

"Men purchase these as an aid to masturbation." Grim amusement tinged John Nickols's rugged face; he held up the postcard of the woman who offered her sex in blatant invitation. "If a woman were present, these would not be necessary to fire our imagination."

There was too much pain in his black eyes. There was too much need in the barrister's hazel eyes.

"I believe," the secretary offered, "Mrs. Hart is suggesting that women, given the opportunity, would also gain enjoyment from viewing French postcards."

"Do you enjoy staring at naked women, Miss Hoppleworth?" Joseph Manning asked cuttingly.

"Not particularly, Mr. Manning, although I certainly found the sight educational," Marie Hoppleworth returned. "However, I would be interested in viewing postcards of naked men. We women occasionally need our imaginations fired, too."

Joseph Manning's handsome, mustached face turned scarlet.

"Pornography is the root of prostitution!" Jane Fredericks burst out.

Frances realized it was not the discussion of French postcards that instigated the young woman's outburst.

"The women who are forced onto the streets, Miss Fredericks," John Nickols retorted acidly, "cannot afford the luxury of pornography. You must look elsewhere for blame."

Jane Fredericks's eyes blazed with anger. "If men did not produce pornography—"

"Prostitution is not the issue here, Miss Fredericks," Marie Hoppleworth firmly interrupted, silver-framed glasses glinting in the too-bright gaslight. "Last week Mr. Whitcox asked if women experience desire. We would not be here, ladies, if we did not. Why do we deny it? Mrs. Hart does not. What are we afraid of, that she is not?"

Frances's heart lodged in her throat, hearing her name offered as if a model by which other women should pattern themselves.

"If we should feel desire, Miss Hoppleworth," Ardelle Dennison retorted; her amber gaze settled on Frances, "we would admit it. But we are guided by a higher moral ground. Education frees women from the shackles of lust. *We* are not animals."

The publicist addressed Frances by all but name.

"Oddly enough, Miss Dennison—" Frances heard her voice over the toll of Big Ben: one bong . . . two bongs . . . three bongs. Impossibly, the meeting had been going on for an hour. "Where I come from, it is believed that *educated* men and women are more likely to engage in acts of moral impropriety."

Ardelle Dennison's lips thinned into a hard, unlovely line.

Frances captured a murky green gaze. "You said pornography is the cause of prostitution."

Jane Fredericks's chin mutinously notched higher.

"In my village, Miss Fredericks, *you* would be said to promote promiscuity, because in my village it is not uncommon for men and women to stand on opposite sides of a dance floor, and converse with members of their own sex rather than dance with a member of the opposite sex. They would not understand how a woman such as you could belong to a club such as this, and still call yourself respectable."

"Is that why you wish to become a member of the Men and Women's Club, Mrs. Hart?" Thomas Pierce's sarcasm sliced through Frances's composure. "So that you may engage in acts of 'moral impropriety?'"

"In three months' time, I will turn fifty." Frances stared down the mahogany table at the man with the baby-blue eyes and cherubic cheeks. There was nothing angelic about his expression. "I assure you, sir, even if I were desirous of engaging in acts of moral impropriety, my body is long past the age to do so."

"Yet, Mrs. Hart"—Joseph Manning deliberately mocked her—"you are here. Why is that?"

Why, indeed?

"You think that I am a 'shopping doll.'"

"Yes." He did not lie. "I do."

"Because I enjoy wearing pretty frocks."

"Clothing does not enrich the mind."

"Yet, Mr. Manning, you are dressed very handsomely."

The bright crimson staining his face crawled down his neck. "The money I spend on my wardrobe is mine to spend, Mrs. Hart."

"I see." And indeed Frances did. "Are you married?"

"I have not found a woman worthy of marriage."

"Why is that, sir?"

Joseph Manning frowned at her presumption.

"Is it because you have not found a woman who is your intellectual equal?" she asked. "Or is it because a servant comes more cheaply than a wife?"

A gasp rifled through the meeting room.

"Servants provide a noble service," Joseph Manning bit out.

"But servants have little time to enrich their minds," Frances said, heart pumping, "because they are too busy taking care of their employers. Whereas a wife takes care of her family and home. She puts the needs of everyone else above her own. If a man's servant is ill, it is his wife who carries out the servant's duties. If a man's child cries, it is his wife who soothes away the child's pain. If a man's property is in need of repair, it is his wife who oversees the repair so that he will not be inconvenienced."

Joseph Manning opened his mouth.

To challenge her. To correct her.

"Surely, Mr. Manning—" Frances did not allow him the opportunity to speak. She would *not* be made to feel unworthy. "A woman is entitled to the same monetary recompense that a servant receives. If she spends what spare time may come her way on shopping rather than enriching her mind—*surely*, sir—that is her prerogative, and of no one's concern but her own. Don't you think?"

Chapter 8

"Mr. President." Marie Hoppleworth's voice rang out over the hiss and pop of flaming gaslight, and the relentless grind of carriage wheels. "Last week we promised Mr. Whitcox an interview. I move that we now vote to accept Mrs. Frances Hart into the society of the Men and Women's Club."

The barrister met Frances's shocked gaze. There was no remorse in his eyes.

He had asked if she would be *interested* in joining the Men and Women's Club. He had never once guaranteed her membership. It was Frances—fresh from the country—who had assumed that all she need do to become a member of this sophisticated club was to attend the next meeting.

"It has been so moved." Joseph Manning's voice was cold and clipped. "Do I hear a second to the motion?"

"I second the motion," the barrister said.

"Discussion on the motion," Joseph Manning said flatly.

The barrister did not take his gaze off of Frances. "I call for the question."

John Nickols's, "I second the question," tumbled through the air.

"The question is called." Frances's gaze snapped toward Joseph Manning. "I move to vote on the acceptance of Mrs. Frances Hart into the Men and Women's Club."

"All those in favor," Marie Hoppleworth briskly instructed, silver-framed glasses glinting, "say aye. Mr. Whitcox?"

"Aye."

The sharp nib of the secretary's silver pen scratched a trail of black ink across white vellum.

Frances's fingers dug into ungiving wood.

She was being publicly judged, and there was nothing she could do to stop it.

"Dr. Burns?" the secretary briskly asked.

The doctor's square face was set. "Aye."

"Mr. Addimore?"

Bright red etched protruding cheekbones, glistened through bristling side-whiskers. "Aye."

"Miss Palmer?"

Purple splotched Esther Palmer's thin, high-bridged nose. "Aye."

"Mr. Pierce?"

Wary speculation darkened the baby-blue eyes. "Aye."

"Mr. Manning?"

Emotion battled with reason in Joseph Manning's gaze. "Aye."

"Miss Dennison?"

The beautiful, amber-eyed publicist glanced toward Joseph Manning; he nodded once, curtly, oiled hair and mustache glinting black.

"Aye," she said.

"Mr. Nickols?"

The man in the wheelchair did not hesitate, black eyes gleaming. "Aye."

"Mrs. Clarring?"

Shadow darkened the woman's cornflower-blue eyes. "Aye."

"Mr. Stiles?"

"Aye."

"Miss Fredericks?"

Murky green eyes sulkily stared at Frances. "Aye."

"Let the records show that on this day, Saturday, the sixteenth of April, 1887, that by unanimous vote"—the scratch of a pen filled the pause in Marie Hoppleworth's speech—"Mrs. Frances Hart is hereby appointed a member of the Men and Women's Club."

Frances could not breathe.

Six men and six women had unanimously voted her into their club.

Despite her age. Despite her lack of education.

Adjusting her glasses with an ink-stained finger, the secretary glanced up. "The Men and Women's Club was established to discuss relations between men and women. However, I am certain you will all agree that before today, we have never obtained that goal. Mrs. Hart—and Mr. Whitcox—have given us a language in which men and women may talk about sexuality."

Sharp sensation stabbed through Frances's chest, hearing her name coupled with that of the barrister.

"That language, ladies and gentleman, is desire." The secretary's gaze lit from member to member. "Mr. Whitcox posed the question as to whether we women are repulsed by articles which incite a man's lust. I pose this question: are you men repulsed by articles which incite a woman's lust?"

There was no repulsion in the hazel eyes that caught her gaze.

"Mr. Whitcox was kind enough to bring French postcards for our enlightenment." Marie Hoppleworth's voice was decisive. "I suggest that we equally share this responsibility. I suggest that in future meetings we each bring items that will further stimulate discussion."

Consternation rippled the air.

Men had access to erotic articles; women did not. Men could openly purchase postcards and widow's comforters.

Could women?

"I do not . . . that is," Rose Clarring hesitantly spoke up, "I do not know of any shops that sell items which would stimulate a woman's . . . interest."

"The shops that sell these pornographic materials are not safe for respectable women to visit," Joseph Manning stiffly intervened.

"Many respectable bookstores sell erotic paraphernalia, Mr. Manning," John Nickols returned ironically. "As you are no doubt aware."

Crimson crawled down Joseph Manning's neck.

Frances realized that this man who so vehemently objected to pornography in public enjoyed it in private.

"There are items which can be purchased at a chemist," Sarah Burns offered. Her square face flushed, darkly defiant. "Machines are surely of interest to women."

"Doctor Burns!" A latent Scottish accent burred George Addimore's voice. "You leave us men no modesty. Why not have us unbutton our trousers for the ladies' enlightenment?"

Frances glanced at the mahogany table which hid George Addimore's trousers from view.

She had cared for her father, her husband, and her two sons. She had seen a man when he was ill. She had never before seen a man when he was in good health.

But she wanted to, Frances realized.

"I will bring a machine," Jane Fredericks offered defensively.

"Mrs. Butler does not approve of machines, Miss Fredericks," John Nickols mocked. "They entice immoral men to sin with moral women."

"Perhaps Mrs. Butler is occasionally overzealous in her campaigning, Mr. Nickols," Jane Fredericks stiffly acknowledged, "but at least she is trying to improve the lives of women."

"I do not see that illegitimate children and disease improve our lives, Miss Fredericks," Marie Hoppleworth retorted. "You have repeatedly spoken against the Malthusian league and the literature they distribute. Why are you now volunteering to bring in a device which you have in the past condemned?"

"I am volunteering, Miss Hoppleworth," Jane Fredericks retorted, too-young face flushing with anger, "because my father would not have infected my mother with a disease if he had taken the time and money to invest in one."

Silence greeted the suffragette's confession.

Frances's stomach lurched in understanding: Jane Fredericks bore the anger of a mother who had been infected by a sexual disease, and the guilt of a father who had infected an innocent woman.

What other secrets did the members of the Men and Women's Club hide?

"What will you bring, Mrs. Hart?" Esther Palmer asked.

"I'm not certain." Frances licked her lips, tongue a hot, slick rasp. "Perhaps Mr. Nickols will be so kind as to suggest the name of a reputable bookstore where I might find postcards more inducive to inciting a woman's"—*lust*—"interest."

"I, too, would enjoy visiting such a bookstore, Mrs. Hart," Marie Hoppleworth said, voice unnaturally loud. "Perhaps Mr. Nickols will be kind enough to accompany us."

Dark red rouged John Nickols's olive-tinted skin. "I would be honored, Miss Hoppleworth."

"I would be interested in visiting this bookstore," Rose Clarring piped in.

There was no sadness in her eyes, only a grim determination.

"We are the Men and Women's Club." Thomas Pierce's voice was a jarring intrusion. "I suggest we all visit this appointed bookstore, and that we each bring to the next meeting an object which stimulates our interest."

"Don't be absurd, Mr. Pierce." Joseph Manning's gray eyes glittered. "It is illegal for these shops to carry pornographic material. You are a journalist, Mr. Nickols. You of all men know the dangers involved. If the bookstore should be raided, we would all be put in gaol."

"It's a risk I am willing to take, Mr. Manning," Thomas Pierce coldly countered.

"As am I," John Nickols said.

"Very well," Joseph Manning bit out. "It has been moved that we next assemble in a pornographic bookstore. Do I hear a second to the motion?"

"This is ridiculous," Ardelle Dennison sharply protested. "I am not going to risk my reputation, and my career, simply because certain members have acquired a taste for pornography."

"You are aware of the rules, Miss Dennison," the barrister said softly.

"I am an original member, Mr. Whitcox," the publicist snapped. "I helped *create* those rules."

"Then I need not remind you," Marie Hoppleworth said, "that if you do not vote in favor of this motion, I will bring it up for vote again. I will continue to bring it up for vote until we reach a majority. If you cannot vote with the majority, then you must stand down. Those are the rules. Are they not, Mr. President?"

The arrogance drained out of Ardelle Dennison's face, leaving behind stunned bewilderment.

Joseph Manning looked as if he had been turned into stone. His voice, when he spoke, was expressionless. "Yes, Miss Hoppleworth, those are the rules."

Triumph gleamed through the secretary's silver-rimmed glasses. "Then I suggest, ladies and gentlemen, that we vote on the motion."

Voices volleyed back and forth over Frances's head.

All of her life she had been a law-abiding citizen.

"How do you vote, Mrs. Hart?"

"I vote—" What would her children say if she were arrested? "Aye."

A sharp nib scratched Frances's answer onto white vellum.

Anticipation battled with apprehension, and won.

"I have a question, if I may," she said.

The barrister leaned forward. "What is it?"

It occurred to Frances that he, too, would be in the bookstore. He would see what aroused her. Just as she had seen what aroused him. He would know why she became aroused, because she would tell him.

"When and where are we to meet," she asked over the dull roar in her eardrums, "and at what bookstore?"

Chapter
9

"Mrs. Hart." A deft hand grabbed the left shoulder of her coat. Hot breath tickled her ear. "You should have more faith."

Awkwardly, she plunged her left arm inside the empty sleeve. "In what, Mr. Whitcox?"

"I told you I wanted you." Heat imprinted her shoulder, fingers tugging at things that had nothing whatsoever to do with a coat seam. "And that *is* all that matters."

Frances pivoted to face him.

Baby-blue eyes blocked her vision.

Hand reaching for the brass clothes tree, Thomas Pierce said in a curiously tight voice: "Well done, Mrs. Hart."

Before she could reply, he drew back, dark wool coat and black felt bowler hat clenched in a white-knuckled fist.

A flurry of activity crowded her peripheral vision.

"I look forward to our venture next Wednesday, Mrs. Hart." Marie Hoppleworth, four inches shorter than Frances, plucked a dark cloak off the coat tree. She briefly nodded in the barrister's direction. "Mr. Whitcox."

A chill draft whipped at Frances's straw hat.

Releasing the brass doorknob, Thomas Pierce stepped through the doorway into the shadowed corridor. He did not close the door behind him.

"Thank you for an illuminating discussion, Mrs. Hart." Rose Clarring was seven inches shorter than Frances. Head tilting back, she squarely met Frances's gaze. "I am looking forward to our next meeting."

A frisson of excitement raced down Frances's spine.

"As am I, Mrs. Clarring," she said. But Rose Clarring had already turned away.

Black motion snagged her gaze.

Cloak in hand, Jane Fredericks stared at Frances in baffled anger. Frances keenly felt the younger woman's perplexity.

A dull *clunk* rang out in the sudden lull of conversation.

Long red face blending into bristling side-whiskers, George Addimore freed a curved wooden grip from a brass hook. Only to stare down at the umbrella as if he didn't know what to do with it.

"Thank you, Mrs. Hart. Mr. Whitcox." Sarah Burns was six inches taller than Frances. "This meeting has been most enlightening."

Images winked through Frances's inner eyes: a woman's clitoris; a woman's nipple. Dark hair curling from under a stiff white cuff.

"Thank *you*, Doctor Burns," Frances returned the woman's courtesy. "You didn't say what the rubber cap that fits inside a woman is called."

The physician unflinchingly held Frances's gaze. "A Mensinga Diaphragm."

"Welcome to the Men and Women's Club, Mrs. Hart."

Frances turned. Frances blinked.

One second she stared up into vivid blue-green eyes; the next moment she watched a vertical line of crimson climb up a row of white scalp like red mercury topping a thermometer.

"Thank you, Mr. Stiles." She smiled warmly. "I would enjoy seeing your sketches one day."

Impossibly, the crimson line grew brighter. Shifting a bulky drawing pad, he reached between Frances and the barrister, and withdrew a coat and a hat.

"I will assist you, Mr. Stiles." Esther Palmer reached past him and lifted his black umbrella free of the clothes tree.

Frances bit back a giggle. The young man stood six feet and seven inches tall; the young woman stood just over five feet. Her chest was nearly on a level with his sex.

Pinched face turning purple, Esther Palmer nodded. "Mrs. Hart. Mr. Whitcox. This day has indeed been liberating."

Tears pricked Frances's eyes. She had never thought to have a liberating effect on anyone, let alone on a schoolteacher.

"Pardon me, Mrs. Hart." A masculine voice feathered Frances's spine. "You are standing in the way of my coat."

"Mr. Nickols." Starting, Frances stepped back, purposefully distancing herself from both the clothes tree and her seesawing emotions. "I beg your pardon."

"There's no need to beg my pardon." John Nickols plucked off the coat tree a squat black bowler hat. "I would say, rather, that we of the Men and Women's Club should beg yours. But you're one of us now, aren't you? An invigorating addition, I might add." Reaching for a short, black wool reefer coat, he asked, "May I hail you a cab?"

"Thank you, Mr. Nickols, but I am riding the omnibus."

"Very well. I will see you Wednesday evening at the Achilles Book Shoppe." Flicking the brim of his hat, he said, "Good day, Mrs. Hart. Mr. Whitcox."

The black-haired man expertly maneuvered his wheelchair through the mahogany door frame.

Frances had been alone with the barrister last Saturday, but she had not then seen what stimulated his desires.

"Good day, Mr. Whitcox." She nodded. "Thank you for inviting me to join the Men and Women's Club."

She ducked outside the door.

Behind her, gaslight flooded the meeting room. Before her, darkness cloaked the corridor.

Metal wheels grated on wood.

The stairs were in one direction, the lift in another. Frances blindly walked toward the stairs.

Shapes materialized out of the dimness: rectangular doors . . . a horizontal bannister . . . a circular newel cap.

Metal clanked, lift opening. Heels clicked, footsteps following.

Frances stuffed her right hand inside a kid glove.

Heat seared the left side of her body—shoulder, hip, leg, foot.

"This could become a habit," she said, face forward, shoulders squared, reticule swinging.

"A pleasant one, I hope."

Frances remembered the stricken look on Ardelle Dennison's face when challenged by the secretary.

She did not know what to think about the members of the Men

and Women's Club. They had by turns terrified her, infuriated her, but always they had invigorated her.

Just like the man beside her.

"It was not my intention to create discord among the members of the club."

"It wasn't you who created the discord, Mrs. Hart."

Carefully she worked a kid-leather glove onto her left hand, gaze focused on a horizontal gleam of wood. "Would you have stepped down if they had not voted to accept my membership?"

Cynicism edged his voice. "It would not have been I who stepped down."

Frances struggled to regulate her breathing. "I take it barristers do not step down."

"Not the good ones."

"Do you always win?" she asked.

"Always," he said.

It was not a boast.

Frances's stomach knotted. "Could we be thrown in gaol?"

"Yes."

There was no apology in his affirmation. There was no passion in his voice. There was just the relentless progress of a man and a woman's footsteps.

"You know my christened name," Frances said. The click of their heels—his dull, hers sharp—simultaneously halted. She grasped the newel cap. And faced the barrister. "But I do not know yours."

His hazel eyes beneath the brim of his hat were black. "My name is James."

Hot, sweet caramel washed over her.

Smell. Taste.

Desire.

Frances glanced away from the eyes that had stared at her while she stared at pictures of naked women.

The white silk of his scarf shimmered seductively against black wool. Beneath the open coat, his waistcoat rode tailored black trousers.

"You said you find the mental imagery of a woman spanking another woman's bare bottom titillating," she said impulsively.

"Yes," he said, voice oddly strained.

Quickly she glanced up. His face was bathed in pulsing shadow.

"Do you ever imagine, Mr. Whitcox," Frances asked, breasts tightening, buttocks tingling, "that it is *your* bare bottom which is being spanked?"

Chapter
10

Light blazed in James's hazel eyes. "Do you ever imagine, Mrs. Hart, that your fingers are a man's phallus?"

Frigid air crystalized inside her lungs.

"No." Masculine laughter drifted up the stairs. "I don't."

"Why not?"

The truth.

"Because," Frances forced herself to reply, "that part of the body does not belong to a woman."

The light in his eyes dimmed. "To whom does a woman's vagina belong, if not to the woman?"

Frances looked back on her life before marriage . . . after marriage. "A man."

"A woman preserves her virginity for her husband," he deduced.

"And then she bears his children," Frances agreed.

A darkness came into his eyes. "A man need not impregnate a woman when he lies with her."

A flirtatious trill of laughter spiraled up the stairwell.

"Because of machines," Frances suggested gravely.

A familiar light filled his eyes. "That are not equipped with cogs and wheels."

Laughter bubbled up in her throat. At the same time tears burned her eyes.

She swallowed both the tears and the laughter. "Thank you, Mr. Whitcox."

Instantly the laughter lighting his face vanished. "For what?"

"For allowing me to speak for myself," she said.

"I would not have it otherwise."

The muscles deep inside her lower abdomen fluttered. He had

said he was not interested in a flirtation. For one heart-stopping moment Frances wished that he *were* flirting with her.

She turned in a swirl of suede and velvet and silk and wire.

The barrister's voice tunneled down the stairwell after her. "Mrs. Hart."

Frances paused, right foot suspended between steps. A man and a woman—they were little more than children, both of them—stood below on the marble platform ogling the dead giraffe, oblivious of the turmoil that raged above them.

"Yes, Mr. Whitcox?"

Her voice sounded tinny, as if it came out of a metal machine—what a London clerk had described as a graphophone—instead of flesh and bones.

"You asked if I ever imagined that it is my bare bottom which is being spanked."

A baby squalled, cry amplified by marble floors and arched ceilings. Frances folded her arms to still the ache inside her.

"Do you?" she asked, watching the lips of the young woman move. Watching the young man throw back his head and laugh at the young woman's sally.

"Not until today."

The yearning his words elicited catapulted Frances down the stairs, past the laughing couple and the giraffe that would never hear laughter again. She could not escape the feeling that the museum was not the same. The dented suit of armor hadn't changed. The chipped Roman sarcophagus hadn't changed. The peat-blackened prehistoric fossil hadn't changed. But things were not the same.

Ignoring her reflection in the brass and glass door, Frances stepped outside the museum.

Moisture slid down her cheek.

She glanced up.

The gray sky leaked rain impregnated with black soot.

Out of the corner of her eye, an omnibus lurched away from the curb.

"Wait!" Holding her straw hat—bustle and reticule ignominiously bouncing—she chased after the lumbering carriage. "Please wait!"

The three horses obligingly halted.

Advertising bills cluttered the omnibus like cuttings in a scrapbook. Frances recognized some of the products that the smiling models endorsed: Ropert's Celebrated Standard Blacking, Hudson's Extract Soap, Yorkshire Relish. And some she did not: Bird's Concentrated Egg Powder, Cuff's Soda Water, Huntley & Palmers Superior Boudoir Biscuits.

Hurriedly digging out of her reticule the prerequisite twopence for a two-mile ride, she clambered upward into the enclosed wagon. The stale odor of cologne, musky sweat and damp wool greeted her. Two dark silhouettes sat in the back of the bus, heads pressed together.

The omnibus lurched forward.

Frances collapsed on a bench in a whoosh of cloth and metal. Feeling absurdly adrift—like a balloon that had escaped from its ribbon—she scooted across the worn wood and pressed her nose against a finger-smeared window.

A bronze coin tumbled through the air.

Her heart leapt as she caught sight of a black silk top hat.

Its owner wore a striped wool coat rather than a black one. It was he who had tossed the bronze coin.

A small, grimy fist snatched the penny out of the air.

The man who wore the top hat held an umbrella over a stylishly-dressed woman while she walked a path the street sweeper swept. Their bodies moved in harmony.

Frances wondered what it would be like to explore London with a man. A man who would shield her from the rain. A man who would share with her the sunshine.

A man who need not impregnate a woman when he laid with her.

A stifled giggle jerked Frances to attention.

The gentleman with the black silk top hat and his fashionable companion were no longer visible outside the window. Reflected in their place was the silver mist of her breath, and the blurred reflection of her face.

"Don't, Molly." A boyish voice anxiously whispered over the grinding and groaning of overweighted wheels. "You'll get us tossed off the bus."

"Awwww, Jerry, no one's going to know . . ." The girlish response carried more clearly than had the boy's voice. "Just a look-see, that's all I want. . . . Ohhhh! Look how blue it is! Is it cold, Mr. Hornsby?"

Frances wiped the mist of her breath off the pane of glass and did her best not to eavesdrop on the young couple.

"Very, Mrs. Hornsby." It was not an easy feat: city-bred folk, Frances noted wryly, talked as if surrounding Londoners were deaf. "Take it in your hands and warm it."

An ice vendor dipping ices for a clutch of children rolled past Frances.

"Like this, Mr. Hornsby?" A giggle—surely too young to belong to a married woman—penetrated the gloom inside the omnibus.

Frances wondered what *she* had sounded like when she married. Had her laughter been filled with girlish delight? When she had given birth to her first child, had it been filled with maternal bliss? When she had held her first grandchild, had it been filled with mature contentment?

Had Frances *ever* laughed in carefree joy?

Outside the omnibus a muffin hurtled through the drizzling rain.

"Oh, yes, Mrs. Hornsby. Just like that." The young man's voice deepened. "You can do it harder. It won't break, you know."

Frances watched a muffin boy—head bowed, cap dripping water—wheel away his barrow while an old woman sat hunched inside a doorway.

"It's so hot, Jerry. And soft. Here. Feel it. It's softer than a silk billy."

The old woman made no move to catch the muffin that hurtled past her shoulder. She was resigned to her station in life.

"Squeeze it harder," the young man urged. "Make it spit . . . like I showed you . . ."

The girl's giggle pierced the creaking, groaning shadows that filled Frances's head. "Like this, Jerry?

The omnibus jerked to a halt.

No one got on. No one got off.

"Gawd." The boy's voice, oddly strangled, rang out in the sudden silence. "Get me kerchief, Molly, or it'll mess my trousers when it spits."

Mess . . . trousers . . . *spits?*

Electric awareness jolted through Frances.

Surely the girl and the boy weren't doing what she suddenly, strongly suspected they were doing . . . ?

The omnibus lurched, rolled backward, jumped forward. Frances strained to hear the boy and girl more clearly.

"Look how purple it's turning. Like a juicy ripe plum." The girl's hushed whisper was unnaturally loud over the creaking of wood and rumbling wheels. Awe reverberated in her voice, along with something that Frances could not quite identify. "It's getting bigger, Jerry. Does it hurt?"

"No . . . right . . . Lor', Molly! Don't stop!"

"Shall I make it spit for you, Jerry?" she asked, sounding far, far older than a mere girl. "Shall I?"

Frances suddenly realized what that extra something was that resonated in the girl's voice. She sounded exactly like the women in the French postcards had looked: secure with her sexuality, and in her ability to give and take pleasure.

A wave of jealousy broke over Frances.

For the girl's silliness. For the girl's boldness.

For the girl's youth.

This was what Frances had been cheated of, married at the age of fifteen with a baby at sixteen.

Shock wiped away the inexplicable crest of jealousy. It was chased by a surge of unadulterated horror.

Frances leapt to her feet. What was *wrong* with her? She loved her husband, her children and her grandchildren. She would not change one single moment of her life with them.

The omnibus jerked to a stop.

Shoulders hunched, face averted from the couple, Frances hurriedly stepped off the bus.

The soot-impregnated drizzle stopped as quickly as it had started.

Fingers fumbling, Frances dug out of her reticule the key to the red brick townhouse that she had leased for the season. Forcefully she pushed open the door. The meaty aroma of roasting beef halted her, mid-step.

A girlish giggle drifted out of the drawing room.

Frances's galloping heartbeat faltered: there were no girls in this household.

Alarm tripped down her spine. Unless one of Frances's children had brought her granddaughters for a London visit . . . ?

"Mr. Denton?" Frances called out, mouth dry, voice echoing in the empty foyer. "Mrs. Jenkins?"

No one answered.

She wasn't ready to be reunited with her family, Frances thought on a spike of panic. She needed more time.

A dull metalic clang rang out in the silence. Following a fern-pattern of dusky green wallpaper, Frances crossed the scarred oak floor, through the entranceway, along a short hallway, and halted outside the drawing room.

The twin walnut doors were closed.

Taking a deep breath, she threw them wide open.

Denton, white head bowed, shoulders stooped, knelt on the floor in front of the black iron fireplace. He held a small bronze shovel. Mrs. Jenkins, lacy white cap and linen apron pristine, stood beside him. She held a bronze-handled brush.

The butler was seventy-two years old; the housekeeper was sixty-six. That girlish giggle had not come from either of them.

"Mrs. Jenkins," Frances said carefully. "I thought I heard some-one laugh. Do I have visitors?"

Mrs. Jenkins glanced up, face flushed. Her Irish accent was oddly thick. "It be the chimney whistling, Mrs. Hart. Mr. Denton and me been inspecting it. He'll knock up the chimney boy, just as soon as we finish here."

The echo of that girlish giggle hung in the air. It had not sounded like wind whistling through the chimney.

Frances hovered indecisively in the doorway.

"Up you go, Mr. Denton. We've cleaned as clean as it'll get. Give me your shovel." The housekeeper efficiently hung the brush and shovel onto the rack of fire-irons. When she faced Frances, her lined face was serene, the flush reduced to a healthy glow. "Would you like a cup o' tea, Mrs. Hart?"

"No—" The butler stood up with surprising dexterity; his face also glowed with vigor and health. "Yes. That would be most wel-come. Thank you, Mrs. Jenkins."

"Not at all, marm."

Frances stepped aside for the butler and housekeeper to pass. Suspiciously she stared around the empty room. An essence lingered, a sense of joy, and something else—

"The post, Mrs. Hart."

Frances jumped.

The butler silently extended a silver tray, head bowed. He was quiet as well as dexterous.

Gingerly she plucked the white envelope off the tray. A childish scrawl monopolized the square piece of paper.

Frances did not need to open the envelope to know from whom it came: the letter was from her eldest granddaughter, seven-year-old Megan, the only family member who had inherited Frances's red hair.

She was feisty. She was fearless.

She was the joy of Frances's heart.

Soon she would be a young woman.

Age pressed down on Frances's shoulders. Perching on a worn, gold-brocaded chair, she prepared to rip open the envelope.

A bronze knife materialized under her nose.

Flushing, Frances accepted the letter opener. "Thank you, Mr. Denton."

London ways were indeed different from country ways. In the country, she did not employ a butler. A housemaid would not have thought to fetch her a letter opener.

"Very good, madam," Denton said placidly. "Will there be anything else, madam?"

"No." Frances carefully slit open the envelope. "Thank you."

Pale sunlight streamed through the window. Holding the letter out at arm's length—diminishing eyesight another reminder of her age—Frances scanned the familiar scrawl, paused, lungs collapsing. Squinting through a glaze of tears, she read the letter more slowly.

Dear Grandmama,

I miss you. Letters aren't the same as talking. I caught a fish yesterday. It was really big. I wanted to show it to you, but you weren't here. When are you coming home? You've been gone weeks and weeks. I know you miss grandpapa, and mama says we must be patient, but we miss him, too, and we're not running away. Please come home.

Chapter
11

"Mr. Bartle took ill on December eighth, 1886. Twenty-three days before he died." James looked up from his notes. "Is that correct, Dr. Dudley?"

"That is correct." George Stewart Dudley, the witness for the Crown, was calm. "Yes."

"What did you find when you examined Mr. Bartle?"

"We—that is, Dr. Leach, who asked me to assist him, and I—found symptoms of mercurial poisoning."

James leaned back. "Why did Mr. Bartle suffer from mercurial poisoning, Dr. Dudley?"

"I would assume, sir, because he ingested mercury."

Tense laughter rifled through the courtroom.

An uncertain grin hitched up the corners of the witness's thin mouth.

George Stewart Dudley had not intended his reply to be humorous. Nor had it been. But the response from the gallery had gratified him. He would now deliberately use sarcasm in order to make James appear incompetent.

The twelve men in the jury box shifted uncomfortably. Today had been another long day in the trial of Mary Bartle. The jurors were eager to get home to their dinner. James was eager to meet Frances Hart at the Achilles Book Shoppe.

"That is a fair assumption, Dr. Dudley." James smiled sympathetically at the witness. "But why would Mr. Bartle ingest mercury?"

The doctor smirked nervously. "I wouldn't know, sir, and the victim being dead, it is not possible for me to ask."

Raucous laughter—both male and female—erupted inside the

gallery. The spectators, too, were tired. The trial had started last Saturday; it was now Wednesday, and James had yet to deliver his opening speech for the defense.

He smiled in mock appreciation at the physician's witticism, his every expression, his every move, his every word a calculated risk. "Did Mr. Bartle suffer from an illness prior to December eighth, Dr. Dudley?"

"I wouldn't know, sir." The witness's gaze uneasily darted away from James. He was hiding, just as Frances Hart hid. James knew what the doctor was hiding; when would he discover the widow's secrets? "I was not his family physician."

Sweat crawled down James's scalp. He could feel his patience slipping with his every heartbeat.

"But you *are* a physician," he gently prodded.

The witness's gaze indignantly snapped toward James.

"Objection, Your Honor," the Attorney General quickly intercepted. "Dr. Dudley is not on trial here. His credentials have been examined by this court, and found to be exemplary."

"Objection allowed." The judge, pharaoh-like wig unruffled, covertly glanced at the pocket watch he kept hidden in the colorful nosegay that perched on the edge of his desk. Like so many judicial traditions, the sweet-smelling flowers were a carryover from the times when bathing and plumbing were even more scarce than they presently were. "Mr. Whitcox, you will not malign the witness's credentials."

"I beg your pardon, Your Honor." James smiled, the self-deprecating smile he had perfected over the years. "It was not my intention to do so."

James had wanted the physician to look at him. And now he did. It had not hurt to have the Attorney General reaffirm the physician's credentials to the twelve jurors.

"Dr. Dudley," James said pleasantly. "In your learned experience, for what illness might one ingest mercury?"

"Objection, Your Honor!"

The judge frowned. "For what reason, Mr. Lodoun?"

"Mr. Bartle's cause of death has been determined to be a result of chloroform poisoning," the Attorney General firmly stated. "Whatever illness he suffered from which might have required the use of mercury has no bearing on this case."

"I beg to disagree, Your Honor," James said cordially. "The illness from which Mr. Bartle suffered has every bearing on this case, which I will shortly demonstrate, if Your Honor will bear with me for a few more moments."

"Very well, Mr. Whitcox. Swiftly, sir." The judge stole another glimpse at the hidden pocket watch. Every Wednesday evening the honorable Justin Aaron took dinner at his daughter's house and played draughts with his grandchildren. He, too, was eager to finish the session. "Objection denied, Mr. Lodoun. Dr. Dudley, you may answer the question."

"There are several illnesses which are treated with mercury," the physician replied, hedging.

The witness had been coached well; he would not volunteer Crown secrets.

"Dr. Dudley." James pitched his voice to reach the gallery. "Is it not true that mercury is used to treat syphilis?"

Feminine gasps filled the cavernous courtroom.

Though venereal disease was rampant throughout London, polite women must feign shock at its mere mention. The silence resulted in many women—respectable women like Jane Fredericks's mother—being victimized by the very vice from which they were socially shielded.

The jurors, their dinners forgotten, leaned forward to hear the doctor's answer. The sins of a man were almost as titillating as the sins of a woman.

"Yes," the physician said reluctantly. "Mercury is sometimes used to treat syphilis."

"And isn't it also true, Dr. Dudley," James asked, "that Mr. Bartle suffered from syphilis?"

"Objection, Your Honor!" the Attorney General sharply protested.

"On what grounds, Mr. Lodoun?" the judge snapped.

James waited, outwardly patient, inwardly assessing the Attorney General's strategy.

"Such information will unduly influence the jurors' verdict, Your Honor," the Attorney General stated more calmly. "Mr. Bartle is the

victim; whatever sexual disease he may have contracted prior to his
death has no bearing on this situation. He was murdered, sir, feloniously, wilfully and with malice aforethought. I move that you
strike Mr. Whitcox's statement from the records, in order that justice
may best be served."

"I assure you, Your Honor," James smoothly intervened, "that
Mr. Bartle's unfortunate illness has great bearing on this situation.
Diseases of the type from which he suffered have a genealogy that is
quite revealing. I believe, by tracing the course of Mr. Bartle's disease, that we may more readily determine who is the villain in this
situation, and who is the true victim, so that justice may indeed be
served."

"Very well, Mr. Whitcox. Objection denied, Mr. Lodoun. Pray
serve *justice*, Dr. Dudley," the judge instructed, quickly glancing at
the bright nosegay, then sideways at the witness box, "and answer
the question."

The physician glanced at the Attorney General for confirmation.
The Attorney General curtly nodded assent.

"Yes, it is true," Dr. Dudley said stiffly. "Mr. Bartle did suffer
from syphilis." Hurriedly he added, "But he did not die from this
disease, sir!"

James knew full well what had killed Thomas Edwards Bartle.

"Thank you, Dr. Dudley," he said.

"Nor did he die from mercury poisoning," the physician anxiously stressed. "There's no doubt that he died from chloroform poisoning."

"That will be all, Dr. Dudley." James smiled, a cynical smile.
The witness for the Crown had been an effective weapon; now it
was time for him to exit the stage. "I have no more questions, Your
Honor."

The Attorney General half-stood up. "I would like to take a moment to re-examine the witness, Your Honor—"

"Tomorrow, Mr. Lodoun, you may re-examine Dr. Dudley to your
heart's content," the judge said dourly. "This court is hereby adjourned."

The Attorney General flushed with anger. "Your Honor—"

"Tomorrow, Mr. Lodoun." The sharp crack of a gavel emphasized the judicial decision. James had never known the judge to a Wednesday dinner with his family. This evening, he thought with satisfaction, would not be the first. "This court is adjourned. We will continue tomorrow morning at ten of the clock."

Anticipation tightened his groin.

"You seem in a hurry, Whitcox."

The groaning of benches and the rustling of clothing filled the courtroom as, singly and in groups, men and women exited the gallery.

James slid his papers into the black leather satchel. "The whole world is in a hurry, Lodoun."

"But not you," Jack Lodoun said. "You live for the courtroom."

"Are you getting nervous?" James buckled the satchel. Lightly he mocked, "Before my opening speech?"

Bitterness sharpened the Attorney General's voice. "Do you know what they call you?"

James's head snapped upward. For long seconds he studied the man who stood on the opposite side of the table for the Counsel.

He was shorter than James. More slender. Chestnut Dundreary whiskers untouched by silver jutted out on either side of a gray periwig.

It occurred to James that the Attorney General's eyes were the color of periwinkle, blue tinged with purple. They matched the silk drapes in his drawing room.

"If I have done something to personally offend you, Lodoun, tell me," he said coolly. "If you're upset because I won't allow you to hang my client, tell Judge Aaron."

Puzzlement fought with anger in Jack Lodoun's eyes. "You don't know, do you?"

James slid out from behind the table, progress aided by the slick slide of silk. "I know exactly what names I'm called."

In the gazettes. In the clubs. In the drawing rooms.

"But do you know why?" the Attorney General challenged.

James stood. *Later* he would puzzle over the Attorney General's unusual behavior. *Now* he had an assignation. "Make an appointment with my clerk if you have something you wish to discuss."

He turned in dismissal, satchel swinging, robe swishing.

"You won't win this time, Whitcox."

Pausing, James reached up and pulled the periwig off his head. Cool air caressed the nape of his neck. Roughly he raked his fingers through his sweat-clumped hair before replying, "I always win, Lodoun."

"But you don't care, do you?"

James thought of all the defendants he had represented throughout the years.

When was the last time he had felt sympathy or empathy for an innocent client? When was the last time he had felt regret or remorse over freeing a guilty client?

"It's what we do," he said indifferently.

The Crown charged. The defense defended. There was no right or wrong inside the four corners of the law.

James walked out of the courtroom. Periwig swaying in his right hand. Satchel swinging in his left hand. Robe alternately swirling and catching at the legs of his woolen trousers.

The Attorney General did not follow him.

His footsteps hollowly clicked a question along the endless corridor: *Do you ever imagine, Mrs. Hart, that your fingers are a man's phallus?*

James's riposte had been impulsive. Frances's response had been devastating.

There had been no anger in her eyes. There had been no regret in her voice. She simply could not imagine a woman taking pleasure in her own vagina.

Listening to her admission, James had more than anything wanted to demonstrate to Frances what a gift her sexuality was.

Shoving his wig underneath his left arm, he halted in front of a door. Light spilled through a crack and turned shadowy wood into polished oak.

His hand froze over the bronze buckle securing his satchel: James did not need his key.

Slowly, silently, he eased out his foot and gently pushed open the heavy door.

Leaning over a large teak desk, a black-haired man rifled through a stash of papers.

A smile eased the tension cording James's shoulders. "Still here, Mr. Tristan? I thought you had a meeting this evening."

"Sir! You gave me a fright." James's clerk, checkered reefer coat gaping open to reveal the traditional black "clerk" frock underneath it, hurriedly scooped up the pile of papers he had dropped in his surprise. "I thought I'd forgotten to write up a message. I came back to give these a quick go-over. I'll just be a moment—"

"No hurry." James carelessly tossed the periwig onto the wig stand behind the desk, then dropped the satchel into his black leather chair. Avery Tristan had been with him for two years; he was both efficient and discreet. "I have an appointment this evening. Is there anything that can't wait?"

"An appointment, sir?" The clerk quickly thumbed through a black leather book on the edge of James's desk. "I don't recall making an appointment for this evening."

Irony tinged James's voice. "It's not that type of appointment, Mr. Tristan."

"Oh." Blushing, the clerk diplomatically closed the black book. "Right-oh, sir!"

James shrugged out of his robe.

"Here, sir. Allow me." The robe slid off James's shoulders. "Did you get a chance to go over the Hart report?"

Faint heat edged James's cheekbones. He had invaded the widow's privacy.

Instantly he dismissed the uncustomary twinge of conscience: a conscience did not gain a barrister the silk.

"Yes, thank you," James said. The report was neatly stacked on top of his desk where he had read it over recess. Frances Hart's life filled three pages, every one of them more telling than the last. It had answered his every question save for why she believed she was past the age of engaging in sexual relations. "Has there been a problem with Mr. Lodoun?"

"No, sir." The clerk paused, hand poised over James's black silk robe to brush off a piece of lint. "Mr. Lodoun's clerk asked for a copy of Mrs. Bartle's medical reports. I told him I would pass on his request."

Was that what had the Attorney General's knickers in a wad?

James wondered cynically. Because he rightfully suspected that information was being withheld?

Lips curling, he unbuttoned his waistcoat, eager to cleanse himself of the deceit and despair that clung to his clothes and skin like coal dust. "Give the reports to him tomorrow morning."

It would be too late for Lodoun to form an offensive strategy. The Crown had no more witnesses to call.

Tomorrow he would present his opening speech of defense. Tomorrow he would call *his* witnesses.

Tonight belonged to James Whitcox and Frances Hart.

Chapter
12

Fear tightened her throat. Excitement hardened her nipples.
The gay tinkle of a bell rang out; at the same time the grind of
carriage wheels invaded the Achilles Book Shoppe.

Frances's gaze snapped toward the front door.

Two fashionably dressed women stepped out of the thickening
darkness into the brightly lit bookstore.

No policemen followed them.

The door closed on the evening, a jarring tinkle; the grind of carriage wheels disappeared.

Eight members of the Men and Women's Club browsed among
the tables stacked high with books, each one determinedly avoiding
the other members' gazes. James Whitcox was not one of them.

Self-consciously, Frances picked up a brown leather book. The
bell over the shop door jangled; simultaneously, a masculine voice
spoke from the opposite direction. "Mrs. Hart."

Frances froze; the book dropped from her suddenly nerveless fingers.

"Mrs. Hart." John Nickols retrieved the fallen book; instantly
Frances became mobile—*what was the matter with her?*—and accepted the leather-bound volume. "There is a door at the back of
the shop which Miss Hoppleworth is now making her way toward. It
is clearly marked by a sign, 'Latin and Greek Classics.' When she
goes through that door, I want you to wait a few minutes, and then
follow her."

Frances's stomach tightened.

"But we're not all here, Mr. Nickols," she protested reasonably.

The black eyes below hers filled with sharp irony. "I doubt very
much that anyone else will show, Mrs. Hart."

Ardelle Dennison, Jane Fredericks, and Joseph Manning, perhaps.

"But Mr. Whitcox—"

Moist heat caressed her neck. "Is standing behind you, Mrs. Hart."

Awareness charged through Frances. Of the too-bright overhead lighting. Of the overwhelming smell of leather and ink.

Of the man who stood behind her.

"Mr. Whitcox," she said, heart racing, breath quickening. "I didn't see you come in."

"You were occupied."

"I'm sorry," she said. And did not know for whom she apologized: the seven-year-old girl who felt that her grandmother had abandoned her, or the fifteen-year-old bride—not yet a mother let alone a grandmother—who had never taken joy in her husband's sex.

"It is I who should apologize." Moist heat caressed her ear . . . her cheek. "I was detained after court."

Frances looked up. Diamond drops of water clung to the barrister's gold and bronze hair. "You're not wearing a hat."

"I forgot it."

"Your hair is wet."

"I showered."

"I've never taken a shower," she said impulsively.

Immediately the eyes above hers narrowed intently. His breath feathered her lips; it tasted of tooth powder instead of caramel. The flavor was equally intoxicating. "You may visit my chambers anytime you wish, Mrs. Hart."

"I am to follow Miss Hoppleworth in a moment," she said quickly, avoiding the intimate insinuation. What must the journalist think of their exchange? "Mr. Nickols will direct you—"

But the journalist was gone.

"*Elements of Social Science* by Dr. George Drysdalc," James Whitcox read. Frances gazed upward. The light in his eyes stole away her breath. "Is there a reason that you need more information about contraception?"

Heat engulfed her.

"I . . . I—" Frances floundered. *Elements of Social Science* was the title of a book about *contraception?* She awkwardly set the leather-bound book back down onto the table. "I must follow Miss Hopple-worth now."

"Then I will accompany you."

"I believe Mr. Nickols wishes us to go in single file."

"Nonsense." Long fingers firmly tugged her gloved hand through his left arm. The muscles in his forearm were hard under the padding of his wool coat; the fingers that clasped her hand were equally hard through the leather of Frances's gloves. "We are everything that is respectable. I assure you, we will not draw undue attention."

Her fingers curled into a fist.

He *touched* her.

She touched him.

Common sense came to her rescue.

Ladies and gentleman often walked hand in arm. There was nothing *intimate* in the gesture. Men in their prime did not become intimate with women who were beyond *their* prime.

No matter that women might wish differently.

"You smelled of caramel at the meetings," she said stiffly, forcing her legs to move when he moved. The closed door bearing the sign LATIN AND GREEK CLASSICS seemed a mile away. "Do you frequently have court business on Saturdays?"

"I have." Her right breast brushed his left arm; electricity bolted from her nipple straight down to her lower abdomen. "In the past."

Frances concentrated on their conversation instead of the heat that raced up and down her spine. "Out of which courthouse do you operate?"

"The Old Bailey."

"It's listed in my tour guide."

"I'll give you a private tour"—his hip bumped her hip—"if you would like."

Frances determinedly stared straight ahead. Their shared goal yawned before them. She had only to endure five more feet.

"You must live very close to the courthouse," she managed.

"Why do you say that?"

"Your hair is damp."

From his shower, she did not add.

"I have private chambers in the courthouse."

To which he had invited her.

"Mr. Whitcox." Frances drew in much needed oxygen; at the same time she jerked her hand free from the crook of his arm and the heat of his fingers. "Only one of us will fit through the doorway."

Face enigmatic, he stepped back with a half bow. "I will follow wherever you lead, Mrs. Hart."

What did he imply? Frances wondered, heart hammering, pulse throbbing.

Why did she think that he implied anything but simple courtesy?

"Thank you," she said, and pushed open the white enameled door.

"Good afternoon, Mrs. Hart, Mr. Whitcox," Marie Hoppleworth greeted.

The barrister quietly shut the door behind him.

"Miss Hoppleworth," Frances said.

But the secretary had already turned back to the wall of gold embossed leather books, studying in rapt absorption the titles that could only be in Latin and Greek. Languages which Frances could not read, but which James Whitcox no doubt did.

The small chamber offered two comfortable armchairs and nothing else of interest.

Turning, Frances forced herself to gaze up into the barrister's eyes. "Have you been to this shop before, Mr. Whitcox?"

"I've heard of it," he said. "Usually I visit a shop outside the courthouse."

Surprise streaked through her. "There is a pornographic shop outside the courthouse?"

"These shops are everywhere," he replied cynically.

"But . . . but barristers, and . . . and *judges* visit the shop outside the courthouse?"

"Of course." The mockery in his eyes turned inward. "There is also a shop outside the Parliamentary House."

Barristers . . . Judges . . . *Parliamentary* members?

Outrage, for the fear that throbbed inside her and the hypocrisy that surrounded her, flared through Frances. "Then why are these shops illegal?"

"Imagine, Mrs. Hart"—darkness played in his hazel eyes; above him a gas globe flickered and flared—"if sex were not a sin."

Puzzlement threaded through Frances. "I'm afraid I don't understand, Mr. Whitcox."

"If sex were not a sin, Mrs. Hart," Marie Hoppleworth interrupted, sliding the library ladder to the far bookshelf, and stepping onto the bottom rung, "then women would have the same legal rights as men."

"Are you suggesting Parliament makes these shops illegal in order to prevent women from gaining the right to vote?" Frances asked incredulously.

"These shops are illegal," hazel eyes recaptured Frances's gaze, "because men govern, and men want their women pure and virginal."

"Men want their women powerless, Mrs. Hart." Marie Hoppleworth stepped off the ladder. Holding a slender black leather-bound book to her chest, she stared up at the barrister. "They take away our power by controlling our sexuality. When women are powerless, men do not have to account for their actions against them. And wife murderers are found innocent."

James Whitcox's lips curved in a mocking smile. "The system is a two-way drive, Miss Hoppleworth."

"Mrs. Hart," a masculine voice intruded. "Miss Hoppleworth. Mr. Whitcox."

"Hello, Mr. Pierce," Marie Hoppleworth said coolly. "We were just talking about the emancipation of women through the legalization of sex shops."

Thomas Pierce flushed. "I hardly think emancipation will occur because of sexual proclivity, Miss Hoppleworth."

"Then what is the purpose of the Men and Women's Club, Mr. Pierce?"

Three pairs of eyes latched onto Frances.

"Isn't the purpose of our being here to learn about our sexuality," she asked, "and through that learning, create a better quality of life?"

"What do you think you can learn in a pornographic shop that will better your life?" Thomas Pierce asked.

"Good afternoon, Mrs. Hart," Rose Clarring interrupted. "Miss Hoppleworth. Mr. Pierce. Mr. Whitcox."

Frances smiled with unchecked warmth. "Good afternoon, Mrs. Clarring."

"Good afternoon, Mrs. Clarring," Marie Hoppleworth said. "Mr. Pierce has asked Mrs. Hart what she thinks she can learn in a pornographic shop that will benefit her life."

Rose Clarring adjusted a smart black bonnet. "If you do not think any worthwhile knowledge can be gained from this expedition, Mr. Pierce, why did you go to such efforts to get us all here?"

"I didn't say that this expedition was without educational benefits, Mrs. Clarring," Thomas Pierce said defensively. "I was merely interested in what Mrs. Hart hoped to learn."

"Well, I certainly know what I hope to learn," the secretary stated briskly.

"What is that, Miss Hoppleworth?" Frances asked.

"The price of a widow's comforter."

It had not occurred to Frances that the bookstore might offer more than French postcards.

Unerringly her gaze found the barrister.

His eyes were alert, glittering with amusement yet softened by a glow of anticipation.

One by one the remaining members of the Men and Women's Club crowded into the small room. Exchanging greetings. Stealing oxygen. Shrinking the floor space until there was no place to stand. And still Frances could hear the timbre of James Whitcox's voice. Could feel the heat of his body. Could taste the salty tang of his tooth powder.

If sex were not a sin . . .

Shifting, Frances bumped into the barrister. Her bustle molded her buttocks.

The painful awareness of his body was chased by an odd sense of expectation, as if she might learn something in this shop that would indeed change the course of her life. Impossible, of course, but Frances could not shake the feeling.

Excitement was a contagious fever.

The faces surrounding her bore the same deliberately blank expression. The color staining their cheeks belied their seeming indifference.

The doorknob rattled.

Frances's gaze shot toward the opening door.

John Nickols quietly wheeled his chair inside the overcrowded room. Two young men dressed in tweed—vaguely she identified them as clerks—followed him inside and closed the door.

"You must stand away from the bookshelves," the journalist instructed.

Easier said than done.

One of the clerks reached out and pressed the middle section of the wall that was filled with gold embossed leather. The panel of books swung inward.

Frances murmured in surprise. A feminine volley of matching *Ohs!* surrounded her.

"Ladies. Gentlemen." John Nickols gestured toward the hidden staircase, now revealed. "Welcome to the Achilles Book Shoppe."

Chapter
13

"After we make our purchases, how do we exit?" Thomas Pierce asked.

He sounded as young as Frances felt.

"There's a separate exit," one of the men in tweed explained. "A clerk will show you."

"Mrs. Hart."

Frances could barely breathe for the tension that gripped her throat. "Yes, Mr. Nickols?"

"We are here this evening because of you." The journalist's expression was enigmatic. "I think it only fitting that you be the first to descend."

Her legs were embarrassingly weak. "Thank you, Mr. Nickols."

A twinge of dampness tickled her nose, along with the smell of leather and ink.

The stairs were carpeted. The incline was steep. The air was noticeably cooler.

Above her, a white ceiling expanded outward. Below her, trestle-like tables branched off, forming a series of aisles.

The private bookstore looked almost exactly like the public bookstore.

Frances hesitated at the foot of the stairs.

A blond-haired man soundlessly appeared at her elbow. "May I help you, madam?"

Frances started, relaxed. He was dressed in the same tweed wool that the upstairs clerks wore.

Cautiously she glanced around. Ten pairs of masculine eyes skittered away from her perusal.

She determinedly raised her chin. "I would like to see a selection of French postcards, if I may."

"Certainly." The clerk's gaze was level with hers. He showed neither shock nor disapproval. "If you will follow me."

Singularly aware of the descending swish of skirts behind her and the watching eyes before her, Frances trailed after the blond-haired man.

Halting in front of what had to be the longest—and busiest— table, the clerk bowed. "By your leave, madam."

Carefully averting her gaze from the five gentlemen who bordered the table, she stared in dismay at the boxes and boxes of postcards.

"Wait!" Frances licked her lips. Lowering her voice, she asked in a near-whisper, "Do you have any postcards that include . . . men?"

The clerk walked a short circle, alternately tapping boxes. "Femmes. Renters. Mothers and Fathers. Billiards."

"Thank you." She gripped her reticule. "There is certainly a nice variety from which to choose."

But the clerk had already deserted her.

A feminine murmur drifted through the shop; Frances recognized the voice of Sarah Burns, the physician. Stiffening her spine, Frances stepped forward and plucked up a card from one of the designated boxes.

At first glance, she saw a young woman rolling up a sepia-tinted stocking while smiling flirtatiously into the camera. A second glance revealed that the woman was not a woman, but a man.

She breathed shallowly to counteract her shock.

A long penis shadowed a lacy garter. Curiously, the head and the shaft were the same size in circumference.

Heat suffused her forehead.

Head snapping upward, she captured the gaze of the gentleman who stood directly across the table from her.

A black bowler sat on graying hair. His face beneath the brim sported an impressive mustache.

Obviously he was a respectable man.

"Hello," Frances said politely. "The weather is rather fine for April. I expect it will soon turn, though."

Dark crimson bled into his suddenly mask-like face. Without speaking, he turned and walked away. The remaining four gentlemen edged farther away from her, their gazes fixed on the boxes of postcards that lined the table.

Frances deduced that talking was not welcome in the downstairs shop.

She self-consciously replaced the "femmes" postcard. And picked up a "renters" postcard.

Heat bolted up her arm.

A naked, dark-haired man knelt on a stool, buttocks provocatively tilted while he leaned forward to kiss a blond-haired man. A second blond-haired man who was also naked stood to the left of the kneeling man; he held a thin cane in his right hand. His erection stabbed at the camera.

It was long *and* thick.

Very long. Very thick.

The plum-shaped head was as large as a fist.

"Oh, my!"

Frances jerked to attention to find Rose Clarring at her side, rosebud mouth a round *O*.

Irresistibly, Frances's gaze was drawn back to the three men.

"The composition is quite good, don't you think?" Rose Clarring observed in a curiously hushed voice.

Frances swallowed. "Quite."

Stepping closer, Rose Clarring chose another postcard from the "renters" box; stepping sideways, Frances investigated a "mothers and fathers" box. Out of the corner of her eye, she watched the remaining four gentlemen scuttle away from the table.

Glancing down at the "mothers and fathers" postcard pinched between her thumb and forefinger, Frances was instantly sucked straight down into the photograph.

Cool air tickled her breasts. Hot flesh prickled her buttocks.

She did not know the man whose naked body molded her body; she only knew that he would touch her, please her, love her for what she was now, and not for what she had been years earlier.

He nuzzled the side of her neck, a question marked with moist heat. She leaned her head back against his shoulder, an answer of trusting assent.
Long, elegant fingers cupped and lifted her heavy breast.
His hand was hot. Her nipple was hard.
She felt as if her body were a well gone dry.
He knew how empty she was. He knew how much she wanted to be filled.
She couldn't breathe. She couldn't move. She could only watch while he squeezed her breast and stroked down her stomach . . . long fingers combing through her pubic hair . . . slipping between her thighs . . . shaping her . . . parting her . . . filling—

A sharp jab jerked Frances out of the postcard.

Esther Palmer with single-minded intent reached for the "billiards" box, unaware of the fantasy she had interrupted.

Frances sucked in cooling air. It did not cool her.

Now she understood why conversation—and women—were not welcome in the downstairs shop. The postcards were more than masturbatory aids. They were windows for erotic fantasies, an intimate peek into the very heart of a man's—and a woman's—most secret desires.

Compulsively she stared down at the postcard.

It pulsated with heat.

The woman. The man.

Frances.

Hurriedly, she replaced the postcard. Only to be riveted by stark hazel eyes.

James Whitcox stared at her from across an aisle.

The hair on the nape of her neck prickled with sexual awareness.

He saw her desire. He saw her arousal.

He saw a forty-nine-year-old woman whose hair was a vivid red and whose body was shaped into a fashionable hourglass, but Frances was not that woman.

Blindly she turned away.

There was no escaping her whaleboned corset: it was hard. Like her nipples. There was no escaping the heels of her half-boots: they tilted her body so that her pelvis jutted forward. Like her breasts.

Furtive eyes stared at her from across the shop. Men who wanted acceptance. Men who needed touch. Men who saw that she, a woman, also wanted and needed.

She swung into an aisle. George Addimore—his back to Frances—bent over a glass case. A clerk discreetly stepped back to the opposite side of the cabinet.

Saturday she would see his purchase, as well as the purchases of the other men and women.

What would she have to show?

Thomas Pierce had asked what she could find in a pornographic shop that would have any bearing on her life. The answer was simple: *nothing.*

Hazel eyes superimposed George Addimore's bowed head.

Frances turned away. From George Addimore, a man who searched for inspiration. From James Whitcox, a man who wanted what she couldn't give him.

Gilded titles leapt out at her: *Letters from a Friend in Paris*; *The Amatory Experiences of a Surgeon*; *The Wedding Night or The Battles of Venus*; *Betsy Thoughtless*; *The Romance of Lust*; *Ups and Downs of Life.* She ducked between the two tables piled high with books.

Hard wood jammed into her stomach.

Her breath escaped in a *whoosh.* Glass bottles leapt into the air.

Quickly she grabbed at the overturning table, caught it, righted it, snatched one sliding bottle, missed six.

Face flaming, she dropped out of sight of the watching eyes—feminine as well as masculine, she had no doubt—and scrambled to retrieve the rolling bottles, carpet a woolen abrasion, gloves a fumbling hindrance, *please*, please *don't let them be broken. Please*, please *don't let James Whitcox see her like this.*

Naked. Vulnerable.

"Madam." A tweed-frocked man hunkered down beside her. Vaguely she recognized him as the blond-haired clerk who had directed her to the postcards. "Are you injured?"

"I'm sorry," Frances said, reaching for a bottle. It eluded her grasping fingers. "I'm sorry."

"There's no harm done, madam." Expert fingers gathered up the scattered bottles. "Nothing is broken."

But something *was* broken.

Her body would never be what it had once been. She felt desire, but she had no means to satisfy it.

Frances jumped up, clutching the lone bottle. It was a pretty container with a crystal stopper; liquid sloshed inside the clear glass. A flowery label identified it as "Rose's Lubrifiant."

"Is this perfume?" she asked quickly before she burned up with humiliation. Oh, *what did it matter* what was inside the bottle? "I'll take it."

It was the least she could do, after having toppled the whole lot.

Silence greeted her offer.

She glanced up. The blond-haired clerk had pointed out postcards of men dressed in women's underclothes—Frances inanely realized she did not know what type of pictures resided in the "billiards" box—without blinking a single eyelash. What could possibly make him hesitate now?

She thrust the bottle toward him. "I said I would take this," she said with an unaccustomed edge to her voice, needing to assert herself, to prove that she was in control—if not of her body—then at least her actions.

A muscle twitched in his cheek. He made no move to take the bottle from her. "It is not perfume, madam."

Not perfume. *Then what . . . ?*

Frances forgot about staring eyes, and gazed down at the bottle with sudden intrigue. "Is it . . . a potion?"

She had heard of potions that enhanced a man's virility. She had only ever heard of potions for women that would ensure fertility.

"No, madam." The clerk's voice was impassive. "It is not a potion."

"What is it, then?" she asked, glancing up.

"It is a *lubrifiant.*"

Rose's Lubrifiant, to be precise.

Frances bit her tongue to stop herself from lashing out in irritation. It was not the young man's fault that she had made a fool of herself because a postcard had cried out to the very depths of her being.

"What is a—" Carefully she pronounced the new word . . . so many new words, soon she would need to start a diary. "*Lubrifiant?*"

Chapter
14

"You smell of vanilla."

Frances Hart swung around, green-and-gold-dyed egret feathers fluttering. She protectively clutched her reticule to her chest. "I beg your pardon?"

Her breath misted in the dim glow of lamplight. Red hair glinted beneath the shadows of her straw hat.

"I said: you smell of vanilla," James repeated.

This night she had truly sampled a taste of the city known for its dreadful delights. How would she now respond to him?

Frances's gaze skidded away from his. "I don't use any products which are scented with vanilla."

"It's the smell of you," he said, purposefully redirecting her attention back to her body. "Of your skin."

She stared at his chin. "Is vanilla a scent you enjoy?"

"I quite like the flavor of vanilla," he said with deliberate intent.

"My middle grandson is fond of vanilla custard," she murmured in a low voice, outwardly impervious to his innuendo. Inwardly battling with thoughts and feelings that she was not yet prepared to share.

James could not see past the darkness that cloaked her face; he could only feel the conflicting waves of desire and fear that radiated from her body.

After long seconds, he said, "You were shocked by what you saw inside the shop."

"Not at all." Head tilting back, she reluctantly met his gaze. "I am merely digesting the forbidden apple."

The corners of his lips kicked upward. "Beware the worm, Mrs. Hart."

"Too late, Mr. Whitcox," she said somberly, her shadowed eyes no longer clear.

The smile slid off James's face.

Tendrils of yellow fog curled around the lamppost.

It was cold. It was damp.

He didn't want her out on the streets alone at night.

A hansom cab clipped toward them, twin lanterns a bright beacon.

"Let me hail you a cab."

"The omnibus will be along presently."

"Do you enjoy riding the omnibus, Mrs. Hart?" he asked dryly.

"Do you, Mr. Whitcox?"

"I've never ridden one."

A silvery gust of surprise burst from her mouth. "Why not?"

Why not? reverberated in James's ears.

Why hadn't he asked his wife which touches excited her? Why hadn't Frances demanded more from her husband than a wedding band?

"I've never felt the urge to do so," he replied neutrally.

"They're quite economical," she assured him.

James would not lie to her. "I've never needed to economize."

He had been born into a wealthy family. He had married into a wealthy family. In his years of practice he had more than doubled his wealth.

"I see."

Her voice was cordial, her tone cool. Her inference was implicit: James Whitcox was wealthy; Frances Hart was not.

His money, she was thinking, was another barrier separating a country woman and a city man.

"I'm not interested in your finances," he said flatly.

"Nor are you interested in a flirtation," she returned unexpectedly.

James studied an illuminated cheek, the bridge of a nose, a curved lip, a line of chin, all that was clearly delineated by the lamppost. The whine of carriage wheels and the clip-clop of horse hooves filled the elastic silence.

"No," he said with finality. "I'm not interested in a flirtation."

He wanted far more from Frances Hart than a superficial dalliance.

Her gaze dropped from his eyes to his chest. "In the shop . . . did you find anything that interested you?"

He remembered the longing on her face when she had viewed the postcard of a woman offering her breast. He remembered the yearning that flushed her cheeks when she had viewed the postcard of a woman with a widow's comforter.

He remembered the pain-filled hunger in her eyes when she had turned away from the postcard of a man and a woman bound by mutual passion.

The way it could be. The way it should be.

The way it would be.

"Yes," he said quietly. Emphatically. "I found something that interested me."

Her head dipped lower, face plunging into complete shadow. "Are all men in Parliament against the emancipation of women?"

He leaned into her warmth, inhaling the spicy vanilla scent that was uniquely hers. "Not all."

"Are you?" she asked in a voice so low that he had to strain to hear it.

James lowered his head until the soft feathers adorning the crown of her hat tickled his forehead. Carefully he chose his words. "It isn't politically advantageous to support women's suffrage."

Her head reared back. "But *do* you?"

"Yes." He inhaled her breath, tasting tooth powder, tasting Frances. "I do."

He didn't often approve of the ways in which women sought equality, but he wholeheartedly endorsed the idea.

"Why did Miss Hoppleworth imply that you have represented wife-murderers?"

James had hoped she would not ask, even as he had known that she would. During the meeting last Saturday she had with courtesy and grace demonstrated an extraordinary intellect.

It was to Frances Hart's innate intelligence that he responded. "I am a defense attorney. The men and women I represent have been charged by the Crown. It is my duty to defend my clients. It is the duty of the jury to judge them."

"But you have represented clients, knowing that they are . . . murderers."

"Yes."

"What happened when the jury determined they were not guilty?"

"They were acquitted."

"Because of you."

"Yes," James said. And waited for her judgment.

The tips of her eyelashes shone like pale gold in the gaslight. "The Crown is not always correct when they accuse someone of a crime."

James tamped down the hope budding inside him. "No, they aren't."

Many blameless men—and women—had hanged in the name of justice.

"So because of you," she concluded, "innocent people who might otherwise hang are also set free."

It would be so easy to lie. She wanted to think that there was something noble in his person. But James would not lie. Not now. Not to this woman. He wanted Frances Hart to want him for what he was, and not for what set best on her conscience.

"I do not accept situations because I feel that the accused have been wrongfully charged," he said.

"Why do you accept them, then?"

The truth.

"Because they can't be won."

"But you said you always win," she puzzled.

"Yes." He had said that. To Frances, four days past. To Jack Lodoun, three hours past. "I do always win."

"Then, regardless of your own personal reasons for accepting these situations," she reasoned with quiet logic, generously sharing the warmth of her body and her breath and her conviction, "you do free those who are wrongfully accused."

Pain fisted inside his chest.

"Frances—" James's voice broke off, realizing he had used her christened name.

"Mr. Whitcox—" Frances's voice broke off, realizing he had used her christened name.

"Frances," he repeated more softly, his breath commingling with hers, "you do not know me."

"But I do know you—" His christened name hovered in the air between them; at the last second Frances lost courage. "Mr. Whitcox."

James ignored a pang of disappointment; at the same time, he felt his heartbeat quicken at the knowledge that she did not object to him using her given name. At the realization that she did not pull away from the closeness that was just short of a kiss.

"You know what I've told you," he corrected her, brutally honest.

She knew that he was a father. A widower. A barrister. She knew what types of postcards sexually excited him. She now knew that he had no scruples inside the social and economical loophole called the law. But she still did not know of what he was capable in his private life.

Frances licked her lips, a dark rose in the flickering light of the lamppost. "We all have secrets, Mr. Whitcox."

He knew everything there was to know about Frances Eleanor Goodrich Hart. Her past. Her present. He wanted Frances to know everything there was to know about James Cordon Whitcox, the Seventh.

James started with his past. "My wife presented me with a daughter on my twenty-sixth birthday."

Frances had told him that she had borne her first child at the age of sixteen; she had not told him that it had been a boy to whom she had given birth.

"I gave my wife a pearl necklace," he said, coldly indifferent to the mist that wet his cheeks, "and then I dined with the Lord Chancellor."

Frances's husband, the investigator had reported, had been a good man. A caring man. A family man. Everything that James was not.

"My wife bore my son just after my twenty-eighth birthday," he continued in that same stark, relentless voice. "I was in court when

I received the message that she was in labor. I delivered concluding remarks to a jury, then I purchased her a diamond necklace."

An icy rivulet of moisture dripped down his cheek. Dimly he realized that the mist had condensed into a drizzle.

"Four years and one miscarriage later, my wife asked to be spared the weekly trial of my conjugal visitations."

Frances mutely gazed up at him.

James curved his body to protect her.

From the rain. From the truth.

"The next day during a court intermission," he said inexorably, "I commissioned a popular architect to build her a house on Queen's Gate."

Her shadow-darkened eyes widened in surprise.

Queen's Gate was home to some of the most expensive properties in London. No doubt it was listed in her tour guide. Perhaps she had even seen the mansion he had built.

"I want you to know that I was with women after I took a wife," James said.

"After your wife left your bed," she quickly appended.

"*Before* my wife left my bed."

Frances audibly inhaled the warm mist of their commingled breaths.

"You gave your life to your family," he said, bluntly underscoring the difference between them. "I gave my family my wealth."

"My life," Frances murmured, "was all I had to give."

"Law," James said unrepentantly, "*was* my life."

Light and darkness glimmered inside her eyes. "But now it's not enough."

His law. Her family.

"No," James said. "It's not enough."

"Why do you want me to know these things, Mr. Whitcox?" she asked over the heavy grind of approaching wheels and jingling harnesses.

James saw what Frances did not. "I didn't take mistresses because I wanted to bed younger women, Frances."

"Why did you take them, then?" she challenged.

"I thought responsible men did not burden respectable women with their lust." His heartbeat clocked the passing seconds. "But now I know differently."

Cold moisture pooled at the nape of his neck.

"I gave my wife possessions." A lone drop of water crawled down his forehead. "You gave your husband children."

The names and birth dates of her children and grandchildren were indelibly imprinted on his brain.

"We didn't allow our spouses to know us, because we didn't know ourselves." Moisture misted the golden tips of her eyelashes. "But I want you to know me, Frances."

Father. Barrister.

Man.

"I want to know you."

Mother. Grandmother.

Woman.

The omnibus jerked to a halt beside the curb. He prepared to let Frances go when all he wanted to do was to touch her, to hold her, to love her in a way that neither of them had ever been loved.

"I don't want a flirtation," James said, need like hunger gnawing at his stomach, "because games are for children, and I don't want a child in my bed. I want a woman who will take as much pleasure in my sex as I will take in hers."

Chapter
15

It's not enough.
Creaking wood and a slap of leather reins sounded behind Frances. The omnibus pulled away from the curb.

She bowed her head against the stinging rain, each step reviving another memory. Another emotion. Each step, each memory, each emotion chased by the decision she must make.

A man raced past Frances, head buried inside the black tent of an umbrella, hurrying home. Or perhaps he hurried away from home. To a family. Or from a family.

Or perhaps he was alone.

She thrust a key into a lock. And saw not the rain-sluiced door, but James Whitcox. Breath misting the night. Gold and bronze hair dripping icy rain.

The door burst open. She collapsed against hard wood.

"Mrs. Hart?"

Frances jerked upright, heart springing into her throat.

"Are you ill?" The white-haired butler peered down at her, his lined face ruddy. "Shall I summon a doctor?"

"Oh." She brought her hands up to her wet hair, encountered wilted straw; the reticule slammed against her jaw. Liquid gurgled. The overwhelming burden that the bottle of Rose's Lubrifiant placed upon her weighted down her hands. "No. I'm fine, Mr. Denton. Just tired. And wet."

And frightened.

"Shall I bring you tea?"

"No, thank you."

Mindlessly she started for the stairs.

"If I may take your coat, madam, Mrs. Jenkins will hang it by the fire to dry."

"Yes." Frances dumbly halted. "That would be kind of Mrs. Jenkins."

"Are you quite certain you wouldn't like a physician, Mrs. Hart?"

A physician had told her to not fight her husband's death, to let nature take its course.

She unbuttoned sodden leather. "Quite certain, thank you."

Frances turned away.

The wool runner was worn, the steps were old. Oil-filled sconces flickered feebly at the top of the stairs.

The gas lighting that had been installed downstairs had not made its way upstairs. It was doubtful it ever would. The lease was affordable because the townhouse was deteriorating.

Frances thrust open the third door: an ember popped in the tiny fire blazing in the small, black iron fireplace.

Hazel eyes stared up from the burning coals. *I want a woman who will take as much pleasure in my sex as I will take in hers.*

She had not been able to respond to James Whitcox. She had only been able to stumble onto the waiting omnibus.

He had not expected a response from her, she realized. He had known the omnibus was coming. He had known that she would take it. While he stood in the rain. With no hat, no umbrella, no protection from rejection.

Frances shut the walnut door, a thud followed by a snick of metal lock.

Blue and yellow flames licked the darkness.

A patch of gray and black squares covered a sleigh bed. Beside it, a table stood squat and sturdy.

Frances carefully laid the heavy reticule onto the nightstand and tugged off her gloves. Easing open the top drawer, she rummaged for the box of safety matches . . . found them. Lungs filling, emptying, she lifted the glass globe off the oil lantern and held a burning stick to the wick.

Flickering light careened off a drab beige wall, danced on her fingers.

She blew out the match, breath escaping in a whoosh of recognition: all her life men—a father, a husband—had been responsible for her sexuality.

Frances dropped the blackened match into a miniature blue glass bonnet.

But now that responsibility lay—not in the hands of men—but in the hands of one woman.

She replaced the clear glass globe and turned the wick up as high as it would go, every movement methodical, as if she had planned beforehand each breath, each turn of the wrist, each step across the worn woolen carpet.

Standing in front of the dressing glass, she reached up and slid the hat pin out of the wilted straw hat.

She hung up the hat, green-and-gold dyed egret feathers a series of drooping question marks.

Purposefully she reached for her bodice.

The buttons were hard. The cashmere was soft.

A widening gap in the leaf-green jersey revealed white cotton . . . rose satin.

The chemise chastely concealed her chest from collarbone to bosom, while below it the corset boldly emphasized her breasts, waist and hips.

It was a ridiculous hodgepodge of mature woman and inexperienced girl.

A soft knock skidded down her spine.

She stiffened. "Yes?"

No doubt another letter had arrived in the evening post. But Frances didn't want to be a mother or a grandmother.

Tonight she simply wanted to be a woman.

"Do you need a cup of hot tea to ward off a chill, Mrs. Hart?"

It was the housekeeper rather than the butler.

"No, Mrs. Jenkins." She took a deep breath. It was not tea that she needed. "Thank you."

"Very well, marm," Mrs. Jenkins's accent was soft, sympathetic. "Good night."

Conversely, Frances wanted to call her back.

But the housekeeper was gone, footsteps as silent as the passage of youth.

Hands trembling, she reached for the steel frogs securing her corset.

Liberation, she discovered, came at a price.

Chapter
16

"Gentlemen of the jury, today I share my duty of defending the friendless lady in the dock." One by one, James gazed into the eyes of the jurors, deliberately impressing upon them the plight of Mary Bartle. She had no friends: they must become her friends.

The bored men and women in the gallery shifted restlessly.

They wanted more sex, more scandal—and James would provide it—but for now he ignored the rough laborers, the conservative middle-class, the privileged gentry, his sole focus on the bond he must forge between twelve men and one woman.

"The Crown has charged that Thomas Bartle died of poisoning. Two questions, therefore, must enter into your consideration: was it death by chloroform poisoning, and if it was, was the poison administered by Mrs. Bartle?"

He paused, allowing the weight of duty to settle on the jurors' shoulders.

"On the first question," James continued, "I concur with our learned prosecutor: we do not dispute the fact that Thomas Bartle died as a result of chloroform poisoning. However, we do dispute the second question.

"Mr. Lodoun claims that Evan Keaton is Mary Bartle's lover, and instructs us to believe that any woman who betrays the sanctity of her marriage vows is more than capable of murder."

To the twelve men in the jurors' box, infidelity was a form of murder in and of itself: an unfaithful wife cost a man his standing in the community.

"But was Mr. Keaton Mrs. Bartle's lover?" he asked, deliberately planting seeds of doubt.

The Attorney General had fed the jurors moral indignation; James fed them moral ambiguity.

"I have revealed to you that Mr. Bartle suffered from syphilis. I will reveal to you that he suffered from this disease before he took Mary Bartle to wife. I will reveal to you that Mary Bartle suffers from syphilis, and that it was her husband—in the sanctity of their marriage bed—from whom she contracted this disease."

Jurors two, five and six were shocked at learning that Mary Bartle had syphilis. Jurors one, four, seven and eleven were horrified that Thomas Bartle had knowingly infected his wife.

"I will reveal to you," James continued, "that Evan Keaton does not suffer from this dreadful malady. Gentlemen, I ask you, how can Mr. Keaton be Mary Bartle's lover if he does not have syphilis?"

Uncertainty ripped through jurors eight and ten. Logic told them that the chemist, with knowledge of venereal diseases and with direct access to condoms, might safely engage in sex with Mary Bartle. Personal revulsion at the thought of a healthy young man knowingly having sex with a diseased woman made them question their very legitimate logic. Jurors three, nine and twelve remained firmly convinced of her guilt.

It was to them that James spoke. "I will further reveal to you that Thomas Bartle was in the tertiary stage of syphilis. It is in this stage that death occurs from this most terrible of diseases. In a desperate attempt to save his life—for Mr. Bartle well knew that the syphilis was murdering him—he sought a cure. Even though, as you will soon discover, several physicians advised him that he sought treatment too late, Mr. Bartle—understandably anxious—took mercury. And he suffered. Hair loss—Mr. Bartle was nearly bald when he died—and loss of teeth are just a few of the casualties of mercury poisoning. There is the extra secretion of saliva that must surely feel like drowning in your own spittle."

The third juror convulsively swallowed.

James addressed the ninth juror. "The learned physicians in this courtroom have testified about the deadly effects of chloroform, but they have not instructed you about the agony from which a man with advanced syphilis suffers. They have not instructed you that syphilis ravages the mind and distorts reason.

"In my evidence for the defense, I will reveal to you that Thomas Bartle was in perpetual pain from the deformity to his joints that this dreadful disease causes. I will present witnesses who will testify that he suffered from acute malaise. These witnesses will tell you that on the night Mr. Bartle died, he confessed his sorrow that he had contaminated Mrs. Bartle, his wife, and he prayed to God to forgive him."

James addressed the twelfth juror. "Mr. Lodoun has told us that it was chloroform—not mercury or syphilis—that killed Thomas Edwards Bartle. You will, therefore, be presented with the question: from where did this chloroform come?

"Mr. Lodoun claims that it belonged to Mrs. Bartle. But I will reveal to you that one week prior to his death, Mr. Bartle visited a surgeon where he was given chloroform before having a syphilitic tumor removed from his neck."

James's gaze passed from juror to juror, assessing the thoughts and emotions that he purposefully created. "Imagine the relief Mr. Bartle must have felt to have his pain numbed for a little while, at least, without the drugging effects of an opiate.

"Yes, Mrs. Bartle had a bottle of chloroform. On the advice of Mr. Keaton, she purchased it for anesthetic purposes, to dull the pain of a minor surgery she was to have on the second of January, also to remove a syphilitic tumor. Mr. Keaton testified, however, that he sold Mrs. Bartle only one bottle. That bottle, upon examination, was found to be full. And still this isn't sufficient evidence to put reasonable doubt in the mind of our learned prosecutor.

"But you and I realize that chloroform may be purchased from any chemist, in dozens of London shops. During the evidence for the defense, I will suggest that Mr. Bartle purchased the chloroform which killed him. I will suggest that Mr. Bartle—suffering from incurable pain and malaise, products of both his illness and the mercury he took for treatment—drank the deadly anesthesia. Perhaps his mind wandered, and in his confusion, he didn't remember how chloroform is properly administered, which is, of course, inhaled rather than ingested. Or perhaps he thought that if a few drops on a cloth that is held to his nose is beneficial, that ingesting it would be doubly so. Mr. Bartle is dead, as Dr. Dudley pointed out, so we will never know *why* he drank the chloroform. We will never know if he intended to permanently end his suffering, or if he merely hoped for one night of respite."

James pinned jurors nine and twelve. "But we do know that Mrs. Bartle is not responsible for her husband's death. Mr. Bartle was dying when he ingested the chloroform. It is your duty, gentlemen, to listen to the evidence I present, and ask yourselves: why would Mary Bartle murder her husband and risk her own life when, if only she had waited . . . a month, three months, six months, a year at the most . . . Thomas Bartle would have died from the natural progression of his disease?"

The twelve jurors as one looked up at the dock.

They thought what James wanted them to think: Mary Bartle was a victim of both the Crown and her husband. It didn't occur to them that she might have taken her husband's life out of simple hatred for the life he had stolen from her.

James had won the trial without bringing forth one single witness.

Periwinkle blue eyes snared James's gaze.

Rage filled Jack Lodoun's face, immediately replaced by the cold mask of law.

Jack Lodoun had lost.

He knew it. James knew it.

James felt no triumph.

Mary Bartle's life would end no matter the jurors' verdict. She would die, day by day, from an unstoppable disease that had been inflicted upon her by the very man who had vowed to love, comfort, and honor her.

What good would Frances Hart see in his actions this day?

Chapter
17

The echo of wood banging wood reverberated inside the meeting room.

Tingling awareness of the twelve men and women who sat around the mahogany table raced up and down Frances's spine.

They had shared danger and excitement, visiting a pornographic bookshop. They would now share intimate thoughts and feelings, discussing the sexual artifacts they had purchased.

"This meeting is called to order," Joseph Manning said.

"Thank you, Mr. Manning," Marie Hoppleworth coolly acknowledged. "I regret that we did not have the pleasure of your company at the Achilles Book Shoppe."

Anger flushed his face. "There were extenuating circumstances, Miss Hoppleworth."

"Then Miss Dennison and Miss Fredericks must have suffered from a similar set of circumstances," the secretary countered.

"There is no rule saying that we must attend every single meeting, Miss Hoppleworth," Ardelle Dennison returned, voice equally cool.

"Quite right, Miss Dennison." Anger—or perhaps it was anticipation of the discussion to come—colored Marie Hoppleworth's face. "Last week Mr. Pierce proposed that we convene at the Achilles Book Shoppe, and bring to our next meeting an item which we found of interest. Today we shall discuss those items, and hopefully, as Mrs. Hart stated at the bookstore, learn more about sexuality, and be able to apply that learning to better our own lives. Who shall go first? Mrs. Hart?"

Frances's heart leapt up into her throat. *She wasn't ready to reveal herself.* "I—"

"Why don't you go first, Miss Hoppleworth?" John Nickols challenged.

The secretary studied the reporter. "Very well, Mr. Nickols."

Frances leaned forward to better see—reckoning deferred, curiosity rising. Out of the corner of her eye, she noted that Rose Clarring also leaned forward.

Marie Hoppleworth whipped out of her canvas satchel a black leather-bound book instead of the widow's comforter that Frances and Rose Clarring had anticipated. "I chose a Greek play."

"You disappoint me, Miss Hoppleworth." John Nickols's black eyes gleamed with mockery. "I was certain you would be able to find something more stimulating than a book."

"I'm afraid not, sir." Crimson dotted the secretary's face. "It is not every day that one comes across a two-thousand-year-old play starring a dildo."

"I am not familiar with the term dildo, Miss Hoppleworth," Rose Clarring said tentatively.

"Dildo is the traditional word for a widow's comforter, Mrs. Clarring," James Whitcox clarified.

He spoke to Rose Clarring, but Frances felt his gaze through every fiber in her being.

Slowly she met the hazel eyes that waited for her. "Why did you refer to it as a widow's comforter last Saturday, rather than a dildo, Mr. Whitcox?"

"Do you prefer traditional words over euphemisms, Mrs. Hart?" he feinted.

"I'm afraid I don't know very many euphemisms when it comes to sexual issues."

"Come now, Mrs. Hart, you have children," John Nickols goaded with gentle irony.

"Indeed I do, sir," Frances returned mildly. "Their use of bodily euphemisms, however, were limited to peewee, tinkle and doo-doo. Which they in turn have passed down to my grandchildren."

John Nickols grinned, a flash of even white teeth. James Whitcox's hazel eyes glinted with amusement.

"Respectable women do not possess the type of vocabulary to

which you are referring, Mr. Nickols," Joseph Manning said repressively.

A militant light gleamed inside Marie Hoppleworth's silver framed glasses. "Really, Mr. Manning."

Joseph Manning's top lip curled. "Really, Miss Hoppleworth."

"Choose a topic, sir."

"I beg your pardon?"

"You inferred that, because you are a man, you know more sexual euphemisms than I. There is only one way to test your hypothesis, is there not?"

Joseph Manning's ears turned red. "I refuse to bandy vulgar words with you, Miss Hoppleworth."

"Such a gentleman, Mr. Manning," John Nickols said sardonically. "I will gladly bandy about vulgar words with you, Miss Hoppleworth."

"Very well, Mr. Nickols," the secretary acceded. "You may choose the subject."

"Thank you," the journalist mocked. "We are at this particular point in our lives because Mrs. Hart very courageously reminded us that we need not suffer from sexual frustration; therefore, I choose the subject of masturbation—masculine, not feminine, I have no desire to put you ladies to the blush—and I'll start with my personal preference, which is 'frigging.'"

The red mottling the secretary's face deepened; her voice remained brisk and professional. "I myself prefer the term 'slaking the bacon.'"

John Nickols's eyes flashed with an odd mixture of speculation and anticipation. "Fiddle."

"Diddle."

"Bob."

"Shag," the secretary promptly returned.

"I didn't realize that the university taught a course on vulgar language, Miss Hoppleworth."

"There are many things you don't know about me, sir."

Deliberately John Nickols said, "Whank."

"Pull one's taffy."

The imagery was unmistakable.

"Box the Jesuit and get cockroaches."

"Bang the bishop," Marie Hoppleworth said.

"Spank the monkey."

"Prime one's pump."

Frances wanted to laugh at the absurd euphemisms. The rising tension choked off her laughter. The battle between the secretary and the journalist involved far more than words.

"Whizzing the jizzum," John Nickols said.

Frances blinked.

"Fetch mettle," Marie Hoppleworth said, undeterred.

"Onan's Olympics."

"One-legged race."

John Nickols's voice deepened. "Play a flute solo on a meat whistle."

Marie Hoppleworth promptly returned, "Burp the worm."

Creaking wood protested a shift in weight. Outside the museum a passing vendor cried: "Pies all 'ot! Eel, beef, or mutton pies! Penny pies, all 'ot—all 'ot!"

John Nickols regarded Marie Hoppleworth with unblinking intensity. "You didn't learn those words at university."

"No, I did not."

"Where did you learn them?"

"In a county orphanage," the secretary said evenly.

The tightness in Frances's throat moved into her chest.

The secretary, an orphan, had experienced the pain of rejection as surely as had John Nickols, confined to a wheelchair.

Blurring motion caught Frances's attention. A brown rubber sheath plopped down onto the middle of the polished table.

"This is what all of you want to see, isn't it?" Jane Fredericks challenged. "To see vulgar artifacts? To discuss what excites us? Pray let us discuss how *this* can excite a woman's interest."

There was so much anger and pain inside the young woman's murky green eyes.

Thomas Pierce reached out and picked up the condom. "Thank you, Miss Fredericks."

"Let us hope that your wife thanks you when you wed, Mr. Pierce," Jane Fredericks scornfully returned.

"I said 'thank you, Miss Fredericks,'" Thomas Pierce repeated; he did not take his gaze off the rubber sheath that he gently stretched between his two hands, "because last Saturday you made me realize why I do not enjoy the company of women."

Protest burst inside Frances's ears.

Ardelle Dennison: "How dare you—"

Marie Hoppleworth: "I demand you—"

George Addimore: "I say, there—"

"My father died when I was seven," Thomas Pierce spoke over their outrage; he continued stretching the rubber sheath, half an inch, three quarters of an inch, one inch . . . "Every day since he's died, my mother has lectured me about the folly of men pursuing women." The rubber sheath snapped back into shape. "'Like dogs chasing bitches in season,' she says."

Baby-blue eyes suddenly looked up from the condom, pinned Jane Fredericks. "Last Saturday, I realized that my father was unfaithful to my mother. When he died, my mother had no one to blame for his infidelity but me. I don't enjoy the company of women, Miss Fredericks, because my mother daily fed me her anger and her jealousy.

"You asked how a woman could find one of these"—he indicated the condom limply dangling from his fingers—"exciting. If I were a woman, rather I would ask: how could I find a man who did *not* use one of these exciting? How could I trust a man who puts his own moral values above the well-being of the woman for whom he is entrusted to care? But I'm not a woman, I'm only a man who has allowed himself to be poisoned against women by a woman."

"My mother has every right to be angry," Jane Fredericks said hotly. "She is dying because of my father."

"Not every man is like your father, Miss Fredericks."

"Really, Mr. Pierce," Jane Fredericks sneered. "And just how many times have *you* used one of those abominations to protect a woman?"

Painful red stained his cherubic face. "I've never been with a woman."

Disparate emotions raced up and down the mahogany table: shock; embarrassment; curiosity.

"What, nothing to say, Miss Fredericks?" Bitterness thickened Thomas Pierce's voice. "It's what you would have all of us immoral men be—a virgin—isn't it? So that we don't corrupt morally pure women?"

Jane Fredericks glanced away from the resentment in his eyes.

"You're not alone, Mr. Pierce."

Frances gazed toward Louis Stiles.

He bent over a sketch pad; dark red dissected his precisely parted black hair. "Neither have I ever been with a woman."

Frances did not know if her husband had come to their marriage bed a virgin or not. Resolutely she turned to Thomas Pierce. In the bookstore he had asked her a question. She returned the courtesy of his curiosity. "What did you select at the shop, Mr. Pierce?"

After a long, tense moment, he reached inside his black wool frock coat, and produced a pair of gold ear bobs.

"Those are very pretty," she said encouragingly.

"The clerk called them 'apple bobs.'" Thomas Pierce steadily held her gaze, his eyes free of rancor. "He said that women wear them on their nipples."

Frances abruptly became aware of the corset that bit into the sides of her breasts.

Gaze dropping to the table, Thomas Pierce meticulously re-arranged the "apple bobs." "When I was a boy, my mother dressed me in a ridiculous sailor's suit, and every Saturday promenaded me about the park. She belittled women who wore jewelry and the men they were with. Wednesday, in the shop—when I understood what these were—I thought how nice it would be if a woman wore them underneath her clothes, so that only she and the man of her choice knew."

Away from prying eyes and maternal condemnation.

Frances's chest constricted.

The faint whine and grind of carriage wheels filled the silence.

Esther Palmer abruptly spoke up. "What did you purchase, Mr. Stiles?"

A loud *snap* jolted up Frances's spine; half of a lead pencil flew through the air.

Head down, gaze locked onto the drawing that no one else could see, Louis Stiles drew out a professional print from the back of his sketch pad.

James Whitcox reached out and gently stretched the sheet of paper between his hands. He studied it for long seconds. "This is an extraordinary work of art, Mr. Stiles."

"I hope someday to be able to draw like that." Still without looking up, Louis Stiles dug into his frock coat and produced another pencil. "To see a woman like that."

Hazel eyes snared Frances's gaze. The emotion in them mirrored the emotion that had resonated in Louis Stiles's voice: the desire to see a woman. To know a woman. Naked in need as well as flesh.

Wordlessly James passed the print to Frances.

It was a simple drawing. There was nothing simple about the affect it elicited: it squeezed her heart and cramped her lower abdomen.

Because of the artist's talent she saw through the eyes of a man: the naked woman who straddled his hips, back a pattern of shadowed vertebrae and smooth skin. Her hips that rose upward while she leaned forward, head turning to gaze over her shoulder as if to gaze upon their intimate union: the loving clasp of her vagina; the vulnerable stalk of his penis; his hands cupping the softness of her hips; her pubic hair mingling with his pubic hair.

"It's beautiful, Mr. Stiles," Frances said truthfully. She passed on the print to Esther Palmer. "I have no doubt that you will someday capture a moment such as this. I hope, when you do, that you'll share your talent, so that others may enjoy it, also."

His chin sank into his chest. "Thank you."

George Addimore's side-whiskers twitched. "What did you purchase, Dr. Burns?"

Square face a dull brick red, the doctor reluctantly laid out a set of braided, black leather laces. Gruffly, she said, "I overwhelm men. I know I do because I'm taller than most men. I'd like to be overwhelmed once, to feel small and vulnerable, like other women."

Rose Clarring curiously studied the laces. "Overwhelmed in what manner, Doctor Burns?"

Sarah Burns squared her shoulders, as if expecting a blow. "By being restrained, Mrs. Clarring."

Frances's wrists tingled. She had never before imagined being tied down in order to feel desirable.

Sarah Burns hid an onslaught of shyness behind a show of aggressiveness. "What of you, Mr. Addimore?"

"I . . ." George Addimore ran a finger underneath his collar. "It's best I not say in front of ladies, Doctor Burns."

"Thank you, Mr. Addimore"—Ardelle Dennison lightly clapped, an outrage to all who had spoken—"for preserving our sensibilities."

"On the other hand—"Anger sparked inside his eyes. Face red, he defiantly reached into his frock coat. A large ring . . . or a very small bracelet . . . rolled across mahogany wood. "I stand by the rules of the club."

The ivory circle lost momentum just short of reaching Ardelle Dennison, wobbled, fell.

The publicist gazed at the object in equal parts intrigue and suspicion. "What is it, Mr. Addimore?"

"A cock ring," he said stiffly.

Ardelle Dennison jerked backward in revulsion.

Frances Hart leaned forward in curiosity. "What does it do, Mr. Addimore?"

Words failed him. "I . . . It . . . I . . ."

Hazel eyes drew Frances's gaze. "It fits over the base of a man's cock . . . or penis, if you will."

Instantly Frances remembered the men she had seen in the postcards, bodies bared, erections jutting. They had not worn any jewelry.

"Why would a—"She paused, breath quickening, wondering in what shape James's penis was formed . . . was the crown larger or smaller than the stalk? "Why would a man wear a ring over his penis?"

"To maintain an erection after ejaculation," John Nickols volunteered, "so that he can continue to pleasure a woman."

Frances slowly inhaled.

"What did you purchase, Mr. Nickols?"

Marie Hoppleworth's question was a direct challenge.

Without comment, the journalist pulled a postcard out of his coat and flicked it across the table.

The picture was upside down. All Frances could make out was a naked woman wearing a feathered mask.

The secretary slowly raised her eyelids. "Surely you could find more exciting postcards than this."

"I have simple fantasies, Miss Hoppleworth." The journalist's face was expressionless. "All I need is one woman."

"Who hides her face," the secretary provoked.

"Who hides her revulsion," John Nickols grimly returned.

Behind the thick glasses Marie Hoppleworth's eyes widened in surprise. "Why would she be disgusted, Mr. Nickols?"

Self-derision roughened the journalist's voice. "What woman wouldn't be disgusted by a man who lives in constant fear, Miss Hoppleworth?"

"What do you fear, Mr. Nickols?" Rose Clarring asked compassionately.

"Why do you think I was the last to descend the stairs at the Achilles Book Shoppe, Mrs. Clarring?"

Rose Clarring did not answer.

"I had to be carried, because there is no lift. I'm afraid that some-day I will be dropped down a flight of stairs. Or that a prankster will push me in front of a carriage. Or that a thief will overturn my chair, and leave me lying in the gutters for the dogs and rats to feed on.

"Every day, Mrs. Clarring," John Nickols said, "I live in fear."

Frances wanted to offer words of comfort, but she knew there was nothing she could say that would bring him solace.

He had told her they were at the bookstore because of her. It had not occurred to Frances that she could cause a man to fear. Any more than it had occurred to her that the two clerks had been with John Nickols so that they might carry him down the stairs.

"My husband contracted mumps shortly after we married," Rose Clarring suddenly confessed. She pulled a postcard out of her reti-cule. Tears glimmered in her cornflower-blue eyes. "He wanted chil-dren very much. After the mumps, of course, we couldn't have any.

He has told me that . . . that having intimacy without the hope of having children is like . . . like what this man is doing."

Frances stared at the naked man in the postcard. He stood upright, unashamedly stroking his erect penis, head slightly tilted back, an expression of sublime ecstasy on his face.

This, she realized, was a "billiards" postcard.

There was nothing unproductive about the man's actions: he took pleasure in touching his own flesh. As she had taken pleasure when touching her own flesh.

It was a beautiful and erotic postcard.

Glancing up, Frances caught Rose Clarring's gaze. Purposefully she said: "The composition is quite good, isn't it?"

A hiccup of laughter burst from the younger woman's mouth, too quick to be stifled by a hastily raised hand. Clearing her throat, Rose Clarring lowered her hand. The memory of the excitement they had shared—two women staring at three naked men—lingered in her eyes. "Quite."

"I hate wool."

Frances's startled gaze swung toward Esther Palmer.

"Dr. Jaeger claims that wool absorbs perspiration and allows the skin to breathe. Mrs. Beasley's Academy for Girls promotes healthy minds and healthy bodies, so wool is our uniform. Every girl. Every teacher. Every item of clothing."

Frances's skin itched in sympathy.

Esther Palmer gazed down at the table. "I know that I am not an attractive woman. My . . . my face turns purple when I'm upset or excited. Even as a child I suffered from this affliction. No man would wed me."

Frances's heart reached out. "That is not true, Miss Palmer—"

"Mrs. Hart, I know what I am." The teacher forced her head upright, caught Frances's gaze. "I know what my future holds. I will teach at the academy until I am too old to teach. Please don't think I'm complaining, because I'm not. I consider myself fortunate. I could have no position, and therefore be forced to live with my parents or, heaven forbid, my sister and her family.

"But I would like the comfort of a man. I long ago realized the futility of saving my virginity for a husband. For years I have used a . . .

a candlestick. But I have wanted to see a man. To—" The teacher swallowed. "To experience what it must feel like, to have a man inside me. To that purpose, I purchased this at the Achilles Book Shoppe."

Daring condemnation, Esther Palmer placed a leather phallus on the table.

The crown was only marginally larger than the stalk. It measured some six inches long.

"I have read that some women in India deflower themselves with stone phalluses," Thomas Pierce offered awkwardly.

"Women have had these needs for over two thousand years, Miss Palmer," Marie Hoppleworth bracingly reassured the mathematics teacher. "I myself cook the occasional sausage. They're much the same shape as your comforter, and far cheaper."

"Many women lose their virginity through regular exercise," Sarah Burns offered. "It is highly unlikely that a man would be able to determine whether you were a virgin or not."

Louis Stiles unexpectedly spoke up: "I would not want to hurt a woman when I took her to wife."

Frances glanced at the young man who rarely spoke. His vivid blue-green eyes were trained on Esther Palmer.

"A man strokes himself and pretends his hand is a woman." Louis Stiles's fingertips were white where he pinched the edge of his sketching pad. "That doesn't make him less of a virgin. He hasn't experienced a woman's body. He hasn't been embraced by a woman's flesh. You're still a virgin, Miss Palmer. You will gift a man with your joy when you first feel his body become a part of you. And he will treasure your gift."

Frances was riveted by the young man's declaration.

As if just realizing that he had spoken aloud, he ducked behind his pad.

"What did you purchase, Mr. Whitcox?" Rose Clarring asked after long moments had elapsed.

Frances's heartbeat quickened. *This* was the moment she had been waiting for.

Reaching into his coat, the barrister slowly withdrew a postcard.

Frances's breathing accelerated.

Holding her gaze, he placed the postcard on the table faceup and pushed it inexorably toward her.

Lightning recognition jolted through Frances.

Of a man. Of a woman.

Of moist heat buried in the crook of her neck, breathing in the scent of her skin. Of dry heat lifting and shaping the heaviness of her breast. Of rasping heat plunging between—

Frances clenched her thighs together. The physical barrier did not stop the acute sensation of masculine fingers finding her, parting her, filling her.

"Last week Mrs. Hart asked why there were no men in the postcards I brought to the meeting." The barrister's voice reverberated throughout Frances's body. "I replied that the sight of men didn't titillate me."

She forced her gaze away from the postcard.

"I was wrong." James spoke at large; he focused on Frances. "I find the sight of a man and a woman together far more stimulating than pictures of women alone. When I look at this postcard, I can smell the woman's excitement—like vanilla and spice. I can feel her desire as keenly as if it were my body that she leaned against. As if it were my hand that cupped her breast. I look at this postcard and I become this man. It is I who touch this woman's sex. It is with me that this woman shares her passion."

The raw need in his hazel eyes pierced Frances to the core. The knowledge that she now possessed the ability to satisfy that need sent her heartbeat tripping with both fear and excitement.

"What did you purchase, Mrs. Hart?" Thomas Pierce asked.

This was the moment Frances had been dreading. For long seconds she was paralyzed with indecision.

Twelve pairs of eyes peered at her as if they could see into her very soul.

There would be no going back if she did this. There had been no going back since the day she had met a man who unashamedly admitted his need for a woman's passion.

Moving as if she were ninety-four instead of forty-nine, Frances reached into her reticule and grasped a glass bottle. Slowly, carefully, she pulled it free of silk-lined leather, and set it on the table between her and the barrister. The soft *clunk* of glass contacting wood clamored in the cool spring air.

Quizzically, James Whitcox glanced down, dark shadow hollowing his cheeks. A stillness settled over his features. Silence settled around the table until the only sound in the meeting room was the dull rumble of traffic and the relentless hiss of gas.

"*Lubrifiant*," he breathed into the quietness, long fingers reaching, wrapping around the pretty bottle. "Lubricant."

Frances realized that she was the only member of the Men and Women's Club who had not known what the word *lubrifiant* meant. No sooner did the thought cross her mind, than James glanced up.

His eyes were dark with knowledge, both of her needs and of the purpose of the lubricant.

Taking a calming breath, Frances met Thomas Pierce's waiting gaze. "Two weeks ago, Mr. Whitcox said that he was afraid it was too late to experience passion."

Hazel eyes burned a hole in the back of her head.

"I didn't believe it was too late for Mr. Whitcox, Mr. Pierce, because he is a man in his prime. But I did believe it was too late for a woman of my age."

"Why?" James Whitcox asked sharply.

"When a woman reaches a certain age, Mr. Whitcox"—Frances forced herself to meet the barrister's gaze and publicly acknowledge her weakness—"she is no longer capable of producing natural . . . lubricants."

His gaze narrowed, a barrister's gaze. "And you thought that would prevent you from experiencing passion?"

"I thought it was nature's way of telling me that I should concentrate on things other than carnal pleasure."

"What do you think now, Mrs. Hart?"

"I think, Mr. Whitcox"—Frances squared her shoulders, refusing to give in to the fear that bubbled inside her veins—"that women have a choice when it comes to their sexuality. I think, because of aids such as Rose's Lubrifiant, that a woman's sex—no matter her age—need never be dry. Neither for her pleasure, nor for a man's."

The light that blazed in his eyes riveted Frances.

He still wanted to know her, *knowing* that her body no longer performed like the body of a younger woman.

"This meeting has been most informative," Marie Hoppleworth announced. "I have learned many things today. I suggest we make plans for next week's discussion."

"I suggest we assemble somewhere outside this coffin," John Nickols stated.

"I second that motion," James Whitcox said.

"Let's go on a picnic," Esther Palmer suggested.

"On a Sunday," Rose Clarring proposed, "so that we do not need to rush."

"I'm free tomorrow," Sarah Burns offered.

"Tomorrow is good," George Addimore added.

Ardelle Dennison's mouth tightened into a thin line. "We have met in this room each Saturday for two years—"

"And we are more strangers to each other now than when we formed this club," Thomas Pierce concluded.

Frances stared at Ardelle Dennison. And saw—beyond the anger that sparked her amber eyes—the desperation that pinched her beautiful face. It had been *she* whom Joseph Manning had hurt with his thoughtless declaration that he had not found a woman worthy of marriage.

"Why can't we have our picnic tomorrow," Frances quietly queried, "and meet here next Saturday?"

"Very well," the secretary agreed. "We will meet here next Saturday. Meanwhile, where do you suggest we convene tomorrow, gentlemen . . . ladies?"

"The Crystal Palace," James prompted.

Chapter
18

Wood creaked, relieved of weight. Wool rustled, propelled into motion. Five men and six women pushed away from the mahogany table.

James gently caressed cool crystal with his thumb. "You used this."

Frances Hart's pale green eyes returned his perusal. "Yes."

Wooden umbrella handles clinked against brass; woolen coats swished around bodies. The odd conversation fell onto the muted noises drifting up from the street outside.

James intently studied the woman who continued to touch him in ways he had never thought to be touched. "You used this on your sex."

Flesh that she had thought a man would not want to touch due to her age.

Frances did not flinch away from the truth. "Yes."

There was a new awareness in her gaze.

"You used this inside your sex," James assayed.

"Mrs. Hart. Mr. Whitcox." Rose Clarring's voice shot down his spine. "Would you care to join us for a spot of tea?"

James purposely projected his voice, eyes trained on Frances. "We'll join you directly, Mrs. Clarring."

Hot color tinged Frances's cheeks.

"We'll be down the street at the coffee shop," Marie Hoppleworth said.

"Thank you, Miss Hoppleworth," he said, again projecting his voice.

The heavy mahogany door closed.

James and Frances were alone. Clearly delineated by the over-head chandelier. No shadows to hide behind.

A private club of two.

"They'll know we speak of personal matters," Frances said.

"They have their own personal matters to discuss," James said in-differently. Caressing the crystal stopper, he repeated: "Did you use the lubrication to penetrate your sex?"

"Yes." She lifted her chin, daring him to judge her. "I did."

"With your fingers."

"Yes."

His chest tightened. His groin tightened.

She would not lie to him.

A sharp need to know Frances Hart drove James. "How many fin-gers did you use?"

He wanted to picture her pleasure in his mind, to be a part of her burgeoning sexuality.

"I used three fingers," she said in a steady voice.

The hum of the outside traffic vibrated inside his body.

"Show me," he said. "Show me which fingers you used."

Frances placed her right hand onto the table, palm down.

She had small hands. Industrious hands.

Her short oval nails were buffed to a shine.

Slowly she hooked her little finger with the pad of her thumb, the heel of her hand rising, three fingers tilting downward.

Heat engulfed the fore, middle and ring fingers on James's right hand.

"Did you take pleasure in your vagina?" he asked.

"Yes." The hot color tinging her cheeks bridged her nose. Her gaze did not waver from his. "I did."

The tension coiling inside James tightened. "You said you didn't use your fingers like a phallus."

"I didn't."

"But you penetrated your body after visiting the bookshop."

"Yes."

"And you took pleasure in your vagina," he probed.

"Yes." She did not look away from either his questions or her sex-uality. "I did."

James remained casually sitting in the medallion-backed chair; his entire being strained to reach out to Frances. "Why?"

Why did she now take pleasure in the flesh that a week earlier she had rejected?

Her gaze glanced off his; she stared at the anemic sunshine that penetrated the window. "You said you looked at your wife, and saw a stranger."

James had looked at his wife lying cold and still in the satin-lined casket and realized that he did not know any more about the woman who had borne him two children, than he had known about the debutante he had married.

"When I looked at my husband," Frances said, face soft and vulnerable as she focused on her past, "*I* was the stranger. Not the man I married. I had never taken the time to be anything other than a wife and a mother. My whole life revolved around my family. I had no existence without them, yet when my husband lay dead, I did exist."

The man inside him wanted to comfort her; the barrister inside held him back.

Resolutely, Frances met his gaze. "I no longer want to be a stranger to myself, James."

Pleasure twisted inside him, hearing her address him by name. Pain cut through the pleasure, understanding the reason she had touched herself: Frances had claimed the sexuality she had sacrificed for others.

"Did you receive the same pleasure from your vagina, as you receive from your clitoris?"

Knowledge of the satisfaction her own body was capable of achieving glowed in her eyes. "No."

James had never explored a woman's sex. Vicariously he explored it through Frances.

"How do the sensations differ?"

The chandelier hissed, gas steadily pumping through copper tubing like blood through veins.

Frances unselfishly shared the knowledge of her body. "Penetration is a deeper, more intimate sensation."

There had been nothing intimate about the pleasure James had received when thrusting inside a woman's flesh.

He had felt duty. He had felt lust.

He had not been touched by either.

"What does it feel like when you touch your clitoris?" he asked, needing to understand the essence that was Frances Hart.

"It feels like my clitoris has a heart," she answered. "Each time I touch it, it throbs."

Like a little cock.

"Which sensation do you prefer?"

"I don't know."

His fingers pulsated against the brittle glass of the bottle; a matching pulsation throbbed inside his groin. "Did you orgasm when you penetrated your vagina?"

Her eyelashes flickered. "Yes."

The truth but not the whole truth.

"How did that orgasm differ from those you experience when you touch your clitoris?"

Frances hesitated. "I don't know."

There was no deceit in her eyes. There was no prevarication in her voice. She simply did not know the answer to his question.

"Why don't you know, Frances?" he asked gently.

Why must it be so difficult for men and women to overcome the burdens placed upon their sex?

The dusky rose that infused her face spread down her neck. "The heel of my hand pressed against my clitoris when I penetrated myself."

"A man's pelvis presses against a woman's clitoris when he comes into her," James dispassionately observed.

Yet no woman had ever reached orgasm when he penetrated her. Would Frances Hart?

Could a man satisfy a woman while he took his own satisfaction?

"What does the *lubrifiant* taste like?" he asked abruptly.

Her pale eyes widened in surprise. "I don't know."

Slowly James took off the crystal stopper. Gaze holding hers, he dipped the tip of his middle finger into the bottle. "Taste."

Frances stared at his finger.

James glanced down to look at what she studied.

A clear drop of oil quivered on the tip of his finger. He could feel a matching drop of liquid bead on the tip of his glans.

Slowly leaning forward, she quickly swiped his finger with the tip of her tongue.

Hot. Wet.

The rasp of her tongue penetrated deep inside his testicles.

Instantly she drew back, gaze uncertain, knowledgeable about her own body, but as ignorant of a man's sexual needs as James was ignorant of a woman's. "It has no flavor."

The oil. The law.

His life.

"I've never tasted a woman's sex."

Her expression told him that she had never been tasted.

"Why not?" she asked quietly.

"Women are taught to place the needs of others above their own."

Her internal battle between self and family continued. "Yes."

"Men," James said, "are taught to place their own needs above others."

Understanding weighted her gaze: she had pleased others, but she had never taken pleasure for herself; he had pleased himself, but he had never given pleasure to others.

James focused on Frances, seeking in her what he had never sought in another.

"Stick your finger into the bottle," he said, his voice remote, a barrister's voice, removed from the needs of the flesh.

Frances's eyes asked a question as she dipped her middle finger into the bottle.

"Not just your fingertip," he said. "Stick your whole finger into the lubricant."

Pale green eyes still questioning, she reached more deeply into the bottle until the oily liquid reached her second knuckle.

"Now penetrate your vagina, Frances, and let me taste your finger."

Her shock ricocheted off the five gas globes that starkly illuminated them.

Mary Bartle's trial would end the following week. The Crown

would present closing remarks, followed by the closing remarks of the defense. Twelve jurors would deliberate the fate of a woman who, regardless of their verdict, would never take joy in her womanhood.

"Share your sex with me, Frances." James needed to understand what it must be like to be a woman. Sold in marriage. Betrayed in marriage. Dependent upon the good will of men who had been raised to put their own good first. "I don't want you to be a stranger to me."

Fear battled with vulnerability inside her eyes. The need to be known overcame the two disparate emotions.

Holding his gaze, she scooted forward onto the edge of her chair.

James could not see Frances below the waist. He could only hear the rustle of her clothing. He could only see the embarrassed awareness that tensed her face. He could only feel the slick penetration in the dilation of her pupils.

Slowly, hand slightly trembling, she offered her finger.

Oil glistened inside the twin indentations of her fingernail, lightly smeared her finger, first knuckle, second knuckle. The rest of the oil resided one and a half inches deep inside her vagina.

James leaned forward and licked her fingertip.

Frances's sharp inhalation of pleasure filled the emptiness inside him. Deliberately—his gaze holding hers—he sucked her finger into his mouth and licked it clean of oil and Frances.

She tasted like spicy vanilla.

Her skin. Her sex.

James licked her finger until the black of her pupils swallowed the pale green of her irises, and the lingering embarrassment tensing her face melted away.

Releasing her finger with a slick lick, he sat back and replaced the crystal stopper. "Let's go have tea."

Chapter
19

The heels of Frances's half-boots tapped sharply in the shadowy corridor. James's steps matched hers, his heel taps an audible reminder of the intimacy they had shared and the bond it had forged.

She had reached into the most private recesses of her body while he watched. He had tasted the essence of her femininity while she watched.

Frances stared fixedly at a dull gleam of brass, her entire being intent upon their forward progression. "Were you a virgin when you married?"

"No," James said. "I lost my virginity when I was fifteen."

Frances would have been seventeen, unaware that James Whitcox existed, married two years already to a man who had given her one baby, with another on the way.

"Was she a virgin?"

"I don't know."

Had the girl saved herself for a boy who had no notion of her gift?

Frances had not bled when her husband had taken her to wife. Had she diligently preserved a hymen that had already been lost through regular exercise?

"Did she enjoy it?" Frances pursued.

James had lost his virginity thirty-two years ago; Frances had lost her virginity thirty-four years ago. Their pasts could not be altered. Why did it matter?

"A chambermaid offered me her body in exchange for five bob," James said in that same curiously passionless voice with which he had told her that he needed her to share her body with him. "At the time I thought it was a fair transaction. She lifted her skirts and bent over. I loosened my trousers and fumbled my way into her. The whole thing was over in less than a minute."

Frances reached out and grasped the brass newel cap, the reticule wrapped around her left wrist swinging, the bottle of lubricant safely tucked inside.

The giraffe below stared with dead eyes.

"Do you still think it was a fair transaction?" she asked.

"My mother found the coin on her the following day and dismissed her."

Frances swallowed. "Did you tell your mother that she didn't steal it?"

"It wasn't for theft that my mother dismissed her," he said cynically.

A primly cloaked woman and a young boy dressed in a sailor suit paused at the foot of the stairs. Frances was irrepressibly reminded of Thomas Pierce.

"What did your mother do to you?" she asked.

"My mother told my father, who that night sat me down and explained the business of sex." There was no emotion in his voice. "He felt I had grossly overpaid the chambermaid."

A girl had lost her livelihood. A boy had lost his innocence. All for a crown.

"Did *you* enjoy it?" Frances pressed.

"Not particularly."

The young boy in the sailor suit excitedly pointed at the seventeen-foot-tall giraffe.

Frances gripped the newel cap. And stepped over the line of the past into the present. "Did you enjoy my taste?"

"Vanilla spice, Frances."

She swung past the balustrade and descended the stairs, her internal flesh slippery with oil. James descended beside her, matching each downward plunge, left foot, right foot.

Louis Stiles's erotic print flashed through her thoughts.

She had never before imagined her pubic hair entwining with a man's. Logic told her that it was inevitable when a couple engaged in conjugal intercourse. She would have experienced the phenomena countless times with her husband. There was no reason why the thought of her pubic hair entwining with that of James Whitcox should accelerate her heartbeat, and swell her breasts.

There was no reason why the memory of him licking her finger should fill her eyes with tears.

"Why did you suggest that we assemble at the Crystal Palace?" Frances asked, throat taut.

"Have you been there?"

"No." The tour guidebook had described it as a two-hundred acre park filled with botanical and geological wonders. Sussex county abounded in botanical and geological wonders.

She stepped off hard wood onto even harder marble.

James stepped down beside her, saying cryptically. "You'll see to-morrow."

Tomorrow.

Frances could not get past the last half hour, let alone plan for the morrow.

She strode past a dented suit of armor, worn for protection. She strode past a chipped Roman sarcophagus, proof of mortality. She strode past a peat-blackened prehistoric fossil, the past ever present.

A man and a woman approached on the opposite side of the brass and glass door. The man was tall and he wore a black top hat. The woman was half a head shorter and wore a plumed straw hat.

"I can no longer become pregnant," Frances said, risking the ulti-mate rejection.

"I have no desire to impregnate a woman," he replied imper-turbably, still not rejecting her.

"Why did you use the word 'cock' when you turned off the faucet?"

There were any number of words he could have used that Satur-day: faucet, spigot, tap, valve.

James's reflected gaze snared hers. "I wanted you to look at me."

"I did look at you," she admitted.

James pushed open the door. "And then you walked away."

Frances stepped over the threshold.

London paraded before her. Rumbling wagons. Shrilling car-riages. Men in bowler hats and women in bonnets hurried past while children, their future lost in the present, unconcernedly raced by it all.

Hot breath feathered the back of her neck, her cheek. A solid presence stepped beside her.

"I'm not walking away now, James," Frances said into the acrid air that smelled of manure and coal.

"Then take my arm—" James offered his arm, the gesture of a respectable gentleman to a respectable lady. There was nothing respectable, surely, about their needs. "And walk with me."

Frances tucked her gloved hand into the nook of his arm.

His hip burned where it nudged her. Her shoulder burned where it rubbed his.

Men and women all around walked together as Frances and James walked.

Did the women yearn to be more than wives and mothers, as Frances yearned? Did the men ache with the need to experience a woman's passion, as James ached?

Their walk was short. The coffee shop was crowded.

Bouncing light and egret feathers danced underneath gaslit globes.

"Mrs. Hart," Rose Clarring called. "Mr. Whitcox."

Eight pairs of eyes openly appraised Frances and James.

Frances instinctively pulled away from the barrister. At the same time she returned the acknowledgment. "Mrs. Clarring."

"Take a seat, Mrs. Hart." John Nickols pushed forward a white-enameled wrought iron chair. "You, too, Mr. Whitcox."

"No, thank you," James politely declined. "I have an errand I must attend."

Frances gazed upward. There was no light in his eyes.

Nodding his head, he turned and walked away.

Loneliness engulfed her.

"I must be off as well, ladies, gentlemen," George Addimore said. "I'm dining with a business associate."

"I, too, must take my leave," Rose Clarring said. "I also have errands to run."

"There was a shortage at the bank today," Thomas Pierce said. "I must audit an employee."

"I must finish an assignment, since I will be otherwise occupied tomorrow," Marie Hoppleworth said.

"I have a patient I must visit," Sarah Burns said.

"I have an article to finish," John Nickols said.

"I have papers to correct," Esther Palmer said.

Frances silently sat at the white-enameled table and watched as one by one the members of the Men and Women's Club took their leave.

Vagina burning. Finger burning.

Letters waiting to be answered.

Frances did not know how to answer them.

She did not know how to tell her thirty-three-year-old son or her seven-year-old granddaughter that it was not grief which kept her in London, but the need to have a life separate from theirs.

Louis Stiles busily sketched.

"May I see your picture?" Frances asked impulsively.

A perceptive blue-green gaze captured hers. Slowly, reluctantly, he turned around the pad.

Frances saw the members of the Men and Women's Club through the eyes of Louis Stiles. Ardelle Dennison gaped in horrified fascination at the cock ring that rolled toward her. Thomas Pierce longingly stretched a condom between his hands. Esther Palmer guiltily warmed a dildo in her fingers. Joseph Manning fixedly stared at a miniature print of a naked woman who sat backwards across a man's hips.

Unerringly her gaze honed in on the man who sat at the opposite end of the table, and the woman who sat beside him.

James grasped a small bottle, his face ineffably vulnerable as he looked at the postcard that a troubled Frances held up.

Chapter
20

The Victoria Station reverberated with the wails of over-excited children, the cries of exhorting mothers, and the commands of herding fathers.

English Sundays were devoted to God and family.

James had never spent time with his wife. He would not make that mistake with Frances.

The door to the public toilet opened. Frances exited behind two chattering women, her face flushed with excitement.

James stepped forward. "Have you got your ticket?"

"Yes." Startled awareness shone in her eyes. "Thank you."

"Then let's take our seats." He drew her hand through the crook of his elbow. "The train's about to leave."

Frances quickly glanced around and through the closed circles of families. "Where are the others?"

"Waiting for us."

She raised her face to his. "Did Miss Fredericks come?"

"No."

Disappointment clouded the excitement in her pale eyes. "I wish she had come."

Some wounds could not be healed.

Frances's face visibly brightened at an inner thought. "What of Miss Dennison and Mr. Manning?"

"They're not here, either," he said.

Some people were more afraid of intimacy than they were of loneliness.

Avoiding the disappointment he knew his words had caused, James wound around the closed circles of men, women, and children, laborer families and middle-class families alike, dressed in their Sunday best.

"James."

He leaned closer to hear over the din of voices and trains. "Yes?"

"I'm sorry I pulled away from you yesterday in the coffee shop."

James opened his mouth to tell her it didn't matter. Only to realize that it did matter. He *had* been hurt by her withdrawal. He simply had not wanted to admit to himself that this woman could wound him.

Shutting his mouth, he straightened.

"James."

Frances's clear voice was gently insistent.

He reluctantly leaned closer; vulnerability set uneasily on his shoulders. "What?"

"Did you know that the toilets here flush by themselves?"

A tickling sensation filled his chest. Laughter, still too new to push past the years of self-imposed solitude, melted away the small hurt Frances had inflicted.

Their train—a blue light train for short trips—belched steam.

"Step up, Frances."

He steadied her as she climbed up steep metal stairs. Third class was the only section that could seat all of them together. James had never ridden third class in his life.

The train—otherwise known as a parliamentary train because of the legislation requiring all trains to include at least one carriage at a penny-a-mile rate—was crowded.

"You can squeeze in here," Thomas Pierce called.

The banker had managed to grab a row of seats by the door.

James squeezed in beside Frances, he in his black silk top hat and she in vivid, striped green serge.

John Nickols sat in an aisle seat, his face grim. Marie Hoppleworth sat in a window seat, her head covered by a black bonnet. Her face in the glass was a distant ghost framed by silver-rimmed glasses.

"Is it far?" Frances asked.

"Not far," Rose Clarring said, dark, conservative hat precisely angled on her head. "About seven miles."

"I haven't been to the Crystal Palace since I was a young girl," Sarah Burns said from behind James.

Frances turned in her seat; the soft press of her breast bolted through James's arm. "What is it like?"

"It's a park," Louis Stiles said behind the barrier of his sketch pad.

"It's an exhibit," Thomas Pierce said.

"It's a cultural smorgasbord," Marie Hoppleworth said into the window.

"Concerts are held there," Esther Palmer said.

"Fireworks are shot off every night," Rose Clarring said.

"We should arrange a place to meet after the fireworks," James interrupted, deliberately redirecting the conversation lest someone spoil the surprise that was in store for Frances, "in the event that we get separated."

"Why not the gate?" Thomas Pierce suggested.

"The gate it is," James readily agreed.

"I will be glad to provide escort for any of you ladies," George Addimore gruffly offered.

James imagined there would be several couples who paired together this day.

"When did you last visit the Crystal Palace?" Frances asked.

"Four years ago," James said, his arm burning, his muscles cramping. He had physically traced the last steps of a murderer and his victim. His client had been propositioned by a young man on the boating lake. The young man had made the unfortunate choice of taking James's client home with him instead of taking him to a public inn.

An awkward silence fell over the small group of men and women, who after two years of estranging one another were now working to develop the comradery they should have established in the beginning.

They did so now because of one woman's honesty.

James inhaled Frances's scent. And remembered the taste of her.

As if aware of his thoughts, Frances glanced up.

It was all there in her pale green eyes. Her penetration. His tasting.

Her breast that now imprinted his arm.

Busily punching and collecting tickets, a conductor called out the next stop.

"Keep your ticket," James murmured. "You'll need it to get into the park."

"How many more stops?" she asked, dropping her ticket into her reticule.

"I don't remember," he said, breathing in the salty tang of her breath. But he remembered the murder case. He remembered the victim. He remembered the accused.

He remembered the jurors who had acquitted his client.

The train braked, metal screaming, steam roiling.

"Your breath smells of tooth powder," Frances whispered.

"So does yours," James whispered back.

More people boarded. No one exited.

A cloud of steam rose up from the train; it slowly chugged forward.

The ticket-collecting conductor, body rocking side to side, called out Sydenham.

"That's our stop," George Addimore said.

John Nickols's face tightened.

It had taken tremendous courage for a forty-nine-year-old woman who had never traveled outside of her small county to come to London, alone. The journalist possessed the same indomitable courage as did Frances Hart, daily traveling alone in a world that was not equipped to handle men in wheelchairs.

James gave John Nickols back some control.

"Mr. Addimore," James said. "Mr. Nickols could descend the train more easily if he grabs our shoulders."

John Nickols's head snapped around. They stared at each other, two men who needed, two men who feared the very thing they needed.

The tension tightening the journalist's face eased. If he fell, it would be because he didn't hold on tightly enough, not because someone dropped him. He nodded.

The train halted with a screech of brakes. Roiling steam obliterated the sky.

Frances's eyes were luminous in the gloom of the carriage.

Silently James offered her his umbrella.

Expression inscrutable, Frances accepted the wooden grip. Every man, woman and child exited the train save for James, John Nickols, and George Addimore.

"Ready?" James asked. A heavy, muscular arm dropped over his shoulders. "Let's go."

Strength and trust bonded the three men, each one using his individual strength to achieve a common goal, each one trusting the other to not fail.

A conductor had retrieved the wheelchair and held it ready in front of the door. James felt the momentary loss of the warmth and weight of John Nickols's trust.

Silently Frances held out James's umbrella.

The sky was gray, threatening rain.

Working-class families set off on foot for the park. Middle-class families boarded the omnibuses that clogged one side of the street. Affluent families waited to be picked up by the cabs that lined the other side of the drive.

James raised his umbrella to hail the latter.

Excitement sparked Frances's voice. "Look, that omnibus has a double deck."

Motion caught James's attention: John Nickols, Rose Clarring, Thomas Pierce, Sarah Burns and George Addimore crossed the street toward a worn Clarence cab.

"There's no need to ride an omnibus," James said, watching the banker and the accountant assist the journalist into the cab. The two women lifted up the wheelchair for the cab driver to secure it on top of the carriage.

"You said you would follow wherever I go, James."

He sharply focused on Frances. "I want you to experience my world, too, Frances."

A world where money was plentiful and privilege was assured.

"Neither of us has ever ridden on top of an omnibus." Face solemn, gaze searching, Frances asked, "Why not make the experience a part of both our worlds?"

A smile twisted his mouth. "You would make a formidable opponent, Mrs. Hart."

Her returning smile took his breath away.

James searched in his pocket for change. Frances dropped into the box the appropriate pennies for two rides.

His stomach knotted. No woman had ever paid his fare.

Marie Hoppleworth, Esther Palmer and Louis Stiles declined the opportunity to get chilled and probably rained upon. They rode inside the omnibus while James rode on top with Frances.

Cool, damp air caressed his face. Warm, scented woman enveloped his senses.

"Look, Frances." His shoulder companionably rubbing hers, he pointed toward the Crystal Palace, a glass and iron construction that was one thousand eight hundred and forty eight feet long and four hundred and eighty feet wide. The largest conservatory ever built, the critics said. "Look at the water towers."

Two water towers flanked the glass palace; they were two hundred and eighty-two feet tall. Hot-air balloons soared high in the background. A roller coaster reared up above a skyline of trees.

"Oh," she said with an audible intake of air.

James looked at Frances's face, and saw the Crystal Palace through her eyes: the beauty; the wonder; the unencumbered joy.

He wanted her to look like that when he joined his body to hers. He wanted to experience the innocence of unashamed sexuality.

A growing crowd gathered outside the closed gates, children restless with excitement, mothers already tired, fathers determined to keep their families together.

John Nickols waited outside the fringes of the crowd, his face moody. Thomas Pierce, Rose Clarring, George Addimore, Esther Palmer, and Sarah Burns silently milled around him.

The wafting aromas of cooking meat, sugar and fruit heightened the anticipation.

Behind the closed gates and throughout the expansive grounds, vendors selling ginger beer, sandwiches, pies, sweets, and other foodstuff finished setting up their stalls.

Excitement crested at the approach of uniformed men. Without further ado the gates were opened wide.

Families flowed around the members of the Men and Women's Club like water around a boulder.

The moodiness darkening John Nickols's face increased as he wheeled toward the glass and iron palace, metal crunching on the paved path. "You're limping, Miss Hoppleworth."

The secretary subtly favored her left foot. "It's nothing, Mr. Nickols."

"Obviously, it is something," the journalist said, matching the speed of his wheelchair to her gait, "or you wouldn't be limping."

"I merely laced my shoe too tightly."

"Then loosen the lace."

"I fully intend to do so"—Marie Hoppleworth limped forward—"when I reach a place where I can sit down."

"I am a traveling chair, Miss Hoppleworth," the journalist challenged. "Unless, of course, you would rather endure pain than take advantage of what comfort I may offer."

James silently watched the struggle between the secretary and the journalist, he to gain attention, she to avoid attention, neither of them used to public acceptance.

Marie Hoppleworth flushed. "I have no intention of flashing my ankle in public, sir."

"We will stand in front of you and act as a screen, Miss Hoppleworth," Rose Clarring quietly offered, an unexpected accomplice.

She, too, knew the pain of loneliness and the fallacy of pride.

One by one Rose Clarring, Thomas Pierce, Esther Palmer, Louis Stiles, Sarah Burns and George Addimore formed a half-circle around John Nickols's chair, their backs facing the couple to afford them privacy.

There was nothing more that anyone could do to lessen the plight of the secretary and the journalist. Either Marie Hoppleworth would accept the comfort that John Nickols offered, or she would reject it.

"It's going to rain," James observed neutrally. "There is something that I wish to show Mrs. Hart before the park gets too soggy. We'll be back in time for lunch."

"Where shall we lunch?" Rose Clarring asked, eyes wide, gazing at the acres of green grass and carefully manicured shrubs that were intertwined with paved walks, terraces and fountains. Gazing anywhere but at the woman behind her who finally, reluctantly accepted what she needed.

"There are cafés inside," Thomas Pierce said.

"If weather permits, we can purchase food from vendors and lunch by the main fountain over there," Esther Palmer said, pointing toward a jet of water that spurted two hundred and fifty feet in the air.

But James was already urging Frances forward.

"What do you want to show me?" she asked breathlessly.

"It's a surprise."

The park covered two hundred acres. It contained a lot of surprises. Statues. Fountains. Gardens. A man offering a woman comfort. A woman offering a man hope.

"I've never been on a scream machine," Frances said, looking with interest at the small line of children and adults who boarded brightly colored carriages.

James steered her past the roller coaster.

His breath quickened, catching sight of a sign. "Close your eyes."

"I can't walk with my eyes closed," Frances said seriously.

"Close your eyes, Frances." James leaned into her, inhaling her scent. "I want to surprise you."

He wondered if anyone had ever surprised her with love.

Gently he ran his thumb and middle finger down over her brows, the black leather of his gloves dull against the radiance of her skin.

He tensed, waiting for her to reject his touch.

Frances closed her eyes.

Carefully he led her to an ornate iron bridge. "You may look now."

Frances opened her eyes.

Her face went completely still, her every emotion so easy to read. Surprise. Delight.

Understanding.

"You remembered," she said, warm breath misting the cool air.

"I remember everything you've said, Frances."

Moisture glinted in her eyes. "Can we go inspect them?"

"I will sue anyone who tries to stop us," he solemnly swore. "And I assure you, I will win."

Frances's laughter rang through the swamp.

James wondered when she had last laughed.

"Look how big they are," she said, hurrying across the green slope of grass toward the group of five garish dinosaurs that were made out of brick, tile and cement. "What are they?"

James followed more sedately.

"That surly fellow there—" Feeding on her enjoyment, he pointed his umbrella toward a forty-some-odd-foot-long beast. "Is a Megalosaurus."

Reaching up to touch a clawed purple paw, Frances with unfeigned excitement glanced toward a bright green dinosaur with spiked vertebrae. "What's that huge one there?"

"I have no idea," James admitted.

He had not been interested in prehistoric fossils until a red-haired woman had defended her right to have interests outside of her family.

She ducked underneath the green monster with the spiked tail, came out on the other side of a thigh that was taller than she. Disappointment dimmed her excitement. "It has no sex."

The emotion building inside James burst; his laughter startled a chipmunk drinking at the edge of the pond.

Frances stared at him, gloved hand resting on the dinosaur's spiked tail. "That was a kind thing you did for Mr. Nickols."

A light veil of rain misted the swamp.

James's laughter died, an echo in the dampening drizzle. "I'm not a kind man, Frances."

"But you will be kind to me."

"I will try to be."

All his life he had taken; never once had he given.

A pigeon whirred over them, landed at the pond's edge.

She did not look away from him. "I want to see you, James."

"You are seeing me, Frances."

He had never revealed to anyone else as much of himself as he revealed to Frances.

"I want to see your sex."

The slow, clacking ascent of the roller coaster distantly started.

"Why?"

"All my life I have thought of a woman's vagina as a receptacle. A place where men deposit their sperm so that women may bear their children."

His wife had been a receptacle. His mistresses had been receptacles. The first to bear his children; the second to bear his lust.

James had divided his life into categories—his seed for his wife, his sex for his mistresses, his ambition for his work—like pigeonholes in a clerk's desk.

"You're not a receptacle," he said.

"I know that, now," Frances agreed. Mist darkened the green silk ribbon banding her straw hat and clung to her face. "But I would like to see a man. I would like to see you, James. I have had five children, yet I don't know what a man looks like when he's excited. I would like to see what it is that men hide from women."

Apprehension and anticipation raced up and down James's spine. At the very least they could be kicked out of the park for public indecency. At the very worst they could be hauled off to gaol.

James propped his umbrella against the surly Megalosaurus.

Stepping forward, he worked off his left glove. Taking another step forward, he worked off his right glove. He took a third step, stuffing his gloves into his coat pocket.

He halted in front of Frances, his back toward the iron bridge.

She glanced down at the open front of his black wool coat.

Hands trembling, James reached for the placket of his wool trousers.

The brim of her hat blocked her eyes, but it did not hide her mouth.

He released the second button . . . the third button . . . the fourth button . . . the fifth button . . . Watching every curve of her lips. Gauging every emotion that washed over her face.

Gentle fingers reached into the placket.

James's gaze snapped downward.

Her gloved hand disappeared inside the black gap venting his trousers.

A sharp inhalation of air sliced through the murmur of clattering wood, trickling water, and rustling rodents.

His. Hers.

Her suede glove was cool. Her fingers were firm.

She disengaged James from his small clothes. She exposed James to misty rain.

"What does it feel like when I touch you?" she asked in a low murmur, warm breath gusting a silvery plume.

"It feels like my cock has a heart," he answered, deliberately using the analogy she had used to describe what it felt like to touch her clitoris. His voice was strained; his body strained toward her. "It throbs when you touch it."

Lifting her left hand to her mouth, Frances bit into the leather fingertips and pulled off her glove. Quickly stuffing the limp suede into her coat pocket, she transferred his cock to her left hand— James sucked in cool mist at the touch of her warm, naked fingers— and pulled off her right glove with her teeth.

He was enveloped in heat.

"Your skin is so soft," she said, softly exploring him. She held him in her left hand, and gently worried his urethra with the middle finger of her right hand. "It cries."

James closed his eyes at the sensation she created. No other woman had touched him simply because she wished to. He felt both agonizing pleasure and humbling vulnerability.

Cool air replaced the hot, slick glide of her finger.

James's eyelids snapped open.

Frances brought up her finger—glistening with the tear she had excited—to her lips.

His breath snagged inside his throat.

She licked the crystal tear off her finger.

Heat ripped through his chest and shot out of his cock.

"Jesus." He gripped the head of his penis. He came into the palm of his hand. "Jesus."

Frances pried loose his grip so that she could peek inside the cup of his fingers.

"James," she said. Watching the spurt of his ejaculate. "James."

A soft finger touched the deflating head that continued to rhythmically pulse, and gathered up a sample of thick, white fluid.

His every breath ripping through his chest, James watched as Frances raised her head and brought her finger up to her lips.

Gaze holding his, she tasted the sperm that he had given one woman out of duty, but which he now gave to this woman for her enjoyment.

"Look, Papa!" A child's distant voice cried out in excitement. "Look at the splendid dinosaurs!"

Chapter
21

The gentle drizzle cocooning the swamp erupted into a rousing rain.

. . . splendid dinosaurs! arced up and down Frances's spine.

Wonder filled her body. Flavor flowed over her tongue.

James tasted of earthy salt.

Before he had ejaculated. After he had ejaculated.

The boy's youthful enthusiasm charged the rain. "May I go visit them, Papa?"

Frances glanced over James's shoulder, still absorbed with the miracle she had witnessed.

On the iron bridge, father and son stood underneath the protective circle of an umbrella. They wore matching straw boating hats. The father's voice, calmer, older, drifted over the pond. ". . . stops raining."

Gaze shifting, Frances stared up at James.

The hazel eyes were dark and inscrutable. Water dripped off the brim of his black silk top hat.

"They're gone," she said, suddenly aware of the cold rain that trickled down the back of her neck.

James reached into his pocket with his left hand. At the same time, Frances released the warm flesh that nestled inside her palm.

Belatedly, she realized: "We could have been seen."

The knowledge did not detract from the excitement that continued to course through her body.

James cleansed his right hand with a folded white handkerchief; the dark lashes that fanned his cheeks were pearled with moisture. "My back was to the bridge; the dinosaur blocks the other side of the swamp."

Silently Frances watched him tuck his flesh back into his trousers.

His hands trembled.

He buttoned the fifth button . . . the fourth button . . . the third button . . .

Voice neutral, James addressed the second button. "Did you enjoy the taste of my sperm?"

"I didn't taste your sperm, James," she gently corrected him while the rain fell down upon them.

His eyelashes fluttered open. The hazel eyes that gazed down at her were dark and stark.

"I tasted your pleasure."

Light blazed in his eyes so brightly that it hurt to look at him. "There are more dinosaurs."

Splendid dinosaurs.

"It's raining," Frances pointed out reasonably.

There would always be rain. He was a sophisticated barrister. She was a simple grandmother. Exploring their sexuality would not change what they were.

The light in his eyes dimmed. "Not underneath my umbrella."

The responsibilities that weighted their lives melted away in a burst of gladness. James had an umbrella, and Frances had a London holiday.

"Yes," she said. "I very much want to see more dinosaurs."

Holding his umbrella over their heads—both of them wet and bedraggled and smelling of damp wool—they picked their way through the dinosaur swamp. Discussing the impossibly long snout on a thirty-foot-long ancestor to the crocodile. Exploring a bird-like dinosaur with huge, outspread wings. Laughing at a group of what James described as "giant carnivorous frogs." Frances ignored a lurking shadow, intent on the rhythmical rub of James's shoulder and hip, and the intimacy he had granted her . . .

A spray of water jetted up in her peripheral vision. Halting, she released James's arm and swirled around.

The head of a submersed dinosaur pierced the murky pond water.

Long minutes passed.

Without warning, a plume of water burst out of the dinosaur's spout.

Frances laughed for the sheer joy of laughing.

Breathlessly, she turned at the pressure of a hand in the middle of her back. "I never imagined that anything like this existed."

James's eyes beneath the brim of his hat were unreadable. "Neither did I."

Around them, a child's laughter filtered through the swamp. Above them, watery sunlight penetrated a gray cloud.

"It's not raining anymore," Frances said.

Five pulsebeats throbbed in the middle of her back where his fingertips pressed into her serge coat. "So it's not."

Anticipation twisted inside Frances. "Would you like to share a ginger beer?"

There were so many simple joys she could share with him, if only he would let her.

The corner of his mouth hitched upward in a lopsided smile. "I would be honored."

The train rocked, metal wheels rhythmically clacking. With each swaying motion the friction of James's arm and shoulder sparked another image, another sensation: a crystalline glint of glass; moist wind whipping her cheeks; the wet gleam of a Megalosaurus; sharp, jagged spines pricking her fingers; the thick length of James's penis; liquid salt pearling on the tip of her tongue.

The members of the Men and Women's Club silently rode the seven miles back to London while all around them overtired children wailed and whined, and exhausted parents slumped in their seats.

Screeching brakes and roiling steam broke through the deafening silence and crying cacophony. Frances instinctively glanced at James.

Awareness simmered in his gaze.

"Take my umbrella, Frances," he said, breath scented with ginger, "and wait for me outside."

Frances glanced at John Nickols. He sat in the aisle seat. As if he had not challenged Marie Hoppleworth to sit on his lap and loosen the lace on her shoe while three women and four men shielded them from prying eyes.

Frances glanced at Marie Hoppleworth. She sat in the window seat. As if after lunch she had not perched on the footrest of John Nickols's chair in the warming sunlight, his legs framing her narrow shoulders, and read from the play—translating ancient Greek into modern English—that she had purchased at the Achilles Book Shoppe.

Frances wordlessly stepped into the noisy herd of exiting bodies.

The whining, wailing cries that vacated the carriage filled the Victoria Station.

"Thank you, Mrs. Hart."

Rose Clarring's cornflower blue eyes had been filled with light while watching the exploding fireworks; now they were dark and somber.

"Thank *you*, Mrs. Clarring," Frances said, throat tightening, wanting to ease the younger woman's unhappiness and knowing there was nothing that she could do to help her. "The fireworks were beautiful."

But Rose Clarring was gone.

"Good night, Mrs. Hart."

Esther Palmer had laughed uninhibitedly at the two-thousand-year-old Greek story of a woman who wanted to borrow her friend's dildo, only to discover that it had been loaned out to another friend. There was no laughter in her eyes now. Nodding briefly, the mathematics teacher stepped into the moving mass of bodies that crowded the station.

Frances's heart leapt into her throat, espying James.

He walked in unison with John Nickols and George Addimore. He leaned down in unison with John Nickols and George Addimore. He straightened in unison with George Addimore while John Nickols straightened his body in the wooden chair.

Sarah Burns, Thomas Pierce, Marie Hoppleworth, George Addimore, Louis Stiles and John Nickols all dispersed in different directions, each club member leaving the station as they had arrived: alone.

Pulsing heat spanned the middle of her back; simultaneously hot, moist air feathered her ear . . . her cheek. "Will you share a late supper with me?"

Frances's gaze followed Sarah Burns, an unmarried woman who dressed in mournful black while she, a widow, dressed in lively green.

If she went with James Whitcox, they would share more than a late supper.

Frances sought out hazel eyes while the woman physician dodged a family of five, wearing the clothing that Frances should be wearing. "I would enjoy that."

A deafening whistle shrilled over the throb of engines and the din of voices.

The darkness in James's eyes twisted her heart. "You took pleasure in my sex."

A hard body struck her between her shoulders.

Frances stumbled forward, reaching for James. He grasped her upper arms, holding her steady.

Her breasts abutted the solid wall of his chest.

Vaguely she was aware of the men, women and children who flowed around them while every nerve in her body focused on the heat that flowed directly from James.

"I have never felt less alone," she said over the din of voices, and the drum of engines, "than when I touched you."

"And when you tasted me?"

A masculine voice rose above the noisy hubbub, syllables disjointed, words unintelligible.

"I felt as if your pleasure was a part of me," Frances said.

Jagged shadow hollowed his cheeks.

She remembered the dark slash of his lashes pearled with rain as he buttoned up his trousers. She remembered the light that had blazed inside his eyes when he told her there were more dinosaurs.

She remembered how alone she had felt in Kerring, Sussex, surrounded by family and friends.

James had not lied to her; she would not lie to him.

"I don't feel like I'm a stranger when I'm with you, James."

Slowly his thick black eyelashes swept open.

"I'm hungry, Frances," he said in a curiously toneless voice.

"Then let's go eat," Frances said with a confidence she was far from feeling.

Chapter
22

A line of carriages waited outside a side door.

James had ridden the omnibus for her. It was now Frances's turn to ride in a cab for him.

With one hand he steadied her as she stepped up, first onto a steep metal stair, and then onto a small, rectangular platform behind a steaming horse rump; with his other hand he reached around her and swung open the cab door.

This was a type of care and courtesy to which she was not accustomed.

Frances hesitantly stepped into mottled darkness.

The leather upholstery was cracked; the wood underneath it was hard.

One moment James's voice drifted over the jumbled careen of traffic; the next moment he invaded the dark cocoon that the interior of the cab created, shoulders stooped, white silk scarf dangling. Hurriedly she scooted over to make room.

There was no room to make. His hip, firmly pinning her skirts, pressed solidly against her hip.

A sharp closure of wood sealed off the vertical splashboard that protected the horse's modesty. At the same time, James leaned back, his shoulder abrading her shoulder. The cab rolled backward before leaping forward into the stream of traffic.

Heat that had earlier flowed from his chest now flowed from his hips and shoulders.

"I'm glad the rain stopped," she said over the drumming of her heart and the grinding of carriage wheels.

His breath warmed her cheek. "I have very fond memories of the rain."

Jesus reverberated inside Frances's ears.

"Only of the rain?" she asked unsteadily.

The cab turned a corner, wheels sliding on muddy pavement: she grabbed a leather pull.

"I also have fond memories of ginger beer."

Frances could not stop a smile of pure pleasure. "You liked it."

Gaslight slashed through the window, framed hazel eyes. "I like everything about you, Frances."

Frances's breath swelled inside her chest.

The grinding progression of the wheels slowed; the cab jerkily crawled to a stop.

She peered out the window. "Are we there?"

A richly liveried doorman—hat and shoulders decorated with Wedgwood blue braiding—stood on a concrete stoop that glittered in gaslight as if strewn with diamonds.

The cracked leather seat shifted. "Yes."

Stepping out onto the peculiar platform that adorned the front of this particular style of cab, James reached up and over the door.

The cabby's voice leaked through the ceiling. "Thank 'e, sir."

Half-turning, his body a shield against passing carriages, James waited for Frances to exit.

She stared up at the streetlight that silhouetted him, and the solitude that cloaked him.

He had in the past committed adultery. He would in the future free men guilty of murder.

The sophisticated barrister was everything an unsophisticated grandmother should avoid.

Knowledge, Frances realized, did not kill emotion.

"I like you, too, James."

Light and shadow traced his features, revealing the corner of his mouth, hiding the bridge of his nose. "Do you?"

"Yes." She could not ever remember liking anyone as much as she liked James Whitcox. "I do."

Solemnly he offered his hand, black leather glove blending into dark shadow. "Why?"

"I respect you." The pressure of his fingers clenched her entire body; James tugged Frances up and out of the cab, a breathless transition from sitting to standing. "I know you."

Wood creaked; harnesses jingled.

"Wednesday night you said I didn't." She turned her face up to his. Outwardly she saw the light that revealed his features; inwardly she recognized the shadows that defined his character. "But I *do* know you, James."

Frances knew every doubt, every fear, every desire he had experienced as a widower; they were the same doubts, the same fears, the same desires she had experienced since the death of her husband.

For long seconds he searched her eyes as if trying to see himself through her gaze.

Black motion caught her eye. Forward sensation offset her feet.

"Easy, Janey," the cabby muttered. "Easy, gurlly."

Between one blink and the next, James's upraised hand dropped and he stepped aside. Steadying heat notched the small of her back. "Watch your step."

Frances took the warning to heart: the lone iron stair was a long way down.

Her stomach fluttered, glimpsing the gas-lit restaurant through mullioned windows.

Crystal sparkled. Silver gleamed. Men in tailored black suits and white bow ties, and women in elegant silk dresses and glittering jewels sat around white linen-covered tables.

James had said that he wanted her to experience his world; Frances only hoped she could afford the luxury.

"The prices here must be very expensive," she confided in a hushed whisper.

"Frances," James murmured; heat singed her ear and danced up and down her vertebrae, "when you're with me—"

Blue flame shot up high into the flickering gaslight.

Frances halted, entranced.

"—you don't need to worry about prices."

One second the blue flame leapt high; the next second it crouched in a dying flicker.

"James." Frances was abruptly, acutely aware of standing outside, looking in. "I did not accept your invitation with the expectation of a free meal."

"Frances, it is my privilege and my responsibility to pay your fare."

"James." Frances took a deep breath. "I am not your responsibility."

"Would it be so terrible if you were?"

"I saw you ejaculate, James."

Pleasure had erupted from his flesh like a fountain.

"I know you did," he murmured, voice moist and hot.

"I never saw my husband ejaculate."

Stillness crystalized the chill night air.

"You asked if it was a man's sexuality that a woman feared, or if it was her own sexuality that she feared." A puzzled crease darkened Frances's expression. "As if it were fear that prevented a woman from taking pleasure in a man."

"Isn't it?" James asked.

The Sussex parson preached that truth made one free. But how hurtful truth could be.

"The home I lived in belonged to my husband," Frances said. "The clothing I wore belonged to my husband. The food that I ate, James, belonged to my husband.

"It isn't fear that makes a woman submit rather than revel in a man's touch. It's a sense of obligation—of having to rely upon a man for one's every physical need.

"I wanted to see you, James"—pain sliced through Frances, admitting to this man what she had previously been unable to admit to herself—"but I never wanted to see my husband."

After a pause, she continued. "Yes, it would be a terrible thing to be your responsibility." Frances turned away from the window. "I gladly share your passion, but I will not be dependent upon your wealth."

Chapter
23

James had wanted to know what it was like for a woman to be dependent upon the good will of a man. Understanding cut far deeper than the blade of a knife.

Sound exploded the night, a burgundy-enameled door opening.

A woman, rubies glittering in her ears—and a man, white silk scarf framing his neck—exited the restaurant.

He knew the woman. He knew the man.

He knew the man's mistress, a former mistress of his own.

James glanced down at Frances. "You said you wanted to see what men hide from women."

Muted voices drifted down the stoop. The doorman hurried down the steps to hail a cab. Less harried footsteps followed . . . the man and the woman, their arms entwined, their lives estranged.

"I trembled," James said.

A short, sharp whistle pierced the grinding hum of traffic.

"*That* is what we hide."

There was no condemnation in her gaze. "But you didn't hide from me."

"No, I didn't hide from you," he said flatly.

A jangle of harnesses rang out, a cab pulling up to the curb.

"Will you share dinner with me, James?"

Independently purchased. Joyfully offered.

He sought out the curve of her back. Heat raced up his fingers, and filled the cold void her rejection had created. "I would enjoy that more than you can imagine."

Frances took the first step into his world.

"James." She paused on the fourth and final step.

He glanced down at the curve of her cheek. "What?"

"You said I tasted like spicy vanilla."

The taste of her sex flooded his mouth. "Yes."

"You taste salty."

"Allow me, sir." The doorman breathlessly raced up the stoop, and opened the restaurant door. "Madam."

Familiar sounds surrounded James: masculine guffaws; feminine titters; crystal clinking; heavy silver striking fine china.

The coat clerk—too old to be a boy, too young to be a man— hurriedly stepped forward. "If I may take your coat, madam."

Frances hesitated, unused to the service James took for granted.

"Mr. Whitcox. What a pleasure." The maitre d' appeared beside James. "A table for two, sir?"

Frances self-consciously reached for a rattan button, suede reticule swinging from her wrist.

James shrugged out of his coat. "My companion and I will dine privately."

The checker boy slid Frances's green striped coat from her shoulders; full breasts strained against her green silk bodice.

"I'm sorry, sir," the maitre d' apologized; there was no regret in his voice. "Our private rooms are spoken for."

"Perhaps"—James dropped a twenty-pound note on top of the lectern—"there's a room you overlooked."

"Indeed, sir. I believe one party is late for their reservation." One party, James surmised without remorse, would have to wait until another room cleared. Silently he surrendered his coat, umbrella and top hat—gloves inside the upturned bowl of the crown—to the coat clerk. "If you will follow me, madam. Sir."

Frances followed the maitre d' across Wedgwood blue carpeting flanked by white linen-covered tables and flickering gaslight. James followed Frances, fingers riding the warm curve of her spine.

"Whitcox, old man!" A silver-and-black-haired man pushed back his chair, blocking Frances's path. "I was just telling Lodoun that I didn't think you'd take the Bartle case. Nasty business, that. You've lost me a bit of money."

Frances glanced up at James uncertainly. She had no knowledge of Mary Bartle.

"Baldwin," James acknowledged. Across the room a periwinkle gaze snared his attention. Jack Lodoun dined with a solicitor and a woman whose face James could not see, but he gazed at Frances. James glanced down. Frances determinedly ignored the men and women who stared at her. Expertly he steered the silver and black-haired man away from the woman whose needs he neglected. "Mrs. Baldwin. Allow me to introduce to you Mrs. Frances Hart."

"Mrs. Hart." Charles Baldwin's nod was cordial; his eyes were coldly appraising. "I don't believe we've met."

"Mrs. Hart is up from the country." James splayed his fingers across Frances's spine; he must soon let her go, but not yet. "Mrs. Hart, allow me to introduce to you Mrs. Barbara Baldwin, and Mr. Charles Baldwin, MP."

"How do you do, Mrs. Baldwin," Frances said courteously. "Mr. Baldwin."

"It is not our intention to interrupt your dinner," James said, acutely aware of the passing seconds. "If you will excuse us."

"Indeed, Mr. Whitcox." Barbara Baldwin's gaze flitted past James; coldly she appraised Frances's silk dress. "Perhaps, Mrs. Hart, we will have the pleasure of meeting Mr. Hart."

"My husband is deceased, Mrs. Baldwin." Frances nodded pleasantly. "Mr. Baldwin."

Making no effort to hide his speculation, Baldwin scooted his chair out of Frances's path.

The maitre d', holding two burgundy leather menus in white-gloved hands, impassively waited at the back of the restaurant.

James was hailed four more times. He introduced Frances four more times.

Each time the gazes turned toward her were filled with cold appraisal. Each time he fielded their curiosity while inexorably obtaining the goal of the private dining room.

"After you, madam." Sketching a bow, the maitre d' opened a burgundy door. "Sir."

Overhead, a gas chandelier flickered and shimmered. A gold velvet divan flanked one side of a white linen-covered table. Three burgundy leather Queen Anne chairs completed the square.

"If madam will be seated"—the maitre d' pulled back the square table—"a waiter will be with you directly. Would madam and sir enjoy an aperitif?"

Face flushing, Frances sat down on the gold velvet divan. "I would like a glass of champagne, please."

"One glass of champagne," the maitre d' repeated as he pushed in the table, too well trained to express emotion. In the world of wealth, men ordered, not women. And men as wealthy as James Whitcox did not order champagne without tacking on a prestigious brand name. With a flourish of a white-gloved hand, he offered Frances a menu; in the next moment he pulled out the chair to her right. "Shall we have our brandy, sir?"

"Yes." Masculine pride rising up like sour bile, James sank into butter soft leather and accepted a menu. "Thank you."

Plucking off the table the two spare place settings, the maitre d' bowed his way to the door. "Your waiter will bring your aperitifs."

A soft click filled the private dining room.

"This is very grand," Frances said, tugging off suede gloves while her gaze flitted from a color-splashed painting of a man and woman taking wine together, to an unoccupied burgundy leather chair, to the silver bud vase and single red rose in the center of the table. "Do you dine here often?"

"Often enough."

His life hadn't changed since the death of his wife: he worked in public; he dined in public; he slept alone.

Frances arranged her reticule and gloves onto the divan. "What did Mr. Baldwin mean when he said you lost him money?"

The solicitor had shopped Mary Bartle around like Newmarket ware.

"No one wanted to take the Bartle case," he said remotely.

She raised her head, gaze shadowed by the brim of her straw hat. "Except you."

"Except me," James agreed.

She opened her menu. "There was no need to introduce me to your friends."

He studied the shadow of her nose and lips. "Did you think I wouldn't?"

"The menu doesn't list any prices," she evaded.

He tugged her menu out of her hands and replaced it with his own.

She opened the burgundy leather. And glanced up in surprise. "Why are prices listed in one menu but not the other?"

"Because one menu," James said, steadily holding her gaze, "is for men, and the other is for women."

Women, by being made dependent, lost their sexuality. But men, by making women dependent, gained self-esteem.

Frances self-consciously glanced down at the menu. James watched the expressive curve of her lips, alternately reading determination, intrigue, shock, dismay.

He knew how much money she had in her bank account; he did not know how much money she had inside her reticule.

Deliberately leaning forward, he reached between the flaps of the leather menu and with his forefinger underlined heavy black lettering.

Frances glanced up, slowly her dismay over the menu prices gave way to awareness of his proximity, and the intimacies they had shared. "Is that what you're ordering?"

James did not draw back. "I thought you might like to order it."

"Why?"

She had stared through the window at the flambé like a child staring into a toy shop.

"Torched food, Frances."

Comprehension widened her eyes. She glanced back down at the menu, and bit her bottom lip in concentration.

James knew that she scanned for the price of champagne. He directed her attention to the bottom right-hand column.

"I would like to try that, yes." She glanced up from the menu, eyes suddenly sparkling, clearly able to pay for both the champagne and the flambé. "What are you ordering?"

A sharp knock prevented his response.

James reluctantly straightened. "Enter."

"Good evening, madam." A waiter in a black evening coat and white waistcoat balanced a round tray on a white-gloved hand. "Mr. Whitcox."

Frances raptly accepted the fluted glass of house champagne.

The waiter—a favored waiter, attentive without being suffocating—deposited a snifter in front of James. "Shall I take your order, sir?"

The Napoleon brandy in front of James was twenty years old, the best that money could buy. The bubbles inside Frances's champagne were fine, but not as fine as the bubbles in the vintage champagne he would have her drink: Moët & Chandon cuvée Dom Pérignon, or a royal favorite, Roedere Cristal.

"We'll be dining lightly tonight, Benjamin." Frances glanced up; the pleasure in her eyes was far more important than the bite of injured pride. "Oysters, followed by a single order of Cherries Jubilee."

"Very good, sir." Nimbly the waiter took the menus. "I'll shuck the oysters personally."

The door closed with a quiet click.

"Shuck the oysters . . . ?" she asked curiously.

The scent of spicy vanilla, cool rain, and warm sunshine enveloped James.

"Shucking oysters"—he grasped the stem of her fluted glass, and set the bubbling champagne onto the table—"is a rare skill."

Carefully he captured her hands. They were soft and warm, slightly resistant.

Lowering his lashes, James pressed the palms of her hands together. She wore her wedding band, just as he wore his. Two gold rings that bound them to a life of deception.

"First you wrap your left hand in a towel," he instructed her. "With your right hand, you cup the bottom shell of the oyster."

Matching words with deeds, he cupped the back of her right hand.

"Why must you wrap your left hand in a towel?" Frances asked, breath catching.

"The shell is sharp," James said simply; there was nothing simple about the sensations coursing through his fingers. "And slippery when wet. The shell mustn't be jostled or tipped during the shucking process, or the oyster's liquor will run off."

"What happens if the oyster's liquor runs off?"

James glanced up. "Then we don't have the pleasure of tasting it."

The thought of how easily he could have missed Frances Hart squeezed his chest.

He could have been held over in court. Or she could have opened another door.

Dusky rose tinted her cheeks. "How do we get the liquor out?"

"We gently insert the tip of a knife into the hinged edge of the oyster's shell." Gently he ran his thumb between the seams of her hands; he watched the effect of his touch in her pale gaze. "Then we push it in, gently twisting"—he penetrated the twin seams of her hands; instantly his thumb was surrounded by warm, pulsing flesh—"until we feel the shell yield."

As Frances's hands now yielded.

Out of desire. Not out of obligation.

"Once the shell is open, we probe against the upper roof until we feel no resistance"—he probed deep inside the unresisting clasp of her hands—"and then we cut through the oyster's umbilical cord."

The green silk ribbon banding the crown of her flat straw hat gleamed in the light of the chandelier; her eyes beneath the brim dimmed with shadow. "What happens when we cut through the umbilical cord?"

What happened when a man and a woman severed their ties to the past?

Could a woman's love survive a man's pride? Could a man's pride accept a woman's need for independence?

"The shells separate"—James separated Frances's hands, his left hand holding her right hand, his right hand holding her left hand—"and the oyster is free."

"To be eaten," she said unevenly.

"To be eaten," he agreed, holding her hands and her gaze.

A quick rap snapped the thread of desire holding them together.

Frances tugged her hands free of James. Just as on the step of the cab James had stepped away from Frances.

Nudging aside the silver vase—a red petal floated free of the rose—the waiter set down onto the linen-covered table a silver serving dish.

A dozen half-shells lay on midnight-green strands of seaweed; underneath the insulating seaweed shaved ice coldly glittered in the light of the chandelier.

Frances dubiously studied the oysters in their slate-gray beds.

The waiter methodically set out a crystal bowl filled with quartered lemons and a silver boat of Worcestershire sauce. "Shall I shuck more oysters, sir?"

"No." James studied Frances. "This will be enough."

The door clicked shut, a dark motion of burgundy.

Moving decisively, he scooted the table out. Startled, Frances glanced up.

Without giving her time to protest, he slid onto the divan beside her. The weight of his body tilted her against him.

"Oysters in the shell aren't chewed; they're swallowed whole." Testicles drawing tight against his body, James reached for a half shell, careful not to spill the delicate liquor. Expertly he added a squirt of lemon and a dab of Worcestershire sauce. Leaning into her warmth, he held the shell up to her lips. "Swallow."

"James"—Frances's gaze darted from his eyes to the pale oyster inside the gray shell, back up to his eyes—"it's not cooked."

"Neither was I."

Inside her eyes he saw the raw essence of his pleasure.

"I've not been fed in a very long time," she murmured.

"Neither had I."

The memory of his tongue licking her finger dilated her pupils.

"Open your mouth, Frances." Pressing the edge of the shell to her lips, James tilted his hand. "Let me feed you."

Frances opened her mouth.

He could feel the solidity of the oyster washing into her mouth. He could taste tart lemon, tangy Worcestershire sauce, sweet oyster liquor. He saw when the involuntary instinct to chew kicked in.

"Swallow," he reminded her, the hardness of his leg pressing into the softness of her thigh.

Frances swallowed.

He wanted her to take pleasure in the foods he enjoyed as well as in the intimacy he needed. "Do you like it?"

"I think"—picking up her folded napkin off the table, she carefully patted dry her lips—"that with a squirt of lemon, and a dab of Worcestershire sauce, you would very much taste like an oyster."

Hot blood engorged his penis. Leaning forward to hide his erection, he racked the empty half-shell inside ice, and grabbed a handful of lemon wedges. "Oysters are said to be aphrodisiacs."

"What is an aphrodisiac?"

James squeezed lemon juice onto the plump molluscs. "It increases sexual desire, and expedites a man's recovery."

"What do oysters do for a woman?"

"Apparently not much," he said dryly, dribbling Worcestershire sauce, "if you need to ask."

The clear peal of her laughter squeezed a tear from his glans.

She reached for a half-shell. "Do oysters increase your desire?"

Deliberately, he turned his head and gazed at her profile, still alight with laughter. "I don't need anything to increase my desire when I'm with you."

Tipping back his head and his hand, James swallowed whole the oyster.

He felt through his hip the shift of her body . . . he felt throughout his entire being her gaze on his throat.

"Mr. Stiles said that men and women who have yet to experience pleasure together are still virgin."

Hand and head lowering, James met her gaze.

"Do you consider yourself a virgin, James?"

"Frances I have obtained orgasm inside a woman's body many times."

"James"—gaze sliding away from his, Frances cradled a shell—"a man obtained orgasm inside my body many times."

Gingerly she brought up her hand, and swallowed down the contents of the half-shell.

Outwardly he watched the muscles inside her throat. Inwardly, he mapped the slippery descent of the oyster. Mussel invading. Throat acquiescing.

James's lashes swept upward. "Did you resent the fact that he took release, but you did not?"

"I didn't then." Gaze averted, Frances placed her empty shell on top of the growing rack of beds. "But I think I would now."

Tentatively she sipped the champagne. Surprise suffused her face. "Oh." She took a drink instead of a sip. "This is very good."

There was nothing complicated about Frances's enjoyment, yet James had never before met a woman who was more complex.

"Champagne and oysters are a perfect marriage."

He felt her gaze. "Then why did you not order champagne?"

James scooped up a half-shell. "I prefer my spirits to lie quietly in my glass."

He could hear the smile in her voice. "It is quite bubbly."

Turning, his thigh pressing into hers, James held the shell up to Frances's mouth. "Swallow."

"Do you enjoy feeding me, James?"

"Yes, I do," he said truthfully. "Don't you?"

Frances swallowed.

"Now chase the oyster with champagne."

She tipped up the fluted glass.

James's cock swelled with the swell of her throat.

Setting the glass down on the table, Frances reached for a half-shell. "Did you resent it when a woman didn't obtain release?"

The tang of lemon and Worcestershire sauce filled his nostrils. Sharp shell prodded his lips.

Frances fed him.

James cupped her hand and gazed at her over the oyster. "I never expected a woman to reach an orgasm."

He swallowed the oyster. Her gaze seared his throat.

The cool slide of mussel. The open expansion of muscle.

Slowly removing the empty shell, staring at his throat, Frances offered the brandy snifter. "Would you resent it now if a woman did not gain release?"

Cupping her hand—"Yes"—he raised the bulbous glass to his lips.

The alcohol burned. Frances's gaze was far hotter.

Without warning, her gaze caught his. "Did you want to see their sex?"

"No."

A soft knock brought home the truth.

"But I want to see your sex, Frances."

Chapter
24

A long second elapsed before Frances realized that the vibration racing up and down her spine was the result of a second knock, and not James's words reverberated in her ears.

Alcohol-scented heat licked her lips. "Enter."

The door opened.

"Shall I shuck more oysters, sir?"

"No." The darkness in James's eyes riveted Frances. "No more oysters"

"Shall I bring dessert?"

"Shall he bring dessert, Frances?" James asked, holding her hand and her gaze while the chandelier above them popped and hissed, and the waiter waited on the threshold.

They both knew James wasn't asking about dessert.

"No." Her voice was strangely husky. "We're not ready for dessert, thank you."

James's focus remained locked onto Frances. "I'll open the door when we require your services, Benjamin."

"Very good, sir."

A burgundy blur shone out of the corner of her eye, the door closing.

"He's gone," Frances said.

The echo of earlier words glittered inside his gaze, words she had said in the falling rain while father and son moved on, and James lay soft and warm in the palm of her hand.

The rain had prevented further exploration. But there was no rain inside the restaurant.

"I'm not certain how I should—"she swallowed. "It's more dignified, surely, for a man to show his sex than it is for a woman."

"Are you offering to show me your sex, Frances?"

"Yes."

The chandelier flared. Or perhaps it was James's eyes that produced the blinding flash of light. All Frances knew was that life wasted could not be savored.

Like an oyster's liquor.

"A woman's breasts are a part of her sex," James said.

Two weeks earlier Frances would have disagreed.

"So I am learning."

"Why did you pass over the third postcard so quickly?"

Indelibly imprinted in her mind was the sepia-tinted image of a woman cupping a heavy breast. Dark nipple hard and swollen. Unashamedly offering her flesh.

"Why did you include that postcard?" Frances countered.

"I imagined that the woman's breasts were yours," he said. "What did you imagine when you looked at it?"

"I imagined what it must feel like to have a man suckle me." Her fingers convulsively flexed in memory. "And I wondered how the sensation would differ from suckling a baby."

James lowered his lashes. "What did it feel like when you nursed your children?"

His gaze on her breasts was a palpable touch.

"A bond is created when a mother suckles her baby." She fought to keep her voice even. "It invokes a tenderness that I've never felt outside of nursing. The suckling contracts a woman's abdomen. It feels as if the baby is drawing directly from the womb. As if trying to take back the nurture it was deprived of by being born."

His fingers tightened around her hand.

Frances held her breath, expecting something to shatter: the glass; her body.

"Is it painful?" he asked, voice oddly taut.

"Sometimes."

One second James stared at her breasts; the next second he pinned her gaze with his. "Is it pleasurable?"

"Yes."

His fingers marginally relaxed. "Did you ever wish it were a man who suckled you instead of a baby?"

The truth.

"Not until two week ago."

Blazing light; searching darkness. "Why not?"

Frances had spent seven and one-half years nursing. Over breakfast. Skipping dinner. Late at night. In the early light of dawn.

"My breasts were for my children."

Her vagina had been an avenue for both conception and birth, but her breasts had been strictly for her children.

"But you'll share your breasts with me," James said.

It was not a question.

Insecurity warred with desire.

Frances saw the breasts in the postcard. Frances saw her breasts in the mirror.

Both full. Both heavy.

Nipples ripe for a man's mouth.

"Yes," she said unevenly. "I will share my breasts with you."

Cold air cupped her hand, abutted her hip, embraced her shoulder. In one smooth motion James pushed back the linen-covered table and stood.

Quickly, neatly, he rearranged the furniture, pushing the table to the side—rose petals scattered—shoving a chair in front of the velvet divan.

Dark color edging his cheeks, James sat down, black frock coat hugging his shoulders, hair glinting gold, bronze, there a thread of silver. "Show me your breasts, Frances."

Outside, in the park, exploring his penis had been as natural as the emerald grass and the misting sky.

There was nothing innocent about the man who sat across from her in the high-backed burgundy leather chair. He had been with women. He had ejaculated inside women. Yet he had never shared a woman's pleasure.

Frances reached for her bodice.

Her fingers trembled. Just as his fingers had trembled when unbuttoning his trousers.

Naked need flared in his eyes, glimpsing the rose satin corset. "You're not wearing a shift."

"No." She stood up; the silk bodice fell open. "I'm not wearing a shift."

If . . . *when* . . . the occasion occurred, she had wanted to offer her sex to James as unashamedly as had the women in his postcards. But oh, it was difficult, shamelessly exposing what a woman was taught to hide in shame.

Taking one step forward, she released the first spring latch securing the corset.

Her heartbeat tripped at the first release of unfettered flesh. At the first gust of cool air.

She remembered the first time she had nursed her firstborn: her breasts had been like firm, ripe apples.

Taking a second step forward, she released the second spring latch. And remembered the first time she had nursed her secondborn.

She couldn't remember what her breasts had looked like.

In what year had they grown from small, firm apples to the melons they now were? Had it occurred at the birth of her second born? Her third born? Her fifth born? Had she been seventeen? Nineteen? Twenty-four?

Frances stopped in front of James and released the third spring latch.

Cool air invaded the valley between her breasts.

Short, dark eyelashes cast jagged shadows on James's cheeks.

He stared intently at the vent of satin and the vee of exposed flesh.

The fourth spring latch was buried below the waistband of her skirt.

She could not further expose herself. But he could.

Frances dropped her arms to her sides.

Slowly, face painfully young in his self-absorption, James peeled back the gaping flaps of the rose satin corset.

The vulnerability she had so carefully held at bay exploded inside her.

She had exposed her breasts to her babies, but babies didn't care about their size or shape, they only cared about the milk they produced.

Dimly she heard a squeal of leather, James scooting forward in the Queen Anne chair.

"Look, Frances." Squeezing pressure, bursting coolness. Long fingers lifted her left breast . . . her right breast. "Look how hard you are."

Frances bit her lip and forced herself to gaze downward.

His thumbs rolled her nipples and pinned them against his forefingers.

Turgid flesh protruded from the twin vises of his hands: her nipples were dark and distended with the desire she could not hide.

"Are you thinking about your babies now, Frances?"

Leather squeaked; at the same time hard thighs gripped the outside of her knees. Plumping together her breasts, James lightly rubbed his cheeks—sandpaper rough with the beginning growth of an evening stubble—against her nipples.

"No." Frances tentatively rested her hands on his shoulders; his muscles underneath scratchy-soft wool were taut. "I'm not thinking about my babies."

Moist heat. Searing regard.

"I didn't know a woman could get this hard."

A soft kiss grazed her left nipple.

Frances hadn't known that a man's lips could produce electricity. It bolted through her womb and exited her vagina.

"Why did you shut your eyes?"

Dark lashes fanning his cheeks, James kissed her right nipple.

"I—"Frances's breath snagged inside her throat. "I was wishing that my breasts were like they once were."

Scalding heat prodded the tip of her nipple, there where she had discharged milk, a quick lick of his dark pink tongue tasting her dark brown nub. "Were they more sensitive then than they are now?"

"They have never—"Frances's hands with a will of their own leapt from his shoulders to his head. Silky warm hair clung to her fingers. "Been as sensitive as they are now."

James sighed, a quick burst of hot air, and opened his mouth.

Scalding moisture. Unbearable tenderness.

He sampled her taste. He tested her texture.

"James." Frances's shoulders bowed over him, as if sucked forward by his drawing mouth. "James."

Sharp teeth measured the length of her nipple.

Frances sucked in his scent, smelling wool, smelling soap, smelling James.

A slurp of release was more felt than heard.

Cold air fanned her nipple. It was dark and wet, and so hard it ached.

Curling his fingers into her softness, he nuzzled her left breast, a gesture so familiar yet so alien coming from a man that it brought tears to her eyes. "What does it feel like when I suckle you?"

"Your mouth is hot."

James sucked her nipple into his mouth.

"Your tongue is hotter still."

James curled his tongue around her nipple.

"When you draw on my nipple, it feels like your mouth and your tongue wrap around my womb."

James drew on her nipple.

Tenderness that was more pain than pleasure ripped through her.

She wanted to protect him, to shield him from his past, to fill up his loneliness.

She wanted to give him the pleasure no other woman had given him.

"It feels as if"—Gently she contoured the rim of his ear with an unsteady finger, mapping translucent skin, firm cartilage—"if you suckled just a little harder . . . I could feed you."

James swallowed the dark ring of her areola, cheeks hallowing with the force of his suckling.

She touched the corner of his mouth—a man's mouth, hard and taut, not the rosebud mouth of a child—with the tip of her finger.

A small, hungry sound erupted from the back of James's throat.

When nursing, Frances's milk had dropped at the sound of a baby's cry. Impossibly, hearing James, Frances felt that same sensation.

Flashing heat. Flooding release.

For one blinding second she was swallowed whole by James: her nipple; her breast; her sex. In the next instant she was cast out of his mouth, gulping air while sound and sensation bombarded her: wafting laughter . . . banding heat . . . hissing overhead light . . . bronze, gold and silver hair glinting . . . stark hazel eyes staring.

Frances gazed down into James's eyes, and saw reflected there her every emotion.

Paralyzing pleasure. Tearing tenderness.

Invasive intimacy.

"I tasted your heartbeat, Frances."

His voice was curiously unsteady.

A dull crash vibrated the air, metal clashing, china shattering.

A waiter had dropped a tray—perhaps the waiter who waited their table.

"What"—Frances struggled to adjust to the distance that separated them, and the tremors that racked her; experiencing his release had been exciting, experiencing her own release had been devastating—"What did it taste like?"

"Vanilla spice."

The starkness inside his eyes squeezed shut her throat.

James lowered his gaze, thick, dark lashes shielding his expression.

Her breasts heaved from the force of her breathing.

"Did your womb contract?" he asked, voice devoid of the emotion that had briefly shone inside his eyes.

"Yes." His fingers that cuffed her forearms pulsed in time with her heartbeat. "My womb contracted."

"Did you feel tenderness for me?"

Frances wanted to cry, but she didn't know *why* she wanted to cry.

"I felt great tenderness for you, James."

The reassurance did not relax the tautness of his features.

Her decelerating gasps for air clocked the passing seconds.

Without warning, the fingers banding her forearms tightened. "I don't want the breasts you had when you were younger, Frances."

She would *not* cry.

"Why not?"

Both dark nipples were hard, but her left nipple was shiny wet and so engorged it jutted out from her areola.

Abruptly drawing backward, James released her arms. "Because I want these breasts." He pulled together her corset and fastened the third spring latch. "Those breasts you had in the past"—he fastened the second spring latch—"they were for others. But these breasts, Frances"—he fastened the first spring latch, reinforced satin biting into her swollen flesh—"these breasts are yours and mine."

James glanced up, no hazel visible in the blackness of his eyes. "Shall we have dessert?"

Chapter
25

"The Cherries Jubilee"—Frances broke the silence, voice hollow over the rumbling wheels of the hansom cab—"was quite excellent."

She had silently watched the preparation of cherries, syrup, and warmed kirsch. There had been no joy in her eyes when the blue blaze of alcohol fumes had shot to the ceiling. No excitement when she had shared the flaming dessert. All that had occupied her had been the knowledge of her orgasm.

"It should be," James said neutrally. "A chef created it in honor of the Queen's jubilee anniversary."

"Have you met the Queen?"

"Yes."

"She must have loved the prince very much to still mourn him."

"Yet loving the prince," James said, deliberately blocking Frances's guilt, "our widowed Queen took comfort in her husband's gillie."

And had let him die alone, unwilling to break protocol.

The flat crown of her straw hat suddenly tilted downward, hiding her face. "I trembled, James."

James *still* trembled. He had watched her breasts quiver with the force of her breathing, and had wanted to weep for the gift she had given him.

Streetlight filtered through the cab and melted into darkness.

"You said men needed women," Frances said over the grind of turning wheels.

The cab slowed to a crawl. A snap sounded, a coin purse opening.

His stomach knotted, knowing the cost of her next words.

"I discovered tonight, James, that women need men, too."

All forward motion stopped.

"My townhouse is rented." The sharp closure of the coin purse reverberated in the darkness. "It's not very fancy, but the tea is quite excellent."

But it wasn't tea that Frances offered.

James spoke past the raw desire that gripped his throat. "Frances . . ."

The cab rolled backward, jarring her into realization.

"I see," she said politely, face a pale mask. Motion a dark blur, she ducked off the seat and swung open the cab door. "Perhaps another time."

Cold air replaced Frances's warmth.

Standing upright in the chill night, Frances turned toward the cabby, her shoulders outlined against a crescent moon. "How much do I owe you?"

The coins she had carefully counted out at the restaurant weighted down his pocket.

Frances stood on tiptoe—breasts straining against the striped coat, breasts he could still smell and taste—and reached across the top of the cab to pay the cabby.

She had told him that she didn't feel like a stranger when she was with him. And James had said nothing. She had told him that she knew him, yet James had not responded.

She had told him that she trembled. And he had let her tremble alone.

With cold precision, James leaned his umbrella into the corner. Reaching out, he grasped Frances around the waist—her flesh was soft even through the corset—and shifted her away from the door. Simultaneously he exited the cab to stand beside her.

The hurt on her face nearly knocked him to his knees.

She had defied her every moral principle by offering up her sexuality, and he had rejected it.

She turned away from him.

James caught the gaze of the cabby, an uninterested witness. "Wait for me."

The wool-muffled man nodded one short nod.

In the courtroom, one round was all that a barrister had. Once he lost credibility, he lost the jurors.

Frances stood in front of a white-enameled door, nape exposed to flickering lamplight, futilely stabbing at the keyhole.

"Frances." He cupped her shoulders, staying the jerky motion of her arm. His voice was emotionless, as it had been trained to be; the emotion he felt for Frances shook his entire body. "I have court tomorrow morning."

"You do not owe me an explanation."

"A woman's life hangs on the outcome of this trial."

"Then of course you must be prepared to defend her."

"This is a part of my life, Frances."

The quiet intensity of his voice reverberated over the jangle of harnesses and the restless strike of a shoed hoof. Being a barrister was no longer who he was, but he would always be a barrister.

Frances remained stiff. "I didn't know that sharing one's sexuality would make one this . . . this . . . *vulnerable*."

James stepped closer, the contact that he needed—that they both needed—frustrated by the bulk of her bustle. "I didn't, either."

"I understand why you can't accept my invitation for"—light and shadow danced on the nape of her bowed neck, flyaway hair glinting dark auburn then bright red—"tea."

"Do you, Frances?"

"Yes," she said. "Of course I do."

But she didn't understand, because James hadn't allowed her to.

"I wanted to spend the day with you," he said.

"Instead of preparing for trial," she deduced.

"Yes."

"Will you get any sleep tonight?" she asked in a low voice.

Her concern twisted something deep inside him that was both a part of, yet separate from, sexual desire.

"I have a couch in my chambers." In the past he had more often slept in his office than in his bedroom. "I'll grab a few winks there."

"Will you win this situation?"

"I always win, Frances."

But there was no pleasure in winning the Bartle case. If he won, she died. If he lost, she died.

"In the park." Frances fixedly stared down at the key that notched the lock. "What did you feel when you ejaculated?"

James tentatively explored Frances's shoulders, the padded line of a clavicle, the rounded joint of an arm.

He had told her he wouldn't hide from her; James shucked away the last of his pride. "I felt ashamed."

"I'm sorry—"

"And humbled." James felt a fleeting sense of kinship with George Addimore. It had required great courage to show the cock ring—a device to aid men who suffered from premature ejaculation—to the members of the Men and Women's Club. "You barely touched me, yet I ejaculated."

The quietness of the street prickled his skin.

"Pleasure shouldn't be a matter of control, surely," Frances said finally, quietly.

"No." His fingers fractionally tightened; her bones underneath the padding of wool and silk and flesh were fragile. "It shouldn't."

But the lives of men and women daily relied upon the control James exerted.

Her voice was so low he had to strain to hear it over the hum of silence. "Were you ashamed by my lack of control?"

Regret for the pain his pride had caused Frances constricted his lungs. James had in the past experienced orgasm with women, but not intimacy. Frances had experienced neither orgasm nor intimacy with a man, until this night. She had nothing with which to compare their relationship. But *he* did.

"When I ejaculated, Frances, I wanted to hold you." He leaned into her, shielding her from the world that would judge her sexuality. Or perhaps it was his own sexuality that he shielded her from, men raised to take. And he would take from her. "But when you came, Frances, I *needed* to hold you.

"I've never felt the bond you felt when suckling your children." He stared at the line of her jaw through the silver mist of his breath. "But I felt a bond when I suckled you. I felt the beat of your heart, and the soughing of your breath. I felt your orgasm, Frances, as if it were my own. The only shame I feel is not having the courage to hold you like we both needed to be held."

James watched the rhythmical gust of Frances's breath, exhalation a stream of silver mist, inhalation a slight expansion of her shoulders.

"When you ejaculated, James, did you need me to hold you?"

"Yes," he said. "I needed you to hold me."

She marginally relaxed beneath the pressure of his hands. "I didn't know a woman could gain release through her breasts."

James had heard men talk over a urinal or in their cups, but he hadn't believed them.

"Nor did I," he said.

"I would enjoy holding you," Frances said, braving rejection again, "if you would still like me to, that is."

The burst of emotion her courage evoked bowed his head over hers. "Frances."

She twisted.

"No." James didn't release her shoulders. "Let me hold you like this for a minute."

If he put his arms around her, he would take her. But he couldn't take her this night. Ejaculating in her hand had rendered him vulnerable; coming inside Frances while she cradled his hips, and embraced his cock, and cherished his flesh would shatter him.

"The cabby is watching," she said breathlessly.

"Perhaps." But the cabby couldn't hear them. "Are your nipples still hard?"

"I"—James felt her inhalation deep inside his groin—"I can't seem to help it."

He carefully kissed the back of her neck. A pulse frantically beat against his lips while the sound of the approaching carriage rattled the night.

"You said you felt tenderness when you suckled your children," he whispered against the fragrant warmth of her nape. "What did it feel like?"

A fine tremor ran through her shoulders. "I felt as if I would die for them."

James felt that for Frances, feeling the thrum of her pulse and inhaling her scent.

"What did you feel when I suckled you?"

"I felt like I would die without you."

The approaching carriage halted; it wouldn't stop indefinitely: there were no stables on a residential street.

James couldn't give Frances the night, but he could give her the few minutes it would take for the carriage to reach them.

He tasted the softness of skin and baby fine hair. "The French call orgasm the little death."

"Is that what you felt . . . 'a little death'"—her voice vibrated through her skin—"when you reached your orgasm?"

James had never felt more alive than when he had come inside her hand. But there wasn't time to tell her how profoundly this day and evening had affected him.

"May I see you tomorrow night?" he asked instead.

"Yes."

His throat swelled; his chest swelled; his cock swelled. "I'll pick you up at seven."

"How should I dress?"

"For a private evening."

The slow start of wheels and hooves jarred his spine.

"Should I dine beforehand?"

The approaching carriage picked up speed.

"Lightly," James said, counting off the seconds before the carriage arrived while he lightly explored her nape. Preparing to let her go. "Shall I protect you?"

"No." She breathed more deeply, back swelling against his chest. "I don't need protection."

Nudas veritas. Naked truth.

James's testicles drew into a tight knot. "I'll try to be gentle."

"What makes you think, James"—Frances's voice vibrated against his lips; the clatter of wheels and the clip of hooves reverberated on the cobbled street—"that I want you to be gentle?"

Chapter
26

"**D**o you think we should tell her, Mr. Denton?"
But it wasn't the butler who answered the cook.

"What would be the purpose, Mrs. Ellis?" the housekeeper asked in a no-nonsense manner. "It can't be pleasant, being the target of gossip."

Three pairs of eyes gazed down at the sectioned newspaper.

. . . our illustrious defender dined privately with widow Frances Hart. Are spring roses blooming, or is Mr. Whitcox wooing a client?

" 'Wooing a client,'" the cook read. "Is he saying that Mrs. Hart is a murderess?"

"Since it is well known that Mr. Whitcox only represents clients accused of murder—" The butler carefully polished a silver spoon. "I think that is exactly what the author is suggesting."

"Fancy!" the cook said. "Do you think she did it?"

The housekeeper pushed back her chair. "Who did what, Mrs. Ellis?"

"That Bartle woman," the cook said. "Not that that scoundrel husband of hers didn't deserve it, mind. Terrible. Simply terrible, what he did to her. But they do say Mr. Whitcox don't care if they be innocent or guilty. Is that pudding done yet, Mrs. Jenkins?"

"Not for a bit." The housekeeper prodded the cheesecloth-shrouded pudding with a fork. "Mrs. Hart said she'd be dining lightly tonight."

"Is she seeing that barrister again?" the cook asked.

"That's none of our business." Boiling water swallowed the clump of dough. "Now is it?"

"Nary it isn't. But it do make life more interesting, thinking about it." The cook gazed at the front page of the newspaper. "Fancy our Mrs. Hart stepping out with the likes of him."

"Why not?" The housekeeper prodded the pudding one last time. "Mrs. Hart is a fine looking woman."

"He's certainly a fine looking man." The cook sighed. "I wouldn't mind taking a tumble with him myself. I wonder how they met. It's not like he and Mrs. Hart run in the same circles."

"Mrs. Hart attends a number of public events. No doubt they share similar interests." The housekeeper set the fork aside. "More tea, Mrs. Ellis?"

"No, thank you, Mrs. Jenkins." The cook, sixty-two years of age to the housekeeper's sixty-six, stood up unsteadily. "I think I'll have a nap before lunch. My Arthur's paining me."

The click of a door sounded over the steady boiling of water.

"She got two more letters today," the butler said in a voice that he only used when alone with the housekeeper.

"Ack." The housekeeper dropped a lid onto the cavernous pot, Irish brogue rising to the top. "Why don't they let the poor woman alone?"

The butler gathered up the polished silver. "You sympathize with her."

The housekeeper grabbed up the cook's empty cup and saucer. "She reminds me of myself when I was younger."

The butler stood up, hands full of gleaming silver. "And you're so old now, of course."

The housekeeper glanced affectionately at the butler's gently stooped shoulders and thick white hair. "Thinking of trading me in for a younger woman, are we, Mr. Denton?"

The butler dropped the silverware into the metal sink basin. "Mrs. Ellis prefers blue ruin to a bit of slap and tickle."

Plunking down the cook's empty cup and saucer on top of the silverware, the housekeeper grabbed the kettle of hot water off the metal stove. "And how would you know that, now?"

Hot water cascaded into the empty cup, spilled over into the saucer.

"She's not the same woman she was a month ago."

The housekeeper froze in a cloud of steam. "Mrs. Ellis?"

The butler swept up the two remaining cups and saucers from the scarred kitchen table. "Mrs. Hart."

Frances Hart had arrived fresh from the country with faded red hair streaked with gray, lost, hollowed eyes and wearing an ugly black bombazine dress.

"She's exactly the same woman." The housekeeper dumped the rest of the hot water out of the kettle. "She just looks differently."

"Others won't think so."

"'Others' aren't here in London."

The butler dunked the empty cups and saucers into the basin. "London papers sell outside of London, Moira."

"And what's wrong, Roger"—the housekeeper added slivered soap to the steaming water—"with a widow enjoying dinner with a widower?"

"Mrs. Hart's not cut out of the same cloth as Mr. Whitcox."

"Why do you say that?" The housekeeper snatched up the damp cloth draped over the gray metal spout. "Because he's a high-flyin' barrister that knows his business?"

"She's as trusting as a lamb." The butler grabbed up a linen towel. "And he's as tough as mutton."

The housekeeper swished the cloth back and forth in the water. "Have you ever been kicked by a wee lamb, Roger?"

"No."

White suds foamed inside the basin. "They're stronger than they look."

"Did you complete the report on the chemists, Mr. Tristan?"

"Yes, sir." The clerk scooted back his empty luncheon plate and rummaged inside a brown leather satchel. "I have it here."

James took the report out of the clerk's hands. The white of the paper blurred against the white linen tablecloth.

Noise momentarily overwhelmed him: men talking; silverware scraping; men laughing.

. . . if you suckled just a little harder . . .

James knocked back strong black coffee. "Mrs. Bartle stands in the witness box tomorrow." He set the translucent china cup onto the silver-rimmed saucer, a definitive click matched all around by other clicking cups and saucers. "Make certain she has a sleeveless bodice to wear underneath her vest." James wadded up his napkin and tossed it onto the remains of an undercooked beefsteak. "I want the jurors to see the syphilitic tumors on her arm."

The clerk paled but otherwise showed no emotion. "Yes, sir."

"Take this with you." James stuffed the report into his satchel. Thrusting the satchel at the clerk, he pushed back the leather-padded chair. "I'll meet you outside the courtroom."

"Sir."

James paused, back to the clerk, and stared through a cloud of cigar smoke at a mahogany-faced clock. It was a quarter to one; court convened at one. "Yes?"

"You have a meeting at five-thirty."

It would be possible to squeeze in a quick meeting before picking up Frances. But he didn't want to.

"Who's the meeting with?"

"Mr. Adam Frowt."

One of the three private investigators James used.

"I don't recall setting up an appointment to see Mr. Frowt."

"He rang today."

But today James was not available.

"Cancel the meeting. In the future, Mr. Tristan, don't make any appointments without first consulting with me."

The clerk's answer blended into the background noise of other "yeses" and "sirs."

James swung through the vestibule into the lavatory. A man stood in front of the second of four porcelain urinals.

Periwinkle eyes met James's gaze in the beveled mirror that bordered the room. "Whitcox."

James stepped up to the first urinal and unbuttoned his trousers. "Lodoun."

"You were out late last evening." The Attorney General did not look away. "Have you found a woman who is more entertaining than preparing for a trial?"

The Attorney General had also dined with a woman.

James stared expressionlessly into Jack Lodoun's mirrored gaze. "Have you?"

"Yes." The Attorney General glanced down; he had long lashes. They were darker than his chestnut-colored hair. "I found such a woman."

"Are felicitations in order?" James politely enquired.

"She died."

Lodoun stepped back from the urinal. The sound of gushing tap water filled the lavatory.

"My condolences," he said shortly: he didn't like Jack Lodoun, but neither could he imagine finding intimacy with a woman only to lose her, "for your loss."

The swinging closure of the lavatory door was Lodoun's response.

Water dribbled into the marble washbasin.

James automatically shook himself before tucking his penis back into soft wool.

Court wouldn't end until five o'clock. He had spent the day and evening with Frances rather than preparing for trial. He had spent the night and morning working on the trial without preparing for Frances.

A boyish chuckle rounded the vestibule.

Hurriedly James buttoned his trousers and washed his hands, firmly shutting off the brass tap that the Attorney General had not. Two young clerks hugged the vestibule wall to give James room to pass.

The courtroom hummed with anticipation.

Avery Tristan hovered just outside the threshold. "Your robe, sir."

James stuck first one arm and then the other into black silk.

"Silence!" The court clerk's command shot through the doorway. "All stand, please."

"Ring the number I gave you Saturday." Cramming his wig onto his head, James grabbed his satchel. "Tell Peasebody to order several dozen roses—coral, I think—and to keep warm a supper *pour deux*. Instruct him to light a fire in the master bedroom at a quarter to seven. He may leave at seven."

James gained the Counselors' bench at the same moment that the judge bowed to the court. A sigh of clothing moved through the courtroom, the result of every man and woman bowing in return.

The judge sat. James sat. A groan of wood announced the seating of all present. While the court clerk proceeded with court protocol, James dug out of his satchel the necessary papers: an autopsy report; the chemist report—

His skin suddenly prickled.

Someone watched him.

Head turning toward the opposite side of the Counselor's table, James met periwinkle eyes.

She died reverberated in the air between James and Jack Lodoun.

Chapter
27

A distant bong penetrated glass and wood. Frances's hand jerked; a sharp pin scraped her scalp.

She froze, arms raised, breasts straining against blue-green silk. The remembered sensation of scraping teeth was so strong her abdomen contracted.

Knuckles rapped softly on the bedroom door.

"One second, please," Frances called out shortly.

A succession of bongs sounded over the pounding of her heart: five . . . six . . . seven.

She had prepared for this moment, only to discover that she wasn't prepared at all. She felt as if she teetered on the edge of a precipice: the past a barren call, the future a certain fall.

Settling a dark blue windsor hat on her head, she carefully slid through the crown a long hat pin. Gold flashed in the mirror, a ring of fidelity.

A second knock ricocheted through her chest.

Hands shaking, Frances snatched up a slippery blue cloak, black leather gloves, and a black beaded reticule. She jerked open the door.

The butler's eyes widened, hand raised in the air.

Did he look at her with approval? Or did he look at her with disapproval?

What did she know about men and what they desired?

"Is anything the matter, Mr. Denton?" Frances asked hesitantly.

"Not a thing, Mrs. Hart." The butler's features dropped into a mask of dignified reserve. Raising his left hand to join his right, he gently pulled down the half-veil that curled over the brim of her hat. "You have a gentleman caller."

Black blotches speckled the butler's ruddy skin and snow white hair.

"Thank you." Frances fought her hands not to reach up and rip off the knotted netting. *Brides* wore veils, young girls shrouded in tradition, not middle-aged widows who abandoned all convention. "Where is Mr. Whitcox waiting?"

The butler dropped his hands and stepped back. "He's in the foyer, madam."

Frances braced herself for condemnation. "Mr. Denton."

"Yes, madam?"

She glanced away from the butler, squared her shoulders, firmly met his gaze. "Please don't wait up."

Face expressionless, the butler lowered his head and shoulders in a half-bow. "Very good, madam."

The corridor was even darker viewed through black netting. She paused at the top of the stairs.

A black silk top hat shielded James's face. He appeared to be studying the faded green wallpaper.

Frances had told him the townhouse was rented. The pang of shame she felt was useless, senseless baggage. She could not change her circumstances, any more than he could change his.

A squeaking step drew his gaze upwards.

Silently he watched her descend the stairs. Iridescent blue-green silk swishing. Bronze kid slipper turning. Ringed hand grabbing.

Dimly Frances noted the stately shadow that followed her . . . that preceded her when she paused at the foot of the steps. James silently eased her cloak out from between her fingers and settled it around her shoulders.

"Have a splendid evening, Mrs. Hart." The butler held open the door. "Mr. Whitcox."

"Thank you, Mr. Denton," she said with a calmness she was far from feeling.

A gray mist aureoled the night. The heat scorching her spine drove her forward.

Frances didn't recognize the address James gave the waiting cabby.

"Where are we going?" she asked inside the darkness of the cab.

James settled beside her, stealing space and oxygen. "You'll see."
The cab jerked forward.

Frances shakily pulled on a black leather glove—invisible inside
the darkness of the cab—every nerve focused on the hard body that
rhythmically rubbed the softness of her body. "Did you catch any
sleep last night?"

"Enough," he said noncommittally.

A wave of vulnerability swept over her.

Tugging on her left glove—leather dry, fingers dry, her *sex* dry—
she tightly asked, "Did you satisfy yourself last night?"

Frances felt rather than saw his sharp gaze. "Did you?"

The bottle of lubricant weighted her reticule.

"I hoped it would make me"—*more in control*—"less agitated."

"Did it?"

"No."

Warm, moist breath ruffled the short veil. "Did you pretend that
your fingers were my cock?"

"Yes," she said. Breasts swelling. Tender still from his ministra-
tions.

Light briefly penetrated the window, the cab passing a street
lamp. James looked as if he were carved in stone, lips chiseled,
cheekbones sharp.

"Yes." Darkness swallowed up his face. "I satisfied myself. When
I got to my chambers, all I could think about was you. The taste of
you. The smell of you. I wanted you, so I touched myself, and I
thought about you. And then I worked, trying to forget you."

For one long second Frances didn't know if the black spots she
saw were the result of knotted netting or lack of oxygen. "How did
you touch yourself?"

Darkness grasped her wrist. Darkness tugged off her glove.

Heat enveloped her hand.

Gently he rubbed her flesh back and forth between his two
hands, creating friction.

It was not the motion she expected.

"When I touched myself," Frances said, straining to see as well as
to feel, "I imagined that you would move your hand up and down."

As she had moved her fingers.

The heat sandwiching her hand dissipated. Only to band her forefinger. "Like this?"

His gently pumping thumb and forefinger slid up and down her womb.

The strength of her reaction was a douche of cold reality.

A man should not be able to affect a woman this strongly.

Frances fisted her fingers. "Where are we going, James?"

She was no giggling girl. He was no inexperienced boy. And the cab was no omnibus. It jerked and bounced beneath them, journeying where neither of them had ever before traveled.

Hard heat momentarily squeezed her knuckles before evaporating in the chill musk of the cab. "Home, Frances."

She stiffened. "To Queen's Gate?"

Was he taking her to the house that he had built for his wife?

His voice in the darkness was devoid of warmth. "Queen's Gate was never my home."

Mist fogged the small square window behind James.

The vapor would turn into rain.

"Where is home?" Frances asked, clinging to a leather strap, hip pulsing, forefinger throbbing, chest aching.

"I bought a townhouse."

"You *bought* a townhouse?" she repeated.

"For us," James said simply.

Surely she could not have heard him correctly.

"You bought a townhouse . . . for"—*cohabitation* stuck inside her throat—"*this?*"

"I bought a townhouse for *us*," was the sharp rejoinder.

Frances's home as a daughter had belonged to her parents. Her home as a wife had belonged to her husband. Now her home belonged to her oldest son.

The full impact of losing the house she had diligently tended and loved for thirty-four years struck her: her family wanted her to return home, but she didn't have a home to return to.

"When did you buy it?"

"Last Thursday."

The day after their meeting outside the Achilles Book Shoppe.

"What if I had decided not to"—deliberately Frances used a euphemism, *their* euphemism—"'see more dinosaurs?'"

"Then I would have sold the townhouse. Or perhaps not." He shrugged, a blur of motion and a creak of leather. "I've been thinking that it's time for a change of address."

A burst of water pelted the windows: the rain had come.

"How long have you known we would come together like this?" she asked.

"I knew the moment you did."

The cab jerked to a halt.

James threw open the door and thrust out his umbrella, blocking the rain. Standing, turning, he reached into the cab and offered his hand. "When you first looked at me."

But Frances had not then thought it was possible for a forty-nine-year-old woman to experience passion.

She reached out and clasped his naked fingers.

It was too gloomy to appreciate the exterior of the townhouse. All that was visible was a glow of light. Shielding them both with his umbrella, James stuck a key into the rain-slashed door.

A veined white marble hallway was lit by an overhead chandelier. Crystal droplets shone like dewdrops.

Frances realized that the chandelier was fueled by electricity.

The differences in their lives had never been more evident.

Wood collided with wood, the closure of the front door. A *swoosh* immediately followed, the collapse of James's umbrella.

Water puddled around her feet. "I've tracked in rain."

Her voice carried hollowly up a marble staircase.

"The servants will clean tomorrow." James's voice, equally hollow, climbed up the staircase after hers. Hot breath feathered her neck. "Allow me to take your cloak."

He took more than her cloak: he plucked her reticule out of her gloved fist.

Her right hand was bare.

"I left my glove inside the cab."

The lined silk cloak slid off her shoulders. "I have it in my coat pocket."

Frances shivered. "Are we alone?"

Had they ever been anything else, he busy with his law, she busy with her family?

"Yes." The sharp pin securing her hat slid free.

Frances reached up. *Too late.* She turned.

James's back faced her, his arms lifting, the muscles in his shoulders stretching. He hooked her cloak on a gleaming brass clothes tree beside his own black wool coat. Her windsor hat hung beside his top hat. The wooden handle of his umbrella protruded from a matching brass stand.

"Do you know, James," Frances asked, hair exposed beneath the chandelier, "that yesterday you wore your hat when you ejaculated?"

She, too, had worn a hat—a boat rather than a windsor—when he suckled her breasts.

"Do you know, Frances," James returned, equally solemn, the blue silk of her cloak outlining the black wool of his frock coat, "that you are a frightfully beautiful woman?"

Beautiful, no. Frightful, perhaps.

"Do I frighten you, James?"

James turned, face guarded. "You terrify me."

Frances could not imagine this man being frightened of anything. "Why?"

"You make me feel," he said enigmatically. "Feeling can be a very dangerous thing."

The deep chime of a Westminster clock announced the half hour.

"What do I make you feel?"

"Hope."

"Is hope such a terrible thing to feel?"

"Men are like boys." A self-deprecating smile twisted his lips; the smile did not reach his eyes. "We tear up a toy to see how it's made. And then the toy exists no more."

The darkness inside James twisted her heart. "I'm not a toy, James."

"But I can hurt you, Frances."

A sudden chill raced down her spine.

"You can only hurt me if I allow you to do so."

"Do you honestly think"—she held still beneath his appraisal that was suddenly coldly calculating—"a woman can control the pain a man wishes to inflict upon her?"

The rain relentlessly hammered the door while electric light mercilessly revealed James.

His sharp cheekbones. His mobile mouth.

His cold hazel eyes.

This is a part of my life reverberated between them.

James had left her last night, but had been unable to forget her while preparing for court. He had returned to her this night, but was unable to forget the day's proceedings in court.

. . . the Bartle case. Nasty business, that, Charles Baldwin had said.

"I think there are things that a woman may do to lessen her pain," Frances said carefully.

Curiosity devoid of emotion shone in his eyes. "What?"

"I think, if a woman takes responsibility for her life rather than allowing her life to be ruled by others, that it provides a certain sense of satisfaction."

"What if a woman is not allowed to make that choice?"

What exactly had happened to this woman that he defended?

"A woman always has a choice, James," Frances said.

If only she was intelligent enough, or wise enough, or experienced enough, or strong enough to take it. Attributes Frances had all her life been short on.

"And once this woman makes her choice?" James impersonally queried.

"It's better to suffer the consequences of one's own actions, surely," Frances gravely replied, "than to suffer from the actions of another."

A low rumble of thunder sounded over the monotonous pounding of rain.

"If you could alter one moment in your life, Frances," James asked, eyes searching hers, "what would it be?"

Frances remembered the drawing Louis Stiles had brought to the meeting. The loving clasp of a woman's vagina. The vulnerable stalk of a man's penis.

"On my wedding night," she said slowly, "I laid in the dark with my nightgown folded around my waist and waited for my husband to come to me." Regret darkened James's eyes. "I remember thinking how ugly the sex of a man and a woman must be; otherwise, why would they lie together in darkness, and hide their bodies from each other in the daytime?"

"But most of all, James, I remember *lying* there. That was all that was expected of me. To lie still with my gown folded around my waist, and my legs spread apart. I wasn't expected to enjoy what was going to be done to me; I wasn't expected to *not* enjoy it. What I experienced was irrelevant. My submission, my mother told me, was my gift to my husband. And I never once questioned the wisdom of what she said."

Frances's pain laced through James's voice. "You were young."

"Was I?" she asked quizzically.

"You were fifteen years old," he said, but there was no conviction inside his gaze.

Complacency was not a disease that age miraculously cured.

"There's a part of me, James," she confessed, "that still yearns for the anonymity of being a wife and a mother."

It had been a comfortable life. Safe. Secure. Whereas it was not at all comfortable being a woman.

"If I could change one aspect of my life," Frances said quietly over the rain, "it would be to erase that image that I have in my mind. Of me, lying there in the darkness. With my gown up around my waist. Holding my body still for penetration."

Chapter 28

"That night set the pattern of my entire adult life." The toll of thirty-four years of sexual submission shone in Frances's eyes, the price she had paid that a man might pass on property—the essence of English law—to a male heir. "But I wish it didn't. I wish I could replace that image."

A pocket of rain slammed into the door.

"Give me your glove, Frances," James said tonelessly.

"What?" Her contemplation turned to confusion, her confusion to realization. "Oh."

Head lowering, hiding the young girl who had lain in the dark, Frances tugged off the black leather glove.

The gold circling her finger banded his chest.

"Last night," he said, taking her glove, "you asked if I felt as if I'd died when I ejaculated."

Le petit morte. The little death.

"Did you?"

James pocketed her glove. "No."

"What did you feel?"

"I felt like I had been born again." Slowly he lifted up his lashes. "Shall we go upstairs?"

"The lubricant is in my reticule—"

"I have a bottle."

Her eyes widened.

"My Saturday errand," he offered.

"Yes." The sudden light in her eyes nearly blinded him; she was pleased simply because he had thought of her. "I would very much like to go upstairs."

With each step the rub of her hip and her shoulder burned away the barrier between barrister and man.

The marble stairs gave way to mirror-bright mahogany wood. Silver-threaded silk lined the walls. A peacock blue wool runner ran the length of a wide corridor. Electric light poured through crystal sconces.

James opened the first door off the corridor. The smell of glue, wood smoke and roses permeated the air.

Frances released his arm and stepped forward into the bedroom.

Feeling uncomfortably bereft without the anchor of her touch, James for the first time saw the room newly redecorated. Peacock blue carpeting. Pale green silk walls. Darker green accents. Gilded furniture. Crystal chandelier.

Burning wood popped and crackled in a gold-veined marble fireplace.

"I thought you said we were alone," Frances said.

"The butler made up the fire before he left." James closed the door behind him. "Do you like our new home?"

Frances glanced at the pale green silk sheets that the turned-down quilt exposed . . . at a peacock velvet armchair . . . at a gilded chest of drawers . . . at a dusky blue silk chaise longue . . . at a crystal vase of coral roses . . . at the cheval mirror in the far corner. "It's very beautiful."

"The wall covering matches the color of your eyes," he pointed out guardedly.

She stared at the pale green silk with sudden comprehension. "You chose the decorations in this room."

"Just the wall covering."

The decorator had designed everything else around the paper.

"During a court intermission," Frances surmised.

"I chose it Friday evening." Heat outlined his cheekbones. "After court was adjourned."

"The air smells of glue."

"I'm sorry," he said, ridiculously hurt that she would comment on the smell of glue but not the flowers he had ordered.

Frances swung around. "It *is* beautiful, James."

It was the best that money could buy, but money wasn't enough.

James pushed away from the door. "You may change the decor."

"But you chose this."

He stepped closer, closer still until the tips of her breasts prodded his chest and he died a little, knowing the loneliness she harbored inside. "Yes."

She raised her face up to his. "Why?"

Her trust bit through him with serrated teeth.

She had said that he didn't remind her of her husband, but James was more like David Hart than he cared to admit. Her husband had bound her with family. James would bind her with passion.

"These are your colors, Frances."

Warm. Vibrant. Everything he was not.

James had never cared for the color green; now he couldn't walk down a street or glance out into a courtroom without it jumping out at him.

Frances glanced down; gold-tipped lashes fanned her cheeks. She reached for his waistcoat. "May I undress you?"

The crackle of fire vied with the drumming of rain.

James took a deep breath at the deft release of one button, two buttons, fighting for control. "May I undress you?"

Her lashes fluttered against her cheeks. "Please."

James had never undressed a woman. He was uncertain where to begin.

Red fire played in her hair. A patch of dull brown dimmed the blaze.

James reached up and found a hairpin.

Cool air invaded his waistcoat.

"Thank you," Frances said, tackling a gold stud.

James found more hairpins. "For what?"

"For preferring the breasts I have now over the ones I had when I was younger."

A loose braid tumbled down her neck.

Pocketing the pins, James carefully combed his fingers through warm silk. "Did you think I wouldn't?"

She removed the third and final stud, carefully pulling it through the front placket of his shirt, then fastening the wingback inside the stud hole. "Yes."

James leaned his forehead against hers and concentrated on the buttons lining her bodice. "Did you touch your breasts last night?"

Frances reached for the front of his trousers. "They ached."

The vivid blue-green bodice parted, revealing the rose satin corset she had worn the day before.

"For me?" James asked, breath quickening. "Or from me?"

Frances's fingers worked against the wool of his trousers until his flesh cried for release. "Both."

Unsteadily he released the buttons fastening the band of her skirt. "Did you squeeze your nipples?"

"I pretended"—she reached into the open placket of his trousers and freed him from his small clothes—"that you suckled them."

The image of her fingers rhythmically milking her nipples squeezed liquid heat from his cock.

A gentle finger prodded his urethra. "I didn't know that a man manufactured lubrication."

Hands trembling, he unknotted a protruding lace: nothing happened. He unknotted another lace just to the right of the first. The heavy horsehair bustle dropped, taking with it the petticoat and silk skirt.

She wasn't wearing a shift. She wasn't wearing drawers.

James stared at the auburn curls at the base of her stomach, gently rounded from the children she had born. And fought not to come inside her hand.

"Does it taste different than my sperm?" he asked hoarsely.

She offered her finger. "Taste."

His nostrils flared, smelling his sex.

Taking her hand, he guided her finger to her mouth. Her eyes widened, her only response to the slippery liquid he smeared on her lips—she opened her mouth—inside her lips, pink tongue quickly tasting before retracting.

He wanted that tongue. He wanted this woman.

The strength of his desire momentarily overwhelmed him.

Leaning down—hiding his need—James licked her lips.

He tasted salt. He tasted vanilla.

He cupped her face in his hands and slipped his tongue inside her mouth. He had kissed before, but he had never before noticed the sharp threat of teeth, or the rich variety of textures. He licked with single-minded intent—reaching higher, he probed the roof of her mouth, swallowing her quick exhalation of air—tasting tooth powder, tasting himself, tasting her, licking and licking until all he could smell and taste was Frances, and the remoteness that had all his life enveloped him like a bubble expanded to the point of pain.

The curious prod of her tongue knotted his testicles.

James leaned back an inch, breath ragged. "Last night, I imagined that you fucked yourself with your fingers."

And he had spurted his release into the air. Alone. As he had been alone each and every time he had ever lain with a woman.

"Last night I *did*"—her gaze searched his face, unfamiliar with the word, clearly understanding what it meant; her breath, too, was labored—"use my fingers."

"I want to see you come."

Her breath fanned his lips. "I thought—"

That he would penetrate her. Like her husband had penetrated her. While she held her body still.

"I want you to show me your sex, Frances." James did not shield her from the force of his need. "And then I want you to show me how you pleasure yourself."

He watched the conflict that blossomed in her gaze. She was still not convinced that he preferred her mature body over the nubile body of a girl, but she would give him what he needed.

Her eyes shone with a sudden gleam of tears. "Will you hold me when I orgasm?"

Gently he ran his thumbs underneath her eyes and wiped away a trace of moisture. "Yes."

"I need the lubricant."

James reluctantly let her go. "It's in the top drawer of the night stand."

Her buttocks were heart-shaped. Twin laces rode the dark crevice between her plump cheeks.

Frances retrieved the lubrication from the drawer, and straightened. James stepped forward, and pressed against her.

His cock notched the crevice to her buttocks.

Her shoulders sharply rose on an intake of air.

Reaching around her, James found the fastening to her corset. "Take off the stopper."

A spring latch snapped free.

Frances unplugged the bottle.

A second spring latch snapped free, more quickly than the first, James quickly learning the underpinnings of a woman's clothing. "Put the stopper on the table."

Frances leaned forward. Her buttocks sandwiched his cock.

A dull thud was accompanied by a third and fourth *snap*.

Leaning back, he worked the corset out from under the silk bodice. The twin laces slid free of her crevice, sharply raking the length of his cock.

Dropping the corset, he eased her bodice down over her shoulders. Frances awkwardly held out her left arm—a pause while she transferred the bottle to her left hand—and then her right arm.

He had felt the fragility of her bones last night; tonight he saw just how fragile she was. The slope of her shoulders. The shadow of a clavicle. The tip of an ear peeking through a curtain of red.

"Dip your finger in the oil," he whispered, cupping her arms to follow her motion.

Smooth muscle worked underneath warm skin.

"Are you ready?" he asked, nuzzling her ear through the warm flame of her hair.

"Yes."

"Lubricate yourself."

Her spine curled away from his chest; the crevice between her buttocks widened.

Heat seared him.

A network of pink lines laced her back. James smoothed away the imprint of the corset.

Frances shifted, legs widening, buttocks flexing.

"Is your finger inside you?" he murmured, tracing her vertebrae to the top of the crevice that embraced him.

A small diamond-shaped indentation marked the end of her spine and the division of her buttocks.

"Yes," she said unsteadily.

He pictured the oil glistening inside the twin indentations of her fingernail.

James reversed his fingers, smoothing up the contoured ridges of her spine. "Did you use three fingers last night?"

"I—" He felt the shaky intake of her breath against the palm of his hand. "Yes."

"Then use three now."

He couldn't visually see her fingers, but he saw them in his mind's eye. Penetrating the bottle. Withdrawing from the bottle. Glistening with oil. The index finger . . . the middle finger . . . the ring finger. . . .

She widened her legs. His cock fused between her cheeks.

He wanted to explore Frances's every orifice, to share with her all the things he had never thought to share with a woman.

"How many fingers?" he whispered while the rain pelted the windows, and he spread apart her buttocks.

The muscles in her shoulders stilled at the unfamiliar touch. "Three."

"Are that many fingers comfortable?"

Frances had said he could only hurt her if she let him. James knew differently.

On the morrow he would devastate a woman.

Slowly she relaxed, accepting his need to know her. "Yes."

But pleasure, James was realizing, was not about comfort. Bending his knees, he thrust his pelvis forward.

The head of his cock hit her knuckles, which immediately became a grip of fingers.

He locked his knees to prevent them from collapsing.

She massaged oil into his skin, around his glans, testing the ring of foreskin, reaching back toward his testicles. The tiny pucker of her vagina kissed the tip of his cock.

He couldn't move. He couldn't breathe.

If she continued touching him, he would explode. If she stopped touching him, he would explode.

Frances took the decision out of his hands.

Slowly, carefully—as if it were she who would shatter rather than he—she straightened. "I ache, James."

James blindly stared at her vertebrae that one by one stacked together to create a vertical column. "Then show me how to ease your ache, Frances."

Chapter
29

Her hourglass-shaped heels wobbled the short distance to the bed.

She visibly trembled. James trembled, watching her.

Turning, Frances perched on the edge of the bed and stared up at him.

Frances would bare herself. James could do no less.

Holding her gaze, he shrugged out of his coat and waistcoat. The wall of his shirt momentarily blocked her from view. He pulled down his suspenders, only to lose her behind his vest. A single button bound his trousers; James freed it. Regaining her gaze, he hooked his thumbs under the twin bands of trousers and small clothes, and in one clumsy sweep pulled them down over his hips. His shoes came off when he stepped out of the woolen legs.

He felt her gaze throughout every fiber of his body.

Frances had seen his cock, but she hadn't seen his testicles. She saw them now: they danced a jig as he jerked off his socks, suspenders attached.

Straightening, James held still for her perusal.

She evaluated the length of his legs, the leanness of his hips, lingered for long seconds on his cock that feinted the air and his testicles that felt like leaden weights, slowly apprised his waist that was thicker than it had been twenty years earlier, the flatness of his stomach that was corded with need, his chest that was now matted rather than sprinkled with hair.

Long heartbeats passed before she met his waiting gaze. "You're a very handsome man, James."

In her eyes, he realized, he was.

His cock swelled. His chest swelled.

"You're a very beautiful woman, Frances," he said.

But she didn't believe him.

"I'm getting oil on your covers."

"*Our* covers," he corrected her. Body opposite in every way—hard where hers was soft, hairy where hers was smooth—he knelt in front of her. "If they're ruined, then I'll replace them."

Slowly he slid his hands up the sides of her legs. Fine golden hair shone underneath the flesh colored silk. White lace and rose silk garters pinched her thighs.

Gently, firmly, he parted her legs; brief resistance melted.

Her pubic hair was spiked with oil. Peeping out from the dark auburn nest was a ridge of rose-colored flesh.

"I touch myself on the tip of my clitoris," she volunteered shakily.

James hunkered down on his knees, heels pressing into his buttocks. "Show me."

Slowly, hand shaking, she touched the tip of her clitoris with a glistening finger.

The bedcovers blocked his view.

"Scoot forward."

Frances wriggled forward until her buttocks were half on, half off the mattress.

Sitting cross-legged—wool carpet prodding his testicles and invading the unprotected crevice between his buttocks—James peeled apart the closed lips of her sex.

The outside of her clitoris was a dusky rose—the color that stained her face when she was excited—but the flesh in between her lips was vermillion. A tiny fissure pouted at the end of the glistening valley.

His throat tightened, seeing just how small was the opening to a woman's body. "Touch yourself."

Frances touched the tiny bud at the top of the small, dusky shaft. It was round and smooth, like the glans of his penis.

"Your clitoris is like a little cock," he said, staring at the proof that a woman was indeed capable of the same enjoyment as a man.

"Perhaps your cock is like a large clitoris," Frances unevenly returned.

He wondered how staunch suffragette Jane Fredericks would react to such a blatantly femininist idea.

The hard little bud underneath her fingertip flexed. Exactly like a cock.

James keenly felt the draw of her sexuality. "Touch yourself like you did when you thought about me."

Slowly, finger glistening with oil, she rubbed in a tight little circle until the hard little bud slickly gleamed.

He hooked his fingers on either side of the small fissure of her vagina, and gently opened her to facilitate the coming penetration.

She smelled of clean soap and tantalizing spice. Glistening vermillion flesh beckoned him inward.

Frances's finger abruptly blocked the small portal. It hovered for long seconds before sinking from view.

James's breath snagged inside his throat, witnessing the ease with which her body accepted the penetration. It seemed impossible that she could comfortably accept anything larger.

"Use three fingers"—he did not recognize his voice—"like you used last night."

His heart slammed against his chest, watching her flesh slip free, and the feminine portal close. Fingertips glistening with oil, she fluted three fingers. The small fissure of her vagina stretched until it formed a pale ring.

James stared, riveted by the delicate bond she revealed.

Slowly her fingers withdrew, exposing her bunched fingertips. Less gently, she reinserted her fingers . . . one knuckle deep . . . two knuckles deep . . . until all he could see was the base of her fingers, and the taut ring of her vagina.

In. Out. Ring closing. Fingertips appearing. Ring stretching. Fingers disappearing.

A stifled sound rode the drum of rain and the crackle of burning wood.

James glanced up, his pulse hammering inside his cock.

Frances's face, eyelids squeezed tightly shut, was tense in a way he had never before seen a woman's face.

Electric energy coiled inside the bedroom.

A flush spread across her face, spilled down her breasts.

He gazed at her sex that had for so many years been a vehicle, first for her husband, and then for her children, but which now was the source of her pleasure.

Her fingers more rapidly pistoned inside her vagina.

Shorter strokes. Deeper strokes. Harder strokes.

Just when he thought the coil of electricity would crush his chest, her fingers froze and a small, choked cry shattered the pelting rain and crackling fire.

Frances's orgasm burst over James.

She needed him in a way that no other woman would ever need him.

Surging upright, he pulled her backward and dropped onto the bed, springs a distant squeal. She fell into the crook of his arm, body rigid. Her back arched, dislodged fingers grasping her breast.

The sound coming from the back of her throat was one of agony.

Hooking his ankle, he dragged her stockinged leg toward him and reached between her thighs. He couldn't breathe for the sensation that gripped him.

Her vagina flowered open, welcoming him. Her vagina snapped closed, embracing him.

He pumped his fluted flesh to provide her with the motion that she, paralyzed by the force of her release, could not.

Three fingers.

Hard. Fast. Deep.

A guttural groan tore out of her throat, and ripped through his cock.

Her eyelashes suddenly lifted. Black dominated her irises.

Even as he watched, her bowed body collapsed and her pupils shrank—black turning into pale green—while the agony etching her face softened into an expression of supreme peace.

She had filled herself with her fingers. But now it was James's fingers that filled her.

A look of such naked vulnerability filled her eyes that his sex cried the tears a barrister could not.

Mutely she stared up at him, her gaze and her body open and unguarded in the aftermath of orgasm.

Gently he rocked his hand, holding his fingers high against the dimpled dome of her cervix. "Am I hurting you?"

"No"—she arced her pelvis, muscles suddenly gripping him— "no."

Feeling her vulnerability as if it were his own, James licked the rock-hard nipple that pierced her splayed fingers.

The outward line of her throat corded. An internal flutter flexed his cock.

"I saw you come, Frances," he rasped, rubbed raw by her honest sexuality.

Women had in the past faked enjoyment. The reality of her orgasm rode him like a summer storm.

He made her ride the storm with him, feeding off her every response. The rise of her breasts. The flush of her cheeks. The renewed vulnerability inside her eyes.

"James . . . God . . . James!" Frances bore down against the short, deep thrusts of his fingers. Riding the end of her previous orgasm. Or riding the beginning of a new one.

Her unrestrained need ripped away his every defense.

"Ride me, Frances." James rolled onto his back, rolling the boneless weight of her body on top of him. Fine hair clung to his lips. The hardness of a nipple punctured his lungs. "I didn't know a woman cried out for the need of a man." He gripped her hips, bending his knees upward between her thighs. "Ride me. Ride me like you rode my fingers. Cry out for me, Frances."

Frances stirred. Arms extending. Hair a flaming curtain.

Slowly she pushed upward. A darkness that did not stem from pleasure shadowed her eyes. "Will you hold your body still for me, James?"

Would he give up his control to Frances?

James urged her upward. "Yes."

Cold blanketed his chest. Heat straddled his groin.

For the first time in his life, he stared up at a woman, a man naked in both body and need.

Eyelashes shielding her gaze, Frances slowly lifted up on her knees. His cock reared up between her legs, crying to give her comfort.

How many times had she lain in the darkness, holding her legs apart, while her husband stuffed his body into hers?

Warm, slippery fingers gripped James, slipping and sliding with every inch she walked backwards on her knees.

"For you, Frances," he said tightly. "My cock is for you."

"Is it, James?" she asked in a voice that was curiously dispassionate.

James slid his hands down over her hips—rounded flesh soft and giving—and fanned his fingers against the outside of her thighs where lace and silk and flesh met. "Yes."

"What if I wanted to touch myself . . . like this?"

She touched his cock to her clitoris, her hard little glans plugging up his urethra until crystalline tears swelled up inside him.

"Then I will watch you"—James forced his hips to remain still—"and relish the pleasure you give me."

"But you said you wanted me to put you inside me."

"I want you to take pleasure in me." He didn't want her to look back on this night with regret. "I don't want my sex to be a burden that you have to bear."

An ember popped over the drum of the rain and the crackling of the fire.

He pulsed around the glans of her clitoris. Or perhaps it was she who pulsed inside him.

"I'm afraid, James."

A fist clutched his heart. "Of me?"

"I've never experienced an orgasm that strongly."

"I've never had an orgasm at all."

He had ejaculated, controlled spurts. When he wanted. Where he wanted. Saving his passion for the courtroom.

Her eyelashes fluttered open. "I don't know what will happen if I reach an orgasm with you inside me."

"You will come," James fought to control the pain and the pleasure cresting inside him, "and I will hold you."

One second she searched his gaze for a reassurance he could not give her, the next second she guided him down the slippery path of her sex.

The mouth of her vagina kissed away the tears of his cock.

Holding his gaze, she lowered her body. He saw the strain of his occupation in her eyes. The initial stretch to accept the blunt head. The long stretch to fully sheath his shaft. Two inches . . . four inches. . . .

Frances grasped his wrists, perched on the threshold of commitment.

He stared at the dark flush that stained her cheeks. At the hard nipples that speared the air. At the spiked auburn hair poised above his own wiry pubic hair. He stared at the thick stalk that bridged their bodies.

The swollen glans on her clitoris glistened with the crystal tear of his lubrication. He envisioned the taut ring of her vagina, glistening between vermillion lips.

"Home," he whispered. Glancing up from their joined sex, he touched her little feminine bud with a fingertip. "You are my home, Frances."

The vise-like grip of her flesh ballooned open and swallowed him.

Frances Hart moved until James Whitcox ceased to exist.

Up . . . Down. In . . . Out.

A woman's gift to a man.

Welcoming his cock. Embracing his cock.

A ring more binding than gold.

"James." Her breasts, darkly flushed, swayed back and forth in time to her movements. She gripped his forearms for balance. Raw need laced her voice. "James."

He viscerally recognized that she was nearing orgasm.

He thrust upward. Giving her every inch he had. Frances bore downward. Taking his every inch.

He gave and she took until suddenly he had no more to give and he froze, back bowing, caught inside the pale band of her green eyes.

"Frances!" rent the squeaking springs and drumming rain and crackling fire. "God! Frances!"

Reaching up—blindly grabbing hot, sweaty flesh and damp,

clinging hair—James spurt against the dome of her cervix. Unable to stop coming. Her vagina milked him, squeezing out more ejaculate. Left hand pressing her face into his throat he rolled onto his side, groaning and grunting with each pulsing release like the animal he had always been afraid of becoming.

Chapter
30

Along dropped.
Frances jerked awake.

Suffocating darkness blinded her. Burning heat surrounded her. James's throat. James's arms. James's thighs.

"I have you." Moist heat feathered her temple. Warm fingers cradled the nape of her neck. "Go back to sleep."

She became aware of the ache, deep inside her. And of the musky scent of flesh, stealing her oxygen.

Frances involuntarily squirmed to free herself.

Blinding light pierced the darkness. Simultaneously, the soft bud plugging her vagina hardened and lengthened.

"Stay." James's muscles were smooth, a man who lived in the city, rather than the corded muscles of a man who farmed the land; they were no less strong. "Stay with me."

The throbbing deep inside her vagina traveled up to her chest.

"I'm not leaving." But she did need to go. There was no delicate way to put it. "I have to visit the water closet."

The prickly thigh imprisoning her legs promptly lifted. She dug her fingers into his side as the hard length of his penis slipped free.

Hazel eyes softened with sleep assessed her. "Do you need assistance?"

The overhead chandelier revealed her every flaw. There were no wrinkles, no evidence of aging skin reflected in his gaze.

"No." Her throat tightened. "Thank you."

"The bathroom is through the door by the dresser," he said, eyes suddenly shuttered.

Liquid spilled out of her vagina when she sat up.

Scalding heat pricked her eyes: the quilt would never come clean.

She stood, heel turning. Memory rushed through her: James had removed her skirt, petticoats, bustle, corset and bodice; he had not removed her shoes and stockings.

Sitting back down—mattress sinking, breasts bobbing, the man behind her watching—she quickly removed her shoes and rolled down her stockings. Deep impressions from the garters bit into her thighs.

The marks left by their intimacy were far deeper.

Frances had reached orgasm with his flesh inside her, and she did not know how she could ever return to Kerring, Sussex.

The carpet was plush, the wool soft rather than wiry. His gaze, a palpable touch, followed every sway of her hips and buttocks.

She opened the door James had indicated. A slice of light penetrated the lavatory, revealing the edge of a mahogany water cistern, gleaming white porcelain, a corner of a mahogany cabinet.

Cautiously, she stepped inside. Her warm toes curled against cold marble.

Electricity did not magically light up the water closet. Nor did the two crystal sconces over the cabinet yield a means to activate them.

Frances shut the bathroom door and stumbled into unmitigated blackness. Her chilled toes stubbed even colder porcelain. She collapsed onto a wooden seat.

Blinding white light flashed on, mid-stream. Frances convulsively stared at the door connecting the bedroom and bathroom, unable to stop the flow of nature.

James stood in the doorway for long seconds, hazel eyes dispassionately watching her.

"There's no need for closed doors, Frances." He walked past the toilet to the back of the bathroom that when fully illuminated was the size of her bedroom in the leased townhouse. The sound of falling rain broke through her paralysis. His voice wafted on a trail of steam. "Join me when you're finished."

Frances grabbed a tissue—Bromo Paper, the same brand as that in the museum—and carefully cleansed herself. The portal to her vagina was tender.

She had fallen asleep with James inside her, the pulse in his penis matching the beat of her heart.

Frances suddenly throbbed with emptiness.

She had cried out her need. And he had held her.

It was too late for embarrassment.

She tugged the porcelain pull, and padded across the marble floor. Steam billowed out of a massive, hooded mahogany tub.

James waited for her, framed by beaded marble. Water-darkened hair clung to his head. Water streamed down his chest, and cascaded off the swollen head of his erection.

"You made me orgasm, Frances," he said, hazel eyes stark.

Steam clogged her throat. "I saw you, James."

His face had contorted in his loss of control, then he had lifted her completely off the bed with the arc of his body.

Silently he held out his hand, fingers long, strong, faintly coated with oil.

"Why?" she suddenly asked, the question rent from the very depths of her body.

"Why what?" he asked alertly.

"Why do mothers teach their daughters that sex is a matter of submission rather than intimacy?"

"Did you?"

Shame rushed over Frances. "Yes."

The hardness edging his features softened.

Frances stepped into the tub and wrapped her arms around his waist. Hot water lapped her toes; moist hair prickled her thighs. She lifted her face to his, seeking the closeness they had shared when his body had been buried so deeply inside her that she had not been able to tell where his penis ended and her womb began. Immediately strong arms enfolded her. James pulled her closer until the hardness of his erection pressed into the softness of her stomach, her feet nestled between his feet, and his chest pillowed her breasts.

"Seven generations of Whitcoxes graduated from Cambridge," he murmured, hot breath and hot water scouring her cheek. "I read law at Lincoln Inn Court, just as my father did, and his father before him. I wanted no more for my son than that he follow in my footsteps, and marry a rich socialite with breeding and education. I wanted him to have the same life that I did."

"Why do we do that to our children?" she whispered.

"Because it's all that we know."

"But now we know differently."

"Yes." A sigh of steam whisked her face. "Now we know differently."

"I've never had a home, James." The heat of his body and the steam of the shower permeated her. "But when you're inside me, I feel like I have a home."

Water-slicked lips rested against her temple. "You'll always have a home with me, Frances."

"You'll always have a home inside me," Frances said, lying to James.

A holiday was enough to last a lifetime, she thought. And knew that she lied to herself.

The hard arm banding her shoulders disappeared. Before she could protest at the break in their closeness, his hand wormed its way in between their bodies. Electric heat singed her clitoris.

"You're still hard."

"You seem to have that effect on me," she said self-consciously.

Pleasure-pain stabbed up through her still-slippery flesh. She buried her face in his.

"I've stretched you."

He was stretching her now.

"You're filled with my sperm." He worked deep inside her, creating a trough. "I can feel it trickling out of you into my palm."

"I can feel it, too."

His lips moved against her cheek; his fingers moved inside her vagina. "Could you feel me ejaculate?"

Emotion swelled over her, remembering the burning invasion. The plunging friction. The exploding pleasure. "Yes."

"What did it feel like?"

"You grew larger inside me, like a fist." The pinch of his penetration dissolved into pleasure. "You pulsed against my womb, and then I felt hot jets of liquid filling me."

"Give me your mouth," James said thickly.

Frances blindly lifted her mouth to his.

The hard pressure of his fingers disappeared. Only to reappear against her lips.

Musk permeated the hot steam. It was not altogether an inviting scent. Before she could turn away, James smeared his fingers on her lips.

"This is us, Frances." Water pearled his lashes; his hazel eyes were intent. "What we experienced together."

Tentatively she licked the pad of a finger. She tasted salt, *him*. She tasted an unfamiliar flavor, *her*. She tasted a heavy musky flavor, their commingled essence.

James's mouth replaced his fingers. Raspy heat licked her lips . . . inside her lips. He filled her with his tongue and his scent until the future dissolved inside the warm rain of the shower and all that existed was the two of them.

"Remember that taste," he said inside her mouth. "That's what passion tastes like."

For a second Frances could not breathe for the pressure of his arms and the moist mist that clogged her throat. "Did you experience passion with me, James?"

"Yes." The prick of his beard and the pelting water stung her. "Turn around, and I'll wash you."

Frances had routinely washed five children and eight grandchildren. She, too, had been a child once, but she could not remember being washed.

She turned around.

Prickly heat plastered her back; hard heat prodded her buttocks. His right hand, slick with soap, trailed up her neck. "You cried out my name when you came."

Frances tilted her head to allow him access. "You called out my name when you ejaculated."

Soapy fingers cupped her left breast. "Did your womb contract?"

"My whole body contracted."

He shaped her breast while with his right hand he cleansed the
length and the circumference of her throat. "I didn't know a woman
could grip a man as tightly as you gripped my cock."

"I didn't know a man"—her breast swelled; her vagina pulsed—
"could penetrate a woman as deeply as you penetrated me."

Slippery fingers slid down her throat, grazed the pointed peak of
her nipple—Frances's lower stomach fluttered—down her abdomen
while with his left hand he continued to squeeze and massage her
left breast.

"You penetrated me, too, Frances."

A tiny penetration for a tiny opening.

"What did it feel like?"

Hot breath and hot water burned her temple; soapy fingers
cleaned her clitoris. "Like you penetrated my throat."

She reached back and grabbed a hair-studded thigh to offset the
jolt of sensation.

"Turn around, and I'll wash your back."

As obedient as one of her grandchildren, Frances turned.

Steam curled around his water-plastered hair; water coursed
down his cheeks.

Emotion shot through her: tenderness; desire; gratitude. She
wanted to give this man the pleasure he had given to her.

"Let me wash you, James."

Light softened the darkness of his gaze. Silently he passed her
the bar of soap.

"When I touch your nipples"—she threaded her soapy fingers
through the wet hair plastering his chest, found a hard nipple—
"where do you feel sensation?"

His forehead weighted her forehead. Grasping her hips—his
head shielding her from the pelting water—he intently watched her
fingers. "I feel it in my cock."

"I never thought about a man having sensation in his breasts."

"Neither did I."

The twin buds, impossibly, grew harder. "You've never touched
your nipples?"

"No," he admitted.

"When did you first touch yourself"—Frances followed the slick line of hair that pointed to his groin—"here?"

He pulsed in her hand—the bulbous head, the thick stalk—just as he had pulsed inside her vagina.

"I think"—he flexed between the band of her fingers—"when I was thirteen."

"You don't remember?"

"No." She could feel him watching her face instead of her hands. "Do you remember the first time you touched yourself?"

"Yes," Frances said, slowly rubbing his rigid flesh, the soap slippery, his erection hard, the water purging. "Of course."

Veins swelled underneath the slippery glide of her fingers.

"How old were you?" he asked in a low voice.

"Twelve." A cap of soap helmeted the head of his penis. "I hid in a wheatfield, and explored my body while the sun warmed my face."

Long fingers plucked the bar of soap out of her hand. "Let me explore your body, Frances."

Frances glanced up. "I don't think I have any new territories to chart, James."

He had held open her vagina, and stared into its very depths.

"Every time I touch you I find something new." The muscles in his arms worked against her ribs and spine as he lathered up his hands. "Put your arms around my neck."

Frances remembered the agonized vulnerability in his eyes when he had reached up to hold her. She wrapped her arms around his neck, breasts sliding between them.

Her face inquisitively turned up to his. His face solemnly turned down to hers.

Impulsively she licked his lips, as he had licked her lips.

A soapy hand cradled the back of her neck. James opened his mouth to Frances, just as she opened her mouth to him.

He tasted faintly of tooth powder.

"I didn't know that men and women kissed like this," she whispered into his mouth.

A soapy hand massaged her back. "Do you like it?"

"Yes." Closing her eyes against the darkness inside his gaze, she stroked underneath his tongue. Tasting him while the rise and fall of his chest prickled her nipples. Teasing him while the thick stalk of him prodded her stomach. Testing him while hot water and steam enveloped them. "I like it very much."

Soapy fingers feathered the crevice between her buttocks.

Frances's eyes flew open with sudden intuition.

James cradled the back of her head. "I've never touched a woman here."

A curious weakness trickled through her muscles, touched where she had never imagined a man touching a woman.

Water streamed down his forehead and dripped off his nose. "Shall I stop?"

Propriety said yes. Curiosity held her still.

"No."

His hazel eyes watched the effect his slippery flesh evoked, circling, pressing, circling—her breath quickened—almost entering, not quite. "I didn't tell you something."

A burning fingertip breached her.

Frances gripped his shoulders, feeling her heart beat in a place she had never imagined it could beat. "What?"

"I never thought I could feel a woman." The full burning length of his finger pierced her. "But I feel you, Frances."

She clenched her buttocks, and didn't know if it was to stop further penetration, or to keep him inside her. "Where do you feel me, James?"

Slowly he pulled out his finger until just the palpitating pad rested inside her. "I feel you in my testicles."

Her internal flesh beat a matching pulse.

Reversing motion, the long finger slid up inside her like a burning brand. "I feel you in my cock."

Frances was melting. From the hot water. From his hot breath. From the hot penetration.

Slowly he slipped out of her, one burning knuckle at a time. She involuntarily pinched her muscles to keep him inside her.

An odd yearning came into his eyes. "I feel you in my heart."

The hot water pounded down around them.

"I know you, Frances"—one soapy finger became two, stretching her, burning her, filling her—"because you're a part of me."

The combined penetration of his gaze, his fingers, and his words were too intense. "James—"

"When I'm with you"—slowly he eased the throbbing length of his fingers out of her, his fingertips a stinging question mark—"I don't feel alone, either."

The burn from the soap climbed up into her chest.

"Is there nothing forbidden between a man and a woman?" she asked unsteadily.

"Nothing. As long as it brings pleasure." She could not escape the water, his eyes, her desire. "Does this bring you pleasure?"

"It shouldn't."

Water clung to his eyelashes, registering the flesh that clung instead of clenched. "But it does."

"Yes." Frances would not lie. "It does."

"Would you like my cock inside you"—he reversed the direction of his two fingers—"here?"

Frances's body opened, accepting James; accepting the pressure of his fingers; accepting the burn of the soap; breathing deeply as he reached deeply inside her. "Yes."

He closed his eyes and angled his head, filling her mouth and her buttocks.

Frances had not known that a kiss could touch a woman's womb. Or that a man's fingers could touch a woman's soul.

And then he was not touching either. With his tongue. With his fingers. With his body.

He turned a bronze cock: the water stopped. Arm stretching, shoulders bunching, he reached for a towel.

Tears burned Frances's eyes. James dried her as if she were a fragile glass ornament that would break with the least hint of roughness.

Entwining his fingers with hers, he led her to the bedroom. Frances watched uncertainly as he scooted a large cheval mirror in front of a blue velvet armchair.

"What are you doing?" she asked unsteadily.

How much more could they share before she ceased being a simple country woman?

He sat on the chair in front of the mirror and lubricated his flesh. "Come to me, Frances."

Frances stared for long seconds at the hard, thick stalk that blossomed into a broad head. The fruit of a man's loins: his pleasure, not his seed.

"Straddle my thighs." James grasped her hips and turned her so that her back faced him, and she saw herself in the mirror, a woman with clinging red hair, round hips and full, heavy breasts. "Now lower yourself on to me."

The first burning stretch took her breath away.

"When I was a boy"—long, elegant fingers dipped between her thighs—"I wanted to know everything there was to know about a woman's body."

The burning spread higher.

Frances grasped hard flesh; the woman in the mirror grasped muscular wrists. "What happened?"

What turned a boy's curiosity into a man's complacency?

"I saw a man hang." James cupped her sex, supporting her while she relentlessly slid down the pole of his flesh. "The Crown needed a scapegoat, and my father gave them one."

James was a defender, representing clients who were accused by the Crown. His father, then, had been a prosecutor, charging the accused in the name of the Crown.

He had hanged innocent men. James liberated guilty men.

The son was not the father.

Tears welled up inside Frances's eyes, taking more of James Whitcox.

Prickly hair scraped her back. Abraded the inside of her thighs. Tickled the exposed skin of her buttocks.

"What did you want to know," she managed to ask, "when you were a boy?"

A hard arm hooked around her lower abdomen, pulling her more tightly against his groin. Simultaneously hot breath feathered her shoulder. "I wanted to know what a woman looked like."

"You've seen me," Frances said, voice thick, filled where no woman should surely be filled.

"I wanted to see a woman like this," he said. The muscular legs in the mirror parted; she felt her knees dragged apart.

Instantly she was transfixed by a Frances she had never before seen.

"I wanted to see the color of her sex." In the mirror, a long finger flicked apart her nether lips, dusky rose on the outside, bright red on the inside. Crystal flashed, a glass bottle. Frances watched while James dipped his fingers one by one into the lubricant. "I wanted to feel how soft her sex was." Glistening fingers glided down the surprisingly colorful valley between her lips. "I wanted to know how deep her sex was."

The long fingers slipped inside the portal that yawned open in the mirror.

Frances gasped at the unexpected invasion.

"This is my cock," James said, outlining the burning length that filled her forbidden passage. "This is your cervix."

Outwardly, she watched the base of his fingers mesh into the thin ring of her vagina; inwardly, she felt a fullness accompanied by pressure.

"What does my cervix"—Frances swallowed a sudden throb of deep sensation—"feel like?"

The skin stretching across his knuckles turned completely white. "Like a little cap with a dimple."

Frances could not tell if his exploration was painful or pleasurable. She only knew that something incredible was happening inside her body.

"Hold yourself open, Frances."

Unbidden, her hands moved toward her sex.

As if her fingers dislodged his, James slithered free of her vagina.

She instinctively tilted her hips to keep him, losing him there but taking him more deeply in that other place.

"When I was a boy—"Soft lips moved against her spine; a prickly cheek scraped her shoulder. Underneath her feminine lips lay a pair of masculine testicles, all that she could see of James's sex. "I didn't know that a woman had a clitoris." He grasped the stem of her clitoris and gently squeezed until a hard little bud showed inside the mirror. "I didn't know that a woman had the same capacity for pleasure as a man." He rolled her extended clitoris, a stab of pleasure that arced between her vagina and her buttocks. "I didn't know how much a man and a woman shared." The testicles underneath the lips of her sex tightened. "A shaft . . . a glans—"A curved thumb further peeled back the skin that capped the hard bud. "A prepuce."

Frances could not speak, she could only gaze into the mirror and feel.

"I didn't know that a woman swelled with need." Relentlessly the long, elegant fingers rolled the shaft of her clitoris until the protruding little bud turned a dark purplish red. "I didn't know that a woman throbbed before orgasm."

She saw the throb. She felt the throb.

Without warning, a flash of heat surged through Frances, and all she could do was arch her back into the burning shaft that filled her, and ride a wave of pleasure.

The arm banding her lower abdomen tightened, hitching her higher, closer, his flesh internally mapping the force of her orgasm through her milking muscles.

Dimly she heard James over the roar of the blood pounding inside her ears and her eyes. "I didn't know that a woman could enjoy multiple orgasms."

He entered her when she was most vulnerable, her vagina relaxed from her orgasm, three fluted fingers gently, deeply thrusting against her cervix until another wave of pleasure broke over her.

"But I'm a man, now, Frances, and I know these things." Prickly beard scraped her shoulder; hot breath seared her skin. "I know that the sex of a woman is a gift to be treasured." With difficulty she focused on the hand that filled her. On the taut ring of flesh that was her vagina. On the tight, hair-studded testicles that seemingly annexed her vagina. "Our sex is not ugly." The white edging his knuckles faded; simultaneously she felt his fingers slide out of her, taking with them her soul.

"Look at us." Her vagina gaped like a red wound where his fingers had stretched her. "Look at us and remember." Long fingers traveled up the glistening red valley between her lips. "You are not that girl who lay in darkness." He touched the hard, distended bud of her clitoris in tight little circles, exactly like she had demonstrated earlier. A choked sound of pleasure escaped her throat; it was too soon to orgasm again. And then it wasn't. Frances exploded, his flesh flexing deep inside her, her flesh flexing against his fingers. The hand gripping her waist lowered, shaping her lower abdomen. "*This* is your gift, Frances: your passion"—he filled the aching gap inside her body, wringing from her a short cry—"not your submission."

Chapter 31

Bright sunlight poured through the sheer green drapes. Morning had come.

He had showered and shaved and dressed. He could not delay the inevitable any longer.

James leaned over Frances and gently pushed aside a tangled red curl. Fear mingled with an emotion so primal that it knotted his groin.

Slowly her eyelashes—auburn red tipped with gold—fluttered open.

James tensed, waiting for disgust to mask her face. Anticipating the regret that would cloud her eyes.

Slowly the sleep cleared from her face, and awareness dilated her pupils.

James saw in her gaze the intimacy they had shared: the deep, burning invasion of his cock; the orgasms that convulsed every muscle. He saw the unguarded vulnerability her sexuality excited. But he also saw in her eyes a new strength that he had not previously seen, a strength born of pleasure.

The fear tensing his spine dissolved, making it possible for him to recognize the emotion that knotted his groin: tenderness.

She had accepted him in the most basic, elemental way that a woman could accept a man. There was nothing he wouldn't do for her.

James kissed her eyes closed so that she wouldn't see the depth of emotion she evoked in him.

"I have to go." Eyelashes as frail as butterfly wings fluttered against his lips. He breathed in the spicy vanilla scent of her, and the musky scent of himself for long seconds before he pulled back. He had not fed her the night before; she must be starved. "Shall I have breakfast sent up?"

Her eyes widened with the realization that the house hummed with activity.

"No." Dark rose colored her cheeks. She protectively clutched the covers to her neck, as if the servants could see her nakedness through the walls. "Thank you."

James could not bite back a smile.

"How can you blush"—he relentlessly peeled down the silk covers and stared at her breasts; gently he touched the tip of her nipple with the tip of his finger—"after everything we've done?"

"Perhaps I'm blushing *because* of everything we've done."

His gaze snapped upward. "Regrets, Frances?"

There was no regret in her pale eyes; there was only the knowledge of their sexuality. "Splendid dinosaurs, James."

Leaning down, hiding from her the relief her words precipitated, he plumped her breast and sucked her nipple up into his mouth.

Soft fingers cupped the back of his head. James felt her touch shoot out of his cock.

He had never felt as close to anyone as he felt to Frances. She was an integral part of him.

Easing backward, he rubbed his lips back and forth over the wet hardness he had created. "I don't want to go."

James could not ever remember not wanting to attend court. To woo the audience in the gallery. To manipulate the jurors in their box.

To win.

Breathlessness threaded her voice. "But we have to."

"Yes."

Their separate lives waited for them.

"May I share a cab with you?"

James curiously tongued the spongy indentation on the tip of her breast, wondering what her milk had tasted like, the milk her children had shared but which he had not.

"James." Frances grasped a fistful of his hair, not hurting, but not gentle. He tongued her nipple until she released his hair and pulled him closer. "James."

He had felt her womb contract. His hand—as if with a will of its own—sought the warm silk of her stomach.

The faint chime of a Westminster clock penetrated the sanctuary of the bedroom. Reluctantly he straightened.

Her swollen nipple gleamed in invitation.

"Yes." James stood up and flipped the covers off of her. "You may share a cab with me."

He suddenly became aware of the tension in the pale green eyes that gazed up at him.

Slowly he perused her naked body in the light of day. There was no part of her that he did not know: her breasts; her hips; her stomach; her thighs; her buttocks.

His gaze returned to her face. The battle she fought not to cover her body was clearly visible.

"You *are* a beautiful woman, Frances," he said neutrally. "Shall I help you dress?"

"I—"Frances swallowed, uncertain of how to respond to his compliment. "Do I have time to shower?"

"No." James was already running late. "I'm due in court."

"I'm . . . oily."

His cock hardened. He knew exactly where she was oily.

Turning, he walked into the bathroom. Turning on the hot water cock, he wet a washcloth. Returning to the bedroom, he cleaned away the lubricating oil.

The flesh between her buttocks was tightly puckered, but the flesh between her thighs was red and swollen.

Frances stared up at him with clear, pale eyes.

"I do believe," she said finally, "that you will soon cure me of blushing."

Laughter crinkled his eyes. "It will be my primary goal. Shall I lend madam a hand?"

Self-consciousness and pleasure mingled in her gaze. "Please."

Frances dressed in quick economical movements, one by one donning the clothes he retrieved for her: corset; petticoat; bustle; skirt. James brushed her hair while she buttoned her bodice; baby fine, it clung to the bristles. She did not use a mirror to pin up her hair, accepting one by one the pins he offered. Quickly she pulled up silk stockings. James smoothed up a white lace and rose silk garter over her right leg. And remembered her thighs clutching his hips while he thrust and ground against her cervix. James smoothed up a garter over her left leg. And remembered her buttocks quivering against his groin while he held himself still and deep inside her as she milked his cock with her release.

Frances watched him lace up her bronze kid shoe. James knew that she, too, remembered the groans he could not stop and the grip of her muscles that she could not prevent.

"I saw you in the mirror," she said unexpectedly.

James had not been able to see their reflection, his vision blocked by her back.

He knotted her laces and moved on to her other foot. His emotions firmly in check—a barrister now—he asked, "What did you see?"

"Your testicles were directly below my vagina."

James blindly stared at the bow he created, envisioning the vermillion gape of her vagina above the hair-studded globes of his testicles.

"I watched them grow tighter and tighter with each orgasm you gave me," she said. "I felt as if they were somehow connected to my body."

James was not a humble man; he was made humble by Frances.

Standing up, he silently held out both hands to help her rise up out of the armchair.

She stared at his left hand. "You're not wearing your wedding band."

He had taken it off before showering for work. "It's not gold, Frances, that binds a man and a woman."

"In the mirror"—Frances uncertainly glanced upward—"my vagina formed a ring around your fingers."

"Your entire body is a ring," he said steadily, offering his hands. "Your vagina. Your anus. Your mouth."

He had been unfaithful to his wife; he would never be unfaithful to Frances.

She took his hands.

The butler greeted James at the foot of the stairs. He showed no surprise at seeing Frances on his arm. He was well-trained, indeed.

"Your cab is waiting, sir."

"Thank you, Peasebody."

The butler held out Frances's cloak. She relinquished James's arm.

Chill air permeated his skin; it was not dispelled by the weight of his wool coat.

Peasebody offered Frances her reticule. Gold gleamed on her ring finger.

The sudden vulnerability in her gaze squeezed his chest.

She must decide which bond was the strongest: the past or the future. It was a decision James could not help her make.

A hansom cab waited by the walk.

"Shall I drop you off?" Frances asked as if they were merely acquaintances sharing a cab. "Or shall you drop me off?"

"I'll drop you off," he said.

He wanted to see that she safely returned to her townhouse.

James followed her up the iron stair and onto the wooden platform, pausing to give the cabby Frances's address before joining her. For long seconds the only sound inside the dim interior was the grinding of carriage wheels, the cab joined by dozens of other vehicles as men and women went about their morning business.

"We're dressed in the same clothes that we wore last night," Frances said at last.

"Yes," James said. He would change in his chambers.

"But we're not the same."

"No," he agreed. "We're not the same."

She had learned to take; he had learned to give.

The left carriage wheel hit a hole in the pavement.

"What does jizzum mean?"

James remembered the meeting last Saturday, and the battle of words between Marie Hoppleworth and John Nickols. It seemed as if it had occurred three years ago instead of a mere three days.

"Sperm," he said dispassionately.

"Miss Hoppleworth used the term mettle."

He did not reply. They both knew that "fetch mettle" was a term for male masturbation.

"My vicar often praises the merits of men who have mettle," Frances said in her clear, steady voice. "I wonder if he realizes that it means sperm?"

Laughter erupted out of James's chest and filled the cab. Reaching out, he pulled Frances close to his side, holding her grounded to him so that she would not bounce away with the motion of the carriage. He buried his face against hers until the laughter died, and her scent filled his senses.

"Frances," he murmured into her temple, his voice thick.

She leaned into his touch. "What?"

"In the shower"—he spoke into her soft skin—"the soap must have burned."

"The sensation was interesting."

He remembered her initial resistance. He relived her spine-melting acceptance.

"Do you still burn?"

"A little."

"I don't know if I'll be able to see you tonight." Her admission of the discomfort he had caused constricted his throat. "I have to prepare closing statements."

"My home will always be open to you, James."

The memory of her welcoming flesh clenched his groin. "What will you do today?"

Her voice vibrated against his lips. "I have an errand to run."

"Send a servant."

James didn't want her to roam the streets of London alone: he of all people knew of their dangers.

"I have to do this on my own," she said.

He of all people knew how impossible it was to protect a woman if a man was determined to injure her.

"Do you have epsom salts?"

"I don't know."

"Send a maid to fetch some." Had anyone ever ministered to Frances's aches and pains? "Soak in a hot bath before you go out."

"I will," she promised.

The words worked up from deep inside his chest. "I won't always say the right words—"

"I don't always know the right words to say," she quickly interrupted.

"But I treasure your home, Frances, more than I can ever say."

She nuzzled his cheek, cleanly shaven for the workday. "I treasure your home, too, James."

There was no reason for the fear that suddenly seized him.

Fear, James realized, was not rooted in reason.

Frances could be killed. As his wife had been killed. Frances could be hurt. As she was bound to be, having an affair with him.

"Frances." He pulled her closer, wanting to absorb her scent, and her taste, and her touch until they were one body like they had been only hours earlier.

"I like hearing you say my name."

The right carriage wheel dropped into a hole, sprang upward. Frances moved with James instead of apart from him.

He would never forget her cry of release.

"I like hearing you say my name, too."

Frances tasted the pulse that pounded in his cheek, tongue a burning flick. "Why are pictures of a man touching himself called 'billiards'?"

James found her hand, slipped her glove off, and slid her unresisting fingers into his front trouser pocket. "Pocket billiards."

Curiously she explored him through the layers of his trousers and small clothes, found his testicles. "Two in the hole."

He held her closer, allowing her to explore the most vulnerable part of his body, unable to shake his fear. "Or one in the side."

"You use the term 'cock' for a man's sex." She measured his circumference through the layers of clothing. "What euphemisms do you use for a woman's sex?"

There were many words for a woman's sex.

Belittling words. Insulting words.

Men needed women, therefore they feared them, and what men feared they reviled.

James didn't want Frances to ever think of her sex in derogatory terms. Holding her with his left arm, he reached down with his right hand and hooked his fingers underneath the hem of her cloak . . . her skirt . . . her petticoat. "A bit of jam."

He found the soft tuft of pubic hair that was auburn like the base of her eyelashes. "Gooseberry bush."

Frances parted her legs. Her clitoris—a little cock—leapt at his touch.

He felt something visceral leap inside his chest. There was no part of her body that did not respond to him.

"Garden of Eden." Delicate lips curled around his middle finger. "Cupid's arbor."

Her flesh was as familiar as his own.

"Honey pot." He kissed the opening of her body—hurt and swollen because of him—with the tip of his finger. "Harbor of hope."

Frances clung to him. "James."

She was so vulnerable.

"What?" he murmured.

"I don't know if I should be eaten, planted, or moored."

A sharp ray of laughter slashed through James. The cab slowed, stealing his smile.

He had to let her go. But not before he heard her laughter.

"Perhaps *madame* prefers 'Buckinger's boot,' 'Jacob's ladder,' 'Cupid's cupboard,' 'mouth that cannot bite,' 'where the monkey sleeps,' or the usual standbys: 'thingamy,' 'thingumajig,' 'what-do-you-call-it,' 'you-know-what,' 'you-know-where' or, of course, 'the name it not,' otherwise known as 'the nameless.'"

The cab halted. The laughter he had anticipated did not come.

"Where the monkey sleeps, James?" she asked in an uneven voice.

He nuzzled her temple. "Do you prefer 'where James sleeps'?"

The laughter he needed filled the cab.

It was clear. Like her eyes. Uninhibited. Like her response to him.

A jingle of harnesses rang out.

"Promise me," James suddenly demanded, withdrawing his hand, his breath, his arm, his face.

Her laughter faded. Slowly the heat filling his pocket withdrew. "Promise you what?"

He clenched his hands to prevent them from grabbing her fingers and wrapping them around his cock. "Promise me that you won't let anyone hurt you."

She searched his gaze in the shadows of the cab. "Why would anyone hurt me?"

"Some people hurt others without realizing they do so."

Men. Women. Husbands. Wives.

Mothers. Children.

"If the hurt isn't intentional," Frances said sincerely, "then it doesn't last."

Chapter
32

"Miss Dennison."

The woman in the tailored dark coat and tall, ostrich-plumed hat froze.

A rhythmical tap-tap-tap permeated the frigid silence.

Frances remembered the chicken at last year's fair that had pecked out an off-key tune on a miniature piano. The comical vision of the speckled hen instantly dissolved into the face of Ardelle Dennison.

She thought of all the ugly words the publicist had said. And wondered if she had lost her mind as well as her morals.

"Miss Dennison." The tap of Frances's heels echoed the length of the corridor. "I wonder if I might have a word with you."

Ardelle Dennison's voice was as chill as the spring air. "This section of the museum is for employees only, Mrs. Hart."

The rebuff wasn't unexpected.

"Mr. Harmon said I might have a few words with you." Heart pounding, Frances stepped ahead of the publicist and turned to directly confront her. "I hoped we might take lunch together. Would you care to join me at the coffeehouse?"

The publicist's amber eyes were on a level with Frances's: they were as chill as her voice. "I'm meeting a client for lunch."

And, of course, she did not consider Frances worthy of introducing to her client. Whereas James had introduced Frances to several members of Parliament.

"Then I won't keep you." Frances squared her shoulders. "But I would like to take a moment to apologize."

Surprise blanketed the coldness in the publicist's eyes. "I beg your pardon?"

"Mr. Manning caused you distress," Frances said. "And for that I am most heartily sorry."

She couldn't mend the hurt she had caused her daughters, but she could aid this woman who was young enough to be her daughter.

"I don't know what you're talking about," Ardelle Dennison said, quickly recovering from her surprise. "Mr. Manning has done nothing to distress me."

Frances studied the publicist in the dim corridor, a beautiful woman reduced to shadow. "I quite think any woman who has affection for a man, Miss Dennison, would be distressed if that man said he did not find her worthy of marriage."

The angry red in Ardelle Dennison's cheeks paled to shocked white. She, too, vividly remembered the conversation that had occurred ten days earlier.

"I know he hurt you," Frances said compassionately, "because I felt your hurt."

"And how, Mrs. Hart"—the publicist's scorn was a strained imitation—"did you deduce that this *hurt* you felt came from me and not someone else?"

Frances had always been able to read her children. "By your eyes, Miss Dennison."

The publicist's soft lips folded into an thin, ugly line, silently refuting Frances's observation.

"I knew, of course, that you held Mr. Manning in high esteem," Frances continued evenly. "But I didn't realize that the hurt I felt came from you until last Saturday. When Mr. Nickols suggested we stop meeting at the museum, I saw the look in your eyes: you were afraid to meet Mr. Manning outside of a meeting."

There was no reaction in the publicist's eyes, just the shocked awareness that she had revealed her secret.

"I think you must be very lonely. But you needn't be. You're a young woman. An educated woman. You don't have to be alone. Unless, of course, you truly wish to be."

But perhaps Ardelle Dennison didn't know for what she wished. Frances had not known at her age.

"I won't detain you any longer." She had said what she came to say; now it was time to take her leave. "I merely wanted to tell you that I am sorry for the distress my actions caused."

If Frances hadn't provoked Joseph Manning, he wouldn't have retaliated in kind.

She turned, heavy skirts swinging.

It suddenly dawned on her what it was that caused the persistent tapping: it was a typewriter. A woman had demonstrated the odd-looking machine in a shop window.

"What would you do, Mrs. Hart?"

Frances stopped short. The question was sharp with pain.

Frances lightly touched her chest. Instantly her flesh leapt to life. Breasts swelling. Nipples hardening.

What would she have done if James had not invited her to join the Men and Women's Club?

"In the omnibus, Miss Dennison," Frances said, "I overheard a young man and his wife. They were both quite young, perhaps eighteen or nineteen years of age."

The tap-tap-tap paused. The ensuing silence was deafening.

"The young girl examined her husband's penis."

Jarring percussion raced up and down Frances's spine: she had twice now shocked Ardelle Dennison.

"It was quite innocent." Frances swallowed a lump in her throat. And knew that her own actions would not be viewed as such. "The girl giggled. There was nothing lewd in her curiosity, there was just a sense of fun and adventure."

The monotonous tap-tap-tap resumed, laborious rather than musical.

"But for one moment, Miss Dennison, I hated that girl." Remembered anger tightened the muscles in her shoulders. "I didn't giggle when I was her age, you see. I listened to her giggle, and I knew that I could never experience what she was experiencing. And I was bitter. I was bitter because I wasn't young. I wasn't innocent. But most of all, Miss Dennison, I was bitter because I didn't possess the courage to take the simple joy that the girl was taking."

Ardelle Dennison responded with scorn. "And you think that Mr. Manning would enjoy having his privates fondled on a public vehicle?"

"I think," she said carefully, "that Mr. Manning admires you very much."

Bitterness lashed out at Frances. "Men admire what they can not possess."

Obviously the publicist had encountered such a man. A man, perhaps, who had taken liberties, and who had then abandoned her.

It's not gold, Frances, that binds a man and a woman.

Frances dropped her hand. "Then you must ask yourself, Miss Dennison, if admiration is all that you want out of life."

The corridor Frances traversed was not familiar. She plunged down a staircase.

Outside the unfamiliar exit, sunlight streamed through gray clouds. The familiar odors of manure, baked bread and coal smoke wafted through the street. Sussex smells. But in Sussex the air did not throb with men and women: buying; selling; wanting; needing. Or perhaps she had been so busy being a wife, a mother and a grandmother that she had never taken the time to notice the wants and needs of those outside of her family.

The voice of a woman who sold cherries mingled with that of a man who sold brick dust: "Cherries groat"—"Brick dust, sharpen yer knives"—"Buy black heart cherries"—"A quart o' brick dust fer a penny!" Overriding the two vendors shrilled a younger voice: "Murder trial! Murder an' may'im fer a penny! Read it 'ere! Murder an' may'im!"

The phrase *murder trial* pricked Frances's attention.

It wasn't the first time she had heard it shouted out while walking the streets of London, but she had not wanted to hear about murder. She had not wanted to acknowledge death in London when it was death in Sussex that had drawn her to the City of Dreadful Delights.

Wearing a billboard almost as large as he, a tousle-haired boy trudged down the street curb carrying an armful of newspapers. "Murder trial! Read about th' woman whot offed 'er 'usband! Penny a paper!"

It dawned on Frances that the boy advertised the Mary Bartle trial.

She had taken James, the man, as deeply inside her body as a woman could possibly take a man, but she knew nothing at all about James, the barrister.

She dug out the obligatory penny from her reticule.

The boy, espying the glint of copper, met her halfway. "Gran' readin', marm! All about a woman wot poisoned 'er mate. Penny a paper!"

Frances stared down at the newspaper the boy thrust into her hands: familiar eyes stared up at her.

Chapter
33

The stench of the courtroom was overpowering.

Behind him, men and women silently exited the gallery. In front of him, men silently escorted Mary Bartle from the dock.

She had unfastened her bodice button by button without a flicker of an eyelash. Men as well as women—the judge as well as the jurors—had gasped at the sight of the syphilitic tumors. Mary Bartle had not flinched at the sound of their revulsion.

Looking into her eyes, James had realized why she did not register either modesty or vanity: Mary Bartle had died during the course of the trial.

The dull thud of a leather satchel slamming onto wood ricocheted down James's spine. "Is there nothing you won't do to win, Whitcox?"

James snapped closed the buckle on his satchel. "Nothing."

"How does it feel to crush a woman's spirit?" Lodoun asked with loathing.

James glanced up, his face expressionless. "How does it feel when you hang an innocent man?"

The sick whiteness of the Attorney General's face turned angry red. "I don't prosecute innocent men."

Righteousness is a well-seasoned dish, James recalled an old professor declaring.

James stood up, silk robes clinging to his wool trousers. His voice was devoid of emotion. "You forget, Lodoun, that my father was once Attorney General."

Shock widened Jack Lodoun's eyes.

James walked out of the courtroom. The reek of despair followed him.

Avery Tristan busily scribbled at his own desk, a smaller version of James's. James shut the heavy mahogany door behind him: it did not block the stink of the courtroom.

"Sir." The clerk did not glance up. "I'm just finishing up a draft for your concluding remarks. Shall I grab us a bite to eat while you go over it?"

The clerk would work right alongside James into the early morning hours. But James couldn't work right now. His mind was filled with Mary Bartle, but he needed Frances Hart.

She filled him with hope, but James felt no hope after his day's work.

Drawings of the syphilitic tumors would on the morrow grace every paper in London. Black and white would not do them justice.

"Finish your draft, Mr. Tristan." He dropped his satchel onto the edge of the larger teak desk. "I'll go grab us something." He jerked off his wig and slung it on top of the black leather satchel; cool air dried the sweat tickling his scalp. "What would you like?"

"Corned beef on rye would be splendid, Mr. Whitcox."

Splendid dinosaurs.

James shrugged off the silk robe.

"Sir."

James grabbed up his coat and hat. "Yes?"

"That was a brilliant motion." The clerk's voice was firm. "No juror will convict her now."

But Mary Bartle would not thank him for her liberation.

In the two years that Avery Tristan had worked for James, James had never asked: "Why do you wish to be a defender, Mr. Tristan?"

Avery Tristan could now don a robe and command his own clients, but after reading law at the Middle Temple, he had chosen to apprentice with James.

"My father liked his billy stick, sir."

The clerk's father had started off as a constable; he was now a sergeant. He wasn't known for brutality, but reputations weren't always earned. Apparently Avery Tristan knew from first-hand experience the darker side of justice: the poverty that invited persecution; the beatings that produced confessions.

"I'll be back in an hour," James said shortly.

"Very well, sir."

The city was already dark; cold fog misted the air. James turned up his coat collar, and crossed the street.

Bailey's Book Shop was crowded. A clerk discreetly escorted James to the back room no one mentioned, but which everyone who was associated with the Old Bailey knew existed.

Familiar faces filled the dark chamber: clerks, court officers, a judge. They did not look at one another.

"Can I help you, sir?"

James glanced down at a blond-haired man who wore wire-rimmed spectacles.

"Do you have Rose's Lubrifiant?" he asked impersonally.

"No, sir, but we can acquire it, if you would like."

"I'll take a dozen bottles."

He wanted a bottle in every room of his and Frances's home.

The store clerk quickly masked his surprise. "Will that be all, sir?"

James had only ever looked at their postcards. "What paraphernalia do you have?"

The variety was not as great as that found in the Achilles Book Shoppe. James carefully studied the objects hidden away inside drawers.

He had never shopped for a woman. The peace he had found inside Frances's body seeped through the miasma of despair as he contemplated which items would give her pleasure.

The peace dissolved the moment he hit the pavement.

An old man sat on a corner tiredly eating a pie; a discarded billboard for *The Times* stood beside him. He had sold his quota of today's newspapers, and was fueling up to sell the morrow's quota.

James ordered sandwiches in a nearby coffee shop. The waiter went out of his way to avoid James's hands, as if he carried the disease of syphilis.

Shouldering open the heavy mahogany door to his chambers, James was immediately inundated with the rich aroma of coffee.

"Oh!" Avery Tristan stepped out of an arched doorway carrying a large, cream-colored mug. He stopped short at the sight of James. "You're back. I made a pot of coffee. Would you like a cup, sir?"

"Yes." He set the parcel of sandwiches on top of his desk. "That would be most welcome, thank you."

The clerk disappeared through the doorway.

James envisioned the empty closet that had been converted into a pantry with a gas burner. Beyond the closet was the lavatory, and beyond that, a conference room.

"The galleries were full today." Avery Tristan's voice carried through the arch. "People stood up against the walls."

"The trial is winding down." James hung up his coat. "They don't want to miss the end."

People liked to watch the face of the accused when the verdict was read.

The clerk stepped through the arch. "Did you notice the woman in the back who was wearing a green-checkered coat?"

A picture of Frances when she had accidentally barged into the club meeting wearing a green-checkered coat popped into James's mind.

"No, I didn't see her." His heart suddenly pounded inside his chest. "Why do you ask?"

Chapter
34

One second David's hand clung to Frances; the next second it disintegrated in her fingers.

"Mrs. Hart." A loud, persistent pounding pierced the darkness of sleep. "Mrs. Hart."

"I'm sorry." Frances jerked up, clutching her left hand to her chest. "I'm so sorry."

She had given David thirty-four years, but she could not give him the rest of her life.

The pounding did not stop.

It occurred to Frances that she was in London and not in Sussex, and that it was the butler who pounded on her door rather than her husband's failing heart pounding in her ears.

Forcefully pulling her thoughts together, she threw back the covers. A dull ache shot up through her pelvis.

Frances remembered the night she had spent with James Whitcox.

Faint light penetrated the window.

The moon was low in the night sky. Or a street lamp filtered through the curtains.

Out of the corner of her eye she saw a dull red coal smoldering in the fireplace.

The air was chill and damp.

Either it was very late at night, or very early in the morning.

"Mrs. Hart." More pounding. "Are you awake?"

Sleep fading, Frances snatched up the wrap lying on the foot of the bed. "What is it, Mr. Denton?"

Had one of her children sent a telegram?

"It's Mr. Whitcox, madam." The butler's voice was harsh through the door. "He insisted that I wake you."

James.

The fear that clenched her stomach was unreasonable: obviously if James was in her townhouse, he could not be ill or injured. Nor could he be a harbinger of bad news, since her children did not know of his existence.

Frances jerked open the door, a plain flannel wrap flapping around a plain flannel nightgown.

Vaguely she was aware that the butler, dressed in a white muslin nightshirt tucked into dark trousers, stepped aside. He held a candle high in the air.

The wool runner was cold; it did not shield her feet from the hardness of wood. Gaslight climbed the stairs, aiding the flickering candlelight.

Frances paused at the top of the staircase, looking down. James stood at the foot of the staircase, looking up.

His face, when he had bade Mary Bartle to unfasten her bodice, had been without expression. He now wore that same expressionless mask.

The wavering darkness squeezed her heart.

She had wanted to see the barrister, only to discover that the barrister was James, and James hurt.

My home will always be open to you, James.

Wordlessly Frances held out her hand.

The worn steps protested James's ascension.

Heat gripped her fingers; uncertainty gripped her throat.

The butler knew she had spent the previous night with a man but, it was another thing entirely for him to see that man enter her bedchamber.

She remembered the fear she had felt, straddling James's hips. She remembered the strain in James's eyes, lying still beneath her.

Squaring her shoulders, Frances led James down the corridor.

"Thank you, Mr. Denton." The butler, waiting beside her door, showed neither approval nor disapproval. "There's no need to see Mr. Whitcox out."

The butler stared for long seconds before bowing. "Very well, madam. Shall I knock Mr. Whitcox up in the morning?"

She swallowed her uncertainty. "Yes, please."

James's voice was as expressionless as his face. "Wake me at seven, Denton."

"Very well, sir."

James closed the door behind him, an almost inaudible click. The small, dark bedroom shrank to the size of a closet.

Frances rummaged inside the nightstand for the box of safety matches, painfully aware of her flannel nightclothes, remnants of Sussex. "Did you finish preparing your closing statements?"

James did not answer her question.

"I couldn't sleep," he said instead.

Yellow fire flamed in the darkness. "Then I shall hold you."

The acrid scent of sulfur permeated the air.

"Why?"

The yellow flame flickered in a sudden draft.

She lifted the globe of the oil lamp and touched the flaming match to the wick. "I needed to see you."

He had said that law was a part of him, but she had not realized just how much a part of him it was until she had seen him inside the courtroom, dressed in a black silk robe and curled gray periwig, peeling apart men and women layer by layer.

"I killed her," he said emotionlessly.

Frances remembered the utter lifelessness inside Mary Bartle's eyes. And understood Jane Fredericks's rage.

She blew out the match, and carefully placed the globe over the burning wick. "Syphilis has destroyed her, James, not you."

In the meeting, the sexual disease had been a name. Now it was a living picture that would forever be a part of Frances. As it was a part of Jane Fredericks, living with a woman who died day by day. As it was a part of James Whitcox, struggling to save a woman who could not be saved.

Flaring light revealed wrinkled sheets and tumbled blankets.

Frances could not stop the question—"Did she murder her husband?"—even as she realized what his answer must be.

"I can't discuss that," was the flat rejoinder.

She dropped the blackened match into the miniature blue glass bonnet. "I'm sorry."

A soft thud resounded over the pounding of her heart. "For what?"

Frances turned. "I'm sorry that you have to bear the burden of so many secrets."

The secrets of every man and woman he had ever defended resided deep inside him where she could not give him comfort.

"We all have secrets."

His words were an eery echo of the words she had spoken six nights earlier, standing outside the Achilles Book Shoppe. He draped his coat across the ladder-backed chair in front of the window; his black silk top hat rested on top of the small writing desk.

A dismal bong sounded over the London night.

Yes, Frances thought regretfully, they all had secrets.

"My bed isn't as comfortable as yours," she said quietly. Quietly apologizing for the secrets she kept from him.

"You'll be in it." James shrugged out of his frock coat, his back to her. "I'll be comfortable."

"Did it disturb you, that I visited the courthouse today?"

James peeled off his waistcoat. And again avoided directly answering her. "Why didn't you come to my chambers after court adjourned?"

She had learned so many new terms. Objection allowed. Objection denied. Chloroform poisoning. Syphilitic tumors.

Willfully and with forethought.

"You said you needed to prepare closing statements," she pointed out reasonably.

She would never interfere with his work.

James jerked his shirt over his head. "We finished the statements around ten."

She wanted to ask who was "we," but was afraid that might be confidential, too.

"Did you see me in the courtroom?" she asked instead.

James pulled off his vest; the rising hem revealed his warm skin inch by inch. "No."

"How did you know I attended, then?"

"My clerk saw you."

Frances stiffened. "Your clerk knows me?"

"He described you to me."

"Why?"

James hooked his thumbs inside the band of his trousers—like he had hooked the sides of her sex—and yanked down two layers of wool. "He thought you made other men and women seem rather drab."

"Really?" Pleasure burst inside her at the compliment. "He said that?"

"Really." James turned around, naked in his need. "He said that."

Frances's gaze involuntarily dropped down to his sex; it swelled beneath her regard, the cap of loose skin sliding back to reveal a large, plum-like head. "I didn't thank you."

His penis flexed. "For what?"

She stared at the thin thread of desire that he cried. "For replacing that image."

He had vanquished forever the passive picture of her lying in the darkness with her gown folded up around her waist.

James crossed the carpet, penis bouncing with each forward step. "Did I give you a new one?"

"Yes." She glanced up, tears pricking her eyes. "You did."

He pushed the flannel wrap over her shoulders, lashes veiling his eyes. "With what?"

"Of you, James." Frances held out first her left arm, and then her right, heartbeat quickening, remembering the feel of his naked skin against her naked skin. Remembering the sight of his sex beneath her sex. "And me."

"Flannel doesn't become you," he said flatly.

Darkness blocked Frances's vision, the exterior of her gown. She held up her arms. Chill air engulfed her buttocks . . . her breasts.

"Flannel is warm," she returned, voice muffled.

"But now you have me to warm you." One second she was engulfed in darkness; the next second she was bathed in flickering light. "Hold me, Frances."

The heat of his skin and the hardness of his muscles and the prickliness of his hair stole away her breath.

"Your sex isn't a burden, James," she whispered against a stubbled cheek. "It's a pleasure that I gladly welcome."

Moist breath seared her ear. "Do you still like me?"

The tightness of her throat choked off a laugh at the absurdity of his question. "I didn't know it was possible to like someone as much as I like you."

She had not realized how tense his body was until it relaxed against her. "I violated a woman today."

Frances held James as tightly as she could, stepping into his arms until her breasts cushioned his chest and her stomach cradled his penis. "You did what you had to do."

"I imagined the humiliation it would cause you," he spoke against her temple, his words short bursts of hot air, "if it were you in that witness box."

"I would thank you."

"Would you?"

"Yes," Frances said emphatically, lips moving against a hard line of jaw, fingers tracing his spine: one vertebra, two vertebrae.... "I would."

"Will you come to my chambers tomorrow?"

Blindly Frances followed the line of his back. "Would you like me to?"

"The jury will reach a verdict."

"How do you know that?"

"Because they won't convict a woman who is already dead."

No matter that she might be guilty. No matter that she might prefer to die.

"Did you know that you have twenty-three vertebrae?" Frances whispered.

Chapter 35

J ames woke with a start. Immediately he became aware of soft
heat. It circled his waist. It bridged the front of his thigh. It prodded his chest. It weighted down his leg.

The scent of vanilla infused his senses.

His eyelids snapped open.

It was Frances's arm that circled his waist; Frances's sex that
bridged the front of his thigh; Frances's breasts that prodded his
chest; Frances's leg that weighted down his leg. She had taken him
into her bed, and he had slept, his sex nestled between the lips of
her sex.

Watery sunlight penetrated drab, colorless drapes.

The ashes in the fireplace were cold and gray: there was no heat
in the poorly insulated bedroom.

Slowly, carefully, he smoothed back a soft red curl. The curve of
her cheek was translucent in the muted morning light.

He had wondered what she would think about the Mary Bartle
case, and now he knew. Frances Hart would never cease to amaze
him.

Gently he brushed his lips against hers, watching her shadow-
darkened face. Instantly her pale eyes opened.

Slow seconds passed. The muffled sounds of household activity
penetrated the bedroom: seven o'clock could not be far off.

"I was dreaming about you," Frances murmured, her breath misting the chill air.

James pushed her hair back off her forehead. "What about?"

"I dreamed you were inside me."

"Did I give you an orgasm?"

"You would have." Her eyes were little-girl solemn. "But you woke me."

With a kiss.

But James was not the stuff of fairy tales.

Solemnly he returned, "Would you like me to give you the orgasm I deprived you of?"

"Please."

He laughed low in his throat. "You are an amazing woman, Frances Hart."

"I think you are rather amazing yourself, James Whitcox."

Her compliment twisted something deep and painful inside him.

He nuzzled her eyebrow, feathery soft, the bone underneath softly delineated. "Where's the lubricant?"

"In the top drawer."

Cold air bit his naked shoulders. With each twist of his body, the bedsprings squealed. Warm covers rode his back, held in place by Frances.

The glass bottle was icy.

Ducking underneath the bedcovers, James warmed the lubricant between the palms of his hands before dipping his fingers inside. Frances squeezed him, forcing out of him his own personal lubrication.

Their shared actions were erotic yet companionable, an aspect of intimacy he had not anticipated. "Did you soak yesterday in epsom salts?"

Her answer was a spurt of silvery vapor. "Yes."

He sucked in icy air at the delicate probe of her fingertip. "Did it help?"

Frances found the bottle underneath the covers and dipped her fingers into it. "Yes."

Stoppering the bottle—careful to keep the covers over their shoulders—he slid his left arm underneath her waist and explored her with his right hand. There was her little stalk . . . her little prepuce . . . her little glans. "You're hard."

She audibly sucked in air. "So are you."

Frances slickly grasped him. James slickly entered her.

Her flesh flowered open and snugly embraced his fingers. James held still at the emotion that surged through him.

He had needed her to hold him. And she had held him. He had needed her to comfort him. And she had comforted him.

He needed her in court. And she would be in court for him.

Fingers abruptly easing out of the welcoming clasp of her vagina, he shifted his weight and rolled on top of her, elbows supporting his upper body. The bedsprings loudly protested the cold air that wormed between them.

Quickly Frances adjusted the covers around his shoulders. "Your house is warmer."

"And quieter," James said dryly.

Catching him unawares, Frances guided his erection into her vagina.

James's back bowed from the tight grip of her flesh, driving him more deeply into her. Frances's knees raised on either side of his hips, taking him more deeply inside her.

She rippled around him like molten velvet. Her face in the morning gloom suffused with wonder.

James stared at her through the silvery gust of his breath and felt his cock cry the tears that he suddenly wanted to cry. Frances was not beautiful in the conventional sense, but she possessed a beauty that eviscerated his emotions.

Carefully adjusting his weight, he lowered his chest to warm her breasts. Slowly her lashes lifted.

The look in her eyes clenched his chest and his testicles: she looked at him as if he gave her the Crown Jewels instead of his cock.

James kissed her eyelids closed. "I didn't know it was possible to like someone as much as I like you, either, Frances."

Warm covers cocooned his shoulders. "Monday night you used the word 'fucked.'"

James gently tasted her spiky eyelashes while her soft vagina squeezed his heart. "Yes."

Slowly she opened her lashes and pinned him with her honesty. "Is that what we do . . . fuck?"

Sliding his arms underneath her warm, supple back, he cautiously rotated his pelvis. "In a sense."

Frances experimented by counter-rotating her hips. "In what sense?"

James pictured her vagina, a ring more binding than gold. "Fuck is the most elemental word in the English language."

He had thought that the respectable sex he experienced with his wife had been a matter of conjugal relations, while the extramarital sex he had experienced with his mistresses had been fucking. Buried so deeply inside Frances that his testicles ached, he realized that all he had ever done was have sex: fucking required emotion, but he had not felt emotion.

"James." Sharp fingernails carved half-moons into his buttocks. "Would you think me terribly forward if I asked you to fuck me?"

James stretched his thighs out and up, knees sliding underneath her buttocks, spreading her apart more widely while at the same time allowing him greater purchase. "I would be charmed beyond belief, Frances."

Her eyelashes fluttered closed at the deeper penetration; her internal muscles fluttered as they adjusted around him. "You kept trickling out of me yesterday."

His cock flexed, imagining her sitting in the courtroom, his sperm trickling down the walls of her vagina. "Did you enjoy the sensation?"

"It reminded me of the pleasure we shared."

The simple joy she took in his ejaculate pierced him; James thrust hard, wanting to pierce her with the joy she gave him.

The springs loudly creaked. Frances's eyelids snapped open.

Holding her gaze, he thrust again, daring her to protest.

The black of her pupils swallowed the pale band of her irises. "They'll hear us."

"They'll hear the bed," James countered.

Each hard, deep thrust produced a tell-tale squeak.

Inside her gaze uncertainty warred with burgeoning need.

If it were warmer, he would sit her on his lap and caress her clitoris until the internal contractions of her orgasms brought them both the release they needed. If he were a gentleman, he would place propriety above passion, and he would stop. But James had long known that he was no gentleman.

Her pleasure was too precious a gift to pass over. He needed her, and he no longer had the strength to fight his need.

"Only I will hear you cry out my name when you come, Frances," James murmured, quickening breath gusting silver in the cold air. "Only I will see your eyes grow wide with vulnerability when your body convulses." Frances's eyes widened, realizing that her desire was stronger than her modesty. "Only I will feel your vagina milk me like a fist." The heat and the scent of her body commingled with the heat and the scent of laundered sheets. "Only I, Frances, will know that underneath your bustle and your petticoats and your drawers, you leak my sperm."

Squealing metal filled the frigid room; James could not hear the squalling springs over the pounding of his heart and the slap of their flesh and the deepening soughs of her breath.

The truth urged him on.

"Only I, Frances, will ever know you like this."

Chapter
36

Frances concentrated on the man in the black silk robe and curly gray wig instead of the men and women—not all of them as hygienic as they could be—who surrounded her.

Passionate words, ugly words—*hateful* words—echoed in the gallery.

"... *feloniously* ... *willfully* ... and with malice aforethought ... *killed* and murdered her lawful husband."

Frances inanely wondered if there were different laws for killing and murdering.

James, seemingly impervious to what was happening inside the courtroom, calmly scribbled notes, bronze hair peeping out from underneath a gray wig that very much resembled that worn by the prosecutor.

He had explained in the cab that the Attorney General would first give closing statements, as he was the prosecutor, and then James, the counsel for the defence, would follow.

They had parted inside the courthouse, he going to his private chambers, she taking an end seat in the rapidly filling gallery.

The Attorney Generals's voice rolled over Frances. "Mr. Whitcox has told us that Mary Bartle had no reason to kill Thomas Bartle. Our learned counsel claims that Thomas Bartle was dying, so why would Mrs. Bartle—a woman who swore to God to love, honor and obey her husband—poison a man who is living on borrowed time?

"And then Mr. Whitcox invites our pity because, he claims, Mrs. Bartle is dying of the very disease of which he claims Mr. Bartle was dying."

Frances glanced at the dock.

Mary Bartle sat with her head bowed, eyes downcast, gloved hands serenely clasped.

The pain she must have endured during the trial—the pain she must be enduring *now*, with the prosecutor mocking her mortality—was overwhelming.

A slow trickle of sperm seeped from Frances's vagina.

It was obscene that she enjoyed the afterglow of illicit sex while the woman on the dock was dying because of lawful sex.

She glanced around at the men and women who eagerly leaned forward to more clearly hear the prosecutor's words instead of jumping up and running away, as her body commanded her to do.

A woman's white-faced profile jumped out at her.

Frances's heart skipped a beat, recognizing Jane Fredericks.

"Thomas Bartle, my learned colleague says, had at the most a year to live. But he is not God," chided the prosecutor. "A physician is not God. No man can tell how long another man may live. How long has Mary Bartle to live?"

Jane Fredericks tensely watched the posturing man who stood in front of the jurors' box.

How long would her mother live? Frances wondered. How long would her father live?

How could the young woman sit through this trial that must surely in so many ways represent the trials of her parents?

"I ask you, gentlemen of the jury." The Attorney General's impassioned voice drew Frances's gaze. "If you were Mary Bartle, and you were dying because of the injustice your husband had committed upon your person—a man who vowed to love, honor and cherish you—what would you do?"

The prosecutor looked vaguely familiar, a sensation that had haunted Frances since her foray into the courtroom yesterday afternoon.

"Our learned colleague says that Thomas Bartle was dying; therefore Mary Bartle had no reason to kill him." Red-brown side-whiskers bristled beneath the Attorney General's gray wig. "And then he proceeds to inform us that Mary Bartle is herself dying.

"Who is to say who—if nature had been allowed to take its

course—would have died first? Perhaps Mr. Bartle would have survived Mrs. Bartle. What greater motive to kill her husband, than for Mary Bartle to take Thomas Bartle's life while she still lives? What better reason for Mary Bartle to kill her husband, than to avenge the life that Thomas Bartle stole from her?

"Mr. Whitcox has tried to convince you that a woman—who is herself dying—would not murder the man who is responsible for her death. Gentlemen, please." Warm comradery filled the courtroom, a man talking to men; the prosecutor conspiratorially leaned toward the jurors' box. Flickering shadow from the overhead gaslight minutely changed their expressions from rabid condemnation to impersonal stoicism. "We are not so naive as to believe that women do not possess the base lusts of men. Women engage in adulterous affairs. Women submit to lustful impulses." Frances flinched. "Women—hiding behind the skirts of their femininity—kill.

"Mary Bartle killed her husband. It doesn't matter *why* she killed him. It doesn't matter if she herself is dying." Out of the corner of her eye, Frances saw Jane Fredericks flinch. "Do not be swayed by pity. The fact remains that Mary Bartle did kill her husband. It is your duty to find her guilty, so that justice may be served."

The twelve men in the jurors' box fidgeted uncomfortably; the prosecutor, with a small bow, took his seat at the same table at which James sat.

Frances tensely gazed at James.

He continued scribbling, as if unaware the prosecutor had ended his closing speech.

A sharp cough stabbed through Frances's spine.

Just when Frances thought that she—or someone else in the gallery—would explode from the gathering tension, James lay down his pen.

Slowly he sat forward and steepled his hands.

Starched white cuffs peeped out from beneath voluminous black silk sleeves.

It is my duty to defend my clients, he had told her outside the Achilles Book Shoppe, so many things clear now. *It is the duty of the jury to judge them.*

Frances saw James Whitcox as the men and women inside the courtroom saw him: a middle-aged man, face clean-shaven, eyes impenetrable.

They did not see his passion; all they saw was his reserve.

Only she, Frances realized, would ever know James.

Only she would know the man who charmed with humorous sexual euphemisms. Only she would know the man who reveled in a woman's sexuality.

Only Frances would ever know of the price he had paid to atone for the innocent men and women his father had prosecuted.

"Gentlemen of the jury." James's familiar voice was not raised in passion, as the Attorney General's voice had been, yet it clearly reached every man and woman in the gallery. "Mr. Lodoun has repeatedly claimed that he would reveal to us that Mary Bartle murdered her husband, when all he has in fact revealed to us is one empty bottle of chloroform, a bottle which I have revealed did not belong to Mrs. Bartle. Mr. Lodoun has filled you with suspicion. But you may not make a judgment that is founded upon suspicion. Mr. Lodoun has today conjectured that Mary Bartle killed her husband to avenge her own imminent death. But you may not make a judgment that is founded upon conjecture.

"The facts are, gentlemen, that there are no facts other than those which I have revealed. It is a fact that Thomas Edwards Bartle took no effort to prevent Mary Bartle from contracting the disease that was murdering him. It is a fact that when Mr. Bartle ingested chloroform, he was in daily pain, not only from syphilis, but also from mercury poisoning. It is a fact that Mr. Bartle *was* living on borrowed time. You've seen the autopsy reports: one does not need to be God to realize that Thomas Bartle was dying at an advanced and horribly painful rate.

"My learned colleague claims that Mrs. Bartle poisoned her husband, yet he has failed to prove that she administered the chloroform that killed Mr. Bartle. There is no murder here, there is only the persecution of one woman."

Frances's gaze snapped toward Jane Fredericks. The suffragette watched James with unblinking intensity.

"First Mr. Lodoun reviled Mrs. Bartle because he claimed she acted outside the legal bonds of marriage," James continued in his cold, clear voice, drawing Frances's gaze toward him. "Now Mr. Lodoun claims that killing her husband is what every law-abiding citizen would do, given her circumstances.

"I don't know what I would do if I were in Mary Bartle's circumstances. I don't know what you would do were you in her circumstances. We are not on trial; Mary Bartle is on trial. For seven years, she has been dying from the disease her husband has murdered her with, yet for seven years, she was a helpmate. For seven years she made Thomas Bartle's house a home.

"Mrs. Bartle is dying—yesterday you saw the tumors that are consuming her—simply because she was a good wife. The wrong person is on trial here, gentlemen. I cannot condemn Mary Bartle." James rested his hands palms down on the mahogany table. "Can you?"

"Mrs. Hart."

Frances jumped at the light touch of a hand, heart slamming into her corset. Gasping, she whipped her head around.

A young, handsome, black-haired man leaned over her: Frances estimated his age to be twenty-five.

He held up a finger to his lips before whispering, "I am Avery Tristan, Mr. Whitcox's clerk. The judge will instruct the jurors now. Mr. Whitcox instructed me to take you to his chambers."

James's clerk. The man who had said she made other men and women inside the courtroom seem rather drab in comparison.

Frances stood up with as much grace as she could muster. Curious eyes watched her: they were not all friendly.

She paused outside the door. "Will the others stay inside the gallery?"

But her question was moot. Men and women were already trickling out of the door behind her.

Frances's heart leapt at the sight of Jane Fredericks.

The suffragette was alone.

"One second," Frances said hurriedly. And then, whisking past the clerk, "Miss Fredericks. Miss Fredericks!"

The young woman twisted around as if she could not believe her ears. The look in the murky green eyes was not welcoming.

"Miss Fredericks." Frances had not allowed Ardelle Dennison to intimidate her; she refused to be daunted by one angry young woman who carried around the weight of too much pain. "I was just joining Mr. Whitcox in his chambers. I understand the verdict may take some time. Please join us."

Surprise quickly turned to stony regard. "Thank you, Mrs. Hart, but I can't wait. My mother is expecting me."

A mother who was living on "borrowed time."

Jane Fredericks turned away with a swirl of a black wool cloak.

Frances wanted to ease the young woman's pain; she knew that it was not up to her: Jane Fredericks must ultimately decide to learn from her parents' mistakes rather than to suffer from them. But Frances could offer her support.

"Miss Fredericks." Jane Fredericks paused, back toward Frances. "If you change your mind, we would both welcome you."

Frances did not know James's personal feelings regarding the young woman, but she did know that he was unfailingly courteous.

Jane Fredericks stiffly dismissed Frances's invitation. "Thank you, Mrs. Hart."

The slender figure in black disappeared behind a cluster of men and women.

Frances stared after her for long seconds.

A warm presence stepped up beside her. "Shall we go, Mrs. Hart?"

Frances glanced around at the churning masses of men and women, some of them richly dressed, some of them poorly dressed, all of them animated with the same avid hunger. "Are these trials often so well attended?"

"Murder trials usually are, although this one does seem to be getting more notice than most." Fingers fleetingly touched Frances between the shoulder blades, directing her toward a long corridor. "Is this your first trial?"

Frances skirted around three men who were excitedly gesturing. *Bartle . . . guilty . . . killed* escaped their tight group. "Yes."

"Are you enjoying it?"

"A man is dead, a woman is dying." Frances sharply glanced upward at the attractive, black-haired clerk. "I see little to enjoy, Mr. Tristan."

Eyes so dark they appeared to be black met her gaze. "Many men and women do."

"I am not one of them, sir."

His face, so very young—not much older than her twenty-four-year-old son—softened. "I beg your pardon, ma'am."

Their heels individually echoed, turning down a dim corridor that was less well-traveled.

"It is I who am sorry, Mr. Tristan." This man had complimented her to James and had been nothing but civil. "I'm afraid I'm not used to this sort of thing."

"There's no need to apologize, Mrs. Hart." The clerk gazed down the corridor. "I don't think one ever really gets used to it."

His voice was as neutral as James's.

"Have you worked for Mr. Whitcox long?" she asked curiously.

"Just over two years, ma'am."

"He's a good man," Frances said firmly.

The clerk glanced down at her, dark eyes inscrutable. "Indeed he is."

"He performs a necessary service," she said emphatically.

"I hope, Mrs. Hart"—the clerk paused and unlocked a large mahogany door; he promptly pushed it open—"to someday be as good as he is."

Frances smiled up at him, imagining James at his age. "Are you a barrister, too?"

"Not practicing." There was no answering smile in his eyes; just grave courtesy. "Please forgive me, I must return to the courtroom. Mr. Whitcox will be with you directly."

Frances stepped through the doorway. "Thank you."

But the door was already closing behind her.

Light infiltrated thick glass windows and reflected off the oak floor. The private chamber smelled of beeswax and coffee. A black leather divan hugged the wall beneath the tall windows—the couch James had slept on in the past but had not been able to sleep on the previous night. Glass-fronted bookcases filled the right wall; they were crammed with leather-bound books. A wig stand guarded a huge teak desk and a large black leather chair; two smaller black leather chairs faced the desk. A black marble fireplace monopolized the left wall; red glowed inside its dark recesses. Two brown leather Queen Anne chairs faced the burning coals; a round, teak-inlaid tea table divided them. A small teak desk crouched in front of a crowded bookcase.

The room was uncompromisingly masculine. Unlike her bedroom earlier that morning, it was also pleasantly warm.

She tugged off tan kid gloves and shoved them inside her coat pocket. At a loss as to what she should do, she took off her suede coat. Only to wonder where she should hang it.

Turning around, she espied on her left an arched doorway. On her right stood a brass coat tree.

The sight of James's black wool coat and white silk scarf constricted her chest.

Carefully she hung up her coat beside his.

Warm fluid dribbled down the walls of her vagina.

Sharp memory stabbed up between her legs.

Only I, Frances, will know that underneath your bustle and your petticoats and your drawers, that you leak my sperm.

Without warning, the mahogany door pushed open.

James paused, gray wig clutched in his right hand which gripped a black leather satchel. Sweat curled his hair, turning bronze into brown and gold into bronze.

Impersonal eyes perused her, gaze settling for long seconds on her lower abdomen before returning to her eyes.

"Are you leaking, Frances?" he asked in the same cool voice in which he had addressed the jurors.

Heat flushed her cheeks, remembering the hard deep thrust and the burst of scalding liquid that had only hours earlier filled her. "Yes."

"Are you thinking of us?"

Frances dropped her hands. "Yes."

Mutely he held out his arms.

Frances slid her hands inside the black silk robe and circled his waist. His arms circled her back, his right hand cupping the back of her neck.

"How long will it be?" she whispered.

Hot breath seared her cheek. "Not long, I think."

"I like your robe."

The silk was as soft as her drawers.

"Do you like my chambers?"

"Very nice."

"Would you like a cup of tea?"

"A little later, perhaps."

Warm lips bussed her temple, and then she was free.

James dropped his wig and satchel into the large black leather chair behind the massive teak desk, then carelessly tossed his robe over the top. "Take off your hat and come sit with me."

Frances wondered how many times he had waited in his chambers for a verdict to be reached.

"Where's Mr. Tristan?" she asked, sliding out the deadly hat pin. Fleetingly she wondered if anyone had ever been murdered with one.

"Waiting to hear news." James sat down, with a creak of leather and a tired sigh, in front of the fire. "He'll come get us when it's time."

Frances set her hat—a straw confection with a swirl of soft green feathers—onto his desk.

"Don't sit there." James held out his hand when she would have sat in the chair on the opposite side of the tea table. "Join me."

"I'm a little big to be sitting on your lap," Frances said, awkwardly perching on the arm of his chair.

"Nonsense." James tilted her across his legs; her bustle skidded to her left hip. "Put your head on my shoulder and relax."

"Like a good wife?" Frances asked, throat suddenly aching.

"By all accounts Mary Bartle was a very good wife," James said, voice utterly expressionless.

Frances leaned her head beside his against the leather chair, legs propped on top of the chair arm; his body was too hard and muscled to make a comfortable chaise longue. Her left arm had nowhere to go but around his neck. "I thought the closing speeches would take longer."

He had worked on his until ten of the clock last night, he had said.

"They vary." James reached underneath her skirt with his right hand; with his left hand he anchored her midriff. "Share our pleasure with me."

"Mr. Tristan—"

"Will knock before entering."

Frances could not see the progress of his fingers, she could only feel . . . hard heat sliding down the back of her stockinged thigh . . . worming in between the fold of her drawers . . . grazing the jointure of her thighs and buttocks . . . delicately probing the moist circle of her vagina.

She was unbearably tight with her legs elevated and her thighs closed.

Frances buried her face into his damp hair and inhaled the scent of soap and musk. His gentleness brought tears to her eyes.

"Home, Frances," he murmured with a ragged sigh.

The thickness of three knuckles filled her until the tips of his fingers abutted her cervix.

"Home, James," she said unevenly. And then, "Does Mr. Tristan know about"—she involuntarily nipped his fingers with her internal muscles—"us?"

"Mr. Tristan is a very astute young man." James tilted his head back and kissed the tip of her nose. "He'll be a good defender when he's ready."

Frances spread her fingers across his chest, stuffed with his flesh and his scent, seeking his skin in between gold studs and underneath a wool vest. "He said someday he wanted to be as good as you."

"Really." James seemed mildly surprised; an accompanying throb probed her cervix. "He said that."

"Yes." Frances twined wiry chest hair around her finger; a single silver hair shone in the curl. "He said that."

A coal burst in the silence. Somewhere in the building a door slammed.

Her internal muscles mapped the slow relaxation of his fingers. "I thought the prosecutor was rather convincing."

"Yes." His lips moved side to side against her nose, as if testing it for softness. "He did surprisingly well. Too well."

She jerked her head away from the chair; her vagina tightly

gripped him, accepting flesh suddenly rejecting. "You think they'll convict her?"

"Relax." Warm fingers spread around her neck; gently he pushed her head back against soft leather. "Men don't convict others of what they themselves would do."

Slowly Frances digested the import of his words.

She remembered the prosecutor: *If you were Mary Bartle, and you were dying because of the injustice your husband had committed upon your person—a man who vowed to love, honor and cherish you—what would you do?* She remembered James: *Now Mr. Lodoun claims that killing her husband is what every law-abiding citizen would do, given her circumstances.*

"The speech you gave—"She stared at the single thread of silver in the wiry curl of chest hair. "It wasn't the one you worked on last night, was it?"

Gently his fingers strummed her throat; she felt a matching caress deep inside her vagina, muscles unwittingly relaxing. "Some of it was."

Slowly his lashes fluttered closed; his fingers and his face relaxed.

Tired shadows smudged the hollows underneath his eyes.

The fullness inside her vagina traveled up into her chest.

She had seen that look of utter relaxation on his face after orgasm, but she had not known that he could obtain that degree of relaxation simply by being with her. But she should have known.

He had come to her last night—not for sex—but for sleep.

A sheet of flame danced over the coals, disappeared into white ash.

Frances curled her left arm around his neck and stared at the gold band circling her ring finger. "When I was a girl, James, I thought that a widow who did not bury herself in mourning for the rest of her life was a shameful woman."

She could feel James's gaze, suddenly alert. She could feel his fingers inside her, suddenly stiff. "And now?"

"Now, James, I'm a woman, and I know that there are many types of love."

The love for a parent. The love of a parent.

The respectful love owed to a Sussex farmer. The passionate love earned by a sophisticated Londoner.

What Mary Bartle had endured was a mockery of marriage. James had said yesterday that he had revealed she had not had an affair. Frances hoped he had lied. Frances hoped Mary Bartle had found a moment of love to compensate her for the horror she must daily experience.

Carefully, she twisted off the gold wedding band: it did not come off without a struggle. With each twist, with each tug, the ring of her vagina twisted around his fingers.

"Now I know that gold doesn't bind a man and a woman." Slowly Frances raised her gaze to James. "Love does."

The darkness of his pupils swallowed the hazel of his irises. Inside their depths she could see a question forming.

Suddenly his lashes blocked his eyes. Sighing, James rested his forehead against her lips.

The cold nakedness surrounding her finger slowly dissolved into the warm fullness of his fingers. She closed her lashes and listened to familiar sounds. Popping embers. James's breath. The internal thrum of their heartbeats. . . .

One moment she was drifting; the next moment she was ripped awake. A second knock ricocheted through the unfamiliar chamber.

Frances was abruptly, acutely aware of where she was, and who was in her bed. The ring clutched inside her palm was a solid reminder of the commitment she had made.

James silently stared at her, his eyes dark and assessing.

For one long second his fingertips throbbed against the neck of her cervix; the next second they slowly, irrevocably slid free of her body.

The jurors had reached a verdict. It was time to return to the courtroom.

James said he always won. But no one *always* won. Someday he would lose, Frances thought. When he did, it would destroy him.

Chapter
37

Frances clutched her reticule against her chest and ducked her head to enter the two-wheeled cab.

Apprehension filled her. The jury's verdict had sent the courtroom into an uproar.

"The cab will drive around to the back of the courthouse." Avery Tristan leaned down and spoke over the roar of voices and the rumble of traffic. "Mr. Whitcox will join you there."

Frances swallowed dryly. "Thank you, Mr. Tristan."

The clerk nodded his head in acknowledgment. "It was a pleasure meeting you, Mrs. Hart."

The cab door gently clicked shut.

Frances held still as the carriage tilted from the descending weight of the clerk, then sprang back with the loss of his weight.

A low voice filtered through the varnished wood.

Frances realized Avery Tristan stood beside the driver's box and was giving the cabby instructions.

There had been no time to question him; she had gladly escaped the cheers and the jeers inside the courtroom.

No sooner did the clerk's voice die than the cab lurched forward.

Her heartbeat lurched with the jerk of the carriage and the jangle of harnesses. She felt like a fugitive slipping away in the night. But it wasn't night. Sunlight pierced wispy clouds of dark smoke.

Without warning, the cab jerked to a stop, tilted to the left, righted itself.

Heart crowding her throat, Frances waited to see who would open the door.

"James," she greeted in relief.

His eyes were guarded above the dangling silk scarf. "What would you like for lunch?"

"I—"Frances hadn't had time to think about her next breath, let alone her next meal. The expression in his eyes told her exactly what she would like. "Oysters, please."

Rearing upward, he spoke to the cabby before sitting down beside Frances with a flourish of black wool and cool air. Leaning forward, he snapped closed the cab door.

"That was . . . quite an experience," Frances said uncertainly. "Why the hurry and the—the secrecy?"

"I wanted you to avoid the mob." He eased back in the hard leather seat. "And I wanted to avoid the reporters."

"Oh." Nothing in her life had prepared Frances for the rewards and the downfalls of James Whitcox. "Is there a mob at the courthouse?"

"A small one."

Outbursts had greeted the verdict. James had not been excluded from either the praise or the criticism.

"Are protests usual after a trial of this nature?"

"Yes."

The rub of his hip and shoulder was a familiar friction; a pothole, a staple of London streets, sent her scrabbling for the leather pull.

"You won," she said, finally, wanting to reestablish the closeness they had experienced an hour earlier but uncertain of how to do so.

"Yes," James said neutrally.

There was no satisfaction in his voice.

"I'm glad," Frances said decisively.

James turned his head and caught her gaze. "Why?"

"Because Mrs. Bartle is—"*Innocent* lodged inside her throat; Mary Bartle could very well be guilty. "Because no woman should endure what she is enduring."

The cab slowed and pulled up to a curb.

Frances glanced out of the window. "Where are we?"

James threw open the cab door and ducked beneath the door frame. Stuffing his umbrella under his left arm—satchel swinging—he offered a gloved hand. "You said you wanted oysters."

Hesitantly Frances gripped his fingers. "I thought perhaps we could dine at the restaurant where we dined Sunday evening."

"This will be better."

Digging a coin out of his pocket, James flipped the cabby a florin.

The cabby seemed as uncertain about the neighborhood as Frances; reins snapping, the cab hurtled forward onto the cobbled street.

The wooden storefronts were old, many covered up with advertisements. Frances did not see a single restaurant.

Readjusting the umbrella under his left arm, James held out his right elbow.

A run-down shop with a small square window bore the sign of "Cockles and Mussels." A dim gas globe shone through what looked to be years of grime. Faded red paint obscured what glass was not streaked with dirt.

"Is this . . . ?" Frances asked uncertainly.

"Don't be fooled by the exterior." Under the brim of his top hat, the strain masking James's face eased. "They have the best oysters in town."

"Are we going to eat here?"

How long before James had to return to the courthouse?

"No," he said, elbow hugging her right hand. "Get the door."

Frances tentatively grasped a blackened doorknob. Overhead a large rusty bell rang out.

Glass tanks filled with water lined shadowy wooden shelves.

Frances's eyes widened, espying large, clawed creatures with bulging eyes and curling, fan-like tails: they were fighting one another.

It was a futile battle: their wicked-looking claws were tied shut.

James stepped in the direction of a water-filled tank that was occupied with murky gray shells.

Frances joined him. "Oysters?"

Hazel eyes glinted down at her. "'Alive, alive, oh.'"

The oysters inside the restaurant had been served shucked. The oysters inside this shop, she realized, would not come shucked.

"Ye be wantin' somethin'?" a quavery voice demanded.

"Indeed," James said, holding Frances's gaze. "We'll take two dozen oysters, packed on ice. Do you have fresh lemons?"

"Aye."

Frances inspected the various tanks while the incurious shop-keeper packaged the oysters. "What are those?"

"Lobsters."

"They look like they'd bite back."

Frances didn't need to see his eyes to know they filled with laughter. "Not after they're boiled."

She inspected the lobsters more closely. "Do they taste good?"

"Quite."

She indicated a tank full of broad, flat creatures that wielded a single claw instead of two; they looked as ferocious as the lobsters. "What are those?"

"Crabs."

There were so many things she had yet to try.

"'Ere ye be."

Quickly Frances turned toward the rheumy-eyed proprietor and reached into her reticule. James had treated her to oysters; she wanted to treat him. "How much?"

The old man didn't mind taking money from a woman.

Stuffing two generous lemons inside her reticule, Frances visu-ally weighed the small, ice-packed barrel before hefting it up to her chest. "Shall we go?"

James opened his mouth as if to say something, immediately closed it and opened the door, rusty bell clanging. "After you."

The street was empty. Invisible eyes followed their progress, bor-ing a hole between her shoulder blades.

Either she had grown lazy from her vacation in London, Frances thought after turning the corner at the end of the block, or the oys-ters were breeding.

"Why did you send the cab away?" she asked, clutching the bar-rel more tightly to alleviate the strain of burning muscles.

"Anonymity. Ah." A tired-tooking hack—four-wheeled instead of two—rounded the corner. "Your chariot, madam."

Frances gratefully collapsed onto a worn leather seat. She recog-nized the address that James gave the driver.

James settled beside her and closed the cab door. "How far would you have carried that?"

She was a hearty country woman, not a London society lady. "As far as need be."

"I would have carried it, Frances."

"You have your satchel," Frances returned reasonably. "And why should you carry it? It was I who wanted oysters."

The left wheel dropped into a hole.

A solid arm anchored her shoulders; hot breath feathered her temple. "How would you like to make a houseful of servants very happy?"

An oddly boyish zest filled James's voice.

Frances tilted her head up to his; his lips—bottom lip full and enticing—were only inches away from her own. "How?"

"By giving them the day off with pay."

She searched his eyes, hazel irises brown in the gloom of the cab. "We have the day?"

"And the night." James readjusted his satchel and umbrella; the heavy weight anchoring her shoulders shifted. "And the morrow. If you want me."

Frances had never wanted anyone as badly as she wanted James Whitcox.

Tears tightened her throat at his unexpected gift. "I need to let my servants know where I'll be."

"I'll send a footman."

"I need fresh clothing."

"Write out a list and the footman can collect what you need."

The advantages of wealth.

"Why did you say you dismissed the cab for reasons of anonymity?"

"Someone at the courthouse could have seen me enter the cab." The light drained from his eyes. "If so, they could take down the number and trace the cabby. I don't want anyone knowing the address to our home."

The mansions in Queen's Gate had been protected by wrought iron gates and tall brick fences; the townhouse had neither a gate nor a fence.

The quickening of desire transformed into a pulse of fear. "Would it be dangerous if someone knew about the townhouse?"

"Dangerous, no." His voice was calm; his face closed. "Annoying, yes. Reporters can be pesky creatures."

Frances deliberately blocked out the angry voices she had heard inside the courtroom. "You must be quite hungry."

His eyes under the brim of the black hat were guarded. "Why?"

"You ordered two dozen oysters."

Light illuminated his face. "Aphrodisiacs, Frances."

Chapter
38

"The shells are clean," Frances said, biting her lip as she carefully scrubbed off a hitherto unseen spot of mud. "Have you finished with the lemons?"

The sharp slice of a blade sank into wood. "I have now."

Erotic anticipation laced the companionable domesticity.

Standing over the kitchen sink, Frances wrapped her left hand in a towel and firmly grasped the bottom of a gray shell inside her right hand.

"Careful." Tantalizing warmth leaned into Frances; the tart scent of lemon enveloped her. "Don't tip the shell."

"I know," Frances said. She quoted: " 'Or the oyster's liquor will run off.' "

James passed her a wooden-handled knife.

Carefully Frances inserted the tip of the thin blade into the hinged edge of the shell.

"Push it in," James murmured, voice low, breath hot. He cupped his hand underneath her right hand. "There. Gently twist now until you feel the shell yield."

The shell fell open.

Frances studied the pale, tongue-shaped flesh. "It's not really alive, is it?"

"Very much so."

"But surely the ice—"

"Kept it alive," James said. "Cut through the umbilical cord."

"Where is it?"

A long, lemon-stained finger pointed.

Frances severed the fragile cord.

"Quickly." His fingers—hot, like his breath—elevated her fingers. "Swallow."

At the restaurant the waiter had cut through the umbilical cords. Ice or no ice, the oysters had been dead when served.

She could suddenly feel the life of this oyster pulsing around her fingers.

Sharp shell bit into her lips; at the same time sweet liquor filled her mouth. Closing her eyes, Frances swallowed; the oyster slid down her throat.

Without warning, hot lips replaced the shell, and an even hotter tongue slid into her mouth. The oyster lodged inside her stomach, pulsing with an imaginary heartbeat. James's tongue lodged against the roof of her mouth, pulsing with a very real heartbeat.

Both heartbeats bolted straight down into her vagina.

Gasping, she turned her head away from the lightning sensation of his kiss to suck in oxygen.

James tilted her head up to his and gauged the raw desire in her eyes. "I wanted to do that Sunday night."

Frances swallowed; his saltiness mingled with the sweetness of the oyster. "I'm not certain I would have appreciated it as much then as I do now."

Warm fingers gently massaged her throat. "Why?"

Turning, Frances set aside the empty shells and grabbed up a fresh oyster from the metal sink.

Fingers sliding away from her neck, James handed her the knife. His fingers—unlike hers—were steady. "Push it in."

Frances pushed in the thin metal blade. And remembered how slowly he had pushed his fingers into her vagina inside his private chambers. Miraculously the two shells parted and the liquor was undisturbed. Carefully she cut through the umbilical cord.

"Bend down," she said shakily. He bent his knees so that his head was on the same level as hers. "Close your eyes."

Dark lashes fanned shadowed cheeks; the rest inside his chambers had not erased the tired smudges beneath his eyes.

Frances held the shell to his lips and tilted the live oyster into his mouth.

Quickly setting aside the shell, she gently grasped the front of his neck, thicker than her own, there a stubble of hair. "Swallow."

She felt the muscles inside his throat expand. At the same time she filled his mouth with her tongue.

The liquor was sweet. His mouth was salty hot.

The oyster slid past her fingers. Frances pushed the tip of her tongue up high against the ridged roof of his mouth.

A harsh sound of desire escaped his throat. Her breasts swelled, responding to his hunger.

Slowly she released his mouth and his throat.

His lips were shiny wet. From her.

Seeing the effects of her kiss tightened something inside her that was deeper than her womb, more erotic than a touch. Frances realized that *this* was what James felt when he saw the desire he created inside her.

Straightening, James glanced down at her with dark, inscrutable eyes. "I don't think either of us were ready for that Sunday night."

He had had to prepare for Mary Bartle on Sunday night. But Mary Bartle was free tonight.

Silently she shucked another oyster.

"Close your eyes and take it into your mouth," James said, voice strained. "Don't swallow until I tell you."

Eyes closed, Frances held the sweet oyster inside her mouth. Preparing for his kiss. Only to discover she was not prepared at all.

Warm pressure fanned the front of her neck. "Swallow."

The muscles inside her throat swelled against the barrier of his hand and the oyster—like a tongue—slid past her tongue. At the same time his tongue penetrated her mouth and the oyster slid down her throat through the ring of his fingers and lodged deep in her stomach while his tongue licked the roof of her womb and she couldn't *breathe* for the two tongues that filled her.

"Open your eyes, Frances."

Opening her eyes, Frances grasped his fingers that seemed to be massaging her every sexual organ: womb, vagina, clitoris, breasts.

The darkness in his gaze twisted her heart.

"You are so beautiful," he murmured, as if it pained him to look at her.

"I feel beautiful when I'm with you," she whispered.

Passionate. Vibrant.

All the things she had never thought to be.

Leaning down, eyes open, watching her watch him, he kissed her.

James did not hide from her; Frances did not hide from him. She showed him the tenderness he evoked. He showed her the need she elicited.

Slowly his eyelashes fluttered shut and he delicately licked the inside of her mouth until she wrapped her arms around his neck and tasted him back. Gratitude for the pleasure he so unselfishly gave washed over her.

"I wanted to do something last Sunday, too," she whispered into his mouth.

The tip of his tongue flicked the tip of her tongue, as if tasting her words. "What?"

The question vibrated deep inside her lower abdomen.

"Sit down."

James had a lively sense of curiosity: he unhesitatingly sat down at the kitchen table.

Frances wondered who had ever taken the time to tempt and tease him. And knew that no one had ever taken the time to do the simple things with him that they had done together this day: warm each other, hold each other, feed each other.

"Scoot your chair out so that you face away from the table," she instructed him huskily.

James scooted his chair out.

"Spread your legs."

James spread his thighs, face endearingly innocent.

Scooping the saucer of lemon wedges off the kitchen counter, Frances knelt between his splayed feet, bones cracking—quickly she glanced up at his face; either he did not hear the tell-tale sound of aging or it didn't disturb him—petticoats and skirt mercifully cushioning her knees against the hardness of the wooden floor.

Catching his gaze, she purposefully said, "Hand me the Worcester-shire sauce, please."

The flare of heat in his eyes took her breath away.

Hands shaking, he cupped her face. "I'm not an oyster, Frances."

Frances reached for the front of his trousers. "I know what you are, James."

Gently he worried the corners of her lips with his thumbs. "If you do this, I'll ejaculate inside your mouth."

An ivory button slid through a too-tight buttonhole.

"I want you to take pleasure in my mouth," Frances said.

Another orifice, rings more binding than gold.

He helped her with his buttons. He released himself from his small clothes. He handed her the Worcestershire sauce.

Frances set the bowl on the floor and sat back so that her heels pressed into her bustle. Gently she cupped his penis inside her hands. It bore a cleft, like a plum. It was purple, like a plum. It glistened with dew, like a fresh, ripe plum. "I never thought your sex was ugly."

A crystal tear welled up inside the tiny eye.

James pressed his hands down flat on top of his thighs. "But you thought yours was."

Frances ducked down and tasted the desire she created.

"I never saw my sex until Monday night," she said truthfully, purposefully bathing his swollen flesh with her breath.

The plum-shaped head was as sensitive as the head of her clitoris. *Glans*, he called them.

"And now that you have?"

She reached down and lifted up a silver spoon. Slowly she dribbled Worcestershire sauce onto the plum-like head that had lodged so deeply inside her that she would always bear the impression of James. "I think our sex is beautiful."

Dark red covered the darkening purple. Frances squeezed a lemon wedge until pale juice glistened like teardrops in the dark Worcestershire sauce.

James sharply inhaled, from more than pleasure.

Quickly Frances glanced up. "Does it burn?"

"Yes," he said, face tense.

"Shall I stop?"

The darkness of desire filled his eyes. Long, elegant fingers trembling, he cupped the back of her head and drew her forward.

Chapter 39

"No."

James's voice lacked conviction.

"Yes."

Frances's voice was decisive.

"Frances." James stared down at Frances, and had the curious sensation of melting. "Where do you get all this energy?"

He had seen more of London in one day than he had as a boy seen in an entire season: the Tower of London, Madame Tussaud's, the National Gallery, and back again to the Crystal Palace.

Solemnly Frances returned his gaze. "It must be the oysters."

James threw back his head, laughter ringing out over the shrill shrieks of tagging children and the admonishing cries of mothers and nannies.

"I like hearing you laugh," Frances said, shoulder a familiar friction, fingers trusting inside the crook of his arm.

The sudden tightness in his chest squeezed his testicles. "I like hearing you cry out my name."

"That is most definitely caused by an oyster."

"I surrender." James's eyes crinkled appreciatively. "Balloon ascension it is."

The weightless elevation clenched his stomach. James gripped Frances's waist and watched people shrink to the size of insects.

"Look, James!" Frances leaned over the carriage and pointed to the swamp; the dinosaurs viewed from above looked more than ever like they were built from a child's blueprint.

He concentrated on Frances instead of the wind that jostled the carriage and the fire that fueled the balloon.

Her cheeks were red; her voice was excited. The enjoyment she took in the ascension was as uninhibited as the enjoyment she took with him.

He had not known that pleasure could be painful or that pain could be pleasurable. Every moment he spent with Frances added to a growing catalogue of sensations.

"Look, Frances." He pulled her up and away from the dangerous rim of the carriage until her bustle flattened against his groin and the feathers in her hat tickled his cheek. "Look at the fountain."

Wind whipped the two-hundred-and-fifty-foot jet of water into a frothing plume.

A sense of peace pervaded him, drifting high up in the sky. There were no judges to placate. No jurors to impress. There was just the heat of Frances's body and the bonelessness of contentment.

The descent of the balloon swelled his heart and ripped away the years. "What next, *madame?*"

Frances tilted her face up to his; pleasure sparkled in her eyes. "You liked it."

"You're with me." He raised a finger and tested the temperature of her cheek. Her skin burned when she was sexually excited. "That's all I need."

"This is ridiculous," Frances suddenly said, voice uneven, she as vulnerable to his touch as he was to hers.

James's senses quickened. "What is?"

"I can't move, or look at you, or touch you without remembering."

"Remembering what?"

"How prickly the hair on your chest is." James felt the stab of her nipples. "How hot your tongue is." James tasted the wet heat of her mouth. "How deeply you penetrate me."

James envisioned the tight ring of her vagina.

A boy whipping a hoop raced past them.

"Good." The heat of her cheek burned his fingers. "I want you to remember." He tucked her gloved hand into the crook of his arm. "Shall we tour the Palace?"

The light glinting off the glass was blinding. The fountains churning the air was deafening. The moisture riding the wind was stinging.

Frances drank in the garden; James drank in Frances.

A heavy glass door eased shut behind them. Immediately the roar of jetted water faded into musical splatters. Overhead the vaulted glass was interspersed by arced iron frames.

"It smells so wonderful," she said in a hushed voice, inspecting a stone fountain fed by lions.

"They perfume the waters," he said, voice a hollow vibration.

"Is the scent for sale?"

Everything was for sale, provided one was willing to pay the price.

"I would imagine so."

The Palace was not as crowded on Thursday as it had been on Sunday. Their footsteps echoed on the wooden floor, bodies moving in harmony.

"James." Inside the Roman court, Frances tugged him toward a larger-than-life-sized statue. "He's not wearing a leaf."

The corners of James's lips hitched upward in a smile, remembering the initial public furor caused by the foliage-free statuary. Most had been appended, but a few had escaped alteration. "*Punch* published a letter suggesting secondhand underwear be sent to the Palace."

Frances's laughter rang through the wooden court.

James lightly swept the length of her back before settling his fingers into the notch between her bustle and her lower spine. Frances melted into his touch, laughter subsiding.

Her uninhibited sensuality squeezed his chest. "I like the sound of your laughter, too, Frances."

It touched him almost as deeply as the little sounds she made before she came.

James wanted furnishings that would stamp their home with Frances: he guided her to the giant showrooms of household goods in the east wing.

"Do you see anything you like?" he asked nonchalantly, walking with her past rows of divans and chairs and lamps.

Frances was not fooled by his machinations. "I like you—*our* home as it is, James."

But she did not yet consider it her home.

Spraying water caught his attention. Curiously he approached the glass-encased apparatus.

"Sir." A shiny-faced young salesman with lank brown hair and anxious brown eyes bore down on James. "This is our most complete combination bath. It is both simple and efficient to use. It's perfectly safe: the hot and cold water supplies are so graduated as to be impossible for the bather to be scalded. The four vertical columns which give the main, or what we call the Needle Spray"— a bony finger pointed to the four pipes in each corner of the glass-plated shower—"are perforated at an angle which throws the spray of water so that it will entirely cover the body of the bather. The two Liver Sprays are fully adjustable, and may be tilted to suit the varying heights of the different parties using the bath." Soft pressure brushed against James's side; absentmindedly, he reached up and found the haven of Frances's spine. "The shower cap is generous, as you can see. And of course, the four distinct sprays may be used either separately or in any combination."

James studied the combination bath for long seconds. The Needle Spray pipes extended from floor to ceiling.

He had never seen anything like it.

"You said there were four distinct sprays, sir," Frances said over the monotonous fall of water. "I count only three."

The young man's pale, shiny face turned red. "There is . . . ah . . . a Rose Jet, ma'am."

"Where?" James asked.

The young man pointed to the metal drain in the floor of the shower.

"The drain is a spray?" Frances asked, puzzled.

"No, ma'am." The young man's gaze avoided both Frances and James. "The Rose Jet must be unscrewed."

"Unscrew it," James instructed, intrigued.

"I—I'd need to turn off the water, sir."

"Then do so."

Hands fumbling, the salesman turned off the water supply cock. Squatting down, he blocked the view of the shower floor for long seconds before awkwardly standing.

James stared intently. "Demonstrate."

Water jetted out of all four sprays.

"We'll take it," he said flatly, suddenly painfully erect.

"Oh, I say, sir." Embarrassment forgotten, the salesman beamed into James's eyes. "What an excellent choice. I'm sure you and your missus will be well-satisfied. It comes with your choice of a marble or slate stall. Which would you like?"

James was quite certain they would be well-satisfied.

Deliberately he asked: "Which would you like, Frances?"

In her eyes he witnessed a silent battle: desire warred with independence; excitement warred with frugality.

Frances took a deep breath, full breasts rising, falling. "May I see samples of the marble, please?"

Satisfaction coiled inside his chest: she had taken the first step in making the townhouse her home.

Frances chose gold veined marble to match the floor in the master bath while he paid for the purchase. Installation was set for the following week.

The warmth of her spine welcomed his fingers. "Shall we go home?"

Frances remained silent until they settled on the train, first class instead of third class. "The salesman thought I was your wife."

In all but name she was.

"Yes."

"I don't think those Liver Sprays are for the liver, James."

"I don't think the Rose Jet, Frances," James returned mock-solemnly, "is for a woman's douche."

Although it certainly could be used as one.

"It's shaped like a penis," Frances whispered, rocking with the train.

"I know," he whispered back, rocking against her.

"I'll pay half, of course."

James swallowed his pride. "Of course."

Excitement filled her eyes. "I'll supervise the installation."

She did not want his money; he did not want her servitude.

"That is why I hire a butler, Frances."

"Will a butler test the Rose Jet, James?"

The thought of Frances sitting on the Rose Jet with water over-flowing her vagina constricted his lungs. "Will you?"

"I'm not certain I'll enjoy a douche."

"Why not?"

"It will wash you out of me."

James could not stop himself; he pulled Frances against him and inhaled her scent, there vanilla, there the faint musk of their satis-faction. "Then I'll just have to fill you up again."

Sexual awareness shimmered in her eyes. "Last night . . ."

James remembered the sharp burn of lemon followed by the wet burn of her mouth. "What?"

"You taste better than an oyster."

She had swallowed his sperm, and looked as if she had swallowed something delicious.

"What did my ejaculate feel like when you swallowed?" he asked in a low voice.

"'Alive, alive, oh,'" she quoted.

The train halted, brakes squealing. Boiling steam blocked the light.

Reluctantly James released Frances, and straightened her hat. Solemnly she reached up and adjusted his top hat.

The din of the rail station was deafening.

"James."

He leaned his head down to Frances. "What?"

"You're much larger than the Romans were."

James laughed. The tension knotting his groin eased. Grasping her hand more tightly inside the crook of his arm, he skirted past a group of work-weary laborers, and exited the side door. "Would you like an ice before we go home?"

Her eyes sparkled with pleasure. "Please."

The streets were alive with people hurrying home for their din-ner. Vendors rushed to intercede, offering pies and muffins.

Arm protectively encircling Frances's waist, James pulled her into a crowded pastry shop. A white enameled table was unoccupied in the back. He seated Frances, and then himself. Impatiently he pushed aside a newspaper, motion stayed by the sudden pallor of her skin. "What is it?"

Her gaze was fixed on the newspaper.

Sudden dread pouring over him, he glanced down.

The headline jumped out at him: "Justice Served: Mary Bartle Dead."

Chapter
40

James's fingers—the same fingers that had only hours earlier stretched her in preparation for the deeper penetration of his sex—in slow motion turned the black and white newspaper.

The woman who had sat in the dock Wednesday morning, hands sedately clasped, stared upside down at Frances. James's bewigged face, every feature indelibly imprinted in her memory, adjoined the photograph of Mary Bartle.

James leaned over the paper, face expressionless.

"Good afternoon, madam, sir. Today's speciality—sir!" A young, effeminate voice—dimly Frances registered through the fog that had filled her brain that it was a waiter—crashed over the deafening drone of surrounding conversation. "You're the one what got that murderess off!"

The young man's voice carried like the ring of a bell.

Heads snapped in their direction. Out of the corner of her eye, she saw a man—dark hair slick with macassar oil—pull out a pencil and a pad of paper from a plaid wool jacket; simultaneously, he pushed up from a white-enameled table.

Suddenly stark hazel eyes pinned Frances. "Don't say anything, just keep walking."

Involuntary words rose to her throat: she was seated, how could she "just keep walking"—

But then she wasn't seated. James's fingers clamped her arm in a vise-like grip and they were walking toward the front of the shop even as the man with the pad of paper pushed between crowded tables to intercept them. "What were you doing Wednesday evening, Mr. Whitcox? Did you know Mary Bartle entertained thoughts of suicide?"

Fingers relentless, James directed Frances around an occupied table; feminine bonnets topped with waving feathers turned.

Embarrassment crashed over Frances at the spectacle the reporter was making of them.

"How does it feel to have a client hang herself on the very day she is acquitted?" the reporter doggedly cried out.

The door loomed only feet away.

"Do you think justice prevailed?" The reporter followed on their heels. "Who were you with when she was putting a rope around her neck?"

Cold air slapped Frances in the face.

"Do you feel responsible for her death?"

James raised his umbrella to stop a passing cab. He did not wait for it to pull over to the curb; instead he urged Frances into the street and lifted up on her arm until she found the single stair eighteen inches up in the air. Her foot slipped; hard fingers steadied her.

"Did she leave a note confessing her guilt?" The reporter followed them into the street. "What did she say—"

"Drive until I tell you to stop," James instructed the cabby.

"—when she was acquitted?"

Legs shaking, Frances collapsed onto a cracked leather seat. "What did—"

The cab door slammed shut, muffling the reporter's voice. Instantly the cab lurched forward.

Frances clutched her chest; her heart pounded through the padding of her suede coat. James sat stiffly beside her, umbrella raised as if he were about to open it.

The cab turned a corner, left wheel tilting. Frances grabbed a leather pull.

"Pull over," James said through the trapdoor in the roof of the cab.

Anonymity.

The cab swerved, jerked to a stop. Without comment James opened the door and stepped out of the carriage. A moment passed before a black gloved hand reached for her. Frances grasped it, needing the strength of his fingers: her legs still shook.

The street was eerily empty, as if in mourning. Their footsteps were muffled in the gathering gloom.

James abruptly halted.

Dazed, Frances glanced down at a boy perched on a doorstep, gulping down a sandwich. A billboard advertising *The Pall Mall Gazette* rested against the brick wall beside him.

Still without speaking, James tossed a copper penny into the boy's lap. Swooping down, he grasped a paper up from the small stack that lay at the boy's feet. Paper tucked under his arm, he waved down a cab.

"You've been through this before," Frances said, joining him at the curb.

Briefly he glanced down at her—"Yes"—before stepping aside for her to climb onto the iron stair.

Frances had felt more anchored in the ascending balloon than she felt inside this cab. She didn't understand the law, but she understood the callous intrusion of the reporter even less. For one heart-stopping moment, she had thought he would jump into the cab with them.

James lit the small lamp in the corner and read the paper, his expression inscrutable.

The grinding wheels of the carriage filled the cab. Frances incongruously wondered how many rotations a wheel made in one second, two seconds, three seconds . . .

Who were you with when she was putting a rope about her neck?

The door to the townhouse opened just as James reached for it, as if the butler inside had been waiting for them to arrive.

Frances reluctantly gave up her coat, reticule and hat: she was so cold. "Thank you."

"It is my pleasure, madam," the butler said in the same voice that Mr. Denton used: urbane and unshakable.

She fleetingly wondered if there was a school where butlers were trained.

The voices of both James and Avery Tristan were bereft of emotion. Had they learned their stoicism while reading law, or had they read law because of their stoicism?

"Peasebody." James offered the butler his umbrella.

"Yes, sir?"

"I need not tell you that any servant here who mentions my name in connection with this address will be immediately discharged."

The butler's face remained courteous. "No, sir."

It occurred to Frances that James had left the newspaper inside the cab. Would the person who next read it think "justice" had prevailed?

"Furthermore, should this occur," James relinquished his coat, face expressionless, "such a person would never find future employment."

The butler draped the black wool coat over his arm. "I understand, sir."

James held out his top hat, crown upturned, stuffed with his gloves. "You and the other servants may have the rest of the day off."

"Thank you, sir."

Familiar pressure nudged Frances's spine: she turned with James.

"Sir."

James paused; Frances paused, needing more than the heat of his hand to ward off the chill of death. "Yes?"

"What shall Cook do with the lobsters?"

Pleasure-pain welled up in Frances, realizing that James had ordered lobsters for dinner as a surprise treat.

"Tell her to write down instructions on how to prepare them," James said.

Frances grasped the bannister and took the first step up the marble stairs. "Are they alive?"

James took the second step. "Not after we boil them."

There was no blaze in the marble fireplace to take away her chill. Closing the bedroom door, James kicked off his shoes and dropped back onto the blue velvet chaise longue.

Dark eyes mutely stared up at her.

Wriggling out of her bustle, Frances perched on the edge of the chaise beside him. James promptly lifted her over his thigh so that she sat between his legs, her ankles between his ankles, her shoes anchored between black silk socks.

Heat cocooned Frances: his thighs; his arms; his breath.

"I'm sorry," he whispered against the top of her head.

Frances warmed the backs of his hands with her palms and rested her head against his shoulder. "For what?"

"I never wanted you to go through this."

Yet he had gone through "this" more than once.

"Pesky reporters, James," she said over the lump in her throat.

"A servant found her Wednesday night, lying in her husband's bed." The fingers beneath hers moved; James unfastened the top button of her bodice. "She hanged herself from the headboard."

Frances turned onto her side and wrapped her arm around his ribs, burying against his chest the image his words created. His sex was firm against her hip. His heart thudded against her cheek. "I'm sorry."

Only she would ever know how strongly Mary Bartle's circumstances affected him.

A second button came open, a small release of silk.

"A very wise woman once told me something," James murmured, lips riffling her hair, fingers diverging.

"What?" Frances whispered.

A *snap* momentarily drowned out his heartbeat. Cool air goosepimpled her chest.

"She said"—a second *snap* accompanied the gust of his breath— "that it's better to suffer the consequences of one's own actions than it is to suffer from the actions of another."

Better to hang at one's own hand than be hanged by the Crown? Frances wanted to ask. Or better to die by one's own hand than die the slow death of syphilis?

But those were questions she could never ask.

Long, sensitive fingers cupped her breast. "I need to be inside you, Frances."

Quite possibly he had been inside her when Mary Bartle took her life.

Stirring—pushing away the guilt that the reporter had planted— Frances sat up. The distance forced his hand out of her corset.

She unbuttoned the rest of her bodice and dropped it over the chaise longue.

James needed her, but Frances needed him, too. She needed him to give purpose to the pain that people perpetrated upon one another.

Husbands. Wives.

Mothers.

Without warning, long, masculine fingers reached around her and freed the third latch of her corset. Seizing the yawning flaps, James yanked hard. Frances sucked in air; at the same time the corset popped free of her waistband. Before she could catch her breath, the fourth latch snapped open and cold air cupped her breasts.

Her satin corset joined her silk bodice.

Caught up in the urgency of his need, Frances shakily stood up to take off the rest of her clothing. Only to have warm hands snake up under her skirt and petticoats.

Grasping her hips, James pulled her down and forward so that she straddled his hips, facing him.

One second she saw the head of his penis rearing up, hard and blunt, a ripe plum pushing up through mourning black wool. The next second her skirt and petticoats spilled over his trousers and waistcoat in a froth of green and white silk and hard heat pierced the open vent of her drawers.

"The lubrication—"

"I'm slippery," he murmured. "Enough for this."

Left hand pressing down on her buttocks, he worked the head of his penis against the portal of her vagina until her flesh opened for him and he was a part of her, and she didn't know how she could leave him when her holiday ended.

Who would comfort him in the future?

"It's always a shock when you enter me," she said unevenly, flesh stretching to hold him, a small pinch without the artificial lubrication.

Quickly he glanced up. "Am I hurting you?"

"No." The walls of her vagina independently nipped at him, claiming differently. "It's just that the head of you is so much larger than the rest of you."

"This is all I need," he said, holding still inside her, only the plum-shaped head of him penetrating her. "Just the ring of you."

The wool of his pants scoured the inside of her thighs.

Frances ran her fingers through his hair; it clung to her fingertips, bronze, gold, fleeting strands of silver.

"And your tenderness."

Frances glanced down into his upturned face in sudden comprehension.

Dark lashes framed dark eyes. "I need your tenderness, Frances."

Lifting her left breast, she held it up for him. Fingers digging into her buttocks—the bridge of his fist butting the lips of her sex so that he wouldn't penetrate her further than the pulsing head that gorged her—he rubbed his lips back and forth against the dark brown nub of her nipple. Electricity jolted from the tip of her breast straight through to the opening of her vagina.

"I need to taste your heartbeat," James murmured against her suddenly painful hard flesh.

She watched his mouth open; simultaneously a sharp shock stabbed through her breast, the incisive graze of his teeth.

Her nipple elongated.

Hot breath batted her swelling flesh. "I need to hear your breath quicken."

The tip of his tongue prodded the tip of her nipple.

Her breath caught inside her chest.

"I need you to feel like you'll die for me."

Frances felt like she'd die for him now.

Scalding heat surrounded her nipple, the curl of his tongue. His breath was hot and moist. "And then I need you to feel like you'll die without me."

Chapter
41

"When did you learn about Mrs. Bartle's suicide, Mr. Tristan?"

The clerk's voice drifted through the arch; it was accompanied by the rich odor of freshly brewed coffee. "Yesterday morning when I read the newspaper."

James had been buried inside Frances. Possibly when Mary Bartle hanged herself. Definitely when Avery Tristan read about it.

He hooked his hat beside his coat onto the coat tree. "Did you try to contact me?"

James had both a telegraph and a telephone in the townhouse as well as in his office. He would not have responded, but the butler was instructed to do so.

"No, sir." There was no apology in the clerk's voice. "I did not."

James turned away from the coat tree. "Why not?"

He would not have left the townhouse with Frances even if he had known.

"You were on holiday, sir." The clerk stepped through the arch; he held two steaming mugs. "You've not had one since I've been with you."

Frances had said that Avery Tristan wanted to be as "good" as James someday.

"And you think I needed a holiday?"

"Yes, sir." The same implacable resolve that fired James filled the clerk's brown eyes. "I do."

James had never slept as soundly as he slept with Frances.

He had not needed a holiday; he just needed a widow from Kerring, Sussex.

"Did Mrs. Bartle have any communication with this office?"

"No, sir."

"Did you contact Mrs. Bartle's solicitor?"

"Yes, sir."

"He accompanied her home." James had very little contact with his clients outside the courtroom; a solicitor initially dealt with the police and wrote up the preliminary reports. "Did she give any indication of what she planned?"

"He said not, sir."

Mary Bartle's father had abandoned her; she had no other relatives. Character references had come from her husband's friends; she had no friends of her own.

"See what arrangements are being made for her burial."

There was nothing else he could do for her. She had lived a private life; he would not further invade her privacy.

James sank down into soft leather.

Frances had held him, and then she had come for him. Tonight he would dine at her townhouse.

A mug of coffee appeared on his desk; gray mist lazily spiraled upward. "You received a letter from the Attorney General yesterday."

"What does Lodoun want?"

"Mr. Lodoun is no longer the Attorney General, sir."

James's head jerked back. "Why not?"

Hot steam blurred Avery Tristan's expression. "He stepped down."

The price of losing.

Leaning over, the clerk tapped the folded newspaper that topped James's mail. "I think you might want to start the day with this, sir."

The aging townhouse smelled of lemon and butter.

James handed his umbrella, satchel, coat, and hat to the butler. "How is Mrs. Hart, Denton?"

"Very well, sir."

"I wouldn't want anyone to upset her."

"Nor would I, sir."

"Reporters sometimes invite themselves into one's home."

"I assure you, sir," Denton's lined face remained impassive, "I am well able to protect this house."

James half-smiled; there was a toughness in good butlers: Denton was a good butler. "In the event something should happen, I would expect to be contacted."

The butler deftly pocketed James's card. "Very good, sir."

A creak on the stairs snagged James's attention.

Frances wore forest green velvet; it darkened her eyes and turned her clear skin into cream. Extraordinary skin. His fingers burned, remembering her soft heat.

"Is dinner ready, Mr. Denton?" Frances asked, face flushing beneath James's regard.

"You have time for an aperitif, madam."

"Thank you."

James used *please* and *thank you* because it got him what he wanted—cooperation—not because he felt respect. Frances's courtesy, he realized, was as sincere as her honesty. He followed her down the hall.

The patterned wallpaper was faded but clean. The oak floor was scarred but polished. Coals glowed in a black iron fireplace. Bronze fire irons gleamed on dark slate.

Frances stood in front of an old-fashioned side table.

"How many servants do you have?" he asked abruptly.

She turned, holding two snifters of brandy. "Mr. Denton, the butler; Mrs. Jenkins, the housekeeper; and Mrs. Ellis, the cook."

James relieved her of a snifter. "The house is immaculate."

"Thank you." Her face softened. "I'll tell them you said so."

A twist of pleasure-pain tightened his skin. James had met very few good people; Frances was one of them.

"I remembered you drank brandy at the restaurant," she said in a sudden rush as he lifted up his glass. "I hope you like it; the shopkeeper said this was a respectable brand."

The brandy was mediocre at best.

Frances cautiously took a sip. Her nose wrinkled at the bite of alcohol.

Amusement shot through James's reserve. "Perhaps *madame* will like it better this way."

Holding brandy inside his mouth, he turned her face up to his.

She opened for him. She drank from him.

"Hold it in your mouth until it's warm and the alcohol diffuses on your tongue," James whispered against her lips, amusement fading into the need she always evoked. "Now . . . swallow."

He chased the brandy with his tongue. Over the burn of alcohol he could taste Frances, vanilla sweet.

For one blinding moment, he wanted to keep the truth from her.

James pulled back from temptation. "It's a very good brandy, Frances."

She glowed, both from his compliment and from his kiss.

Frances was as private as had been Mary Bartle. He didn't know how to gently tell her that her privacy had been invaded, so he told her bluntly: "Your name was in the paper today."

The Pall Mall Gazette, John Nickols's newspaper.

The reporter in the sweet shop, striking out in retaliation at being deprived of a statement, had written that defender James Whitcox had cavorted with widow Frances Hart while Mary Bartle hung herself.

The glow on Frances's face dimmed. She glanced down at her brandy. "I purchased a paper when I went shopping."

So she had known. Yet still she had welcomed him.

"This, too, is a part of my life," James said watchfully.

The law. The mobs.

The reporters.

She swirled the brandy in her glass. "How did he know my name?"

James had wondered the same thing.

"We were previously linked in a gossip column."

Her gaze snapped upward. "When?"

The columnist had seen them together at the restaurant.

"Last Monday."

Oysters and orgasm.

Betrayal flickered inside her gaze. "Why didn't you tell me?"

"I don't read gossip columns."

"Then how did you find out?"

"Mr. Tristan."

Realization shone in her eyes. "You knew there would be gossip when you took me to that restaurant."

"Yes," he said unrepentantly.

"And you introduced me by name."

"Reporters thrive on secrets, Frances."

"I don't have any secrets, James."

She lied.

"Then you have nothing to fear."

He lied.

Frances closed her eyes, fingers white around the globe of the glass. "I feel empty when you're not inside me."

James took the snifter from her fingers and set their two glasses onto the side table. Carefully he wrapped his arms around her. "Then I'll fill you."

"But you won't always be with me."

James sighed with relief, feeling her hands slide inside his frock coat and her arms encircle his waist. He nuzzled her temple, such soft skin, everywhere he touched her she was warm and soft. "If I'm working, Frances, and you need me, come to the courthouse. I promise I'll make time for you." Heat prickled his eyelids. "I promise I'll fill you."

With his fingers. With his tongue. With his cock.

"Will you stay the night?" she whispered.

He didn't know what hurt him the most: the fact that she was afraid, or the fact that she wouldn't share her fear with him.

James tightened his arms until he felt the fragility of her bones. "I plan on spending every night with you."

Chapter 42

"**M**rs. Hart, you have a visitor."

"Is it Mr. Whitcox?" Frances asked, anticipation spiking.

"No, ma'am."

She fought down an unreasonable pang of disappointment. She and James had agreed to meet at the museum, and that is where they would meet. "I'll be down in a moment, Mr. Denton."

"You don't worry about a thing, Mrs. Hart." Deft fingers smoothed out a wrinkle from Frances's dark green velvet coat. "Mr. Denton and I will watch the townhouse this weekend."

The housekeeper must have heard the bed creaking, if not Tuesday morning, then last night. She surely must have noticed her finger that had worn a wedding band, but which now was bare.

A surge of gratitude tightened Frances's throat. "Thank you, Mrs. Jenkins."

The housekeeper stepped back. "For what, ma'am?"

For not judging the needs of a forty-nine-year-old widow.

"You and Mr. Denton have made my visit to London quite pleasant."

"Now, then, Mrs. Hart," the housekeeper said comfortingly, "you're not rid of us yet—"

"Mrs. Hart," the butler interrupted, voice toneless. "Your visitor."

"Yes, of course." Sunshine streamed through the window. "Who is it, Mr. Denton?"

But the butler merely stepped out of the doorway so that she could pass through.

"Did you explain that I have an appointment?" she asked over her shoulder.

The butler's face was as expressionless as his voice. "No, ma'am."

Frances paused at the top of the stairs and raised her hands to adjust her hat, swollen breasts straining against her corset. "Where—"

The dark shadow standing behind the newel post stepped into the light.

Frances's breath caught in her throat at sight of the man who gazed up at her.

She had known this moment would come. She just had not thought it would come now, not when her body was warm and moist from James, and she had never felt more like a woman.

Chapter
43

A second bong echoed inside the burgundy-papered room: it was two o'clock. Immediately the sharp rap of a gavel raced down James's spine.

"This meeting is called to order." Joseph Manning, hair and mustache glinting like black oil under the overhead gaslight, gripped the wooden mallet uncertainly. The men and women in the meeting had changed; he no longer knew in what capacity to chair them.

Rose Clarring's voice carried over the dying reverberation of impacting wood. "Is Mrs. Hart unable to attend the meeting this week, Mr. Whitcox?"

There was no need to ask why she assumed he would know Frances's plans: everyone in the meeting read *The Pall Mall Gazette*.

Common sense told James that there were a thousand and one things that could delay Frances. Common sense did not stop the fear that fisted inside his stomach.

"Something has detained her," he said.

But what?

"Then we will proceed without her," Joseph Manning decided.

The founder would enjoy it if Frances were no longer a part of the club, James thought while the fear rose up inside him: she had breathed life into the dying meetings, bringing spontaneity to order, honesty to academia.

"Without me, as well," James said, grabbing up his satchel.

He had learned over the years to follow his instincts, and his instincts now told him to get to Frances as quickly as possible.

The silence inside the boardroom was complete. Quickly he threw on his coat, silk scarf swinging, and dropped his top hat on his head. Grabbing his umbrella, he turned to go.

John Nickols stopped him. "Mr. Whitcox."

James paused, hand on the doorknob.

"I apologize for the article my paper printed."

James wondered how the reporter would feel if it were his name in the paper. If it were his life that the press juggled in the palms of their hands.

Immediately he realized that John Nickols—a man who had been stabbed while investigating a madam accused of stealing young girls in order to satisfy her clients' appetites for virgins—would know exactly how it felt.

"I do not expect you to apologize, Mr. Nickols," James said.

"You will contact us if misfortune has befallen Mrs. Hart?" Sarah Burns asked.

He opened the door and walked out of the meeting.

It would kill the club, he thought, if they lost Frances.

The dim corridor echoed his fear; the sunshine mocked it. A man and a woman exited a hansom cab; before the door swung closed behind them, he hopped up onto the platform and took up the vacancy.

James stared out of the window, foot propped against the side of the door to anchor his body against the bumping, grinding motion. And remembered his first cab ride with Frances.

He wondered what would have happened if he had kissed her, there on the step of the hansom. He wondered what would have happened if Frances had accepted his proposal of carte blanche.

James more than anyone knew the futility of wondering *what if*.

He had not kissed her, because he was the man he was. She had not accepted his money, because she was the woman she was. Neither of them had been ready for more, but now they had more. He would not lose Frances Hart.

James threw the cabby a florin.

"Thank 'ee," carried above the creak of wood and the jingle of harnesses.

He used his hand instead of the small, bronze, lion-shaped knocker. A dull echo reverberated through the white enameled door.

No one answered.

The fear coiling inside James leapt up into his throat.

He turned the doorknob: the door was locked.

"Hold on. What do you want?" The door wrenched open. The grimness lining Denton's face was wiped away with relief. "Mr. Whitcox. It's you."

The butler's sudden ease compounded rather than relieved James's fear. "Where's Mrs. Hart?"

Denton didn't hesitate. "Upstairs, sir."

James took the steps two at a time. The door to the bedroom was closed; James threw it open.

Light glinted off sharp metal.

Frances froze in front of the dresser, arms raised to secure a round straw hat crowned by dyed green ostrich tips.

She had worn that same hat, without the ostrich tips, the first time he had seen her.

It occurred to James that she had very few hats; the few that she did possess she altered with new ribbons and feathers to give them a new appearance. Frances didn't look the way she did because of a dressmaker or a hairstylist or a milliner: she alone was responsible for the warmth and vibrancy she exuded.

Slowly James closed the door behind him.

A cursory glance told him that the bed he had vacated only hours earlier was neatly made. The pleasure they had shared lingered in the air. An emotion that had nothing to do with sex superimposed the intimacy.

Frances did not look in his direction, but he knew she was aware of him.

The need to see her eyes drew him forward. Tossing his satchel and umbrella onto the neatly made bed, he stepped up behind her.

Inside the oval mirror her breasts strained against green wool. The pain in her eyes squeezed his lungs until he labored to breathe.

He had known that someday she would be hurt. He had not known how much it would hurt him.

Carefully he clasped her waist, soft and supple through his gloves.

As if brought back to life by his touch, Frances pushed the steel pin through her hat.

"Are you all right?" he asked carefully.

Gold-tipped lashes shielded her gaze. "My son visited."

It dawned on James what it was that superseded the emotion between a man and woman: the emotion between a mother and son.

Women in his circles hired wet nurses to feed their children, as if
having their breasts touched or suckled was lewd or obscene. The
thought of meeting Frances's child whom she had nursed and felt
tenderness for touched something inside James that was both a part
of yet apart from her sexuality.

"Is he still here?"

Frances lowered her arms. "No."

"Was he upset by what he read in the newspaper?" he gently
probed.

"No. I don't think—" Her face suddenly became an expressionless mask. "He doesn't know about the papers."

But her son knew something. Something that Frances was not
sharing with James.

The shadow of her lashes suddenly lifted; her eyes were dry. "I
hurt my son very badly."

But not as badly, James thought, as the son had hurt the mother.

James wanted to comfort her, but he didn't know how. The love
between a woman and her son was as foreign to him as the love between a man and a woman.

Suddenly Frances caught his gaze in the mirror. The flatness in
her voice hurt him more than any tears. "I need to feel you inside
me, James."

Releasing her waist, he stepped back, simultaneously turning.
Only to be stopped by her voice.

"What are you doing?"

The afternoon sunlight was a dark shadow outside the narrow
window. "I'm getting the lubrication."

"I don't want it."

James slowly turned back and stared at her reflection in the mirror. Darkness masked the pale guilelessness of her gaze.

He had seen that look in the eyes of defendants, overridden with
guilt.

Frances didn't want comfort, he realized with a dull pang: she
wanted him to hurt her. As she had hurt her son.

James felt her innocence dangling like a noose.

"Lean over," he said tonelessly, "and grasp the edge of the dresser."

She leaned over, her gaze dark underneath the brim of her straw hat.

He stood above her, darker still, and lifted the heavy hem of her dress.

Briefly he glanced downward. She wore a frilly apron instead of a horsehair bustle.

Using his left hand to hold the bunched skirt at the base of her spine, he gripped her petticoats and pulled—sweeping along the apron and gored skirt—the flounced silk up to her waist. White silk drawers clung to her heart-shaped buttocks. Reaching inside the vent, James unerringly found the cleft of her sex.

She burned him. Even through his glove.

Lifting his eyelashes, gaze capturing hers, he penetrated her. Three leather-clad fingers.

The darkness inside her gaze flickered, acknowledging the pain he caused while she clung to the pain she had caused her son.

He hurt her, but not as badly as he could hurt her. Over the course of five days and nights he had stretched her so that her vagina fit him like a custom-made glove—like the gloves he now wore.

"Is this what you want, Frances?" James asked neutrally.

She had not said which son she had hurt; it could only be her eldest: David Matthew Hart, the thirty-three-year-old heir to her deceased husband, David Matthew Hart Senior. The man who now owned her home, and who was now head of her family.

Financially. Legally.

"No," Frances said tightly as he slid his gloved fingers more deeply inside her. "I want your cock, not your fingers."

Frances had never before used the word cock while they were engaged in sexual intimacy; James's flesh leapt in response. Deliberately he pulled his fingers out of her body and guided his erection to her vagina. Slowly, carefully, he probed . . . past the inner ridge of muscles . . . through the tight tunnel of velvety soft flesh.

Her eyes in the mirror darkened until all he could see was the blackness of her pupils. "I feel you, James."

He pressed up high inside her, the dimpled head of his cock fitting against the dimpled dome of her cervix. "Where do you feel me, Frances?"

Sliding his gloved hands inside impeding silk, James gripped her hips. Inside her he found a narrow pocket that was deeper than her cervix.

"I feel you in my womb," she said, the flatness in her voice breaking.

Curving his fingers up and around and over the softness of her stomach, he pulled her upright.

The change of position shortened her vagina until he felt as if he were a foot long. "Where do you feel me now?"

"I feel you in my heart." Frances threw her head back, straw biting into his chin. Her eyes were luminous under the brim of her hat; her pale throat above the green wool collar corded. "You're a part of me, James."

But she did not now take joy in their bond.

James stared at their reflection in the mirror, the image of respectability—he in his black top hat, white silk scarf and black wool coat, and she in her feathered straw hat and green wool gown—and wanted to thrust into Frances until he split her apart. And then he wanted to glue her together with his ejaculate so that they would always be like this, one body united against a society that elevated duty over desire.

Right hand sliding downward, he found her clitoris, hard even through his leather glove.

"I know that you hurt, Frances," James whispered, watching the dark flush of sexual excitement spill over her chin and trickle down her neck, "but I won't hurt you. You want me to take away the pain. And I will. But not like this." He had never thought he would deny Frances anything, but he would not give her pain. If he thrust inside her now without benefit of oil or ejaculate to lubricate him, he would cause her pain. "Come for me, and then we'll go home, and I'll fill you. I'll fill you until you're so full of my pleasure that you overflow like a fountain. But there is no pain inside our home, Frances. I won't allow pain inside our home."

Chapter
44

Hot water overflowed the washcloth and spiraled inside the gold-veined marble basin.

Without warning the wet heat spilling over her fingers bathed the nape of her neck. Simultaneously, a muscular arm curved down her stomach and familiar fingers probed between her thighs.

Frances sucked in warm, thick steam.

"I love the feel of you when you're filled with me," James murmured, testing the wetness he had created.

He stepped closer, the moist heat of his penis pressing against her buttocks. Frances turned off the hot water cock while James sloshed his fingers inside her and tasted the nape of her neck.

She wanted to cry for the tenderness his penetration evoked.

"I'm sorry I woke you," she said unsteadily.

James ignored her apology with single-minded intent. "I love my sperm inside you"—moist heat licked the nape of her neck—"but even more, I love how you open up and welcome me."

"It's our home," Frances said, fighting back tears.

And he would not allow pain inside their home.

"I didn't intend to fall asleep." His concern touched her deeply. "Did I squash you?"

They had both been boneless with exhaustion. She had felt battered yet liberated.

"No." Frances inhaled thick steam, filled with his fingers and his sperm. "I liked it."

The heat of him. The weight of him.

The scent of him.

"Did I chafe you?"

"A little." Frances reached down and pressed his fingers upward, hugging him deep inside her. "I didn't know a man could ejaculate more than once."

"Three times," he murmured, sliding an arm around her waist. Hand spanning the roundness of her stomach—as if he could map the motion of his fingers inside her—he pulled her more firmly against him. Lips warm and moist explored her cheek while his fingers, slow and gentle, explored her vagina. "You're very full."

Prickly chest hair prodded her back; prickly pubic hair tickled her buttocks. Heat permeated her womb and trickled down her thigh.

He had told her he would fill her until she overflowed: he had kept his word.

"Yes." Frances leaned against him. "Thank you."

"You're welcome." Sharp teeth nibbled her earlobe. "Although I may never be able to get another erection."

A smile streaking through her, Frances reached behind and grasped hot, moist flesh. "What's this?"

"That, *madame*"—warm breath gusted inside her ear—"is what is vulgarly known as being 'piss proud.'"

"Oh." The embarrassment Frances should feel would not come. "Shall I leave?"

"Why should you?" One second she was filled; the next moment she was empty to the point of pain. The warm, muscular arm cocooning her stretched; James tugged the damp washcloth out of her fingers. "You're overflowing."

The distant murmur of pain crept closer. "Like a fountain."

Frances stared in the mirror and watched the play of electric light in his gold and bronze hair.

She had nurtured her family, Frances thought, throat tightening, but the man behind her nurtured her with every breath that fanned her shoulder. With every wiry hair that prickled her back and buttocks. With every push and pull of the washcloth he wielded, cleansing the folds of her clitoris and the deep creases of her sex.

"Are you tender?" she asked past the lump inside her throat.

Did a man feel the aftereffects of intimacy?

James gave a final swipe. "A little."

Frances remembered the care he had taken at her townhouse:

stretching her until she teetered just on the other side of pain but never hurting her.

But she had wanted him to hurt her. She had wanted him to punish her. She had wanted the painful tug between mother and woman to end once and for all.

She had come to London to live her own life: witnessing the pain she caused had pierced the dream and slammed home the reality.

Turning, Frances grasped the washcloth from between James's fingers. His penis was firm, but not as firm as it had been while inside her. The smooth flesh in between blue veins was a tender pink.

"Do you think God minds if we call out His name when we orgasm?" she asked, part whimsically, part earnestly, gently cleansing underneath partially capped skin.

James pushed up her chin to meet his dark, stark gaze. "Why should He?"

If sex were not a sin.

"I like the sounds you make when you orgasm," she said.

"Like an animal," James said neutrally.

The hair on the nape of her neck pricked with sudden alertness. Gaze searching his eyes for any pain she might have inadvertently caused, she said, "I assure you, sir, I have cared for animals, and I have never been moved by the sounds they make."

His face lit up. "Not even the bellow of a lonely gentleman cow?"

"I was quite moved when a gentleman cow chased me across a pasture," she said, inviting his laughter.

The light inside his eyes faded. "Parents do what they do because it's all that they know."

Frances dropped the silky-smooth penis that overflowed the palm of her hand.

She had not been raised to hurt her children; she had been raised to comfort them.

The pinch of his fingers was too acute. "But so do children, Frances."

Frances turned away, the truth too raw, and rinsed out the washcloth.

Sharp sound came from her left, wood smacking porcelain.

Twisting off the water faucet, she wrung out the washcloth and draped it over the basin. Turning, she froze at the sight of James.

His back arched. His buttocks dimpled.

Impulsively she padded across the cold marble floor. Standing slightly behind James—her hip abridging a concave cheek—she reached around his waist. "My first son liked his nappies."

James stiffened at her touch, but did not pull away.

Gently Frances grasped him; wiry pubic hair tickled her fingers. "I finally happened upon an idea to break him of them."

James drew his hands away from his flesh and cupped her fingers, guiding her. "How?"

Heat flowed through him; liquid splattered into the bowl, abruptly stopped.

Memories flooded Frances, images filled with love and laughter. A baby boy with white-wheat hair and chocolate eyes. A tiny rosebud mouth dribbling milk, greedily nursing at her breast.

"He liked boats," Frances said, caught between the past and the present, "so I cut out little paper boats and floated them in his potty."

The flesh between her fingers stiffened; water streamed.

Frances directed James. "There's a boat there, don't let it get away." She redirected him. "Sink that big boat there, down it goes." She suddenly jerked him to the side. "Don't let the warship get away, James, shoot it down!"

All of a sudden masculine laughter burst through the splatter of water and Frances couldn't hold onto the past. It slipped free of her fingers, and then James was slipping on the floor and Frances was falling with him, and they were both laughing so hard that she couldn't stop the tears.

She had loved her young son, but he was no longer young. She loved her family, but her family would never again be enough.

The price of being a woman.

Chapter
45

Margaret bit back tears. And did not know from what she ached the most: a son's love for his mother, or a mother's love for her son.

David Senior was dead, but David Junior would not let him go.

Concern had propelled him to visit Frances Hart. He had returned from London silent and grim. Margaret knew from experience that David would talk when he was ready: it was blatantly clear he was not.

Reaching under the freshly laundered sheet that smelled of soap and sunshine, Margaret found a work-callused hand and placed it on her bulging stomach. "The baby is restless."

The baby missed its father. Margaret missed her husband.

For long seconds square fingers curved to fit the tiny foot that kicked. "Mama should be here to help you."

David's voice was curt and tense: it was not the voice of the man she had vowed to love and to honor.

"David, the baby and I are doing well." Holding her breath at her own temerity, Margaret drew his hand up to a swollen breast that throbbed with need. "The midwife said so yesterday."

David slid an arm underneath her shoulders and turned her into a spooning position. "There's nothing more important than family, Margaret."

Margaret stared out the window at a line of black night that was darker than the curtains. "I'm your wife, David."

"I'm your husband, Margaret."

But he did not sound like a husband; he sounded like a keeper.

How hard it was, admitting a desire that she had never before openly acknowledged; it had been their secret, the love they had shared at night, communicated only in the occasional glance across the dinner table or in a passing touch. "I need you, David."

"And I'm taking care of you the best way that I know how." David's voice was rough; his body that spooned hers was tense. "But I can't do it alone."

Hot moisture trickled down her temple into the pillow. "David, you're not alone."

"This baby is my responsibility." David's body was tense; his hand clung to her rippling abdomen. "All of you are my responsibility."

Dread burned in her solar plexus like heartburn.

"Your father was a good man," Margaret said carefully.

"My father knew how to keep his family together."

Margaret realized what David did not: women kept families together, not men. Frances Hart had been the backbone of the family, not David Hart Senior.

"David, Timothy wanting to farm his own land is not the end of the family."

David had been the only one surprised by Timothy's declaration over the dinner table last Sunday.

"Abigail missed Sunday dinner."

"She's with child, David."

"You never missed Sunday dinner."

"I didn't have to travel fifteen miles."

She had lived in Frances Hart's home, the home in which she was now mistress.

"This family depends upon me, Margaret."

The grimness in David's voice broke her heart. Family should be joyful, not this onerous burden.

"Your family loves you, David, but you aren't your father. You surely can't expect them to act as if you were."

"If I don't hold the family together, who will?"

"Love, David." Margaret clasped her hand over his larger hand and pressed it against her swollen abdomen where the consequences of their love demanded attention. "Love holds a family together."

"My father said decency and hard work is what holds a family together."

Margaret had never been afraid for her husband. She suddenly felt very afraid for him.

David rolled away from her and the child their love had created. "Timothy can drive you to church tomorrow morning. I'm going early to talk to the vicar."

Words worked up into her throat: *What did you do, David?* But the words wouldn't come.

Mother Hart had laid the groundwork for the Hart family: women loved unconditionally. But it had never before been this hard to unconditionally lie next to her husband.

Chapter
46

Frances stared at the elongating pearl of black ink.
The words on paper were no better than the words she had spoken out loud.

"Mrs. Hart." A short knock followed the familiar voice of the butler. "You have visitors."

It had been five days since David had visited.

"Who is it, Mr. Denton?"

"A man and a woman, ma'am."

Black ink plopped onto the sheet of white stationery.

"What do they want?"

"They say it is in reference to the Men and Women's Club."

"Oh." Pleasure filled Frances. She swivelled around on the ladder-backed chair to face the butler. "Show them into the drawing room. I'll be down directly."

Quickly she tidied her hair. The sudden thought of taking tea with Ardelle Dennison and Joseph Manning froze her hand, which secured a metal hairpin.

She resolutely squared her shoulders. James gave her his nights, but his days belonged to others. Taking tea with the publicist and the professor would certainly be an interesting diversion.

But the man and woman who sat side by side on the brown horse-hair divan were not members of the Men and Women's Club.

"I beg your pardon," Frances said, hovering on the threshold between twin walnut doors. "Do I know you?"

"Mrs. Hart, I presume?" The man—several years Frances's senior—stood up. He was impeccably dressed in black wool and starched white linen. "I am Mr. Steward, and this is my companion, Miss Shell."

Miss Shell dressed very much like the young women in the Men and Women's Club. Her age was approximate to theirs, as well: she looked to be in her late twenties or early thirties.

"How do you do, Miss Shell, Mr. Steward," Frances said. Her stomach fluttered. Aside from James, these were her very first London visitors. "May I offer you tea?"

"Thank you, that would be very nice," The man returned cordially.

Frances turned to seek out the butler, but he was standing behind her.

"I will bring tea, madam."

"Thank you, Mr. Denton." Frances perched on the edge of a brocade chair across from the sofa. "My butler said you are here on account of the Men and Women's Club?"

"Yes, we are interested in joining," the man said, "but we would like more information."

"I see," Frances said. And did not see at all. Joseph Manning was the president; Marie Hoppleworth was the secretary. It should be they whom the man sought out, not Frances. "Why is it that you have come to see me, and how did you gain my address?"

There was no guile in his dark eyes. "Mr. Harmon at the museum thought you would be more easily available than the other members."

"No doubt," Frances agreed. Unlike the others, she had no career, she did not attend university, nor did she have a husband to look after. "What would you like to know?"

"The club is for men and women, I take it."

A faint, ironical smile curved Frances's lips. "It *is* called the Men and Women's Club, sir."

"Yes. Yes, it is." The man's pleasant smile did not falter. "We are curious about the type of discussions you hold."

"I'm afraid I've not been a member for long, Mr. Steward," Frances said truthfully. "You will need to consult with one of the other members for more detailed information."

"But you do discuss topics pertaining to the relationships between men and women, do you not?"

"Yes, of course."

"We are very interested in the relationships between men and women, are we not, Miss Shell?"

"Oh, yes." There was no interest in the young woman's eyes, just a curious expression of waiting. "Very interested, Mr. Steward."

"Could you give us examples of the types of discussions you have?" the older man asked.

He had an extraordinarily soothing voice, Frances thought.

"We've discussed the use of"—James had said the word "condom" was vulgar—"machines."

The younger woman's face turned crimson. Exactly like the faces of the women in her first meeting with the Men and Women's Club.

"Do you condone the use of prophylactics, Mrs. Hart?" Mr. Steward asked, unperturbed at her disclosure.

"Yes, I do." Did her daughters know of such things? she wondered. But how could they, shielded as Frances had been shielded. "I'm sure you've heard of Mary Bartle. She would still be alive if her husband had protected her."

The dark eyes were curious. "Do you think Mrs. Bartle was justified in killing her husband?"

"I—Oh, Mr. Denton. Thank you." The butler set the heavy silver tea tray on the table between Frances and her guests. "What would you like in your tea, Miss Shell?"

"Nothing, thank you."

Frances poured from the china teapot. Pink roses trailed down the matching cup and saucer.

The younger woman set her tea on the table in front of her and folded her hands. She had not removed her gray kid gloves.

"How would you like your tea, Mr. Steward?"

"Just tea, thank you." The older man balanced the cup and saucer on his knees. "You were saying?"

"I'm sorry." Frances poured tea for herself. "I was saying . . . ?"

"You said you thought Mrs. Bartle was justified in killing her husband."

"No." Memory bolted through her. Firmly she set down the china pot. "I said no such thing, sir."

"Surely you did, Mrs. Hart. You said Mrs. Bartle would still be alive if her husband had used machines."

He did not blush at the use of "machine." Yet how strange the word sounded, spoken in his soothing, sexless voice.

"The jury determined that Mrs. Bartle was innocent of murdering her husband, Mr. Steward," Frances said crisply.

"Don't you think the jury could have been unduly influenced by that barrister . . . what was his name, Miss Shell?"

The young woman did not touch her tea; steam spiraled upward in the cool morning air. "Mr. Whitcox, sir."

"Yes. That's his name. Mr. Whitcox." Frances noticed that the man's dark eyes were small for the size of his face. He reminded her of a mole, digging where he had no business digging. "Don't you think that men such as Mr. Whitcox are capable of seducing the innocent minds of vulnerable women, Mrs. Hart?"

Frances had no doubt whatsoever that James could seduce whomever he wished, if he had a mind to.

A trickle of unease slid down her spine. Surely the older man realized that the barrister was a fellow member of the Club?

Carefully she added two cubes of sugar and a generous serving of cream to her tea. "I fail to see what this has to do with the Men and Women's Club, sir."

"Isn't this the type of discussions you have in the Club?" The older man touched rose-patterned china to his lips before returning the steaming cup to the saucer balanced on his knees. "I find conversations such as this fascinating."

"No, Mr. Steward," Frances said emphatically. The last meeting she had attended flashed through her mind: John Nickols asking if women didn't find fear in a man disgusting; Esther Palmer admitting she was not an attractive woman; Thomas Pierce challenging the morality of not using condoms. "These are not the types of conversations we have."

"You are wise to our deception, I see." The older man set his cup and saucer down on the table. "I confess to a bit of chicanery, Mrs. Hart."

Frances stiffened.

"You see," he continued in his soothing, sexless voice. "Miss Shell and I are not interested in joining your club; rather, we are interested in creating a club of our own. But as you see, we do not have the slightest idea of how to do so. Would you mind terribly if I brought a friend to hear more? It will give us such an advantage."

"The other members are more knowledgeable than I, Mr. Steward," Frances reiterated. "They would be of far more service."

"But we had hoped to set up our club as soon as possible," he gently persisted. "Won't you help us?"

"I . . ." Frances wavered; she really did not have anything to offer. Manners dictated her choice. "Of course."

"Excellent. Thank you so much for the tea. We must be on our way, mustn't we, Miss Shell? There's no need to rise, Mrs. Hart; pray enjoy your tea. We will see ourselves out."

Frances felt as disoriented as she had felt that day when she accidentally walked into the meeting of the Men and Women's Club.

A faint murmer drifted from the front door; immediately a soft closure sounded inside the townhouse. She scooped up her tea.

"They are an odd couple, Mrs. Hart."

Creamy liquid sloshed into her saucer: she had not heard the butler enter the drawing room.

"They've disturbed you." He plucked up the two abandoned sets of cups and saucers. "I will say you are not at home should they call again."

"No." Much as Frances would like him to do just that, she couldn't permit it. "They are due back today sometime. I told them I would see them."

Frances did not have long to wait. No sooner did she drink her tea and finish the letter that she would never send, than the man and woman returned. She stared in dismay at their "friend." The man sat on his spine and gazed at her as if she were a strange species of insect.

"So the men and women in your club discuss the use of prophylactics, Mrs. Hart?" Mr. Steward asked.

Frances squared her shoulders. "I have said so, Mr. Steward."

"Isn't that remarkable, Mr. Wedon, that given the opportunity, men and women can be so democratic?"

The oily-haired man who sat on his spine nodded and grinned. "Indeed, Mr. Steward."

Frances bit her lip to stop herself from telling him to sit up straight, he was getting macassar oil on the couch.

"Do the other members advocate the use of prophylactics, Mrs. Hart?"

Frances did not like speaking for others. "Some do."

"What else do you discuss?"

"We have talked about"—Frances had openly admitted to touching herself in front of the members of the Men and Women's Club; with this man she could not force herself to bring up the subject of self-pleasure—"erotic art."

"Indeed!" Mr. Steward seemed pleased. "Do you enjoy erotic art, Mrs. Hart?"

"Yes." Frances licked her top lip. "I find it quite"—*stimulating* caught inside her throat—"interesting."

"Surely a gently bred woman must find sexually explicit art offensive."

Three pairs of eyes keenly watched her.

Frances lifted her chin. "Why is that, Mr. Steward?"

"You do not find pictures that are intended to excite the senses distasteful, Mrs. Hart?"

"I have said that I do not, sir."

"You are a widow."

Frances's heart leapt up into her throat. "How do you know that?"

"Mr. Harmon, the curator," was the soothing response. "He's a friend of mine. He thinks very highly of you."

Neither the older man's voice nor the curator's endorsement soothed her. "Yes, I am a widow."

"Did you enjoy erotic art before you became a widow?"

"I didn't know that erotic art existed until I came to London."

The moment the words left her mouth, Frances knew she had said something wrong. Suddenly she could not bear being in the same room with the peculiar trio, the one man sitting on his spine, the older man in his too-stiff collar and cuffs like a mortician, and the young woman with her drab clothing and staring eyes.

"I have a previous engagement, Mr. Steward," Frances lied.

"Pray forgive me. It was very nice meeting you, Mr. Wedon. I wish you a pleasant day, Miss Shell."

"Certainly, Mrs. Hart." The older man smiled his soothing smile. A curious light shone in his eyes. "You have been most generous with your time. Miss Shell. Mr. Wedon. We have obtained what we needed. Let us go and allow Mrs. Hart to prepare for her engagement."

The front door closed. They were gone. So why did her stomach churn?

The need to be with James was a sudden, physical pang. How tempting it was to turn to him for her every need. Frances had well learned the damage such dependency created.

All she needed, she thought bracingly, was a bit of fresh air: the City of Dreadful Delights still had plenty to enjoy. She had not yet visited Kew Gardens; that would surely be restful.

Determinedly she climbed the stairs. James's presence pervaded the townhouse. He slept in the bed in which she slept. He relieved himself in the toilet in which she relieved herself. He washed at the sink in which she now washed her hands.

Frances pinned on top of her head a simple straw hat banded with green silk, and grabbed up her suede coat and reticule.

A sharp rap of banging metal halted her at the foot of the stairs.

The knock excited a surge of anticipation that was as painful as it was pleasurable. She knew it could not be James, but it could very well be her son.

Frances stepped down off the stair.

Hurried footsteps echoed along the corridor. "I'll get that, Mrs. Hart."

Heart in her throat, Frances watched the yawning door.

The oily-haired man who had earlier sat on his spine stood between two women. Frances did not recognize either of the ladies: they were tall, large boned and looked quite grim.

"There you are, Mrs. Hart." The oily-haired man peered around the butler. "If you'll come along quietly now, we'll get you the rest you need."

Frances stared at him in surprise. The butler, she briefly noted, was just as amazed.

Without warning, two women swarmed around the butler and grasped her arms, one on either side of her.

Frances was too shocked to be alarmed. "Release me at once!"

They were as tall as Frances: they didn't listen.

The oily-haired man flapped a sheet of paper in front of the butler's face, as if he had a warrant for her arrest.

Frances remembered her foray into the illicit shop. *If the bookstore should be raided, we would all be put in gaol,* Joseph Manning had said.

But the bookstore had not been raided.

"Release me," Frances insisted, jerking her arms to free herself.

"It will not fare well if you struggle, Mrs. Hart," the oily-haired man spoke from the door that the two women were slowly dragging Frances toward. "Come along now, we have a court order to collect you."

Frances's bones suddenly turned into jam: she *was* being arrested.

"Release Mrs. Hart at once." Frances recognized Mrs. Jenkins's voice; it came from the direction of the stairs that led down to the kitchen. The housekeeper was reassuringly calm. "Or she will charge you for assault."

The unclean smell of rank sweat and other less pleasant odors that arose from the two bullish women momentarily overpowered Frances. Surely they must tell her for what she was being arrested?

Yanking with all her might, Frances gained the freedom of her arms.

Immediately the housekeeper stepped between Frances and the two women; she wielded a broom as if it were a weapon. "If you touch me, not only will Mrs. Hart give you in charge for assault, but I shall give you in charge for assaulting me, as well."

"You're interfering with the law, ma'am!" the oily-haired man indignantly yelped.

"The police will be the judge of that, sir." The housekeeper's voice was resolute. "Take yourself off to the drawing room, Mrs. Hart, and wait there until Mrs. Ellis returns with the constable."

Frances was not going to be sent to the drawing room like a child. This was a mistake. A horrible, horrible mistake. But a mistake that could be rectified, surely.

"This is ridiculous, I've done nothing illegal," Frances lied.

An empty bottle of chloroform had been used as evidence against Mary Bartle. Would the police search Frances's house for the bottle of lubrication she had purchased?

The two women stepped forward, one on the right, the other on the left.

"Lock yourself in, Mrs. Hart." The housekeeper thrust a hand backward; a small ring of keys jingled. "These are the only keys; these hooligans won't be getting you."

A sense of unreality settled over Frances. James was a well-known barrister: he would be able to help her. But perhaps even he was being presented with a court order for arrest.

Perhaps *all* the members of the Men and Women's Club were now being arrested.

"I am not going to hide away, Mrs. Jenkins." Frances had broken the law: she would pay the consequences; however, "I demand to know why I'm being arrested."

Chapter
47

The shadow-pitted door silently swung inward.

Frances's eyes, upon seeing James, lit up with emotion: fear; confusion; relief.

"It *is* you!" she said unevenly, breath gusting in the chill air.

She wore a suede coat, gloves, and a flat straw hat.

The vultures had arrived just as she was going out, he realized, delayed fear slamming through his body.

James walked into her outstretched hands. And wanted to rage at the pain he was going to cause her. "Indeed, it is."

"I was afraid they had a court order for you, too," she whispered, arms banding his waist, breath searing his ear.

She trembled.

If they had caught her outside the townhouse, they would have taken her. She could not have stopped them.

Throat aching, James nuzzled her cheek; it was cold with fear. "Why did you think they had a court order for me?"

"I—" Frances fisted her gloved fingers into the wool of his coat, drawing him closer, trying to take back the control that had been wrested from her. "How is it that you're here?"

"Denton."

"Mr. Denton fetched you?"

"Yes."

"How did he know where to fetch you?"

James lifted his head to read her expression. "He has my card."

Puzzlement squeezed out her fear. "But how are you here so quickly?"

She was unsophisticated still in so many ways.

"He telegraphed me."

"We don't have a telegraph machine."

"A neighbor does."

The puzzlement inside her eyes abruptly gave way to dread. "Are they still out there?"

James pulled her more tightly against him, knowing that soon she would fight him. "The policeman sent them away."

Frances's arms worked up through his and looped about his neck; the softness of her breasts pierced his chest. "Then it *was* a mistake."

"No." James thanked his courtroom experience for the emotion he did not show. "It wasn't a mistake."

"I don't understand." The moist heat of their combined breath misted the air between them. "A lunacy order was issued because I visited a pornographic book shop?"

He bowed his head over hers until the straw brim of her hat scraped his forehead.

"Is that what you thought, Frances?" James briefly closed his eyes to block out the innocence he was about to shatter. "That a lunacy order had been issued because you visited the Achilles Book Shoppe?"

"Why else?" she asked.

James raised his lashes and stared down into her questioning gaze. She had recovered from her son's visit; he didn't know if she would ever recover from the news he was about to impart.

"Frances." He shared the warmth of his body, knowing it would not be enough. "Only the male head of a household can sign a lunacy order."

Slow comprehension seeped into her eyes: her husband had been the head of the Hart family, but now her husband was dead.

"No." The arms looping his neck stiffened in denial. "No."

"Yes." James would not let her go. "Yes, Frances."

A low rumble of a passing carriage filtered through the chill air.

The cold stiffness looping his neck suddenly dissolved into warm acceptance. Forgiveness flooded Frances's eyes, inviting him to deny the truth. "That's ridiculous, James."

James imagined that she had looked just so at her son when catching him in a childhood lie. But James had never lied to her.

His silence spoke for him.

Slowly Frances slid her arms down from around his neck, and wedged them between their chests. "I don't believe you."

James ignored the shard of pain her rejection evoked. "I saw the lunacy order."

He had arrived just before the policeman sent the madhouse director packing.

"I'm *not* insane," she swiftly denied.

"Nothing is easier in England than to get a sane woman into a lunatic asylum."

Denial flashed in her shock-darkened eyes. "I can't believe that!"

She had been equally outraged upon learning that officers of the court visited the same pornographic shops as the people they charged. There was so much from which he could not shield her.

"You can't *not* believe it," James said brutally.

The policeman who had told the madhouse director to leave could just as easily have ordered the servants to hand her over.

"My son wouldn't do that," she said firmly.

Sons did it. Fathers did it. Husbands did it all the time.

"I saw his signature, Frances."

Frances wriggled to escape the truth. "No!"

She was surprisingly strong.

"Yes." James purposefully drew her closer. "Yes."

"You're lying."

"No." He pulled her closer still until her wedged arms lost purchase and he held her safe. "I would never lie to you."

"Then it's not his signature."

No doubt every woman who had ever been confined had said those same words. Men relying upon the law; women relying upon men.

"Who else, Frances, would do this?"

"No," she repeated. "You're wrong, James. I can't believe it. My son loves me. He wouldn't do this."

James flinched at the pain in her gaze.

"You have to believe it," he said flatly.

"Why?" she challenged.

Why should she believe the man for whom she merely felt she would die without, over the son for whom she would die?

"Because the lunacy order is in effect for seven days," James said, brutally honest.

Horror filled her eyes. "They can come back?"

"They *will* come back."

"They can take me?"

The sudden vulnerability in her voice brought tears to his eyes. "Yes."

And there would be nothing he could do to stop them.

"English law will allow my son to confine me in an insane asylum?"

James couldn't change the law, but he could circumvent it.

"In order to take you, they have to find you." He steeled himself against the betrayal blossoming in her eyes. "No one knows about our home."

"So my alternative to being confined to a madhouse is to be confined in your townhouse?"

The home in which he had promised he would not allow pain.

"Just for seven days."

"What happens when the seven days are over?"

That depended entirely upon her son. And the law.

James did not know lunacy law. But he soon would.

"The order will no longer be in effect," he said neutrally.

Hope flickered in her eyes. "I'll be safe?"

James wanted to lie; the lie stuck inside his throat. "No."

Chapter
48

"The men are here to install the combination bath, Mrs. Hart."

Frances stared out the bedroom window incuriously. "Send them up, Mr. Peasebody."

The plumbers were not as silent as the butler: they tromped through the bedroom and banged inside the bathroom. Muffled guffaws and grunted responses meandered through the chill silence.

"Mrs. Hart."

Water dripped down the glass pane like tears. When had it started raining?

"Yes, Mr. Peasebody?"

"Mr. Whitcox is on the telephone."

"Please tell him I am supervising the installation of the combination bath."

She didn't hear the butler leave, she only heard him return.

"Mr. Whitcox said I should tell you he's sorry you can't come to the telephone."

The butler waited for her to speak. But Frances had nothing to say. She had thought to become a woman. Only to discover that mothers were not women. Else how could the law allow them to be locked away on the whim of a son?

Slowly she became aware of a faint image inside the tear-streaked glass.

"Mr. Peasebody."

"Yes?" the butler asked with a peculiar hitch in his voice.

"Would you supervise the installation while I—" What could she do to give substance to that ghost imprisoned inside the window? "While I go downstairs for a moment?"

"Certainly, madam."

For long seconds, Frances stared through dry eyes at the pale reflection surrounded by falling tears. Picking up her reticule off a gilded dresser, she walked out of the bedroom that held so many memories.

The butler's voice drifted down the marble stairs: apparently he was not pleased with the installation. Her suede coat and green banded straw hat hung on the brass clothes tree, exactly where he had hung them the previous day.

The biting cold of rain drenched her clothes but did not penetrate her body. She didn't know where she was going, she only knew she had to go somewhere.

"Cab, ma'am?" Wheels rattled on the cobbled street; they kept pace with her strides. "Take ye where ye want."

Frances stopped. The cab stopped.

"Yes." Water poured off the brim of her hat and leaked down the neck of her coat. "Thank you."

Frances sat down on worn black leather and pulled the door closed against the driving rain.

The cab didn't move.

It occurred to her that she must give the cabby directions. But she had no directions to give.

Where are we going, James?

Home, Frances.

Standing up, she lifted the trapdoor.

The Victoria Station was damp and noisy and drafty. Steam roiled and billowed outside the train. Frances boarded third class. A young mother wearing a drab bonnet and dark wool cloak sat beside her, a sleeping baby cradled in the crook of her arm.

Tiny eyelashes fanned chubby cheeks; a rosebud mouth puckered, as if dreaming of nursing.

Frances's breasts suddenly ached.

"Ain't they grand when they're asleepin'?" asked a heartbreakingly young woman.

Frances glanced up.

Pride shone in the mother's clear blue eyes.

Glancing back down at the sleeping baby, Frances gently touched a miniature hand. "Indeed they are."

Tiny fingers grasped her forefinger. Frances's lips quivered.

"Would you like to hold him?" the young mother asked.

"No." Frances realized she was drenched; the cold suddenly penetrated her very bones. "I'm wet."

The sleeping baby yawned and released Frances. No doubt her finger was wet, too. And cold.

"May I get you something?" she asked the beaming mother. "Some tea, perhaps?"

Immediately the young woman's face stiffened. "No, thank 'ee, ma'am."

Frances was not wealthy, but she was comfortably well off. Unlike the young mother.

"I would consider it a favor if you would share a pot of tea with me," she said gently. "I don't like drinking too much when riding the train."

Understanding relaxed the woman's face; sanitary facilities on the rails left much to be desired. "That's awfully nice of ye, mum."

Crowded boroughs gave way to rolling hills. There was no rain in Kerring, Sussex, just ripening fields of wheat that glistened in the noonday sun. A man dozed on a pony cart underneath the shade of a flowering beech tree. Frances woke him.

A Georgian house loomed in the distance, faded bricks a mellow brown. Leafy oak trees shaded green grass cropped by sheep.

Her children had climbed the trees and chased the sheep. The distant echo of their laughter riffled the leaves.

Frances paid the driver of the pony cart and instructed him to return in two hours.

"Grandmama! Grandmama!" A hurtling body knocked the wind out of Frances; thin arms wrapped around her waist. "You're home! I told Papa you'd come home!"

Kneeling, Frances hugged Megan. Her granddaughter smelled of innocent childhood and boundless energy. Red braids trailed down her narrow back. Dirt smeared her neck and white pinafore.

Frances's chest constricted: how much the little girl had grown since she had last seen her.

"What did you do with your fish, Megan?" she whispered huskily.

"I dumped the wax fruit and filled the fruit bowl on the dining room table with water," Megan said against Frances's neck; remembered grievance filled her childish voice, "but Mama wouldn't let me keep him there."

Another time Frances would laugh. Or perhaps not. Adults could indeed be unjust.

"Mother Hart!"

Surprise and trepidation resonated in the warm spring air.

Reluctantly releasing her granddaughter, Frances stood and smiled at the golden-haired woman dressed in flowered muslin. "Hello, Margaret."

Margaret came from a resort town near the coast. David had met her when buying seed from her father. There was a sweetness about the doe-eyed woman that went straight to the heart.

Frances knew that her daughter-in-law loved her. She didn't want the young woman to be caught between mother and son, but the price of keeping peace was too high.

"Oh, Mother Hart, it's so good to see you!" Margaret, shorter than Frances by several inches, leaned forward and hugged her as close as her pregnancy would allow. She whispered close to Frances's ear. "I'm so sorry!"

Frances closed her eyes on a wave of pain and warmly returned her daughter-in-law's hug. "You look wonderful."

Frances lied: Margaret looked haggard.

"So do you, Grandmama," piped in Megan. "Look at her hair, Mama! It grew as red as mine!"

Stepping between mother and grandmother, Megan grabbed Frances's hand and pulled her toward the house. "Come see what Mama's done!"

"Welcome home, Mrs. Hart!" Mrs. Pippins, the sturdy cleaning woman who had been at the house almost as long as Frances, grinned from the doorstep. "Shall Mr. Pippins fetch your luggage from the station?"

An awkward silence followed the well-intentioned question; slowly the smile on the cleaning woman's face faded.

"Mother Hart must be tired from her journey, Mrs. Pippins," Margaret said, pushing trailing blond hair behind a dainty ear. "Please tell Mrs. Tilley to prepare a tea tray. Come inside, ma'am, it is grand seeing you!"

Memories swelled over Frances, stepping inside the house that she had lived in for thirty-four years. She had entered this front door wearing a veil. Her husband had lain in wake inside this drawing room.

But the house had changed in the short month and a half that Frances had lived in London: red silk drapes replaced gold velvet drapes; gold brocade and red silk upholstery replaced tan leather and brown velvet upholstery. It was a home, but it wasn't her home.

"It's beautiful," Frances said truthfully.

Margaret's soft brown eyes pleaded. "You don't mind?"

"This is your home now, Margaret."

For a few fleeting years. And then Margaret's home would pass on to her son, Matthew.

"What about you, Mother Hart?" The pleading inside Margaret's doe-brown eyes melted into feminine searching. "Have you found a home?"

. . . when you're inside me, James, I feel like I have a home.

"Grandmama, is London really dirty and full of squel-squeal-*squal*or?"

Obviously squalor was a new word to the seven-year-old girl.

Yes, the City of Dreadful Delights contained dirt and squalor—David's words, no doubt—but there was so much more to the metropolis than pollution and poverty.

"London throbs with life like a heartbeat, Megan. One moment you can hardly breathe for the smoke and the fog, and the next moment everything glitters like a newly minted penny. There are restaurants, and parks, and museums, and gardens, and even a crystal palace with giant dinosaurs that guard a lake. One of them," Frances said solemnly, "spat at me."

Megan's pale green eyes—Frances's eyes—opened wide. "*Really,* Grandmama?"

Frances felt the hot press of James's hand in the middle of her back, sharing her laughter as the submersed dinosaur sprayed water.

"Really." Frances's throat tightened. "Where is Matthew, and little Peg?"

"Napping, thank God," Margaret said with heartfelt relief. "Megan, sweetheart, why don't you run take a peep at your brother and sister?"

"Mama, you know I can't do that." Megan crossed her arms with a confidence that Frances had never possessed. "Why don't you run along while Grandmama and I have a nice cozy?"

Frances bit her lip to restrain a smile. "Megan, I brought you a surprise, but you can't have it if you don't do as your mama says."

The tangled sash of Megan's pinafore whipped behind her like a white tail.

Frances stared at the gleaming oak doorway that the seven-year-old girl had disappeared through. She would miss the daily transformations of young girl into young woman.

"You look beautiful, Mother Hart," broke through her thoughts. "I've never seen you look more beautiful."

Frances turned her gaze away from the doorway and smiled disparagingly; she raised a hand to ensure that the repairs she had performed on the pony cart still held. "I no doubt look like a drowned rat; it was raining in London."

"No." Tears glittered in Margaret's soft brown eyes. "Your skin glows. You are . . . simply . . . beautiful."

James had said so.

Frances blinked to clear her vision. "Where's David?"

"He's in the east field."

Briskly Frances pulled out of her reticule the three small tins of chocolate that she had purchased on the train. "Give these to the children, please."

Frances did not think she'd be able to face them after the coming confrontation.

"That barrister. Mr. Whitcox." Small hands—reddened from too much housework—gathered the three tins out of Frances's kid-gloved hands. "Is he a good man?"

Frances stiffened. She had not told David about James.

Immediately she remembered the first meeting with the madhouse doctor and the silver spiral of heat escaping rose-patterned porcelain. David hadn't known about James when he'd visited her, she realized, but he had known about James when he'd visited the lunacy doctor.

"Yes," Frances said. The citizens of Kerring, Sussex, would not think so, but, "Mr. Whitcox is a very good man."

"I think, Mother Hart, that after all these years, you have found your home." Throwing her left arm around Frances's waist, Margaret pressed a quick kiss against her cheek. "God go with you."

The house had changed, but the land had not. Acrid manure and musky earth filled Frances's nostrils. A light breeze rippled a fence of bushes. David leaned against a lone maple tree eating a thick sandwich while he looked out over a ripening field of wheat.

Tenderness ripped through Frances's chest. He was her son, and she would love him always.

Suddenly his head snapped toward her, sandwich suspended in the air. The shade of the tree and the drooping brim of his hat hid his eyes.

Frances stepped underneath the umbrella of the tree. "Hello, David."

David lowered the sandwich. "What are you doing here?"

"As opposed to being in an insane asylum, you mean?" Frances asked quietly, controlling the pain.

"It's not an insane asylum," David retorted defensively. "It's a sanatorium for women."

His eyes were clear of the breach he had caused.

"I told you about the Men and Women's Club, David, because I wanted you to understand."

"What did you want me to understand, Mama? That Papa's love— that our love—wasn't enough for you?" David's pain lashed out at her. "Is that what you wanted me to understand?"

A bee droned nearby, oblivious of the hurt a mother and a son inflicted upon one another.

"Or did you want me to understand," David asked raggedly, "that the love your family bears you is a burden that prevents you from being a 'woman'?"

"I never said that, David." Tears pushed upward for release; Frances tamped them down. "I never said that the love of my family wasn't enough. I never said that you were a burden."

"Pray tell, Mama, what, then, did you say?"

How hard it was to remember the words she had said, buried as they now were in a dense fog of hurt.

"I told you that I loved your father, but your father is dead now, and I need something—" *More*, dear God, she had said that, she had made him think that the love her family bore her wasn't enough, and it *wasn't*, but not because of anything they had done or not done. "I need to fill that gap in my life, David, that the passing away of your father created."

His eyes softened. "That's what family is for, Mama."

But family didn't do what David had done to her.

Frances stared at the man who was a replica of her husband: he had the same chocolate brown eyes; he had the same white-wheat hair. But her husband David would never have done what her son David had done. Or perhaps he would have done exactly what her son had done. Frances could no longer differentiate between the truth and what she had thought was the truth.

"David." Maternal tenderness vied with a deep sense of betrayal. "A man and two women tried to drag me off to an asylum for lunatics."

Without the servants they would have succeeded.

"It will only be for a short while." The knowledge of his betrayal briefly shone inside his eyes. "Until you regain your reason."

Joseph Manning had spoken about "reason," but he was an educated man.

"I can't believe that you did this on your own." Frances searched his face for the little boy who had shared his every secret. "Tell me you didn't do this on your own."

How would he know about "lunacy orders" and "sanatoriums" for women?

David looked away, unable to meet her eyes. Moodily he stared at his sandwich, sliced roast beef wedged between slabs of hearty wheat bread; brown mustard filled the imprint of his teeth. "I'm responsible for you, Mama."

The truth was more bruising than physical violence.

"Do you still like boats, Davie?" she asked suddenly, tears clogging her throat. There must be something of her mischievous little boy inside this grim, "responsible" man.

"I'm not a child."

"Must one be a child in order to experience pleasure?" she asked, regret filling her. Is that how she had raised her children?

"You are not a child, Mama."

But she was acting like one, his voice implied.

"And so I should not be allowed a holiday?" she asked reasonably.

"You have responsibilities to your family."

"I have *never* shirked my responsibilities."

She had been a good daughter. A good wife. A good mother.

"My father isn't even cold in his grave"—David's accusation sliced through her heart; his chocolate brown eyes riveted her with his grief—"and look at you! I thought you loved us, but you don't grieve for my father. You don't wear mourning. You took off his ring as if he never existed. How could you? How could you do this to his memory?"

Frances stared at her son and wanted to weep for their loss of innocence.

Taking a deep breath, *knowing* how she looked—her straw hat wilted, her suede coat water-stained, her hair flat and lusterless from the drenching it had taken in London—*knowing* that her son would not understand her explanations, but knowing that she must try one more time, Frances spoke. "I loved your father, David."

"You loved him so much," David said contemptuously, "that you couldn't wait to put him in the ground so you could go off to London and spend his money."

Some people hurt others without realizing they do so, James had said.

Frances was not naive enough to believe that David didn't realize he hurt her. She was mature enough to understand that it was her son's pain that spoke rather than any inherent malevolence. The pain wouldn't last. But oh, it hurt now.

"You know I loved your father, David," Frances returned steadily, gazing up into his face that was so familiar. "I know you know that."

"If you loved him, then explain to me, Mama." His eyes filled with tears: Davie, her baby, who leapt off haystacks into her waiting arms; not David, who signed a lunacy order to confine her. "Explain to me why you ran away to London when Papa was dead for only three months. Explain to me why you dye your hair like a cheap tart, and you dress like you're a young girl primping herself up. Explain to me what happened to my mother who five months ago planned the birth of my next child but now that my wife is almost near her time, cavorts about in London with men and women who talk about things that no man and woman should talk about. Explain it to me, Mama, because I don't know you."

Frances braced her legs against the combined weight of a mother and her son's pain. "Margaret and the baby are doing fine."

"We need you, and you abandoned us."

"But Margaret and the baby are fine," Frances persisted.

"If Margaret and my baby were important to you, you'd come back to Kerring."

"If Margaret and the baby needed me," Frances said more sharply, "I would have packed my bags and returned to Kerring immediately. But you don't need me."

"Margaret's too big with pregnancy to run after the children."

"Then hire a woman to watch over them."

"Family takes care of family."

"Is that what you see me as, David? As someone to take care of your children, in order to make your and Margaret's lives easier?"

"You know that's not true."

"Then tell me why you want me back in Kerring."

"Abigail's housekeeper left; she needs help until she can find another woman."

"So now I'm a housekeeper."

"You're a mother and a grandmother," David retorted angrily.

"But I'm a woman, too, David."

For long seconds David's face went blank; then it turned brick red.

"I will not listen to you defile the memory of my father," he said in a low voice.

"It's because of Mr. Whitcox, isn't it," Frances asked, "that you signed to have me committed to a 'sanatorium for women'?"

"It's disgusting!" The ugly red that boiled his skin came from both embarrassment and anger. "A woman your age carrying on like you are."

"But you don't think it's disgusting that your father married me." The words came unbidden. "Do you?"

"My father was a man."

So it wasn't just her age that provoked David's response.

"Women have needs, too," Frances said gently.

"This isn't you," David said grimly.

"This is me."

This was the woman she should have been, but had not possessed the courage to be.

"You weren't like this before you went off to London."

Frances remembered the lunacy man's question: *Did you enjoy erotic art before you became a widow?* Frances remembered her response: *I didn't know that erotic art existed until I came to London.*

How well she had played into the doctor's hands.

"I love you, David." David would always be her baby boy. A child herself, he had been as much playmate as son. "I love all my family. But I will not sacrifice my life simply to make your lives more comfortable."

David drew back as if she had slapped him. "You wouldn't talk like that if you weren't under the influence of that man."

Sadness welled up inside her. Her son could blame her for many things, but she would not allow him to lay blame on a man whose only crime was in caring for her.

"David, I did not know James Whitcox when I left Kerring."

"So like a whore," David said stonily; a breeze sighed through the ripening stalks of wheat, "you've taken up with anyone who would have you."

"Is that what you think of me, David?" she asked carefully. "That I'm a whore?"

David flung his sandwich into the field. "I ordered the solicitor to stop depositing money into your account."

David shouldn't be able to hurt her anymore; he could.

"Your father requested in his will that I be allotted a monthly stipend."

Even as the words left her mouth, she realized the double betrayal. Her husband had *requested* that she be paid a monthly stipend. She didn't need to be a barrister in order to know that no law could force her son to follow a request. As her husband must have known.

"You said you don't know me, David." The tears she held back burned a hole in Frances's heart. "I don't know you, either."

"I love you, Mama." The cry startled a perching sparrow; a white-tipped feather drifted down between them. "There's help for women such as you. The doctor explained that you're going through"—David faltered; a painful blush darkened his sun-kissed skin, embarrassment unmarred by anger—"through changes . . . *physical* changes . . . that affect your mind. It's not unusual for women of your age to want to feel young again, he said. But he can help you, Mama. He can make you like you were before you went off to London."

"And if I don't want to be like I was before?" Frances swallowed. "What then?"

"The doctor explained that's another sign of your illness," David earnestly explained. "If you were well, he said you would understand that your behavior is irregular. Please let the doctor help you."

Frances strove to understand the masculine reasoning that justified confining a woman: "What is this illness?"

David didn't respond. Frances realized that he didn't know how to respond. He had not done this alone, but he believed wholeheartedly that what he was doing would benefit her.

"Does this doctor think I'm ill because I am no longer able to bear children?" Frances queried.

Doubt flashed inside David's eyes; it was immediately swallowed up by resolution.

"Or does this doctor think I'm ill because I enjoy the company of a man?" she persisted. "Exactly why do you think I'm ill, David?"

His answer was all too damning.

Chapter
49

The sun had shone in Kerring. The rain continued to pour in London. It drove Frances forward into darkness.

No light burned in the rented townhouse.

Frances had told the servants she would not be home for the duration of the court order; the fact that they didn't expect her did not lessen the utter sense of aloneness she felt at not being welcomed.

Cold liquid streamed down her cheeks, dripped off the tip of her nose. It tasted of soot and salt.

The truth almost brought her to her knees: her son *had* signed the lunacy order.

Groaning, like battering rain, filled her ears.

Her son had snatched something away from her that she did not know how to replace. She didn't know if it could ever be replaced.

Behind her, water pummeled the door. Beneath her, water puddled the floor.

From far off Big Ben bonged the hour. It was five o'clock: she had missed high tea.

In her absence, the servants had no doubt taken the opportunity to enjoy a little holiday. Frances couldn't blame them.

Reaching out—feet shuffling, fingers fumbling—she found a table. Removing her gloves and extricating the loop of her reticule, she set the wet leather on a pewter tray and found a box of safety matches in a drawer.

Blue flame illuminated two bronze sconces: Frances lit them. Darkness gave way to the shiny polish of oak floors and the dull fabric of green wallpaper. Blowing out the match, she laid the smoking stick beside her reticule.

The scarred walnut table beneath the pewter blurred.

The rent was paid through the season, but she had no money to pay for necessities. Her son had seen to that. But she couldn't think about that. Her son had said that he loved her. But she couldn't think about that either.

Slowly, carefully—afraid of the emotion that clamored for release—Frances ascended the worn stairs.

Only to discover that she was not alone.

A man stood beside a flickering brass sconce at the end of the hallway, back to her, bowed head a shining cloud of white. He did not wear a coat. His white shirt was rucked up around his waist. Black braces looped his elbows. Sagging black trousers revealed a round moon. It steadily pumped back and forth.

A guttural groan cut through Frances's paralysis: it was chased by a soft moan: masculine need calling; feminine need answering.

Frances stepped back. And slid in a puddle of water. Frantically she grabbed the banister to stop her fall. The slap of flesh on wood rang out in the flickering light. It did not halt the pumping rhythm of the pale buttocks.

The emotion she had been holding at bay crashed over her. Turning, Frances descended the steps as quietly as she could.

The servants' stairs were steeper than the upper stairs. The narrow kitchen was empty. Gaslight hissed and popped above a scarred walnut table. A blue-speckled kettle sat on the back of a black iron stove; it was filled with warm water.

Frances found a squat blue willow-patterned pot in the cabinet above the metal tea canister. Blindly she brewed a cup of tepid tea.

"I'm sorry you witnessed that, Mrs. Hart."

There was an unmistakable Irish brogue in the housekeeper's voice.

Frances remembered the girlish laughter coming from the drawing room.

Setting down her cup of untasted tea, she met the gaze of the sixty-six-year-old servant. She saw emerald green eyes that were bright with intelligence. She saw glossy black hair threaded with silver. She saw the sexual satisfaction that flushed softly lined cheeks.

She gazed at the housekeeper and saw a woman.

Frances became aware of her wilted straw hat and sodden suede coat.

She had looked at the housekeeper in the same light as her son looked at her: as an old woman whose sole purpose was to serve others.

"I'm not, Mrs. Jenkins," Frances said.

The bright eyes were curiously sharp. "Why is that?"

"Because I needed to see that a woman who reaches a certain age—" Frances squeezed closed her eyes. Her son wanted to take away her sexuality, and she didn't know what to do. "I needed to see that men and women of all ages enjoy"—she opened her eyes—"'that.'"

The emerald green eyes suddenly twinkled. "And just what did you think happened to women who reached 'a certain age'?"

Shame burned Frances.

"I didn't," she said honestly.

Women discussed housekeeping and child rearing. Women did not discuss feminine need.

Not once in Frances's life had she imagined that her mother or her grandmother might desire more out of life than a home and children.

Leaning forward, the housekeeper deftly scooped up blue willow-patterned china. "And now that you have?"

Buffeting rain tattooed the kitchen door.

Frances no longer knew what to think. Only one thing was clear . . .

"I could have you dismissed."

One word from Frances and the rental manager would dismiss both the housekeeper and the butler.

"Aye, Mrs. Hart." The older woman paused, willow-patterned saucer and cup suspended over the scarred walnut table. "That you could."

"Doesn't that frighten you?" Frances asked.

She could have the housekeeper discharged. Her son could have Frances confined.

"I'm not afraid of loving, Mrs. Hart." The older woman straightened; compassion softened her gently lined face. "It's a sorry thing not to love."

Frances remembered the fan of tiny eyelashes, the flush of chubby cheeks, the pucker of a rosebud mouth.

"Do you have children, Mrs. Jenkins?"

"Aye." The housekeeper's face lit up in an unmistakable glow of maternal pride. "I've got two lassies. They've done right fine for themselves. They've given me six grandbabies, and three great-grandbabies."

"Do you not feel that your place is with your family, rather than . . . ?"

"Sinning with Mr. Denton?" the housekeeper asked shrewdly.

This was blunt speaking indeed.

Frances held the older woman's gaze. "Yes."

"Youth is a funny thing." The housekeeper stepped behind Frances; porcelain clattered, deposited inside a metal sink. "When you've got it, you don't appreciate it. It seems like you're always afraid of something—another lassie's got a prettier dress, or your sister's got more beaus."

Twelve years older, Frances's sister had died before Frances's birth. Their mother had silently suffered a succession of miscarriages until successfully delivering another girl child: Frances.

"When you don't have it"—the door to the iron stove creaked open—"the past plays tricks with your mind. You think of the dances you didn't go to, or the boys you didn't kiss."

A sheet of rain slashed the window.

"And then one day you wake up"—coal thudded iron; the acrid stench of sulfur filled the chill air—"and you realize you're all alone. Grandbabies don't take the place of a man, Mrs. Hart; they don't warm your arse at night, or get your blood pumping in the morning. A woman's got one life: she's got to reach out and grab it with both hands, or it'll pass her by and leave nothing but a smelly old fart in her face."

The door to the iron stove clanked shut.

"At what age were you widowed, Mrs. Jenkins?"

"Mr. Jenkins"—water splattered metal as the housekeeper emptied the kettle into the sink—"passed away when I was sixty. I remember the night well: he was late for his supper. Mr. Jenkins had a healthy appetite; he was never late for his supper. But he was late that night. Come bedtime, a wagon pulled up to the door. A neighbor had found him on the side of the road; it was too late to help him. He was dead, most likely his heart gave out. Working the land does that to a man."

Frances digested the information that the housekeeper's husband had been a farmer. As her own husband had been a farmer.

A burning coal burst inside the stove.

"Did you"—Frances hesitated—"mourn him?"

"You English are a funny lot. Take your Queen," the housekeeper said matter-of-factly, as if she were used to discussing sex and death with a woman who had caught her in the act of carnal congress. Water spewed from a faucet, thundered inside the empty tin kettle. "Even when she was playing Mrs. Brown, she wore her widow's weeds."

Mr. Brown, Frances thought, must have been the gillie in whom the Queen had taken comfort.

"She should have given the Prince a good Irish wake. A pint of whiskey down the gullet, and a body realizes you mourn in your heart; the rest is just window dressing." Abruptly the roar of water stopped. "Death is no reason to stop living."

But was death a reason to *start* living?

A metal lid stoppered a metal kettle.

I'm afraid, Mrs. Jenkins, surged up inside Frances's chest.

Fear like a fist stopped up her throat.

She could not admit fear. She could not admit defeat. But she was afraid. Because she could see nothing but defeat.

Fixedly she stared at the vee of light slashing the narrow stairwell. "I didn't thank you for saving me."

When the madhouse keeper had told her he wasn't arresting her—that he had an order to take her to an asylum—Frances's feet had stuck to the floor. Yanking out of her hands the ring of keys, the housekeeper had pushed Frances into the drawing room and locked the door.

"Women do—" Cotton petticoats and wool skirts rustled. Tin struck iron, the sound of the kettle deposited on top of the stove. "What they must do, Mrs. Hart."

The madhouse man had waved the paper in front of the butler.

"Did Mr. Denton see the signature on the court order?" Frances asked, voice low, rain a relentless pattern.

"Aye." A metal lid collided with a wooden counter. "That he did."

The pungent aroma of dried tea leaves permeated the coal-scented air.

"My son loves me, Mrs. Jenkins," Frances said. But for whose benefit?

"And you love your son, Mrs. Hart." Dry tea leaves hit the bottom of the porcelain teapot, a comforting *ppfff* that resonated over the crackle of fire and the patter of rain. "Nothing ever changes a mother's love."

"But is a mother a woman?" Frances asked, voice cracking.

"When all is said and done"—tin struck tin, the lid to the tea canister replaced—"being a woman or being a man is all that any of us can ever be. Babies and grandbabies have their own lives; we can't live it for them, and they can't live our lives for us. But being a woman isn't any easier than being a man. We've got to fight for ourselves, Mrs. Hart. Or we're not worth fighting for.

"You're wet through and through." The housekeeper's Irish brogue lightened, the woman stepping into the role of housemaid. "Mr. Denton's running you a bath. I'll bring up your tea while you dress in warm clothes. When you're ready, Mr. Denton will put you in a cab and send you off to Mr. Whitcox."

Chapter
50

Footsteps echoed hollowly down the length of the dim corridor. Frances paused uncertainly outside a shadow-darkened door. Muffled sound came from behind it.

Searching for the strength to do what she must, she grabbed the brass knob. The door wasn't locked. Silently the heavy mahogany swung inward.

Flickering gaslight filled the private chamber. Avery Tristan bent over a small desk, face illuminated by a green lamp, fingers busily tapping a round, circular button on a small machine. James Whitcox sat back in his black leather chair, hair glinting bronze and gold, the handset of a telephone cradled to his ear.

It was the clerk who first saw Frances.

The tap-tap-tap—faster and more rhythmical than had been the tapping of the typewriter in the museum—paused. Dark brown eyes studied her for a long second before returning to the odd button. The spasmodic tapping ended.

It occurred to Frances that it was a telegraph machine that Avery Tristan operated, the same machine, no doubt, upon which James had received the message from Mr. Denton.

Standing, the clerk walked toward Frances—swerving, he grabbed a gold-and-brown-checkered coat off the coat tree—then he walked past Frances and closed the door behind him.

"Mr. Tristan—"

James's sharp voice instantly died. Cold hazel eyes appraised Frances.

"Lieutenant Inspector, thank you for your assistance. There's no need to search further." He spoke into the telephone. His voice was as cold as his eyes. "Mrs. Hart just stepped into my office."

A clean click concluded the conversation.

"I've never talked on a telephone," Frances offered.

"You could have talked on one this morning," James said.

Instead of running out in the rain with no note and no word, he did not need to add.

"I had to see my son."

"I would have taken you to see your son any time you wanted."

There should be no greater heartbreak than seeing David's chocolate brown eyes fill with contempt: seeing the unyielding coldness inside James's gaze hurt far worse.

The pop of an ember sounded over the steady drum of rain.

She had confronted her son. She searched for the strength to confide in James.

"I married when I was fifteen years old."

But James already knew that.

"My husband was forty-four years old."

Only three years younger than James was now.

There was no flicker of surprise in the hazel eyes: older men frequently took younger wives.

Frances forced the words out of her mouth: "He died four and one half months ago."

David Hart Senior had been seventy-eight years old, six years older than Mr. Denton.

"He had been ill for some time when he suffered an apoplexy. I sat with him, day and night. He died peacefully in his sleep." Frances's bottom lip quivered, confessing her selfishness. "I loved him, but I couldn't mourn him. I held his hand between my own hands, and all I could feel was that my own life had slipped away. So I buried him. And I pretended to mourn him for three months. When I could no longer keep up the pretense, I fled to London."

Darkness shone inside his stark hazel eyes. "Did you think I would condemn you?"

Yes.

"My son does."

"Your son is a young man who can't see beyond his own wife and children."

The blindness of youth.

"How long have you been a widower?"

"Seven months."

"Would your children condemn you, if they knew about . . . us?" she asked past the lump inside her throat.

His gaze was watchful. "Neither my wife nor I were loving parents."

"So only loving parents are condemned by their children?"

"More atrocities are committed in the name of love than for any other reason."

"But is it love, James—when someone deliberately hurts another—or is it something else that masquerades as love?"

The pain she felt leaked into his eyes.

He abruptly held out his hand. "Come home, Frances."

Frances blindly walked around the large teak desk. James held her away from him long enough to take off her suede coat and free her hat, and then he pulled her onto his lap and her bustle shot out onto her hip and he held her so tightly she couldn't breathe.

He trembled.

Frances combed her fingers through his hair—beautiful hair, thick and shiny and clean—and buried her face in it until his scent filled her lungs. "I'm sorry."

"I thought they'd taken you," James said rawly.

"I know."

"I couldn't believe you would voluntarily walk away from our home."

"I walked away from a house that had become a prison, James." Frances found his hand and carried it to the vee of her thighs. "This is our home."

Cool air tunneled up her skirt; it was followed by the hard invasion of masculine fingers. He slipped past the slipperiness of her silk stockings into the open vent of her drawers and under the curve of her buttocks. She was tight and dry; he was blunt and hard.

"Just one finger, Frances." She closed her eyes and opened her body. The penetration burned. She had neither oil nor the remnants of his ejaculate to ease his way. Without any lubrication his finger felt larger than a penis. "Now we're home."

The rain pelted the windows. The heat of his finger seeped into her bones.

Turning his head, James brushed his lips against her chin. "Tell me."

Frances allowed the past five days to fill her thoughts.

"David stood in the hallway when I came down the stairs to meet you last Saturday." She took a fortifying breath of James's scent— salt and musk and soap—more beguiling than the perfume in the Crystal Palace. "He didn't recognize me at first."

She relived the stunned disbelief on David's face when he realized that she was indeed his mother.

"He didn't say anything, he just looked at me as if he couldn't believe his eyes." The fullness of James's finger displaced some of the remembered pain. "I took him into the drawing room and tried to explain."

A sheet of rain crashed into the window.

Frances flinched. James waited.

"Those madhouse people . . . David told them what I told him. He told them about the—" Renewed betrayal surged through her; she couldn't continue the sentence. "Yesterday morning Mr. Denton said a man and a woman wanted to see me in reference to the Men and Women's Club. I told him to put them in the drawing room. But they weren't from the Club."

There was no judgement in his voice. "Why didn't you send them away?"

"I wish I had." Frances swallowed. A tiny heartbeat pulsed inside her vagina. "I wish—he said they were interested in joining the Club. He wanted to know what types of subjects we discussed." She briefly closed her eyes in disgust at her gullibility. "But then he said that he had tricked me to gain entrance to my house, that what he and the woman actually wanted was to start a club of their own. So I agreed to see a friend of his, to explain more about what we discussed. How could I have been so stupid?" she asked in an agonized whisper, squeezing eyelids blotting out the clean shine of his hair.

"This is what the madhouse doctors do, Frances," James said matter-of-factly, "and some of them are very good at doing what they do."

Snatching away lives, not restoring lives.

"My son claims he did it because he loves me." Her vagina fisted around his finger in denial. "But he didn't do this alone, I know he didn't."

"There was a second signature on the order."

"Who?"

"It was co-signed by a Reverend Samuel Petty."

Stunned recognition shot through her. "Our vicar."

Frances had actively participated in the Church of England all her life.

"I guess he doesn't realize that mettle is another word for sperm," she said bleakly.

James had laughed when she had said that the vicar often praised mettle in a man: he did not laugh now.

The rain relentlessly pelted the window.

"'You're my responsibility, Mama,'" Frances suddenly whispered against his ear, hard cartilage and warm skin. "That's what David said today. He told me that I was ill, and that the doctor at the asylum would help me. He's cut off the monthly stipend my husband set aside for me. He said he swore to his father that he'd take care of me, and that he will do so."

Frances moved her head until her lips pressed into bronze and gold, there a thread of silver. "I can't live like this, James. I can't live knowing that at any moment my son can sign another lunacy order and confine me to an asylum, simply because he thinks it is what's best for me."

The living heat of his hair slowly seeped into the coldness of her lips.

"Marry me."

James's proposal was bluntly unexpected.

The pleasure his offer engendered was exceeded by pain. "I can't."

"Your son can't confine you if you're my wife."

Deliberately she hurt him, because the law hurt her. "But you could."

"I would never hurt you."

"But you *could*," Frances said harshly. "My son has made me a victim—like Mary Bartle's husband made of her—and I can't escape the disease of knowing that at any moment I can be confined by a man whom I love.

"I can't live like this, James. You tell me that this is the law, that it's the easiest thing in the world to commit a sane woman, but I can't live like this. I can't live knowing that I'm a victim, simply because I'm a woman." Each harsh truth, each harsh breath jarred her home anew. "I refuse to be a victim. I refuse to believe that the law will allow this to happen to me. There must be something I can do. There must be, James, or I might as well go to the asylum tomorrow and turn the key in the lock, because I will never feel safe again."

Her voice reverberated over the burning snap of coals and the pounding drum of rain. His profile was sharply etched in the dim light, his nose straight, his lashes still against his cheek, his lips carved out of flesh. The finger buried inside her frantically pulsed, his heartbeat catching up to her heartbeat.

"Did your husband provide for the monthly stipend in his will?" he asked neutrally.

"He requested in the will that David pay me the stipend."

James suddenly turned his head and snared her gaze. "There's nothing that can be done in the criminal courts, Frances."

Tears scalded her eyes.

"But," James said, voice expressionless, "you can fight in the civil courts."

"How?"

"You can sue your son."

"I'm not concerned about money—"

"You can sue him for emancipation."

Freedom. From a son whom she had nursed and nurtured. It was obscene that the law made this necessary.

"How?" she repeated thickly.

But James didn't answer the question she asked.

"If you do this, Frances, your name will be smeared in every newspaper in London. Everything you've ever done or said will be held against you, both in the papers and in court. Perhaps your son—when he discovers how strongly you feel, and to what extent you're willing to go—will acquiesce, but he may not. A lawsuit will have a profound effect, not just on you, but on your family. The Men and Women's Club has been cited as a contributing factor to your lunacy. Marie Hoppleworth keeps meticulous records. Those records will be seized as evidence. The members of the Men and Women's Club will be brought to court to testify against you. Your servants will be questioned. They will reveal that you and I are engaged in a sexual liaison. They will reveal this not because they want to, but because they will be compelled to. Are you willing to take your son to court? You may win, but you may lose. Are you willing to allow a judge, who is a man, and a jury—who are twelve men, all with mothers of their own—to determine the outcome of your life?"

Chapter
51

James stared at the twenty-foot-long mahogany table. Behind him, the entry of six women and five men one by one filled the burgundy-papered room. The door alternately swished open and clicked shut. Wooden umbrella handles clinked against brass. Woolen coats rustled, hooked onto the coat tree. The odd greeting fell onto the muted noises drifting up from the street outside.

Today James would discover just how deeply the members of the Men and Women's Club had been affected by Frances Hart.

Wood groaned, medallion-backed chairs individually protesting the weight placed upon them. John Nickols silently wheeled his chair up to the table.

A spate of "Good afternoon, Mr. Whitcox," rang out.

Jane Fredericks hunched her shoulders and stared at him like a small animal burrowed inside a black woolen hole.

She claimed to be a devout suffragette. James cynically wondered just how dear women's rights were to her.

A distant bong floated over the sighs of clothing and the groaning of wooden chairs. Joseph Manning reached for his gavel.

James intercepted, deliberately projecting his voice as if he were in trial—and in a sense, he was: this afternoon would lay down the foundation of his case. "I would like to address this meeting before it is called to order."

Eleven heads snapped toward him. A second bong announced it was two o'clock, time for the meeting to convene.

Joseph Manning impatiently fingered the gavel. "What is it, Mr. Whitcox?"

"Is it Mrs. Hart?" Rose Clarring anxiously asked.

"Has some misfortune befallen her?" Sarah Burns asked.

"Is Mrs. Hart not able to attend any more of the meetings?" Esther Palmer asked.

"You may speak, Mr. Whitcox," Marie Hoppleworth said firmly.

Louis Stiles stared at James over the top of his sketching pad. Thomas Pierce and John Nickols leaned forward over the table, chairs creaking.

"This information will shortly be made public, so I am not violating privileged information by divulging it." James carefully chose his words. "Last Wednesday Mrs. Hart was served a lunacy order. The Men and Women's Club was listed as a primary contributing factor to her lunacy."

"What?" John Nickols asked incredulously.

"Is Mrs. Hart confined in an asylum?" Sarah Burns asked sharply.

"Why would this Club"—Joseph Manning angrily interrupted—"be listed as a contributing factor to her lunacy?"

"Mrs. Hart is not a lunatic, Mr. Manning," Marie Hoppleworth said scathingly. "Please explain, Mr. Whitcox."

James alertly assessed the response of each and every member. "Mrs. Hart is safe, Dr. Burns."

"Who would sign a lunacy order against Mrs. Hart?" Thomas Pierce asked.

James frankly met the banker's gaze. "Her son, Mr. Pierce."

The rumbling grind of passing carriages filled the silence; overhead the five gaslit globes hissed and popped.

No one spoke. No one moved.

James carefully advanced. "Many facts will be brought out in trial—"

"This Club will feature in a trial?" Ardelle Dennison lashed out.

"Yes, Miss Dennison," James said neutrally. "Should this matter go to trial—and there is every likelihood that it will—then this Club will be scrutinized."

"Why is this matter going to trial?" demanded Joseph Manning, lips white with anger.

"Because men have the legal right to confine a female relative for no other reason than because they wish to, Mr. Manning," James said coolly. "Mrs. Hart refuses to allow her life to be ruled by laws created for the convenience of men."

Shock exploded in Jane Fredericks's face.

James's gaze passed over the suffragette. "I am telling you this as a courtesy because this trial will affect each and every one of you."

"This trial has nothing to do with me," Ardelle Dennison hotly denied, fear flaring in her amber eyes.

"This trial and its outcome affect every man and woman inside this room, Miss Dennison," James flatly refuted. "Your father"—he glanced at Jane Fredericks—"and your father"—he glanced at Esther Palmer—"and your father"—he glanced at Rose Clarring—"and your husband, Mrs. Clarring, have the legal right to confine each and every one of you."

James caught John Nickols's gaze. "We men want women to trust us with their sexuality"—gaze sliding away from the journalist, he one by one caught and held the gazes of Thomas Pierce, Joseph Manning, Louis Stiles and George Addimore—"but how can they, when we men may imprison them because of it?

"During this trial your names"—James swept the gazes of both men and women—"will be paraded in the newspaper, just as Mrs. Hart's name will be. You will be called to testify, whether you want to or not. The minutes to your meetings will be used to corroborate your testimonies. Your lives are at stake. It is up to you to preserve them. You may do so by supporting Mrs. Hart, and by proudly identifying yourselves as members of this Club. If you act as if you are ashamed of Mrs. Hart—and of this Club—then you will send out a clear signal that what you discuss here is morally reprehensible, and you will lose both your jobs and your reputations."

Some of them would no doubt lose their positions no matter their presentation.

"And what do you stand to lose, Mr. Whitcox?" Joseph Manning sneered, livid with anger that control of his Club was being wrested from his hands.

"Frances Hart," James said simply.

If he did not win this case, he would lose the only woman that would ever matter to him.

"Rest assured, the decision to go to trial was not lightly made. Mrs. Hart deeply regrets any pain or inconvenience this suit will bring. Your support will mean more to her than I can say.

"You have much to discuss." Grabbing up his satchel, James stood. "You'll be receiving subpoenas."

"Mr. Whitcox."

James paused, already planning for his time with Frances. First he would pick up fresh oysters. Then he would concentrate on bringing back to her eyes a spark of joy. "Yes, Miss Fredericks?"

"Why is Mrs. Hart doing this?"

The suffragette was about to get a real lesson in women's rights.

"What would you do, Miss Fredericks," James asked impersonally, "if a man whom you loved and trusted decided that it was in your best interests to be confined in an asylum? What would you do if the police would not help you, because no law was being broken? What would you do, Miss Fredericks, if you realized you would never be safe unless you sued the man you loved?"

"Mrs. Hart is suing for money?" gasped Ardelle Dennison in outrage.

James remembered the look of disappointment on Frances's face in the Victoria Station when he had told her Ardelle Dennison and Joseph Manning were not accompanying them to the Crystal Palace.

"Mrs. Hart is suing her son, Miss Dennison," he said coldly, "for emancipation, so that she may live her life as she sees fit."

Chapter
52

The door definitively closed behind James Whitcox.

Six women and five men stared at one another around the conference table.

"A woman cannot be confined unless she's ill," Ardelle Dennison suddenly snapped.

"Yes, she can," Sarah Burns said in a small voice.

John Nickols dismissed the publicist's disbelief. "It's done every day, Miss Dennison."

"And how would you know, Mr. Nickols?" Ardelle Dennison countered.

"Because I'm a reporter," John Nickols returned flatly.

"Then why don't you report on that instead of all your sex crimes?" Jane Fredericks flared.

"Why didn't your Mrs. Butler campaign against the wrongful confinement of women, Miss Fredericks," demanded Thomas Pierce, "instead of repealing the Contagious Diseases Acts?"

"If women were freed from the demands of masculine sexuality, then women would not be incarcerated," the suffragette said defensively.

"Mrs. Hart's son signed the lunacy order, Miss Fredericks—" Sarah Burns's square face was grim. "Not a husband. I once signed such an order for a father who wanted to teach his daughter obedience."

All eyes trained on the physician. It had not occurred to any of the members that one of their own had the authority to sign a lunacy order.

The indistinct cries of a passing vendor floated up from the street.

"I report on sex crimes, Miss Fredericks," John Nickols suddenly said, "because sex sells, and because no one cares about the women who are incarcerated inside asylums."

"The women care," Rose Clarring said quietly.

"Yes, the women care," John Nickols grimly echoed.

"Mr. Whitcox said Mrs. Hart is safe," Esther Palmer nervously piped in. "Why must she sue for emancipation? Obviously the lunacy order did not present a great threat to her."

"A lunacy order lasts for seven days," Sarah Burns said. "They can seize Mrs. Hart at any time during those seven days."

"Well, then—"

"She's living underground, Miss Palmer," Marie Hoppleworth said briskly. "They cannot cart her off to an asylum if they cannot find her. But if they find her, they will confine her, and there's nothing that anyone can do to stop them."

"No doubt *he's* hiding her in his house," Joseph Manning said with distaste.

"Would you rather she were committed, Mr. Manning?" Rose Clarring asked, aghast.

"We will lose our reputations and our careers, Mrs. Clarring," Joseph Manning bit out, "because Mr. Whitcox and Mrs. Hart have turned this Club into a society encouraging sexual misconduct."

"A man and a woman's desire for intimacy is not a matter of misconduct, sir," Rose Clarring returned icily.

"What do you think will happen when your husband reads your name in the paper?" Joseph Manning asked waspishly. "His name will also be discredited. He, too, could lose his standing in the community."

"He said the minutes would be seized," George Addimore interrupted, face a dark red. "What if they reveal that we visited the bookshop?"

Esther Palmer's face turned purple. "What if they reveal what we purchased?"

"I have not recorded our private conversations," Marie Hoppleworth broke through the sudden fearful tension.

"It is your job, Miss Hoppleworth, to maintain accurate minutes," grated Joseph Manning.

A bark of laughter ricocheted around the mahogany cornices.
Ten pairs of eyes focused on John Nickols.

"Would you listen to yourselves?" the reporter asked mirthlessly.
"You, Mr. Manning, first complain that Mr. Whitcox and Mrs. Hart
have turned our little corner of academia into a sex orgy, and then
you berate Miss Hoppleworth for not recording every lascivious de-
tail. You, Miss Dennison, claim that men can't incarcerate innocent
women, because if you admit that, you'll have to admit that the
ideals you embrace with such vehemence are less than just to your
sex. Miss Fredericks, you are prepared to attack anyone who has not
liberated your fair sex, yet you yourself have done nothing to advance your cause.

"Mr. Manning clearly pointed out the dangers of visiting the
Achilles Book Shoppe, yet we voted to visit it. Neither Mr. Whitcox
nor Mrs. Hart are to blame for that vote. The decision we must now
make has nothing to do with them, and everything to do with us.

"The truth is, ladies and gentlemen, that after two years, each of
us finally has to decide if we truly believe that men and women are
equal. Having arrived at a decision, we must then decide if we have
the strength of character to stand by our convictions. I, for one, am
looking forward to finding out just exactly what we're made of."

Chapter
53

"**D**r. Burns!"

Sarah suddenly became aware that the footsteps behind her belonged to George Addimore, and that he followed her.

In the two years they had been members of the Men and Women's Club, he had not once singled her out for conversation.

Forcing her heart to calmly lay in her chest instead of jumping into her throat where anatomically it should be impossible to lodge, she slowed her gait so that he could catch up with her.

"Dr. Burns." The accountant sounded winded. Sarah glanced sideways and noted that his face beneath the brim of his brown felt bowler hat was red. "I wondered if I could walk with you."

"Why?" she asked bluntly.

The accountant did not glance up at her.

Following behind them, Marie Hoppleworth, Ardelle Dennison, Thomas Pierce, Joseph Manning, Esther Palmer, Jane Fredericks, Louis Stiles and Rose Clarring walked alone.

The clank of the iron lift opening reverberated in the dimly lit corridor.

John Nickols did not have the use of his legs, yet he, too, walked alone.

"Well, Mr. Addimore?" Sarah asked, as gruff as a man but unable to present herself otherwise: it was how she had managed to become a physician.

"I wanted to explain my comment in the meeting."

"Which comment is that?"

"About my concern over . . . certain . . . facts becoming public knowledge."

The image of an ivory cock ring rolled behind Sarah's eyes.

"You have good reason to be concerned, Mr. Addimore."

James Whitcox had neatly summed up the consequences of their names being publicly associated with the Men and Women's Club.

"Aren't you concerned about the repercussions of a trial, Dr. Burns?"

"You advocate Malthus's thesis for population control, sir."

The dimness of the corridor opened up to the light of a stairwell. Sarah swung past the newel post and plunged down wooden steps, petticoats, skirt and coat kicking up around her ankles. The motion made her feel strangely feminine.

George Addimore fell slightly behind, his legs shorter than hers. "Yes."

The stuffed giraffe towered over Sarah.

"So you are aware," she said over her shoulder, "that the purchase or distribution of literature promoting preventive checks is illegal."

"Yes, of course," he said over the tumbling echo of footsteps.

Sarah stepped off the wooden stairs onto the marble floor. "I have a small library of such books and pamphlets that I lend to my patients."

The accountant hurried to catch up with her. "Aren't you afraid that a patient will report you?"

Sarah had seen too many deaths and destroyed lives, women with tuberculosis expending what little energy they had left in pregnancy, men unable to feed the babies their seed planted.

"It's a risk, sir, that I am prepared to take."

She had long lived with the knowledge that she could be arrested and brought to trial: neither event would turn away her loyal patients.

"What of your father?" George Addimore caught up with her. "Does he not object to your involvement in the Malthusian program?"

Sarah passed a cracked Roman sarcophagus. "My father died some time ago."

"What of your mother?" the accountant pursued.

"My mother lives with her sister in Bath."

It had taken Sarah's father two years to die of the cancer that daily fed on him: Sarah's mother had never recovered from the exhaustive care he had required.

Somehow George Addimore managed to pass Sarah by and hold open the brass and glass door for her to exit the museum. A flush of pleasure rushed through her; it was tamped down by acute self-consciousness: she was larger than George Addimore in every way.

"It's a beautiful day, ma'am," the accountant blurted. Sarah looked dubiously up at the gray, misty sky. "Would you care to take a drop of tea?"

Approaching footsteps rang out on marble.

"Have you invited the other members to join us, Mr. Addimore?"

The red coloring the accountant's face turned brighter than the highlights in his beard. "No, ma'am."

"Let us invite them, then."

His side-whiskers twitched. "I would enjoy the opportunity to get to know you better, Dr. Burns."

Sarah passed through the door, momentarily tongue-tied.

The accountant offered his arm.

Women decorously draped on men's arms passed them by: pretty women, petite women.

"Mr. Addimore." Sarah flushed. "I am several inches taller than you. We would look utterly ridiculous if we walked down the street, arm in arm."

"You did not seem to mind when we were at the Crystal Palace."

"We were not alone at the Crystal Palace."

"But it was pleasant, was it not?"

Sarah remembered gushing fountains and cresting excitement. Thomas Pierce, George Addimore, and Louis Stiles had alternated squiring the women. She had felt like a young girl, uncaring of her size and her unfeminine nature.

"It was quite pleasant," she admitted.

Joseph Manning, head down, looking neither left nor right, passed by Sarah and George.

"I didn't know that a woman could be confined on the whim of a man," the accountant said abruptly.

Tentatively Sarah placed her hand in the crook of his arm. The heat of his body warmed her gloved hand. "Do you have a woman relative you would like to be rid of?"

"Of course not!" he said indignantly, gray eyes sparking.

"Then why should you know?" Sarah asked practically.

There were many things she had yet to share with the members of the Men and Women's Club: things that only physicians and their patients knew. Women routinely turned to doctors to give them the orgasm their husbands did not. The medical world referred to the practice as relieving congestion to the pelvis: apparatuses operated by steam had greatly relieved the stress of cramped fingers.

"The girl you spoke of"—George Addimore interrupted her thoughts—"is she still confined?"

Sarah matched her mannish gait to his. "No."

Relief infused George's voice. "Then Mrs. Hart does not face permanent confinement."

"The girl was released because her father was satisfied that she was well and truly brought to heel, Mr. Addimore," Sarah said frankly. "He had the authority to confine her for the duration of her life, if he so wished."

The young woman had never recovered from the ordeal. Sarah would always be ashamed of the role she had played in her incarceration.

The aroma of cooking meat and fruit wafted over the less savory smells of coal smoke and dung.

The accountant maneuvered them around a crowd of people who watched a pie man through plated glass. "Your word would go a long way in convincing a jury that Mrs. Hart is not insane."

Sarah was only a simple physician, and a woman, at that. "Let us hope so."

"So you have decided."

"There was never any doubt in my mind as to what my decision would be." Sarah stepped over the remains of what she hoped was a pie. "What about you?"

"She is shocking sometimes."

"*I* shocked you, Mr. Addimore." Sarah surreptitiously studied the accountant. "You said I left you men no modesty."

"You suggested that a woman demonstrate a machine."

"And so Miss Fredericks did," she said. "Do you now feel that your modesty has been compromised?"

Sarah enjoyed the blush that came and went in his long face.

He averted his gaze; just as quickly he turned back to stare up at her. "Do not tell me that she did not shock you, too."

"Yes," she admitted. "It was rather shocking to hear her speak pragmatically about sexuality, rather than couching it—as Mr. Nickols said today—in academia."

The coffee shop loomed ahead of them.

"You weren't shocked at what I purchased at the bookstore," the accountant said.

"I'm a physician, Mr. Addimore." Sarah could not stop the heat that filled her face. "I'm fully aware that in order for a man to remain erect, blood must be trapped inside his penis."

He searched her gaze. "And it does not disturb you that a man might have . . . difficulties?"

"If you knew how frail the human physique is, sir," she said, heartbeat accelerating, "you would realize what a miracle it is for a man to be erectile at all."

"But I'm not a patient, Dr. Burns."

Sarah was fully aware that he was not a patient. It had seemed natural to reveal to the members of the Men and Women's Club her fantasy, but alone with this man . . .

"Were you shocked by my purchase?" she asked, masking uncertainty with aggressiveness.

The gray eyes above the glinting side-whiskers and bright red skin were warm in a way she had never before seen. "I have never thought of you as anything other than feminine."

Sarah could not hold back a snort. "I imagine you have never thought of me at all, Mr. Addimore."

He opened the door to the coffee shop. "Then you would be wrong, Dr. Burns."

Frances gently scrubbed a hard shell, concentrating on the oyster within rather than the shame without. "Did anyone ask about my whereabouts?"

"Mrs. Clarring. Dr. Burns." A sharp slice cut through the kitchen; lemon scented the air. "Miss Palmer. They were all concerned about you."

"Mr. Manning, too?" she asked dryly, setting the cleaned oyster on top of its companions.

A sharp blade bit into wood, quartering a lemon half. "Mr. Manning has his own way of demonstrating concern."

Frances glanced at James, at the white towel draped over his shoulder, at his face that was little-boy solemn, at the short, dark lashes that fanned his cheek, gaze trained on his task. He was amazingly helpful in the kitchen.

"Have you ever before prepared food?" she asked curiously.

"Certainly. In school we pilfered sausages, sliced them up quick and ate them before their owners could find us." James carefully quartered the second half of the lemon. "We took our Latin lessons to heart. *Potior est conditio possidentis*, you know."

No, she did not know. "What does that mean?"

His dark lashes swept upward. "Possession is nine points of the law."

Laughter rose inside her chest; it did not make it past the tautness that squeezed her throat. "Did you tell them?"

Hazel eyes intently studied her. "Yes."

Turning away from his gaze, Frances unplugged the drain. "What did you say?"

"The truth."

She pictured the various expressions on the faces of the members of the Men and Women's Club. "I suppose they would eventually find out."

But she wished they needn't.

The scent of lemon surrounded her; simultaneously warm, wet fingers lifted her chin. "You have nothing to be ashamed of, Frances."

Frances glanced up into his eyes; his irises were a thin band of color. "If this goes to trial, my son will need to hire a barrister."

Releasing her chin, James rubbed his fingertips over her lips. "Yes."

"He will refer to me like"—lemon seeped into her mouth; it was pure acid—"like the Attorney General referred to Mary Bartle."

Adulterous. Lustful.

Sticky fingers cupped her face; regret swallowed the thin band of his irises so that all she could see was the darkness of his pupils. "Yes."

Frances drew in a shaky breath. "Will I sit where Mrs. Bartle sat?"

Chapter
54

"Mrs. Humphrey Ward, an esteemed English novelist—but I'm certain I don't have to identify her, as many of you here are no doubt familiar with her works"—feminine titters rippled across the rows of women—"claims that 'the special moral qualities of women' will be eroded if we should involve ourselves with what she calls 'the ordinary machinery of political life.'"

Thomas Pierce slipped into a hard wooden chair.

"Across the pond"—the woman, dressed in unadorned black, leaned over a dull, scarred podium, white egret feather quivering with the force of her emotion—"Miss Catherine Beecher claims that it is *natural* for the society of men and women to be divided."

Thomas had never heard of either Mrs. Humphrey Ward or Miss Catherine Beecher. He glanced at the woman beside him, profile pale in the flickering gaslight. She avidly drank in the speaker's words.

"She advises us to seek out 'new ways to maintain the boundaries between men and women.' We have husbands, Miss Beecher says. We have sons, Miss Beecher proclaims. Why do women need to vote, when we women influence those who do vote?"

The woman beside him had neither a husband nor a son.

"Does your father provide for you and your mother?" Thomas asked, voice overriding that of the speaker.

Jane Fredericks's head snapped around.

She dressed in the uniform of a suffragette, dark dress and cloak without adornment, round hat sporting a single egret feather. It waved at him.

Below a black brim, dark green eyes widened in recognition. "Mr. Pierce!"

"Good evening, Miss Fredericks," he returned calmly.

"What are you doing here?" she asked in a hushed voice.

Her breath vaporized in the chill air between them.

What *was* a junior executive banker doing in a cold, damp hall surrounded by what his mother called 'shrieking sisters and canting brothers'? he wondered.

The speaker promptly wrested away Jane Fredericks's attention. ". . . Beecher is amply supported by the American government. In 1866 Senator George H. Williams said . . ."

Suddenly Thomas knew exactly why he had come to the hall. "I wanted to find out what it is that fires your passions."

She visibly stiffened, her gaze if not her attention focused on the speaker. "You will not hear pornographic confessions here, Mr. Pierce."

What he did hear was the speaker quote the United States Senator George H. Williams. "'When the women of this country come to be sailors and soldiers . . . when they come to navigate the ocean and to follow the plow . . . when they love the treachery and the turmoil of politics . . . when they love the dissoluteness of the camp . . . and the smoke of the thunder . . . and the blood of battle . . . *better* than they love the affections and enjoyments of home and family,'" with each pause the speaker pinned the eyes of another woman, "'then it will be time to talk about making the women voters . . .'"

Thomas very much doubted if the senator had followed the plows: poor men could not afford politics. The American politician reminded Thomas of his mother, holding women up to standards to which he could not aspire.

"You are not responsible for the sins of your father," Thomas offered. Three chairs down, a bonneted head swivelled around. "Nor are you responsible for the suffering of your mother."

"I believe it would be best if you leave, Mr. Pierce," Jane Fredericks said in a low, stilted voice.

Thomas did not move. Instead he demanded, "Convince me that women should vote."

Convince him that a woman's liberty was worth a man's reputation and career.

Jane did not gaze at him, the line of her nose and chin a sharp silhouette. "If you wish to know why women should vote, sir, I suggest you listen to the lecture."

"These last two years," Thomas countered, "you have endlessly repeated the words of Mrs. Butler and other esteemed leaders of women's movements. I would like to hear your words, Miss Fredericks, and not those of someone else."

A volley of *Shh!* rang out over the drone of the speaker's voice.

Jane Fredericks looked neither right nor left. Dark color blurred her cheek.

He had embarrassed her. Having lived all his life in fear of being embarrassed by a woman, Thomas felt strangely free of embarrassment.

"Come have an ice with me," he said unrepentantly, "or I shall get us both evicted."

Another row of heads swivelled toward them.

"How did you know to find me here?" Jane Fredericks hissed.

"Where else would you be on a Saturday night?" he countered.

Without comment, she stood up. For one brief second his face was buried in the softness of her hip—an intriguing sweet scent that was decidedly feminine permeated the smell of damp wool—the next second she wormed between his body and the back of the chair in front of him.

Thomas made a surprising discovery: Jane Fredericks did not wear a wire bustle. He followed her.

Behind him, the speaker's voice boomed out, "It is not 'natural justice' that keeps us chained to our husbands and our sons, but *un*-natural justice! Our very own prime . . ."

The door to the cold, dank hall swung shut behind Thomas.

Scurrying cabs and carriages choked the street. Bobbing gas lanterns wove jagged streaks of light. A woman leaned against a lamppost, her cloak open in blatant invitation.

Jane Fredericks whirled around. "I do not wish for an ice, Mr. Pierce."

The suffragette was three inches shorter than he. In the glow of passing gas lanterns, the hair edging the brim of her round hat alternately shone burnished brown and shadowy black.

"Why not?" he asked intently.

Her nose shot up into the air. "I did not join the Men and Women's Club in order to fornicate."

Pale eyes the color of peridot superimposed the turbid green eyes glaring up at him.

Shame swelled over Thomas. "Is that why you think Mrs. Hart joined the Club?"

"Don't you?" Jane challenged.

He remembered his sarcasm, asking Frances Hart if she had joined the Club to engage in acts of impropriety. He remembered the sadness in her eyes, answering that her body was past the age of doing so.

There had been no sadness in her eyes at the Crystal Palace. She had looked at James Whitcox in a way that no woman would ever look at him.

"Why do you believe pornography causes prostitution?" he asked, deflecting her challenge.

"Because it does," she flatly insisted.

Men denied women the vote *because*. Women denied men their favors *because*.

Thomas was suddenly tired of the games men and women played with one another. "Shall we ask the woman over by the lamppost?"

Jane Fredericks glowered at him. "Don't be ridiculous!"

Thomas did not feel in the least ridiculous. What he did feel was a growing urgency to understand the woman who had weekly sat across from him for two years.

"Are you a virgin, Miss Fredericks?"

"I beg your pardon!"

"Do you use candlesticks or sausages, and wish that they were a man?"

"Do not confuse me with Miss Palmer or Miss Hoppleworth."

Jane Fredericks was younger and prettier than both Esther Palmer and Marie Hoppleworth; he suddenly did not find her nearly as attractive as the plainer, older women.

"What makes you think you're better than they, simply because your father gave your mother a disease?"

"My mother would not have a disease if it were not for women such as they!" she lashed back.

A faceless, nameless man approached the woman who leaned against the lamppost.

"Have you ever thought," Thomas asked remotely, "that your father might not have sought out a prostitute if your mother had been more like Miss Palmer or Miss Hoppleworth?"

The woman calmly pocketed whatever it was that the man paid her.

"You know nothing of my mother, sir!"

"Nor do you know anything of those women, Miss Fredericks." The man and woman disappeared into the shadowy depths of a doorway. Turning his head, Thomas studied the suffragette. "But you would, had you joined our party at the Crystal Palace."

The sounds of snorting horses and groaning carriage wheels filled his ears.

"Are you not afraid," Jane Fredericks unexpectedly asked, "that you have inherited your father's propensity toward licentiousness?"

Understanding cut through him. "I am more afraid that I have inherited my mother's frigidity."

"This is her fault," Jane Fredericks said with sudden violence. "Mrs. Hart is forty-nine years old; she's a *grand*mother. She dresses like a—a trollop, she talks about . . . about self-abuse as if it were perfectly acceptable for women to act upon their animalistic urges, and then she defends women and their marital rights, and how *dare* Mr. Nickols say I have done nothing to advance the cause of women. We will never, ever escape servitude if we do not sublimate our desires. Women *must* be above reproach!"

"Yet," he said quietly, "you voted for her to join."

"Why did you vote for her?" was the swift report.

"Because she didn't judge us."

Frances Hart had not judged any of those who stood in judgment of her.

"He freed her," she said abruptly, "and Mrs. Hart invited me to join them in his private chambers to await the verdict. As if I wanted her to be freed."

It occurred to Thomas that she referred to the Mary Bartle trial, and that the "he" she spoke of was James Whitcox.

"Didn't you want her to be acquitted?" he asked curiously.

"She killed her husband," she said tightly.

"How do you know that?"

"She hung herself."

"Do you ever wish your father were dead?" Thomas asked, probing her prickly emotions.

"I would never harm my father!" Jane Fredericks hotly denied.

But in her thoughts she had.

"Perhaps Mary Bartle, having wished her husband dead, could not live with the guilt of having her wishes come true."

Thomas, much as he hated his mother, still clung to the hope that someday he could care for her.

"My mother claims she loves my father."

A thought suddenly occurred to Thomas. "Where did you get the condom, Miss Fredericks?"

The pain in her green eyes was palpable. "He hides them in a tin—a tin that has the Queen's picture on it, as if that would make them respectable!—and keeps them in their bedroom."

A curious pang pierced Thomas's chest. Too late to protect her from disease, Jane Fredericks's father at least protected his wife from pregnancy.

"They didn't used to sleep in the same bedchamber." Jane's confusion was not feigned. "Why do they do so now?"

A dark shadow leaned against the lamppost. The prostitute had finished with the man and returned to attract another.

Thomas did not know why men and women did the things they did, but he did know the answer to one of her questions. "They come that way."

Jane traded one confusion for another. "What does?"

"The condoms."

"They come in tins bearing the likeness of the Queen?"

"Yes."

"How do you know?"

Thomas remembered the shame he had felt two weeks earlier, approaching a chemist. "Because I purchased one."

He had wanted to know what a rubber sheath would look and feel like peeled over his penis.

"But you're a virgin!" Jane Fredericks gasped, as if his celibacy had earlier elevated him in her esteem, but his purchase of condoms had once again relegated him to the status of "man."

Heat burning his ears, Thomas steadily held her gaze. "I someday hope to find a woman who will help me overcome that obstacle."

When he found such a woman, he would protect her.

"You said you did not enjoy the company of women," she said frigidly.

"I find that I quite enjoy their company when they're not belittling others." And when he stopped looking at them through his mother's eyes.

He had enjoyed escorting the women at the Crystal Palace. But now Frances Hart was in hiding for her liberty. Because of her son. While his mother was free to read the papers.

Thomas had never told her about the Men and Women's Club: it had been his secret. But now his secret was about to be made public to both his mother and to his employers.

"And you think that women who support women's rights denigrate men," Jane Fredericks sneered, sounding uncomfortably like himself three weeks earlier.

Thomas glanced away from the antagonism in her eyes. He was not certain that he cared for Jane Fredericks, or even if he could care for a woman. He was not certain Jane Fredericks could care for him, or for any other man. But he could hope. He could hope that her anger would not exclude love. He could hope that his frigidity would thaw with passion.

He could hope that they could heal the damage that had been inflicted upon them, and which they continued to inflict upon themselves.

"I think, Miss Fredericks—" He reached inside his coat pocket; grasping a stiffly resistant hand, he pressed into her palm two gold bobs. "That you might like to have these."

Her eyes widened with shock. "Why do you think I want these?"

"Because we have to make a decision." Thomas stepped back into the night. "And we both need strength to stand by that decision."

Chapter
55

"Are you certain you want to do this, Frances?" James asked, kneeling at her feet on hard marble.

Harsh organ music ground out over screams and shrills and skidding wheels.

Underneath the brim of her round straw hat, Frances's pale eyes were solemn. "Don't you, James?"

He would do anything to put joy back into her eyes.

"Ice skates have blades instead of wheels." He sat down beside her on the hard wooden bench. "But it's the same principle."

But Frances had neither ice-skated nor roller-skated.

"Are you afraid of falling?" she asked quietly.

"Not at all." James grimly laced on his own skates. "If I fall, I'll make sure I land on top of you, so that you take the brunt of impact."

"Just for that," humor seeped into her voice, "I think I'll find another teacher."

The tightness in his throat loosened, hearing the promise of laughter in her voice.

"Too late." Standing up—quickly he jerked out of a spin—he imperiously held out his hand. "You've solicited me."

"And I suppose you'd sue me for breach of promise," Frances said.

"And I'd win," James said, aiding her.

Bracing her arms to push herself up, Frances stood.

"Steady on," he said, struggling to hold his own feet in alignment. "There. That's not so bad, is it?"

He wondered for whose benefit he spoke. Inside a courtroom he was a master. Inside a skating rink he was a novice.

She took a step and plunged forward. James grabbed her, top hat tilting, both of them skidding around in a dizzying whirl.

A seven-year-old girl with blond hair streaming out from under a paisley bonnet pushed past them and hurtled forward onto the crowded rink.

"James."

He caught his breath, holding them both steady, his heartbeat racing. "What?"

"I don't believe you can skate."

"Frances." A laugh worked its way up into his chest at the total absurdity of what they did. She was a woman hiding from a lunacy order. He was a member of the Queen's Counsel surrounded by men and women who would no doubt recognize his name if not his person. "You wound me."

Challenge sparked in her voice, the old Frances surfacing. "Prove it, sir."

"How can I." He mockingly glanced down at her, her softness and her scent and her resiliency a pleasure so keen it hurt. "You're clinging to me like a limpet."

Immediately Frances snatched back her hands, which had been clenched around his waist. She tilted precariously before awkwardly regaining her balance.

James had not ice-skated since he was a boy in Cambridge. Holding his body stiffly upright—staring at both his feet lest they misbehave—he rolled to the outer perimeters of the marble rink.

Roller-skating, a popular Sunday pastime, appealed to both the middle and the working classes. Bonnets, bowler hats, round hats, boater hats and sporting hats in every size and color raced by.

By weaving his feet in small figure-eight motions, he managed to gain the opposite end of the building.

Triumph surged through him. Glancing up, he caught Frances's gaze through the bobbing, ducking hodgepodge of men, women and children. Leather-gloved hands steepled her mouth. Her eyes shone with his success.

She would have applauded her son's accomplishments with the same exuberance, he thought with a twinge of pleasure-pain. Holding her gaze, drawn by the pride in her eyes, James skated toward her.

His feet, without supervision, flew out from under him.

James landed flat on his buttocks. Pain shot up his spine.

"Bloody hell," he muttered. Only to be riveted by the sight of Frances: she was laughing uninhibitedly.

The corners of his lips hitched upward: a little pain and humiliation were well worth her enjoyment. He grabbed up his silk hat; the brim bore the imprint of a wheel.

James had told Frances that roller skates operated on the same principle as ice skates: they didn't. Blades gained purchase on ice; wheels rolled on marble.

"D'ye want a 'and, ol' man?" asked a cheeky boy who wore a sporting cap pulled down over one eye.

James scowled. "I can manage."

Several minutes later, he still had not gained his feet.

Tan suede flashed out of the corner of his eyes.

Balancing with one knee and one skate on ungiving marble, James caught sight of Frances, straw brim curling, suede coat flapping, green silk skirt fluttering against her legs. Men, women and children glided around her on either side, singly and in couples. She precariously rolled through the skaters, arms raised out from her sides to counteract her body, which tilted back and forth, side to side.

He could not breathe for the sudden fear that tightened his chest. If she fell, he would not be able to catch her.

"James." Pale green eyes suddenly sparkled down at him; her voice was breathless with laughter. "How could I ever have doubted your abilities?"

"I would never have taken you for a woman who gloated," he said drily.

Her clear laughter pealed over the heavy throb of the organ. Grabbing Frances by the waist, James used her stationary body to climb up to his feet.

Her laughter abruptly stopped; awareness shimmered in her gaze. She took his pleasure deep inside her body, her gaze said. She held him when he was at his most vulnerable. She knew him like no other woman would ever know him.

And she liked what she saw.

The heat of her gaze crawled up his spine until he wanted to take her into his arms and protect her from all the hurt that men did to women, simply because they could.

"It's not so easy to laugh at a man when he's on his feet, is it?" he goaded, legs unsteady.

A chain of boys with linked hands whipped around them.

"It's *very* hard to laugh at a man when he stands fully erect," Frances solemnly agreed.

Laughter burst from his lungs and carried on a deep bass chord.

"You're laughing, James," Frances said, as if his laughter were a gift.

James's laughter faded; the emotion she evoked within him did not. Impervious to the curious gazes directed at them, he gripped her waist. "You're skating, Frances."

The joy in her eyes gave way to sudden realization: one must live with the consequences of pain as well as pleasure. Mary Bartle had taught both of them that.

Realization metamorphosed into resolve. "Teach me how to skate faster."

Chapter 56

Rose stood by the glass-topped desk and stared down at her husband. His brown hair—lighter than the wing-backed leather supporting his head—was endearingly tousled. Dark lashes fanned thin, sensitive cheeks. With the afternoon sun streaming through the windows behind him, he looked like the man she had married, sneaking in a quick nap before Sunday dinner.

A cigar butt smoldered on the edge of a heavy silver ashtray.

The ashtray, Rose remembered, had been a wedding present from her younger brother.

Gently she lifted the brandy snifter from between her husband's limp fingers. Tears sprang to her eyes at the familiar warmth of his hand.

An amber splash of liquid sloshed in the bottom of the snifter. Incuriously she lifted the glass to her lips and swallowed.

The liquor burned all the way down her esophagus. Immediately a tiny lump of well-being formed inside her stomach.

A wink of crystal caught her eye: he had drank only two-thirds of the brandy in the decanter.

Impulsively she poured the balloon-shaped glass full of amber liquid and pulled up a wing-backed chair. For long seconds she adjusted to the cold, stiff leather and drank in the silence.

The den was at the back of the townhouse; it faced a small, walled-in garden. Dust motes shimmered in the slanting sunlight.

She had never before realized how peaceful a room it was, with its carved cherry furniture and heavy leather chairs.

"We never talked, Jonathon," she said impulsively. An odd sense of companionship settled over her, drinking his brandy and sitting in his den. She almost felt as if he listened to her, here in his masculine retreat. "We planned, but we never talked."

Cigar smoke hazily rose up from the desk; it smelled of sweet cherry and rich tobacco, a familiar scent. He had always loved his cigar.

"I remember our wedding night. My mother told me you'd hurt me, but I knew you'd never hurt me. And you didn't. You kissed me. You kissed me until I thought my body would melt."

Rose closed her eyes against the brightness of the past, and tasted the burn of brandy and the sweetness of cigar: then; now. Blue eyes as soft as a summer sky smiled at her, sharing the memory of their wedding night.

He had been filled with such gentleness. When he laughed, she had wanted to cry from happiness.

"I didn't know I felt desire, of course. I don't think you did, either." She cradled the fragile snifter against her stomach. "We were both so young. Every night you told me you'd plant a son inside me."

But the seed had never taken. And then the mumps had taken away the seed.

"I didn't know then that what you did was called an ejaculation." She took a long sip of brandy; the long burn was pleasant. "Girls are kept so ignorant." The lump of well-being expanded inside her stomach. "I felt a deep, hot spurt, and I thought it was your love that you released inside me. I thought it was love that made children, Jonathon. I didn't know anything about sperm or the value that men placed upon it."

A dove cooed outside the windows, the mating call more mournful than a lament.

Rose opened her eyes and watched a lazy spiral of smoke form a lopsided circle. "I still don't understand why sperm is more important than love."

A muffled laugh worked up from the kitchen below.

Dinner would soon be served, and she would eat alone. Jonathon would wake in due time, and retire to his solitary bed.

"But I do know"—she rested her head against the comfortingly masculine chair, insulated from the world in which men judged themselves by the children they sired rather than the happiness they inspired—"that I have to make a decision, and I find it's not as simple as one might think."

She took a swig of the liquor and warmed it in her mouth: there was flavor beyond the burn. "I belong to a club, you see. I joined it because I was lonely. I hoped that someday I would learn how to make you love me again."

Jonathon's dark brown lashes flickered. Or perhaps it was her own lashes that flickered, lulled by brandy and the illusion of companionship.

"In the meetings we talked about relations between men and women. At least, that's what we pretended to discuss. The club was much like our marriage. We pretend to be married, but we're not. In the club we pretended to share our thoughts, but we didn't."

James Whitcox had said she was an expert on erotic composition in still-life art. But Rose was no more knowledgeable about erotic composition than she was about the pain infertility caused men.

"One day a woman interrupted our meeting"—she swallowed the lump inside her throat—"and something rather wonderful occurred." She remembered Frances Hart with her impossibly red hair, and James Whitcox with his riveting hazel eyes. "A man looked at this woman, and he asked her a question. A question that in two years of meetings, we had never asked each other. He asked: 'What does a woman desire?'"

Rose stared through a lazy spiral of smoke. "It was such an absurd question. As if it mattered what women desired."

Sunshine illuminated the corner wall of the garden, turning cold brown brick into warm gold.

"But she answered. She answered as if a woman's desires *did* matter"—a blue butterfly fluttered over the golden wall into dark shadow—"while we sat there, too shocked and frightened to respond to this man whom we thought we knew, only to discover that we didn't know him at all."

She glanced down at the crystal snifter cupped inside her hand; gold gleamed on her ring finger. "We had talked about all the reasons why there should be inequality between the two sexes, but we never asked each other—a roomful of men and women—if, for all our differences, we might share the same needs." Raising her hand, she swallowed swirling amber regret. "But he asked. And she answered. And then she said something that I will remember for as long as I live."

Rose closed her eyes, savoring the bittersweet memory. "She said: 'I believe there are women who may want more out of marriage than what their husbands are capable of giving to them, just as I believe there are men who may desire more than what their wives are capable of giving. I do not believe either are at fault.'"

She relived the overwhelming rush of emotion, hearing Frances Hart cast aside marital blame.

"I can't begin to tell you the relief I felt." Rose opened her eyes and stared at the empty garden through a screen of smoke and shimmering dust motes. "All these years, I wanted to believe that the failure of our marriage was my fault. Or that it was your fault. Or that the doctor was to blame. I needed someone to blame. When all along it didn't matter whose fault it was."

She blinked back tears and studied her husband. The light brown hair that was baby fine. The dark lashes that were longer than her own. The pale, sensitive face that was somber even in sleep.

"We have come to this point in our marriage, Jonathon, and I have to make a decision." For twelve years she had ignored the fact that her husband—a successful broker—only drank when he was at home, alone with her and the broken dreams she represented. "I have to accept that I do desire more from this marriage than what you desire."

Rose's tears crawled down Jonathon's cheeks, a brandy-induced illusion, surely; her husband could not cry her tears.

"I love you, but I have to let you go." The smoldering cigar dropped off the edge of the ashtray; burning ashes spilled across the glass-plated desk. Setting down the empty brandy snifter, Rose leaned forward and stubbed out the cigar; the fire inside the ashtray died. "For both our sakes, I have to end the pain."

Chapter
57

"Three years ago Georgina Weldon successfully sued the doctors who signed her lunacy—are you all right, sir?"

"Yes, of course." James glanced up from the stack of papers he was flipping through. "Why do you ask, Mr. Tristan?"

"You keep shifting in your chair as if you're in pain."

Amusement sparked through James. His buttocks sported several bruises, as did his knees. "Mrs. Hart took me roller skating."

Avery Tristan's eyes widened incredulously. "You, sir?"

James remembered the pride in Frances's eyes. "Do you doubt my ability to master eight wheels that simultaneously move in differing directions?"

The clerk's dark eyes lit up with laughter. "Did you?"

It occurred to James that he had never before seen anything other than impersonal courtesy or grave consideration inside Avery Tristan's gaze.

"Yes, I did rather well, I think."

"And Mrs. Hart?"

"She was born on wheels," James said dryly. "Did Mrs. Weldon sue her husband for petitioning the lunacy order?"

"I'm not"—smile fading from the clerk's lips, he thumbed through his notes—"no. She did successfully sue him, but it was for failure to perform his conjugal duties."

The press had dubbed the spiritualist a "lunacy lawyer in petticoats." She had escaped confinement by hiding at a friend's house.

Denton had reported that the madhouse doctor daily called at the rental property.

"See what you can find on suits citing poor steward—"

"Why are you doing this?"

James's head jerked toward the door that had but a few moments earlier been closed. A man who clenched a folded letter in his fist stood on the threshold: he had pale blond hair and deep brown eyes.

"These are private chambers, sir," Avery Tristan said sharply. Out of the corner of James's eye, he saw the clerk push back his chair. "If you wish to question Mr. Whitcox, do so through your solicitor."

The man standing in the doorway ignored the clerk; he focused solely on James. "What have you done with my mother?"

James froze. His clerk froze in similar recognition.

Equal parts of agony and anger reverberated inside the younger man's voice. "Does she know that you're doing this?"

"Prepare a tray, Mr. Tristan." James did not take his gaze away from the man who stood in the doorway. There was nothing of Frances in his features. A small coil knotted his stomach, realizing that this must be what her husband had looked like at the age of thirty-three, eleven years before he took her to wife. "Mr. Hart and I will take tea in the conference room."

The younger man's handsome face flushed an ugly red. "If I were a pig, I wouldn't take slop with you, sir."

"You will take tea with me," James said coolly, rising up from behind his desk, "and you will remember that you are Frances Hart's son, and not mine. If you cannot behave like a gentleman, then Mr. Tristan will escort you from my chambers."

Humiliation ate at the anger burning inside David Hart Junior's eyes. Curtly he nodded his acquiescence.

James gestured toward the arced doorway between them. Stiffly Frances's son preceded him through the arc, heels echoing on the hardwood floor.

The lavatory was immediately to the right; the conference room was further down the hallway. Gray light shone through a curtainless window at the head of a ten-foot-long mahogany table. A long, narrow painting of sun and water bathers relieved the monotony of cream-painted walls.

James firmly shut the door behind him. "Sit down."

The younger man stiffly pulled out a brown leather chair and sat down.

James sat across from him on the opposite side of the table, swivelling forward to fully face him. "Your mother did indeed direct me to file this suit."

Incredulity flickered across his face, one side shadowed, the other side lit by gray light. "She wouldn't know about lawsuits."

"No more than you knew about lunacy orders," James evenly returned.

Humiliation. Anger. Guilt. The three disparate emotions raged inside the younger man's eyes. "My mother wouldn't sue her son!"

"Do you know, David," James said deliberately, "that's exactly what your mother said about you in reference to the lunacy order."

For one second the guilt in the dark brown eyes surpassed the humiliation and the anger. And then the anger superseded all else. "That's Mr. Hart to you, sir."

"When you behave like an adult, I will accord you the courtesy of treating you like one."

"What have you done with her?" David Hart asked tightly.

"I'm keeping her safe from your lunacy order."

Tomorrow the order expired. Tomorrow David could obtain another one.

"You have no right to interfere with this family," David said angrily.

James studied the younger man for long seconds, trying to see the little boy who had learned how to piss in a pot by sinking paper boats. "Do you realize the profound hurt that you have caused your mother?"

There was no acknowledgment in David's eyes.

"I demand to know where you're hiding her," David said instead.

James thought of the love Frances had lavished on her children.

"Do you *care* that you've hurt her almost beyond repair?" he probed.

"If you don't tell me where she is, I'll go to the police and say that you've abducted her."

"David," James said gently, "I know that you've read the newspapers. You must know the influence I have in London."

"This is a heathen city!" David lashed out, so predictably that James almost closed his eyes in embarrassment for him. Frances had said that men who lived in the country were different from men who lived in the city, but they weren't. "My mother would not be like she is now if she had stayed home."

Neither Frances nor James would be as they were if she had not left Kerring, Sussex.

A curious sensation seeped through him, talking to the son who had as a child suckled the woman that James now suckled. "Your mother is deserving of happiness, David."

"What would you know of my mother?" the younger man asked with loathing. "She cried at the birth of my children. Every Sunday we worshipped together—we, her family—and then we sat down and ate dinner together. You see the money my father left her, but you don't know her."

David Hart, James realized, didn't want to see Frances as a woman, because he was still very much a child who needed to bask in the limelight of a mother's love.

I hurt my son very badly, Frances had said. James suddenly understood just how well Frances knew her son.

"You can end this, David," he said quietly.

"How?" David asked suspiciously.

"Sign a contract stipulating that you absolve all legal rights over your mother. And that you will pay her the monthly stipend your father requested in his will."

Shocked silence met James's proposal.

"You'd like that, wouldn't you?" David suddenly sneered.

"Yes, I would," James said honestly.

Frances had been hurt enough.

"You'd like that, because then you'd have access to my mother's money."

If it were a different set of circumstances, James would laugh. He had an annual income of over twenty thousand pounds; the Hart estate brought in an average of one thousand three hundred pounds a year, of which Frances was to receive a monthly stipend of twenty pounds. There was nothing remotely humorous about the hurt that radiated from David Hart, or the pain he could yet inflict upon Frances.

"Yes, I want you to sign that contract," James said bluntly. "I want this to end. I want this to end now. Yet, as your mother's barrister, I want this to go to court. I want her to sue you, and I want her to win. I want her to be able to hold her head up and know that in the eyes of the law she has as much worth as any man. What do you want for her, David?"

A soft knock reverberated through the conference room, Avery Tristan with tea.

"Come in," James called out, gently projecting his voice, watching David Hart's every reaction.

The door swung open; china rattled. David Hart's gaze widened as he took in the heavy silver tea service.

James watched uncertainty flicker off and on inside the brown eyes like an electric switch. "How would you like your tea, David?"

Denial hovered on David's lips; he reluctantly swallowed it. "Cream and two lumps of sugar."

Frances also took her tea with cream and two lumps of sugar.

The clerk neatly deposited white eggshell china rimmed with gold in front of David.

Lemon scented tea wafted under James's nose; at the same time, china clinked against the mahogany table in front of him. "Thank you, Mr. Tristan."

The door softly closed behind the clerk.

Steam coiled upward from David's tea, dissipated into gray light. "I want to see my mother."

"I will pass on the request." For once James the barrister and James the man were in complete harmony. "If she agrees, we'll meet at a place that I designate."

"I am her son." Renewed anger flared in David's eyes. "I am entitled to see her without you twisting her every thought."

James intently studied the younger man. "Do you have so little faith in your mother, David, that you really think I or anyone else could persuade her to do something she didn't want to do?"

"She's a woman," David said curtly. "Women are guided by men."

James picked up the little silver spoon resting beside his cup and gently stirred clear black tea; slowly he glanced up through a cloud of gray steam and captured David's dark gaze. "You acknowledge that your mother is a woman, then."

Violent crimson flooded the younger man's tanned face. "How dare you."

"How dare I what?" James asked calmly.

"How dare you talk about my mother when my father is not even cold in his grave."

"What exactly is it that bothers you, David?" James tapped the silver spoon against the edge of his cup, one sharp, definitive tap. "The fact that your mother is a woman with her own needs, or the fact that she isn't there to take care of you?"

David stood up, table rocking, tea sloshing. "I will not listen to this."

"You will listen to this, and worse, if we go to court."

"I want to see my mother."

"I will pass on your request."

"I want to see my mother now."

"What does the rest of the Hart family think about the lunacy order?" James set down the spoon onto the saucer, a small clink of silver and china. "Do they think their mother belongs in a mad-house?"

The flush of anger darkened with guilt; promptly the guilt was swallowed by anger.

"It doesn't matter what they think," David retaliated. "I am the eldest, and I am responsible for my family."

The younger man did not realize just how revealing a face he had: it was as revealing as his mother's face.

"You will find, David, that what they think will matter very much in a court of law."

"I want to see my mother," he stubbornly repeated. "Alone."

"I don't trust you." James remembered the tears Frances had cried, cradled in his arms on the bathroom floor. He remembered the pain in her voice, whispering the words David had told her. "You will see her in my company, or you will not see her at all."

"*You* don't trust—" David choked back the rest of the sentence. Stiffly he capitulated. "Very well. But I want to see her today."

Chapter
58

"Mr. Tristan." Frances tentatively accepted the bare masculine hand and stepped down onto a small iron step. A warning jangle of harnesses rang out. Awkwardly she leapt to the curb. "You needn't have come out into the cold. I know my way to Mr. Whitcox's office."

"Fresh air is never unwelcome, Mrs. Hart." The clerk's fingers tugged her forward onto the pavement before releasing her hand. "Mr. Whitcox is concerned for your safety."

Frances flushed, remembering the worry she had caused when leaving the city. "I'm sorry for the extra work I'm causing you."

"On the contrary, ma'am." Companionably the young man cupped her elbow, deftly guiding her around a clutch of men and through the courthouse doors. "I work fewer hours now than I've ever worked."

A thrill of concern raced down her spine. "I'm not interfering with his work, am I?"

"Only in the best possible way."

A familiar corridor loomed ahead of them. "How is that?"

"Murder trials are draining, Mrs. Hart."

And lawsuits were not? But perhaps a lawsuit would not be necessary, after all.

Cautiously Frances probed. "You met my son."

"Very briefly, ma'am."

There was no expression in his voice. The meeting could have been pleasant. Or the meeting could have been distasteful. Avery Tristan would never betray his clients by revealing his emotions.

"You are very much like Mr. Whitcox, sir," Frances said ruefully.

The door to James's private chambers loomed ahead of her.

"I take that as a compliment, Mrs. Hart."

"It was intended as one, Mr. Tristan."

The clerk swung open the heavy mahogany door.

Uncertainty clogged her throat. The hope precipitated by David's request to see her dimmed with the knowledge that David and James had now met face to face. The mother inside her wanted the two men to like each other; the woman inside her realized that the circumstances were not conducive to liking.

James rose up from behind his desk and intercepted her by the door. There was no expression on his face, either.

"Where is my son?" she asked, head tilting, throat tightening.

Lashes shielding his eyes, James reached for the buttons on her coat. "He's in the conference room."

Acutely aware of the clerk who was hanging up his coat on the brass coat tree behind her, Frances quickly assisted James in releasing the short row of rattan buttons. Her progress was hindered by kid gloves. "I didn't know you had a conference room."

Every day she learned something new about James. She wasn't certain she was prepared to learn how he and her son dealt with one another.

As Avery slid the suede coat off her shoulders, James tugged her reticule off her wrist; her gloves quickly followed.

"You two would make excellent coat clerks," Frances said.

Amusement glinted in James's eyes.

"Thank you, Mrs. Hart," the clerk murmured, exactly like James, as he plucked the gloves and reticule out of James's hands.

"Does he still want to see me?" she asked, heart suddenly gorging her throat.

"Shall I make a fresh pot of tea, sir?"

"Not now, Mr. Tristan." Familiar heat lightly swept the length of her back before settling into the intimate notch between her bustle and her lower spine. "This way, Frances."

A dim corridor was made even darker by mahogany paneling. Flickering gaslight lit up a windowless lavatory.

Frances peered inside, purposefully delaying the coming meeting. "You don't have a combination bath."

"An oversight I shall remedy," James said, breath a wisp of moist heat against her ear.

He was teasing her. Or perhaps not.

The closed door at the end of the short corridor loomed larger than life. It could only be the door to the conference room.

Frances turned into the comfort of James's body. "Do I look . . . respectable?"

"Frances." The darkness in his eyes squeezed her heart. "You *are* respectable."

She automatically smoothed out a wrinkle in his gray-striped waistcoat. "But I don't look the way he wants me to look."

Firm fingers cupped her face, his skin melting into her skin. "Do you look the way *you* want to look?"

Guiltily Frances glanced upward, torn between the son that waited for her and the man who touched her.

"I—" She slipped her hands inside his frock coat and circled his waist; the memory of his eyes when he looked at her naked body welled up inside her. "Yes."

"Then that's all that counts."

Frances had learned from firsthand experience that what her son thought counted very much indeed.

"I showered this morning, and then I showered again when you rang me, but I still feel you, James." Her fingers independently dug underneath his waistcoat, seeking the silk of his shirt and the warmth of his skin. "I'm going to greet my son with you inside me, and I know that he would consider that the greatest betrayal of all."

"You could have used the Rose Jet."

"But I'm not ashamed of what we do."

"I'm glad." The stark planes of his face softened. Lowering his head, he kissed her, a press of warm lips that briefly clung like burning resin. "Let's go talk to your son."

"Yes." Frances tucked the back of his shirt more firmly into his trousers and then smoothed down his waistcoat. "Let's."

David wanted to see her. That was a positive sign, surely. He loved her. She loved him. Together they would work through their pain.

The sudden stiffness of James's body should have alerted her.

Frances turned and stared into chocolate brown eyes. Her husband's eyes. Her son's eyes.

Chapter
59

"I didn't believe it, Mama." David Hart's face and voice were expressionless with shock, and something far more dangerous. "I read in the newspaper that you were cavorting with this man, but I didn't believe you'd lost all sense of propriety. I came to London to admit that I may have acted hastily, but I see the doctor was right. You need help. Until you receive the help you need, you may not set foot in my home. Nor may you contact my wife or my children. I will not have you taint them." Curtly he nodded his head. "I will see you in court, Mr. Whitcox, although I fail to see how you can represent my mother when it is you, sir, who have made her a whore."

David Hart shouldered past James; instinctively James drew Frances closer to the wall to allow her son passage.

Frances turned to follow, her pain fisting inside his chest. "David—"

James grasped her around the waist and pulled her back against him. "Let him go, Frances."

Her diaphragm rapidly expanded and contracted against his fingers.

"That's not—" *That's not my son*, she wanted to say, but they had both seen that it was. Wood slammed against wood, the door to James's chambers. "He didn't—"

James stopped her lie. "He meant every word of it." And then, projecting his voice, "Mr. Tristan."

Immediately the clerk stepped into the narrow corridor. "Yes, sir?"

"Two brandies, please."

"Very good, sir."

"We have to talk, Frances," James murmured against her ear; her scent of vanilla blended with the fresh scent of soap. "Come into the conference room."

Stiffly Frances turned and preceded him through the open door. Unlike her son, she chose the chair nearest the door, facing the window at the opposite end of the table.

Leaning behind her, James opened the double doors of the credenza; he pulled out a notepad and a handful of sharpened pencils. Straightening, turning, he dropped the supplies in front of Frances, yellow wooden pencils rolling across mahogany wood.

Her face remained pale with shock.

"Frances." James knelt down beside her chair. Gray light silhouetted her. "Your son loves you."

She turned toward him; the features he knew as well as his own were pinched. "I know that, James."

But knowledge didn't stop pain.

Frances had said that if hurt wasn't intentional, then it didn't last. James hoped she was correct.

"He's doing what he thinks is right," James said, trying to ease her pain, "even though it hurts him." Righteousness was both the hardest yet the easiest emotion to exploit. "You're doing what you think is right, even though it hurts you. You are very much alike."

"I used to think so." The pain in her eyes cut him in places he had not thought could hurt. "I'm sorry for what he said about you."

James grasped the arms of her chair and swivelled the seat so that she more fully faced him. "Is this the first time he's called you a whore, Frances?"

Shame slashed through her eyes. "No."

"When else?"

"When I returned—" Her lips pursed to form the word *home*, but David had made it clear that her home was now his home, and that she was not welcome in it; immediately her mouth relaxed into a flat line. "To Kerring."

David had twice mentioned that Frances needed "help."

James turned the chair so that Frances fully faced him. Her knees pressed on either side of his groin. They instinctively widened to accept him. "Tell me why your son thinks you need help."

Her eyes were luminous in the gloom of the conference room.

"His father—" She bit her lip; James felt the bite of her teeth. "My husband has been dead for only four and one half months."

"What else?" he asked, hips widening her knees, arms boxing her in.

Frances glanced away from him, holding back. "I'm not wearing mourning."

"What else?" James relentlessly pursued.

"I'm not . . . I don't dress like I did before I came to London."

This was the type of information of which the private investigator would have had no knowledge.

"How did you dress before you came to London?" he asked gently.

A soft knock, more a whisper of knuckles, reverberated inside the conference chamber.

Frances's knees burned his hips through the wool of his trousers. "Come in, Mr. Tristan."

Delicate rose flushed her pale cheeks; she did not pull away from the intimate contact. The dull impact of glass on wood sounded in the silence. Out of the corner of his eyes, he glimpsed two brandy snifters beside the pad of paper, amber liquor sloshing, retreating hands a flash of olive-tinted flesh.

"Will there be anything else, sir?"

"Cancel my appointments for the rest of the day."

"Yes, sir."

James addressed Avery Tristan, but he focused on Frances. "Did you talk to the clerk?"

Frances, suddenly inquisitive, met James's gaze.

"Yes, sir, he's looking to squeeze us in."

"Very good, Mr. Tristan." James wanted the trial over with as quickly as possible. "You may leave as soon as you've cancelled my appointments; I won't need you for the rest of the day."

"Thank you, sir."

The door softly clicked shut.

"Was Mr. Tristan referring to squeezing in my—our—trial?"

"Yes." He returned to the point of concern. "How do you dress differently?"

The flush tinting her cheeks darkened. She was so clearly afraid of telling him something that would lower her in his esteem.

"I dressed more . . . sedately."

Practical attire like the flannel nightgown and wrapper, James deduced.

"You're not a sedate woman," he said, reassuring her.

"But I was, James." Sadness filled her eyes. "My son said he didn't know me. I'm not certain I know myself. I'm not the same woman that I was in Kerring."

David Hart's counselor would use the changes in Frances to his every advantage.

"Why else does your son think you need help?" he asked softly.

Denial flashed inside her eyes. She glanced away from him. Her breasts underneath the green silk bodice rapidly rose and fell.

"Frances." James released the leather chair arms and cupped her face, her skin soft and warm. "There is nothing you can say that will change the way I feel about you."

Her gaze snapped back to his. Defiance leapt into her eyes. "How do you feel about me?"

He addressed the fullness of her top lip instead of the question in her eyes. "I asked you to marry me."

"To protect me," she swiftly asserted.

Raising his lashes, he pinned her gaze. "And you turned down my protection."

She closed her eyes against the truth: she didn't trust her son, but neither did she trust James. Simply because he was a man.

There was only one way she would ever trust him again.

The heat of her skin singed his coaxing thumbs. "Tell me, Frances."

Dark rose spilled out from underneath his fingers. "I dyed my hair."

Delight at her feminine vanity tickled his chest.

"I like it," he murmured, fingers sliding over the hot velvet that was her skin. Gently he touched the loose tendrils of hair at the nape of her neck. "It becomes you."

She had stood on the threshold of the boardroom like a beacon of hope with her blazing red hair and fertile green dress.

One moment his compliment lit up her face; the next second the light drained out of her eyes. She reached out and trailed a finger down his cheek; sensation tightened his testicles. "Were I my son, James, I would be very concerned about my well-being."

"Perhaps." He grasped her hand—smaller than his, softer than his—and planted a kiss inside her palm. Standing he dropped down into the chair to her right and plucked up a snifter of brandy. "Drink up. I want you to tell me everything that has transpired between you and your son."

Frances gingerly accepted the glass. "Are you trying to make me bosky, Mr. Whitcox?"

James cupped the second snifter in the palm of his hand, warming the brandy as he warmed her breasts while she slept, her buttocks snug against his groin. "*In vino veritas.*"

"What is that?" she asked. Crinkling up her nose—James noticed a smattering of freckles that had not been there before her sojourn to Sussex—she took a sip of the liquor.

"In wine there is truth," he said, watching her reaction to the twenty-year-old brandy.

"Oh." Frances looked in surprise at the amber liquid. "This tastes different than what I purchased."

"Better?" he asked curiously. "Or worse?"

"I'm sure it's a very good brand, James," she hastily assured him, fear of hurting him pushing aside her own damaged emotions.

"Here." James's eyes crinkled with laughter. "Taste it properly."

Frances instantly leaned over the table toward him.

Taking a sip of brandy and holding it in his mouth, James met her. Her lips blossomed open for him.

He leaned back an inch. "What do you think now?"

She licked her lips, unaware of how utterly seductive she was in the simple pleasure she took in him. "Much better, thank you."

Frances's love of sensation went beyond sexual into the realm of sensual.

He sat back and picked up a pencil to keep himself from taking more than a kiss. "Tell me word for word what occurred between you and your son."

"There's not much else, really. I told him I"—Frances hesitated for long seconds; James glanced up from the sharpened lead—"I told him I loved his father."

Bittersweet emotion filled him, hearing her declaration of love for another man.

"And?" he prompted neutrally.

Shame shone in her eyes. "David said I loved his father so much that I couldn't wait to get to London to spend his money."

James glanced down at the blank notepad. "He implied I was interested in your money."

"I'm sorry."

Twice now she had apologized for the actions of her son. James had not, nor would he ever, apologize for his son.

He scribbled the word *money* and crossed it out. "Did he say anything about our relationship?"

"He said it was disgusting."

James jotted down the word *sex* before warily glancing up. "What did you say?"

The shame she had felt for her son turned inward. "I asked him if he thought his father was disgusting for marrying me."

Touché, James thought with a twinge of admiration. "What else?"

Frances cradled the brandy snifter between her hands for long seconds before lifting the glass and taking a fortifying drink. "The doctor has convinced him that I am ill because my body has gone through the change."

James wished he was surprised. He had long ago ceased being surprised by the words of men.

"Tell me what life was like before you came to London," he said, underlining the words *change of life*.

James had seen the worst of David; Frances made James see the best. He was a good father. He was a loving husband. He was a devoted son.

Yet he now called his mother—a woman who had nurtured him, nursed his father, embraced his wife, and cared for his children—a whore.

"What do the rest of your children think about David's actions?"

"I don't know."

"You didn't see anyone besides David?"

"Margaret, my daughter-in-law." Remembered pain inflected her voice. "My granddaughter."

David had two daughters: seven-year-old Megan and two-year-old Margaret, named after her mother.

"What did Margaret say?"

"She said I was beautiful."

James's head snapped up. "She likes the way you look now?"

Frances stared at the amber liquor in the bottom of her glass. "She said she did."

James watched the strain on her face. "Had she ever before said that you were beautiful?"

"No."

Had anyone ever praised Frances?

"Why did she compliment you when you returned to Kerring?" he probed.

"I don't know." Taking a deep, shuddering breath, Frances glanced up. "Margaret had bade Megan—my granddaughter—to check on her brother and baby sister. Megan"—reminiscent laughter briefly sparked Frances's eyes—"said she couldn't do that, that Margaret should check on the children while she and I had a cozy."

An ache traveled through James's chest, seeing the love she bore her granddaughter: a granddaughter whom her son had expressly forbidden her to contact.

"I told Megan that she couldn't have the surprise I'd brought her if she didn't obey her mother. When Megan left the room, Margaret said: 'You look beautiful, Mother Hart,' and then, 'I've never seen you look more beautiful.'"

Mother Hart. How strange to think of such a bland appellation applied to Frances.

"So Margaret said you're more beautiful now than you were before you came to London." James absentmindedly balanced the pencil between his fingers. "What happened next?"

She glanced away from him. "I told her it was raining in London, and that I no doubt looked like a drowned rat."

Frances was as uncomfortable with compliments from her family as she had been from him.

"What did she say then?" he asked gently.

"She said"—Frances toyed with the stem of the snifter—"she said, 'No.' She said my skin glowed. And then she said I was . . . simply . . . beautiful."

Margaret was remarkably perceptive.

"Your skin does glow."

But the compliment didn't light up her face.

He tossed down his pencil; it bounced on the legal pad, rolled onto the table. "I'm going to subpoena Margaret."

Confusion flickered in her gaze. "I don't understand."

Marie Hoppleworth had claimed that he and Frances had given the Club a language in which men and women could discuss sexuality: the language of desire. All too soon they would learn the language of law.

"A subpoena," he said shortly, "is a writ ordering a person to testify in court."

"Do you mean"—incredulity superimposed her confusion—"that a subpoena makes a person testify whether they want to or not?"

James watched Frances's face to gauge her reaction. "Yes."

The expression blossoming in her pale green eyes sent a warning chill down his spine. "You would *force* Margaret to testify on my behalf?"

Chapter
60

"Please wait up, Mr. Nickols."

John gripped hard metal.

A pigeon clattered upward into the sky.

Pushing a hooded black perambulator, a man in a dark blue striped coat walked around the left of his wheelchair. Simultaneously a woman wearing a gray cloak—hands thrust inside a dark blue velvet muff—walked around the right of his wheelchair.

Stomach clenching, he forcefully pivoted his chair.

Afternoon sunlight momentarily blinded him.

Perambulator wheels clacking—heels clicking—the family of three converged behind a dark, motionless shadow.

"Miss Hoppleworth," John curtly acknowledged. "Are you lost?"

"No," Marie Hoppleworth said; she pressed her fingers over a braided frog that fastened the front of her black wool cloak. "I'm not lost."

John involuntarily followed the movement of her hand. Small breasts rapidly rose and fell around a gray wool glove.

A pulse leapt to life inside his palm.

It had been six years since he had cupped a woman's breast. Six years since he had felt a woman's heartbeat.

John felt it now, a vulnerable fluttering like the wings of a bird.

"Have you come to take comfort from me?" he asked sardonically, fighting down a ridiculous surge of hope.

"Would you give it?" Marie Hoppleworth returned.

"I offered you comfort at the Crystal Palace."

"I sat on your comfort, Mr. Nickols."

Heat burned his ears, remembering his erection that had sought the pressure of her body through the double barrier of their clothing. "Did you go home to a sausage?"

"Did you go home to French postcards?" she riposted.

He had gone home to loneliness, as had she.

John stared past the black-cloaked figure that cast a dark shadow over him. The family of three rounded the corner of a square brick building plastered with advertisements. Beyond the jumble of pictures and words, men and women and horses and carriages passed by in a blur of motion.

He lived only a few blocks from the newspaper office. A sharp sense of invasion—that the secretary had followed him nearly to his lodgings—pierced him.

"This is not a convenient time," he said shortly, head averted, left hand gripping a metal wheel more firmly to turn the chair. "I have work to do." John did not lie: there was always another story to edit; another sex scandal to expose; another night to get through. "If you'll excuse me . . ."

"You're not the only one who's afraid, Mr. Nickols."

John hadn't wanted to know about the lives of the twelve members of the Men and Women's Club, because he hadn't wanted them to know about his life. But now he did know them. And now they knew of his fear.

"Really, Miss Hoppleworth. Of what do you have to be afraid?" He tilted up his head, eyes narrowing against the sunlight. "Are you afraid I'll mug you?"

Silver glinted around the shadow of her eyes. "Are you afraid I'll mug you?"

John's fingers fisted around metal. "You don't think a woman can mug a man?"

"I think a woman can do anything a man can do, Mr. Nickols."

"If that were the case, Miss Hoppleworth," John retorted, "Mrs. Hart would not now be hiding in order to escape a madhouse."

"*Can*, Mr. Nickols, designates ability, not legality," the secretary replied as correctly as any schoolteacher.

A sudden spurt of wind whipped at her skirts; at the same time, a shock of hair swept across John's forehead.

"Will you lose your employment when the trial goes public?" he asked abruptly.

"I privately tutor students," she returned. "They can barely read their assignments, let alone a newspaper. Will it affect your position with the paper?"

"Not likely." John stared up at the black bonnet and swaying feather surrounded by blinding sunshine. And couldn't remember what it felt like to not look up at a woman. Had his neck ever cricked from looking down? "I'll bring additional attention to the *Gazette*."

Newspapers didn't care about lives, they only cared about sales.

"She must have informed someone: a friend or a relative," Marie Hoppleworth said, voice puzzled rather than condemning. "She told us that the people in her village wouldn't understand how a woman who belonged to the Club could call herself respectable. Why do you think she told?"

Frances Hart had not once eluded their questions, no matter how impolite.

"I don't think she's capable of duplicity."

"Unlike us."

Familiar scents wafted the air: manure; coal; baking bread; cooked cabbage. The sour aroma of fear.

"Unlike us," John repeated grimly.

Chill air invaded the wool of his coat.

"*Have* you ever been mugged by a woman?"

John remembered his excitement, bandying vulgar slang with the secretary. He wanted to feel that excitement again. He wanted to see the exhilaration in her eyes, the woman in her challenging the man in him.

"I was mugged by a prostitute during sex," he said, deliberately crude.

He had been drunk. He had been lonely. A woman on the street had been readily available.

"Did you use a machine?" she asked pragmatically.

"It never got that far." Remembered humiliation poured over him. "She didn't want sex, she wanted money."

A constable had found him in an alley, cursing and crying, sitting on a bed of dung and rotted refuse, unable to mount his overturned chair.

"There is a phrase for orgasm that I never understood until recently."

"Which phrase is that?" John asked harshly, eyes narrowed against the brightness of the sun.

"'Get home,' Mr. Nickols."

The sexual slang for orgasm elicited a sharp pang of longing.

The clip-clop of a lone horse echoed on the cobblestoned street.

John had not ridden prior to the stabbing that had paralyzed him: now he would never ride. A horse. A *woman*.

"Why are you here, Miss Hoppleworth?" he asked flatly.

She had felt the impotence of his legs that had lifelessly hugged her shoulders. And then she had walked away from him.

"I came to apologize."

It was the sun that caused the burning in his eyes, only the sun.

"I don't want your pity," he bit out. "Obviously you were repulsed by my attentions at the Crystal Palace. No more need be said."

"I am not repulsed by you, Mr. Nickols."

"And so, overwhelmed by my attractions"—he gripped the metal wheels more tightly—"you couldn't wait to get away from me."

"Yes."

Searing sun rays stabbed his eyes.

"Yes, you couldn't wait to get away from me?" he jeered.

"Yes, I was overwhelmed by your attractions." John was all of a sudden painfully aware of the woman who eclipsed the sun while the lone horse and rider passed him by. "It was not from you that I turned away."

For one galvanizing second John almost believed her.

"Do tell, Miss Hoppleworth," he mocked.

"Life in a county orphanage does not foster confidence," Marie Hoppleworth finally said, egret feather a dancing shadow. "Children die. Children run away. Sometimes, Mr. Nickols, children simply disappear."

Sold into child labor. Or sold to brothels.

"You're afraid to trust a man," he said tonelessly.

The clopping hooves grew fainter; the silence between them grew longer.

"Orphans who trust, Mr. Nickols," she agreed in her best secretarial voice, brisk and no-nonsensical; piercing sunlight crossed the feather, forcing him to look away, "don't survive."

John had thought men in wheelchairs could not afford to trust. And then a barrister had offered his shoulder. He had never felt as intimately bound to another man than when clasping James Whitcox and George Addimore and exiting the train like other men.

The receding horse lifted a cropped tail and left behind a reminder of its passage.

John's gaze snapped upward to the dark silhouette of a black bonnet. "And having apologized, Miss Hoppleworth, what then?"

A gloved hand nervously fondled a braided frog.

Marie Hoppleworth had high, conical breasts.

Anger and pain and desire roiled inside his stomach.

Breasts were the first thing a man in a wheelchair saw of a woman. Every day he gazed at women's breasts. Every day women walked away from him.

And every day he died a little.

"If my apology were accepted," she said, "I would ask a boon."

John's head snapped upward. "What boon is that?"

"I laced my shoe too tightly"—the burning heat of the sun invaded his chest—"and I am in need of a chair."

Chapter 61

*F*rances echoed down the dim corridor.

Heels tapping, bustle bouncing, spine straight, Frances walked alone. Closed doors silently witnessed her decision.

Familiar footsteps followed. Familiar footsteps advanced.

Frances had the curious sensation of walking two corridors at once: the museum; the courthouse.

"Frances." One second she faced the light at the end of the corridor; the next second the corridor twirled, and she was in the courthouse, facing James. Long fingers curled around her upper arms. "I told you that a lawsuit will affect the lives of others."

The white silk of his scarf glowed in the dim light. Heat penetrated the leather of her coat and the silk of her dress: it throbbed like a heartbeat.

A calmness that had nothing to do with brandy and everything to do with conviction spread through her veins. "I will not force anyone to testify on my behalf, James."

Hot breath gusted her upturned lips; he smelled of the brandy she had drank from his mouth. "Frances, a subpoena is merely a formal procedure to summon witnesses."

Her mouth tightened with resolution. "No."

His fingers tightened, almost hurting her, but not quite. "Do you think Margaret wants you to be committed to a madhouse?"

"Margaret and David love one another."

Their faces lit up as if they were touched by sunlight when they were in the same room. Frances would not step between her son and the woman he loved.

"What about you, Frances?" James asked harshly. "Don't you deserve to be loved, too?"

Love.

David claimed it was love that had compelled him to sign a lunacy order, but it wasn't. The vicar claimed it was love that made a family, but love wasn't enough.

"James." She grasped the dangling ends of his scarf. "This is between my son and me."

"Frances." James's voice and face were implacable. "I'll only call Margaret to the box if it's strictly necessary, but we must subpoena the members of the Men and Women's Club."

She remembered the excitement they had shared, visiting the Achilles Book Shoppe. She remembered the confidences they had exchanged, sitting around a mahogany table. She remembered the comradery they had experienced, exploring the Crystal Palace.

She remembered their vulnerability, walking away from each other inside the Victoria Station.

Frances had betrayed them by telling her son about the Club; she would not further betray them by forcing them to testify. "I can't let you do that, James."

"Don't you think that if we don't subpoena them"—Frances had never before witnessed anger in James: the hazel eyes staring down at her blazed with it—"the defense attorney will?"

"I'm not responsible for what David's barrister does."

"But I am responsible for you, Frances."

"Are you, James?" Frances asked evenly, fingers clinging to the threads of white silk.

"This isn't a matter of who pays for whose dinner," he bit out.

"James." Frances took a calming breath. "This is my fault."

The blazing anger in his eyes stilled.

"*I* did this." Frances's throat tightened, acknowledging responsibility. Releasing the anchor of his scarf, she slipped her hands inside the black gape of his outer coat, unerringly found the inner gape of his frock coat. She fanned her fingers over the front of his waistcoat. His heart pounded against her palm. "I am responsible for my son. It is because of *me* that my son has done this. Only I, James, can right this situation."

Pain bled in his eyes. "Frances—"

Frances didn't want his pain. She had felt David's pain until she had thought she would choke on it. She wanted James's support.

Deliberately she interrupted him: "What can Margaret or the members of the Men and Women's Club say that I can't?"

Regret replaced the pain in his eyes. The fingers cuffing her arms curved to span her shoulders. "The law doesn't operate on the principles of right or wrong, Frances."

"Of course it does," she said firmly. "What would be the purpose of a court system if it didn't?"

"There is a difference between right or wrong, and legal or illegal." A familiar remoteness shone in his eyes. "Jurors are instructed to reach a verdict based upon law, Frances, not good will."

He loved the law, but he did not believe in it.

"They acquitted Mary Bartle," Frances said.

Cynicism curved his lips. "They acquitted Mary Bartle because she made a better victim than her husband."

Frances refused to be a victim, even to win emancipation.

"Perhaps, James," she said evenly, "jurors are not as cynical as the men who practice law."

"If I summon you to the witness box, Frances"—the dark shadow of his lashes hollowed his cheeks—"the defense attorney will also examine you."

The heat of his body offset a chill of apprehension: the Attorney General had not been kind to Mary Bartle. But the Attorney General was a prosecutor for the Crown; he would not be questioning Frances.

"Then let him," she said with a confidence she was far from feeling.

"I can't allow that," he said flatly.

Her heart beat in time with his.

There was not one single part of her body that he had not minutely examined. There was not one single part of his body that she had not minutely examined.

Caressing. Probing.

Tasting.

Loving.

He was a part of her, but she could not let him tear apart the people whom she valued.

"Then I will solicit another barrister."

The thick lashes snapped upward; his heart rhythmically pounding against her palm accelerated. She knew that he simultaneously felt the acceleration of her pulse. "Frances, I will not lose you."

Frances didn't know what would happen when the trial ended—when she won, or when she lost—but she did know that she would have to live with the consequences. "James, it's my life that will be on trial. You said so. You said that everything I've ever done will be held against me. I have the right to speak in my defense, surely. The doctor has convinced my son that my age"—no, not her *age*—"that the change women go through is a sickness." The memory of Rose's Lubrifiant—proof that there were other women such as herself who desired but who were unable to produce the fluids associated with womanhood—fortified her. "I can't believe that men . . . that *jurors* can look me in the eye and believe that my happiness is a symptom of illness." Frances looked into James's eyes and let him see the truth. "And I am happy with you, James. I didn't think it was possible to be this happy.

"Perhaps, if my son sees this happiness, he'll be able to accept the fact that I do not belittle the memory of his father. Perhaps he'll understand that because of his father—and because of the love I bear my family—I am now able to make a new life for myself."

The darkness inside his eyes grew so stark that it hurt to look at him. "What if you lose, Frances?"

"I can't, can I?" she asked, tears pricking the back of her eyelids. "You're my barrister, and you never lose."

James closed his eyes while his fingers cradled her shoulders and she timed the rhythm of his heartbeat against her palm. Slowly the drumming cadence settled.

Hands falling, eyes opening, he said, "Let's go home."

An image of the sprawling brick building in Kerring, Sussex, flitted through her mind's eye. Her past. Not her future.

Tonight, Frances thought, was the last night that she would know with any certainty what awaited her: the lunacy order would expire on the morrow. She wouldn't know if her son signed another order until doctors came knocking on her door. She wouldn't know if she won the lawsuit until jurors awarded a verdict.

She didn't know if she and her son could ever reconcile, but she wouldn't worry about that anymore.

"Let's dine out," she said impulsively.

His lashes slowly lifted; light illuminated his face. "Where?"

She had last taken him roller-skating.

"You decide," she said magnanimously.

His eyes narrowed. "What of gossip, Frances?"

She took a deep breath. "Mrs. Jenkins says that a woman has one life."

"And what does Mrs. Jenkins suggest a woman do with that life?"

"She suggests a woman grab it with both hands, or it will pass her by and leave nothing but a smelly old fart in her face."

Chapter
62

"We have a date, sir," Avery Tristan murmured. "I've prepared the subpoenas."

James stared down at his notes. The underlined words *sex* and *change of life* dominated the page. "Tear them up."

"Sir?"

Slowly James glanced up at the young clerk. "Mrs. Hart doesn't want us to summon witnesses on her behalf."

The clerk's dark brown eyes flickered. "Why?"

"She believes that moral right supersedes the principles of law."

"Shouldn't it?"

"Law doesn't operate on 'should,'" James said cynically.

"Mrs. Hart is a charming woman."

"Are you an admirer, Mr. Tristan?"

James flinched at the harshness in his voice.

"Yes," the clerk said simply.

James leaned back in his chair. "I don't want her to be hurt."

"I think she's stronger than what you may think, sir."

James knew from firsthand experience just how strong Frances was: she had fully faced his anger without a flicker of an eyelash.

And he had been angry. He had been angry because he was frightened. He had never lost a case. But he had never cared if he lost.

James cared very much about Frances.

"I've never been a plaintiff," James said flatly.

He would open the trial with a statement, instead of tailoring his opening on that of the plaintiff. The counsel for the defense would close the trial, tailoring his closing speech on James's.

"I think it will work very well, sir," the clerk said bracingly.

James glanced up into the younger man's honest brown eyes.

The clerk saw his vulnerability. The clerk saw his fear.

What would the twelve jurors see when they looked at Frances? A whore who betrayed her deceased husband? A mother in need of "help" because she could no longer beget children?

James held the clerk's gaze. "We must win this trial, Mr. Tristan."

"I can't imagine you losing, sir."

"I have heard it said that one never hears the bullet that kills one."

"My brother, who is a lieutenant in the army, claims differently."

"Your brother is alive, sir," James said, eyes crinkling with amusement.

The clerk did not share his laughter. "But many of his comrades are not."

The brief spark of humor died. "She doesn't want to hurt anyone, Mr. Tristan."

All Frances wanted was twelve men—all with mothers who more likely than not lived in their household aiding with the cleaning of their clothing, the cooking of their food, and with the care of their children—to vindicate a woman's right to happiness.

"Then we shall launch a friendly offense, sir."

Chapter 63

"**Y**ou have a letter from Mr. Hart's barrister."

James alertly glanced up from the draft of the opening statement that he was writing. The clerk's face was expressionless.

"Who is it?" he asked, in his mind going over the list of barristers who most frequently handled civil suits.

"Mr. Lodoun, sir."

James had the curious sensation of the chair falling out from underneath him.

You won't win this time, Whitcox.

"Who is David Hart's solicitor?" he asked tonelessly.

"Mr. Seaton, sir."

Images formed in James's mind. Of a man with silver-laced black hair blocking an aisle. Of uncertain green eyes staring up into his. Of periwinkle eyes staring at Frances over white linen-covered tables.

Seaton, James remembered, was the solicitor who had publicly dined with Jack Lodoun while James privately dined with Frances.

Frances had asked if she would sit in the seat that Mary Bartle sat in. How could he tell her that the man who had tried to convict a woman who was dying of a disease inflicted upon her by her husband, was representing her son?

How could he tell her that Jack Lodoun would examine her in the witness box?

Warm lips brushed the nape of her neck. Familiar heat bubbled up inside Frances.

"Look at what Mr. Peasebody found in a bookshop." She turned in a flurry. "It's about the Crystal Palace."

James cursorily glanced down at the purchase. "Does it have pictures of the dinosaurs?"

"Yes." She flipped through the brightly illustrated pages. "Look."

The dinosaurs were garish and lurid likenesses that Megan would love.

"I'm going to shower before dinner," was the neutral response.

Excitement arrested, Frances glanced up at James: there was no light illuminating his face.

Concern pierced her chest: the dark shadows under his eyes had not faded. Realization that his solemnity might arise because of the upcoming trial dried out her mouth. "Is anything the matter?"

James linked his fingers with hers. "Come join me."

The heat of James's body did not dispel the chill that raced up and down her spine. "Have you heard from my son?"

"Mr. Whitcox." The butler hurried out of the hallway that led to the kitchen stairs. "Welcome home, sir."

"Thank you, Peasebody." James did not look at the butler. But neither did he look at Frances. "Tell Cook to keep dinner warm. Mrs. Hart and I will serve ourselves later."

"Very good, sir."

"Please tell the staff they may go home, Mr. Peasebody," Frances instructed. Something was terribly wrong. "I hope your grand-daughter is feeling better."

"Thank you, Mrs. Hart."

"Is Mr. Tristan well?" she asked, tugged up the stairs by the heat of James's fingers.

"Mr. Tristan is quite well," James said in a voice devoid of feeling. "He's an admirer of yours."

"No," Frances said, heartbeat accelerating. James had not been this distant since the news of Mary Bartle's death. "Why do you say that?"

"He told me so."

"When did he say that?" she asked, striving for lightness, falling short.

"Yesterday."

They reached the top of the steps.

Fleetingly Frances remembered the first night she had climbed the stairs: how ignorant she had been. Of sons. Of lovers.

The peacock blue runner silenced their steps.

"What did he say today?" Frances asked, stepping into their bedchamber.

It was as chill as the bedroom in the rented townhouse.

James closed the door. "Today we talked about other things."

But suddenly Frances didn't want to know what he and his clerk had discussed.

She set the illustrated book on top of the gilded dresser. "Shall I scrub your back?"

Warm, moist breath feathered the nape of her neck. "I'd rather scrub you."

A smile worked through the tension that prickled her skin. "What part of me would you like to scrub?"

"Your lips."

Turning, she tilted her head up to him.

A smile briefly touched his mouth. "Your other lips."

The heat of his breath clogged her throat. "Do you ever think about us, when you're in the midst of something else?"

"All the time."

She clung to the pleasure his admission created. "What do you think about?"

His lashes lowered; simultaneously, fingers tugged at the buttons securing her bodice. "I think about how soft your skin is."

She reached for the buttons on his waistcoat.

"I think about how hot and wet you are, filled with my come."

James reached for the waistband of her skirt; Frances reached for his gold studs.

"I think about the sound of your breathing, fast and shallow, until it catches inside your throat and you cry out my name."

James untied the laces of her bustle; it fell, taking with it her silk skirt. Frances dropped his studs inside a waistcoat pocket and tackled his suspenders.

"I think about our home, closing around me tighter than a fist until everything in the world becomes you."

James unlaced her petticoats; Frances blinked back tears.

"I think about you lying in the darkness with your gown folded up around your waist, and I want to cry."

"But barristers don't cry," she said unevenly.

Her drawers slipped down over her hips so that all that covered her was the corset.

"No," he said tonelessly, "barristers don't cry."

Frances reached for the front of his trousers. "Please don't think about that girl in the dark, James."

Unyielding hands cupped her face. "But that's what this trial is about, isn't it, Frances?"

She unfastened one button . . . two . . . three buttons, gaze fastened onto the widening vent in the black wool instead of the truth unveiling before her eyes. "Yes, that is what it's all about."

A woman's right to say no: to a husband; to a son.

The unyielding fingers relentlessly pushed up her face until she had to meet his gaze. "David's barrister contacted me today."

Frances reached inside his small clothes. James was long and thick and hard. She held onto him instead of the fear that coiled inside her. "Is he a good barrister?"

"Yes."

Slippery tears moistened the plum-shaped glans: it throbbed like a heart. "Who is it?"

"Jack Lodoun."

The heat of his sex scorched her suddenly icy fingers. Frances opened her mouth to speak, but no words came out. She licked her lips to give them moisture. "How is that possible?"

"He's no longer Attorney General."

Frances met his gaze. "Since when?"

His voice was as dispassionate as his gaze. "He stepped down after the trial."

Frances had thought Mary Bartle hung herself because of guilt. Or to end the syphilis that daily ate her. She had not thought until now that Mary Bartle may have hung herself out of shame at exposing herself to the public.

Eyelashes shielding her eyes, she freed James from the soft

woolen drawers: he wore the softest wool she had ever felt. "Are you frightened, James?"

"Yes."

She smoothed his tears until the large purplish head shone between the shadow of their bodies. "Why?"

"I'm afraid that if you lose you'll lie back in the darkness."

Lifting up her head—holding his gaze—Frances brought her finger to her lips and tasted the essence of James; underneath the salty tang was the sourness of fear. "Then we mustn't lose, must we?"

Chapter
64

"You don't know, do you?" Jack Lodoun asked, gaze hot and angry.
A periwinkle curtain draped the bench.
James slid out from behind the counselors' table, his silk robe clinging to
the wool of his trousers. "I know exactly what names I'm called."
"But do you know why?"

James awoke to darkness. And suddenly knew why.

Frances's buttocks snugly cushioned his groin. Three muffled Westminster chimes pierced the night. Each chime was matched by the echo of a distant bong: it was three in the morning.

He closed his eyes and inhaled the scents of vanilla and musk. The proximity of Frances held emotion at bay, emotion with which he must reckon. But not now. James didn't yet know how to respond to what he should have known all along.

"Frances," he whispered, sliding his hand over the roundness of her hip and dipping into the closed vee of sleep-warmed thighs.

Her buttocks wriggled; his cock immediately responded. James worked his fingers into moist pubic hair and found a little mound of flesh: she was soft as he was not.

"Hmmm . . ."

He rubbed his middle finger in short, tight circles around the sleeping flesh, deliberately awakening it.

"Mmmm . . ."

A smile twisted his lips, hearing her sleepy protest become a murmur of pleasure. "Turn over, Frances."

James helped her, leaning upright on his elbow so that she rolled into the indentation made by his body. She snuggled against him, soft and warm and boneless.

He pushed her hair—bright red leached out by night—away from her face. Seven months ago he had not known that the lobe of a woman's ear was as soft as her clitoris, or that the nook of a woman's neck was as warm as the crease of her thigh.

Slowly he swept his hand down over a soft breast—her nipple reflexively hardened; over her stomach—rounded to fit the palm of his hand; into the space her shifting legs provided.

The welcoming heat of her squeezed his heart. Words struggled upward in James's chest, but he had never before said the words.

Slipping his fingers out of the haven of their home, he smeared their essence against a soft cheek—quickly he realigned his finger—onto her lips.

She had not enjoyed their flavor in the shower; her lips now readily parted. She licked the tip of his finger with a sensuality that the jurors would damn. Or maybe not. Maybe they would recognize a moral right that superseded morality.

Leaning down, he smelled the aroma that was the scent of their union. Unerringly he found soft skin. Their passion tasted like it smelled: spicy and musky. He licked the damp spot off her cheek.

Her breath quickened in the night.

Slowly he licked a path to her lips. They were moist with their essence. Beyond the outer perimeter of her lips was the sleepy vanilla flavor of Frances.

Warm fingers cupped his ear. James felt her touch throughout his body.

"Lie still," he whispered. Grasping her fingers, he tucked her hand underneath the warm covers, his eyes safely hidden by the darkness. "This is for you."

And for him.

He needed to touch her. He needed to taste her.

He needed to come to terms with the past.

Sliding underneath the covers—darker than the night, but unlike the night, filled with heat—he lodged between soft, giving thighs, his shoulders forcing them wider until all that existed was Frances.

"James." James wormed his hands underneath her buttocks, tilting up her hips. Frances stiffened slightly; her voice permeated the warmth and the weight of the cocooning bedcovers. "What are you doing?"

The words wouldn't come. Drawing her closer—tilting her hips higher—he found her clitoris: she was fully awake.

He tasted her hardness, there the little glans that men ignored. He tasted her softness, there the little prepuce of which men were ignorant.

He licked her, and he tasted her until her hips strained upward to escape the grip of his hands, and he could feel the ache she had experienced, married to a man who had given her his children but who had withheld his body, her fingers her only satisfaction.

James gave Frances his fingers to ease the pain of her loneliness. Her thighs stiffened. Her clitoris jerked.

There was a rhythm to a woman's pleasure. It gripped and ebbed . . . gripped and ebbed . . . gripped and ebbed.

Pulling his fingers free of the clamp her vagina had become, he fluted his tongue and wore the ring of her flesh.

Slowly the contractions ebbed away. Gentle fingers tangled in his hair.

James felt the hot moisture of their passion and knew that he could not judge his wife.

He lay with his head pillowed on Frances's thigh—his breath lulling her sex to sleep—until her fingers relaxed. Slowly, gently, careful not to awaken her, he slipped out of bed.

Her face was a pale blur surrounded by shadow.

He had forced one woman to live in darkness. He would not let this woman suffer for his mistake.

Grabbing up the clothes Frances had earlier discarded, James softly pulled the bathroom door shut behind him. Electric light momentarily blinded him.

He stared at the naked man in the mirror—at the lines that radiated outward from hazel eyes, at the silver that glinted in tousled hair—and saw the man that Frances saw: it was not the same man his wife had seen over the breakfast table.

Quickly he washed and dressed.

Regret filled him. Frances would wake alone. As his wife had woken alone.

Turning off the light, he eased open the bathroom door. Frances sighed in her sleep; the dark mound of covers shifted, stilled.

Carefully he opened the bedroom door, gently closed it behind him. Inside the den that he had yet to use, he found pen and paper. James left the note in the foyer.

He walked for what seemed like hours before finding a cab: breath gusting a cold, silvery cloud, he gave the cabby the designated address.

The distant echo of Big Ben identified the half hour. Men and women—members of the working class—slid through the early morning darkness, skirts fuller than trousers, the shoulders of both sexes bowed as they plowed to or from work.

The cab jerked to a halt, jingling harnesses and creaking wood echoing in the night. James sat for long seconds, staring at the dark stack of windows. No light illuminated the shadowy door.

He stepped out of the cab.

"That'll be three shillings six, sir," the cabby said, voice muffled by a wool scarf.

"I'll give you five pounds if you wait," James said tonelessly. He didn't know how long he would be. "Drive around the block if you need to exercise the horse."

The cabby nodded assent.

A pale band of pink edged the darkness, the dawn of a new day.

James lifted a brass knocker. It took six knocks before a garbled voice penetrated the wood. James lifted the knocker a seventh time.

The door swung open. "What d'ye want?"

James stared remorselessly at the butler, caught without dignity and uniform. "Jack Lodoun."

"He's asleep, like all good men should be," the butler grunted.

James had never claimed to be a good man. "Wake him."

The butler—graying blond hair standing on end, striped night shirt sticking out of hastily donned trousers—scowled. "Come back when God-fearin' men are about their business."

James held out his card. "Mr. Lodoun will see me."

"Mr. Lodoun will discharge me without a notice," the butler said, reluctantly taking the card, "if'n I wake him up at this hour."

"Mr. Lodoun will discharge you without notice if you don't wake him up," James returned flatly.

Standing taller, the butler squinted down at the card. Slowly he raised his head. "Step inside, Mr. Whitcox."

The servants were the first to know, James thought with irony. And the husbands were always the last.

"If you'll wait here, sir."

"Certainly."

The truth had waited this long; it would wait a few more minutes.

Jack Lodoun's townhouse was very much like his own: marble floors, a gaslit chandelier, a sweeping stairway.

The butler returned, his dignity if not his attire intact. "Shall I take your coat, sir?"

"That's not necessary."

"If you will follow me, please."

James followed the butler to a masculine den that was obviously well used.

"Would you care for refreshment, sir?"

James espied the liquor tray. "No, thank you."

The door closed behind him.

James wondered what secrets lay inside the barrister's drawers.

Crossing a worn Oriental rug, he poured two brandies.

"Did you finally listen to what people say, Whitcox?"

James picked up the two snifters and turned. "No."

Jack Lodoun, legs naked beneath a blue velvet robe, took the proffered glass. "Then, how?"

"Periwinkle drapes."

Lodoun raised his snifter in a brief toast. "And it only took you two years to notice."

"Why didn't she ask for a divorce?"

The full sleeve of Lodoun's blue velvet robe—like a barrister's robe—fell back when he lifted his arm; his Adam's apple bobbed, swallowing brandy.

Jack Lodoun had less hair than did James. On his arms. On his legs. Red and gold glinted underneath his armpit.

The blue velvet sleeve dropped down. Periwinkle eyes snared James's waiting gaze. "Would you have granted her one?"

James lifted his glass; the Napoleon brandy was quite excellent.

Pale green eyes shone in the amber depths. The truth swelled up inside his chest.

Swallowing, he lowered his glass. "I don't know."

"Spoken like a Queen's Counselor," Lodoun jibed.

"But I'd like to think I would have," James said evenly.

"What if Frances Hart weren't a widow, Whitcox?" Lodoun walked a half-circle around James. "Would you ask the old man for a divorce?"

"This is a useless game, Lodoun."

"I loved her," rang out in the den. "But you were the one who received the condolences. I grieve for her every minute. Do you even remember what color her eyes were?"

For one charged moment, James did not remember.

"Gray," he said, finally. "She had gray eyes."

"Bully for you, old chap." Lodoun took a large swallow of brandy. "Bully for you."

"Did she love you?" James asked, hope fluttering.

"Did you love her?" Lodoun sneered.

"No." He would not lie. "I didn't."

"Do you love Frances Hart?"

Damned if he answered. Damned if he didn't.

"I don't know what love is." James steadily met the angry periwinkle gaze. "But if love is feeling like you'll die without, then yes, I love Frances Hart."

"The problem is, Whitcox, you don't die." The bright anger in the periwinkle eyes flickered. "Every day you keep on hurting."

James knew Frances throughout every sinew in his body. Her smell. Her taste. He knew the sound of her breathing.

"Tell me about—" *My wife*; but she had been his wife in name only. The man before him had worn the ring of her flesh. "Tell me about Cynthia."

Lodoun's nostrils flared, as if scenting a trap.

James tried to see his wife's lover, but all he saw was a man. Jack Lodoun hurt. As James would hurt, should he lose Frances.

"I represent David Hart," Lodoun said suddenly, stonily.

"I'm not here as Frances's barrister," James said. "There's nothing unethical in my visit."

A partial truth: he was not here as a barrister; he was here as a man.

"What do you want to know about your wife, Counselor?" Lodoun asked bitterly. "Do you want to know if she liked my prick better than yours?"

James ignored the man's bitterness. "I want to know if she found happiness in you."

"Yes," Lodoun bit out. "She was happy when she was with me."

James remembered her laughter when they married, the trained laughter of a debutante. She had not cried out when he had taken her virginity; she had simply held her legs apart while she kept herself apart from him.

"Did you satisfy her?" James asked.

Long seconds passed.

Glancing away from James, Lodoun stared down into his brandy. "Does it matter?"

"Yes."

Lodoun's head snapped up. "Why?"

"Because I didn't give her satisfaction."

A faint stirring sounded in the silence: the servants were rising.

James pictured Frances. Had she awoken and found him gone?

He had instructed the butler to let her sleep, and to tell her that he had left early for the office.

"Yes." Lodoun's voice drew James's focus. "I satisfied her."

Relief filtered through James. "I'm glad."

"Why?" Lodoun asked sharply.

"Because no woman should live with the image of herself lying in the darkness, with her gown folded up around her waist."

Pain contorted Lodoun's face. James saw the grief with which the former Attorney General daily lived.

The younger man turned away. "I saw Frances Hart in the museum."

James watched him. "She didn't mention meeting you."

"We didn't meet." Liquid splashed into glass. "She was looking underneath the giraffe."

A smile broke over James, remembering Frances's disappointment when emerging from underneath the dinosaur.

"It's sexless," he said easily.

"As every boy who's ever visited the museum can testify," Lodoun said dryly.

"But not the girls," James said.

A clank of iron colliding with iron penetrated the floor, the cook readying the kitchen stove for breakfast.

"You haven't subpoenaed the members of the Men and Women's Club," Lodoun said abruptly.

They were treading on very dangerous ground.

"No," James said.

They both knew he had not filed any subpoenas.

James would examine the witnesses that Lodoun summoned. Just as Lodoun would examine Frances.

"Family matters are slippery," Lodoun returned in an expressionless voice.

Glass clinked onto wood, Lodoun setting down the brandy decanter.

All James could say was, "Yes."

"If you were to file a subpoena"—Lodoun straightened; he kept his back to James—"for whom would it be?"

Chapter 65

"Mr. Tristan." Lightly grasping the clerk's fingers, Frances hopped from the iron step to the curb. "What a pleasant surprise."

"I thought I mentioned, when I rang, that I would meet you, Mrs. Hart."

"So you did." Her stomach roiled at the encroaching evening. "I thought merely to make light conversation."

"Mr. Whitcox says you are talented on the skating rink." Firm fingers grasped her clenched hand and pulled it through the crook of his arm. "More so than he."

A smile froze on her face: flickering light streamed out of the courthouse. It grinned like a jack-o-lantern.

"Look at me, Mrs. Hart." Frances started. "Don't look around. Concentrate on what I say."

She forced her gaze upward. "I'm sorry."

"Mr. Whitcox will instruct you on courtroom protocol."

"What does courtroom protocol have to say about a woman who regurgitates her breakfast into the lap of a judge?"

A smile lit up the shadows in the clerk's brown eyes. "You won't be near enough the judge to hurtle at him, ma'am."

"I'm frightened, Mr. Tristan."

It was a testament to her fear that she should even mention it to James's clerk.

"Court is not this evening, Mrs. Hart." His arm under her fingers tightened reassuringly. "Concentrate on one day at a time."

It was easy for the clerk to say *concentrate on one day at a time*: it wasn't he who would sit in front of London and be examined by a man who had shown blatant contempt for a woman's sexuality. It wasn't he who must face her son in a courtroom. And for *what?*

Frances clamped down on rising hysteria. She had never been hysterical a day in her life; she was too old to start at this late date.

"Mr. Whitcox showed great aptitude on the skating rink," she said evenly, staring up into dark brown eyes instead of the courthouse they entered. "I think all the clothing that women wear helps us keep our balance."

Approval glinted in the clerk's eyes. "I think you're being modest, Mrs. Hart."

"Perhaps." Gray shadow engulfed her. "Mr. Whitcox and I raced."

"Who won?"

The dim corridor lacked oxygen. The thought that the courtroom on the morrow would be equally deficient accelerated her breathing.

Frances dug her fingers into the clerk's arm. "Need you ask, sir?"

A warm, masculine chuckle rippled down her spine.

Frances blinked; Avery Tristan *laughed*. It transformed an attentive clerk into a charming man.

Reaching to open the mahogany door—laughter still sparkling in his eyes—the clerk confided, "Mr. Whitcox said you were born on wheels."

The panic gripping Frances loosened its hold; nothing terrible could happen, surely, if a man laughed. "Do you skate, Mr. Tristan?"

The door swung open; the clerk straightened. "Indeed I do."

Frances stepped over the threshold on a wave of intrigue. "Perhaps you wouldn't mind giving me a lesson one day."

"I'd be honored."

The private chamber was empty. Frances fought back disappointment. "Where is Mr. Whitcox?"

"He'll be with you directly." Warm breath stirred her cheek. "Shall I take your coat?"

"Yes." Frances quickly pulled off her gloves and tackled the buttons. "Thank you."

The suede coat slid off her shoulders.

Frances remembered the last time that the clerk had taken her coat, and suppressed a shiver of apprehension.

"Why don't you wait in the conference room?" he asked, voice slightly muffled.

"Oh." Fear still simmered inside her, but it was now manageable. "Yes. Of course."

Frances determinedly turned and faced the clerk. He hooked her coat onto the brass coat tree.

"Thank you, Mr. Tristan," she said with genuine gratitude, "for averting a fit of hysterics."

The clerk turned, eyes solemn. "Always focus, Mrs. Hart."

"Yes." Frances forced out of her mind a man in a gray wig with bristling side-whiskers and purplish-blue eyes. "Thank you."

"There's tea in the conference room."

Frances paused to check her hair in the bathroom mirror. Hazel eyes stared back at her.

I think about our home, closing around me tighter than a fist until everything in the world becomes you.

Muted voices penetrated the closed door to the conference room.

Frances paused uncertainly. Surely the clerk would have told her if the room were occupied?

Taking a deep breath, she pushed open the door.

Four heads snapped toward her, three women and one man. They all possessed white-wheat hair and chocolate brown eyes.

Chapter
66

A distant clang reverberated through wood and brick.
Louis could feel his alienness, he a man in a world of women.

The ornate Georgian door promptly cracked open. Wide blue eyes framed by gold ringlets openly appraised him.

Painful heat gorged his face. "I would like to see Miss Palmer, if I may."

The blue eyes widened. Incredulity gave way to a peal of laughter.

Louis stiffened in embarrassment.

"Miss Alders!" halted the girlish laughter. "You have been warned not to answer the door."

"Henley wasn't about, Miss Werrimen." The adolescent girl turned her head so that Louis stared at a delicate cusp of an ear. "Fancy. Miss Palmer has a caller!"

The announcement dissolved into another peal of laughter.

Anger pushed up through Louis's embarrassment.

"Up to your room at once, miss!" the crisp feminine voice commanded. "And not a word of this. I've a good mind to report you to Mrs. Beasley."

Anger and embarrassment colored the young girl's ear. Without another word she fled.

Immediately the crack in the large enameled door widened. "May I help you?"

Confronting the dark-haired woman with the wide, attractive face was a thousand times more painful than confronting the spoiled young miss who aimed at nothing more noble than making the lives of others miserable. Louis clutched his pad to his chest and stared down at the tips of his black patent shoes. "I would like to see Miss Palmer, please."

"We are not in the habit of receiving evening visitors, Mr. . . . ?"

"Stiles, ma'am." Louis briefly glanced up and almost drowned in heat. "Louis Stiles."

"I see." The crisp voice softened. "Is Miss Palmer expecting you?"

"No, ma'am." Purpose gave him a backbone. "Surely Miss Palmer is allowed visitors?"

"Indeed, she is." The woman hesitated for long moments while Louis wondered how he could convince her to allow him entrance: he was not good with words. "Follow me, sir."

Gratefully he stepped into Mrs. Beasley's Academy for Girls.

It had once been a great house, the architect in him thought, casting a sweeping eye over the painted vaulted ceiling and the flowing marble staircase.

"If you will step in here," the dark-haired woman pushed open a paneled door. "I will get Miss Palmer."

"Thank you," Louis said, darting her a quick smile.

Women were sometimes kind to him, but he had never been able to divine their motivation. He was tall and gangly, certainly not the type of man to inspire feminine appreciation.

Nervously he paced the small antechamber. Oil paintings of every size crowded the walls, as if the room were a miniature gallery.

He promptly became lost in the pure lines of color.

"Mr. Stiles." Esther Palmer jarred Louis out of the world of painting. She hovered in the doorway as if she did not know whether to enter or to exit. "What a surprise."

Anger at the young girl's laughter surged anew through his spine. Esther Palmer had a delicate bone structure, and coloring not often seen. Her skin did not turn "purple," a meaningless word that grouped together thousands of varying hues; rather, it blushed like a sun-kissed aubergine.

"I received my subpoena," Louis said, staring down, not at his toes, but at the toes of the mathematics teacher. She wore sensible, sturdy shoes. They did not do justice to her narrow feet. "And I thought of you."

"I received my subpoena, also." The sensible shoes shuffled, weight alternately resting on first one foot and then the other. "Why did you think of me?"

If only he could put into words what he saw in his mind.

"Mrs. Hart said that I would someday capture a special moment such as," briefly he faltered; swallowing, he continued, "such as the one in the print I purchased at the Achilles Book Shoppe. It occurred to me, when I received the subpoena, that I had an opportunity to capture such a moment." Before he lost his courage, he blurted, "Miss Palmer, will you do me the honor of sitting for me?"

Silence interspersed with the faint hum of voices filled the small chamber.

"Is this a practical joke, Mr. Stiles?"

He glanced up from the uncomplicated study of color and form. Hurt and anger colored Esther Palmer's eyes, a tinge of red superimposed with gray. But it had not been his intention to cause either hurt or anger.

"I take art very seriously, ma'am."

"Then I fail to see what it is that you wish to capture in me."

Weekly he had sketched the members of the Men and Women's Club; always he had come back to Esther Palmer.

"You have such passion, Miss Palmer." Louis searched for the words to convey his feelings. "I would like to capture that passion."

Her skin turned waxen white. "I cannot sit here."

"I have a studio."

A trill of laughter wormed through the ceiling.

For one heart-stopping moment, he thought she would turn him out.

"I'll grab my coat," she said, instead.

"And your purchase, Miss Palmer." For once Louis did not have to force himself to hold a woman's gaze. "Please bring your purchase."

The waxen white of her face transformed into a satisfying rich aubergine. She ducked out of the doorway.

Louis studied the paintings in her absence: they were curiously flat and colorless.

"Shall we go, Mr. Stiles?"

Quickly Louis turned. Esther Palmer wore a black cloak and bonnet, her face a fragile palette. He suddenly did not feel awkward and gangly.

Fog streaked the night.

"Is your studio far?"

"Not far." The heavy rumble of an omnibus pulled up to the curb. Three women and a man stepped out of the back of the vehicle. "We can catch the bus here."

Louis dropped in the box the necessary coins for their ride. Esther Palmer found two empty seats near the back. Louis sat beside her, and stared at the shadow that hugged the nape of her neck. There was no black in shadow, contrary to what people thought; there were only pigments of color: slate blue; shades of violet; burnt umber.

"Are you frightened by the trial, Mr. Stiles?"

"Yes," he said simply.

The pigments of color merged into searching eyes. "Why?"

"What is to keep men from becoming monsters, when the law makes it so frightfully easy?"

"You think Mrs. Hart should take her son to court?"

"What else can she do?"

Esther Palmer looked out the window. "I'll lose my position."

He remembered the pleasure in her face while listening to the band of musicians play at the Crystal Palace. "Do you really want to wear wool for the rest of your life?"

Louis met Esther's gaze in the reflective glass. Her eyes under the brim of her bonnet were filled with blue and violet and burnt umber, the exact shadows that hugged her neck.

The distance, as he had promised, was short. Louis's fingers shook—he did not know if it was from excitement or from fear—when he unlocked the door to his small studio. Quickly he hurried about, lighting the gas and building a fire in the rusty iron fireplace.

Turning, he caught Esther Palmer—small, fragile—watching him. "How shall I pose, Mr. Stiles?"

Louis purposefully picked up his pad. "I think you know how I want you."

He sketched her while she unfastened her cloak, head lowered in vulnerability. He sketched her unfastening her bodice, face averted. He sketched her unsnapping her corset, eyes defiant.

Louis drew quick studies until she stood before him, naked, and he stared, entranced, at the crisscrossing of light and shadow, of smooth flesh and sharp bone. "You're beautiful, Miss Palmer."

She glanced away from him, unable to see her beauty.

"May I position you?" he asked.

She was malleable beneath his fingers, her skin warm and supple. Louis positioned her on the edge of a footstool so that just the edge of her buttocks contacted the worn velvet. "Where's your comforter?"

Her face flushed the same wonderful shade of aubergine that tinted her delicate, bell-shaped breasts and slender hips. "In my reticule."

He retrieved the widow's comforter and knelt in front of her. "Shall you have difficulty inserting it?"

The lashes shielding her eyes were raw sienna. "No."

He hunkered back as she spread her thighs. She smelled of fresh lavender, like the lavender sold on the streets before the fragile blooms wilted and died.

The rounded head of the phallus slowly disappeared from sight. Unbidden, Louis reached out and carefully peeled apart the sun-kissed aubergine lips that hid the mouth of her sex.

She froze, a virgin who had never known a man's touch, poised in a moment of self-discovery.

He gazed up from the glistening circle of flesh that encompassed dark leather, to the face that was thrown back in pained pleasure. Raw sienna streaked fly-away hair and trailed down her corded neck.

Louis gathered together sticks of lead—softer than blunt charcoal—a small dish of turpentine, and his sketch pad.

Chapter
67

Frances leaned her head against the leather seat; overhead gaslight pressed down on her lids.

A door opened, a muted click that resonated inside the conference room. "Are you all right, Mrs. Hart?"

Frances squeezed back tears. "He brought my children to me, Mr. Tristan."

"Yes." The echo of her children's voices filled the room. "He thought they would make you feel more comfortable."

"It must be quite late."

"It's a quarter to nine."

James had worked on Mary Bartle's closing statements until ten of the clock. Had he and the clerk been working on her opening statements while Frances visited with her children?

"Where is he?" she asked.

"Waiting for you."

Moisture trickled down her cheek. Hastily she wiped it away and stood up.

But James wasn't in the outer chamber.

"This way, Mrs. Hart," the clerk said, opening the door.

They did not head toward the light at the end of the corridor.

"Where are we going?" Frances asked, stomach coiling.

"This way," the clerk repeated, heels tapping a clear direction.

Frances had no option but to follow. She had the peculiar sensation of walking a path that was no longer hers, but instead belonged to all the men and women who had walked the corridor before her. Men who had been freed. Women who had hanged . . .

Without warning, the clerk opened a door that was smaller than the one to James's private chambers. The tension coiling inside her stomach clenched in recognition: she was inside the courtroom.

James sat at an oak table, gray wig covering his hair, black robe swathing his body, calmly writing. A tiny worry niggled at the back of her mind. Suddenly it dawned on her what was wrong: he was sitting on the other end of the table, where the Attorney General had sat during Mary Bartle's trial.

Slowly he raised his head. Hazel eyes pinned her gaze. "Thank you, Mr. Tristan, that will be all."

"Very good, Mr. Whitcox."

"Welcome to my den, Frances," James said.

Frances could not tell if he said it in a joking manner or in all seriousness. Slowly she stepped forward.

"Close the door."

The command stopped her mid-step. Breathing too shallowly, she closed the door before stepping into the courtroom.

Nervously she glanced upward at the gallery. Men and women had jeered as well as applauded the jury's decision. Women as well as men had leaned forward to better see Mary Bartle's affliction.

A slick slide of silk captured her attention. James stepped out from behind the curved oak table and held out his hand.

Footsteps echoing in the silence, she stepped forward. The heat in his fingers was familiar; instantly the coiling inside her stomach loosened to an almost bearable state.

"This is the counselors' table," James said, indicating the table he had vacated. "Lodoun will sit there at that end."

"Where you sat," she said unevenly.

"Yes." He gazed down at her assessingly. "Where I sat as Mary Bartle's defender."

Breaking free of his hand lest she do something totally unacceptable like cry—or worse, scream—Frances walked around the large oak box in which the jurors sat. Recklessly she stepped up and sat down on a padded wooden chair.

James looked different from the jury box. And why wouldn't he? she thought. The verdicts that past jurors made permeated the polished wood, weighting the shoulders of all who sat inside the box.

"Thank you for bringing my children to London." Desperately Frances fought to regain a sense of normalcy. "That was kind of you."

"They love you, Frances," he said quietly.

Her throat tightened. "Timothy is leasing his own farm."

"He's making a new life, too," James observed.

"Yes."

Her two youngest babies had wholeheartedly endorsed her actions. The two elder children had been reserved: family did not sue family.

Frances had deeply felt David's absence.

James's voice broke through her contemplation. "Step down."

Reluctantly she stepped down: it was so much more comfortable judging as opposed to being judged.

Long, elegant fingers stretched toward her. "I am the man who has touched, and tasted, and probed every part of your body, Frances: a wig and a robe doesn't change that."

"I know that." Frances grasped his hand. "I just . . . you . . . I'm frightened."

"And I am going to remedy that."

"Please do," she said fervently.

His lips kicked up in a smile. "Notice the curtain behind you."

Frances turned, sandwiched between the curtain and the jurors' box. "Yes."

James climbed the short, narrow steps and drew the curtain aside. "After you, *madame*."

Knees trembling, Frances maneuvered the stairs without mishap. A short corridor led to another door. Tentatively Frances opened it. Only to find herself in the witness box.

She backed up.

James pressed her forward. "Tomorrow, Frances, when you're in this box, I want you to look at me."

Frances fought down a surge of vertigo. "Mr. Tristan said earlier I should focus."

"Yes." Heat penetrated the silk of her bodice and the satin of her corset. "When I examine you, focus on me and nothing else. I'll guide you through the questions. Just listen to my voice."

She licked her lips; the air inside the courtroom seemed unaccountably dry. "When I first met you, you smelled of caramel."

"Lodoun had presented his opening statement." Warm, moist heat licked the nape of her neck. "I didn't have to worry about examining a witness with a mouthful of sweets."

But tomorrow morning, James would open with his statement. And then he would examine her. Or perhaps not.

"Will Mr. Lodoun give his opening statement after you?"

"No." Immediately the hope of reprieve died. "Mr. Lodoun will examine you immediately after I."

"Do I focus on him?"

But James didn't answer. Instead he pulled her away from the oak railing and led her toward the huge desk-like structure at which the judge would sit.

"This is called the bench." He collapsed in a huge leather chair. "The judge determines which questions will be allowed, and which will not."

Frances stared in horror at James. "You can't sit there."

He tugged her forward. "Why not?"

"That's where the judge sits."

"And now it's where I sit." Frances was pulled off balance. "And you."

She collapsed across his lap. Her bustle, an apron rather than a horsehair hump, cushioned her legs. Cool air tunneled up her skirts.

Protest welled up inside her throat. "James—"

"Home, Frances."

It was ridiculous to fall back on propriety at this late stage.

Frances leaned back against him. "My home is always open to you."

Warm fingers slid over her silk-clad thighs, found the vent in her drawers.

She involuntarily widened her legs for him while the gallery looked on. Familiar heat stretched her: James, the barrister; James, the man.

"You've never been a barrister to me, James." Tears filled Frances's eyes; she gripped a hard thigh. "You've always been a man."

But now he was her barrister.

"My sperm keeps you lubricated now."

"Yes."

Carefully he rocked his fingers, wrist pressing against her clitoris. "Does this hurt?"

She tightened her vagina to stay the gentle thrusts; it was wrong, surely, to experience sexual excitement inside a courtroom. "No."

"Does it excite you?"

Her shallow breathing deepened. "You know it does."

"Court can be exciting, too, Frances."

"No," she whispered, clenching her legs. Too late.

"Don't look at the gallery." The gentle rocking continued unabated, tugging at her womb. "Look down in the bar. The bar is your domain, Frances."

Frances reluctantly glanced down.

"Feel the power swell over you." Her internal muscles adopted his rhythm, clenching when he withdrew, opening when he thrust. "In this court, Frances, you rule. I am here for you. The jurors are here for you. They want to feel that excitement, Frances. They will look to you to provide it. And you have it in your power to give it to them."

Frances stared down at the jurors' box and felt the thrusting heat of James rise up into her chest. "But they have the power to judge."

"Do they, Frances?"

Without warning, her body was empty and she was standing on her feet, her skirts falling down around her ankles.

"Sit down." James pulled her forward. "This is where you'll sit tomorrow."

Where London would see her. As they had seen Mary Bartle.

Frances's legs collapsed: she sat.

"Look down." James sat down beside her; his hip and shoulder rubbed her hip and shoulder. "Always look down at the jurors."

Frances gazed down at the empty box. She pictured it occupied, filled with twelve men, all of them staring up at her.

"When I'm giving my opening statement, watch their faces." Her body focused on the pulsing heat that was James; the excitement he had elicited somehow sharpened her mental acuity. "The way they sit, the way they move. They're not stationary when they're in that box. They constantly move: their hands; their arms; their legs; their heads. You'll know when I have them. The feeling will grow, like an orgasm."

An orgasm felt as if it were growing inside her now.

James stood, hand cupping her elbow, lifting her up with him. Frances stumbled after him.

The ache of sexual frustration warred with the anxiety of the pending trial.

They exited through the white enameled door off the witness box and down the little corridor, through the dark velvet curtain, and down the short flight of stairs. James stepped up into the jurors' box and took a front seat. Frances followed.

Head bent—gold and bronze hair peeping out from under the back of the gray wig—he unbuttoned his trousers.

Frances stared down at the bulbous crown of his penis and the blue veins crisscrossing the thick flesh that rose up from a bed of dark wool.

She didn't need the invitation of his outstretched hand.

Cool air invaded the back of her legs . . . the globes of her buttocks. She sat on his lap and bit her lip at the stretching fullness that was more than fingers.

This was their home, and no court or jury could take it away.

A slippery finger found her clitoris.

Frances jerked. Dimly she realized that he must have moistened his finger with his own lubrication.

"Look up at the witness box, Frances."

Frances involuntarily glanced upward, neck craning for a better view.

"The jurors will know if you lie." Slowly his finger glided across the tip of her clitoris, the glans that matched his. "Don't ever lie."

Frances fixedly stared at the box where on the morrow she would stand, *because* she had not lied.

"The jurors are simply men who want to feel," James whispered, lazily circling his finger while she tasted his heartbeat. "Like I'm feeling. Like you're feeling. They don't care what they feel, as long as they do feel."

Frances gripped with both hands the cool oak wood that penned her inside the jurors' box.

"Talk to them, Frances, like you talk to me." Slowly his finger rimmed the right side of her clitoris; it burned like his flesh inside her burned. "Share your life with them. Your joy. Your heartache. The love you bear your children."

She gritted her teeth; it was inconceivable that she should have an orgasm in the very box where jurors would judge her.

"Make them feel your passion, Frances." The pressure banding her midriff disappeared; instantly it cupped her breast. "Make them laugh the laughter you laughed when the dinosaur shot up water." Hard, hot fingers kneaded her breast in time to the pulsing heartbeat that her body had become. "Make them cry the tears you cried when I held you in the bathroom."

Laughter tickled her chest. Tears tightened her throat.

"Give them a slice of your life, Frances," James said over the heat that gorged her like a burning brand, "and they will love you like I love you."

Chapter
68

"Gentlemen." James stared at the twelve men who sat in the box where he had only twelve hours earlier ejaculated inside Frances. "We Englishmen hold liberty more dear than any other property. It is the basis of our law. The reason we are here today, is because of our love of liberty. And because of one woman who shares our love." Deliberately he directed the jurors' attention to Frances. "Allow me to introduce to you Mrs. Frances Hart."

She wore the clothing in which James had first seen her: a green-checkered velvet coat with matching walking skirt and green silk polonaise.

She was beautiful. She was unashamedly feminine. She was his life.

James must make her as important to the jurors as she was to him.

"Look at her closely, gentlemen," James urged. "Look at her clothing. Look at her hair. Look at her face."

The twelve men intently studied Frances; Frances returned their perusal with a courteous nod.

Jurors two, five, six, eight and ten were captivated. Jurors one, three, and nine were taken aback. The remainder looked on with interest.

A pained smile prodded his lips. It was Frances herself who would win or lose this case.

James had never felt more out of control.

"I tell you to look closely at her clothing and her hair," he said, "because the law gives us men—as stewards of our families—certain recourse: if we do not like a woman's hair, whether that woman be our wife, our mother, or any other female who is in our care, we may sign an order of lunacy to have her confined in a madhouse. If we do not like a woman's clothing, we may sign an order of lunacy."

Jurors one, three, four and nine sat back in their chairs in patent disbelief.

"That strikes you as ludicrous," James said, addressing the four jurors, young men who had wives and children. "And so it should. Responsible men do not sign orders to put away their womenfolk simply because they do not like the way they wear their hair, or the color of their clothing." Out of the corner of his eye, James glimpsed David Hart's anger. Frances outwardly remained calm; James could feel her hurt like nettle stings. "And yet, gentlemen, that is what happened to Mrs. Hart.

"Her son, David Matthew Hart, signed such a lunacy order. He doesn't like her hair and her clothing, so he signed an order to have her confined in an asylum where the good doctors would prescribe her to dress her hair and her person in a manner that he finds more acceptable.

"Our learned counselor"—James was intensely aware of Jack Lodoun, the man who had been his wife's lover and who now sat at the other end of the counselors' table—"will tell you that it was not Mrs. Hart's hair or dress that led Mr. Hart to sign a lunacy order. He will tell you that it was because of the company she kept. Or perhaps he will tell you that it was because, three months after the death of her husband, Mrs. Hart came to London. Or perhaps Mr. Lodoun will tell you that Mrs. Hart's son signed a lunacy order because Mrs. Hart is forty-nine years old, and is no longer capable of bearing children."

Jack Lodoun had granted James the boon of subpoenaing the witness James could not; James did not fool himself into thinking he would not fight to win this case with every breath in his body.

"Regardless of why her son signed that lunacy order—whether it was because he didn't like her hair . . . or he didn't like her clothing . . . or he didn't like the company that she kept . . . or he didn't like the manner in which she mourned her husband . . . or because Frances Hart has experienced the 'change' that all women experience—the fact remains," James continued, "that he did sign a lunacy order.

"David Hart, as head of his family, has the serious charge of protecting his mother. But he didn't protect her. He betrayed her in a manner that has profoundly affected her life.

"The purpose of this trial, as my lord judge will instruct you, is to determine if Frances Hart should be released from the stewardship of her son.

"I have said that David Hart signed an order to confine Mrs. Hart to an insane asylum. But this hearing isn't about what constitutes insanity, gentlemen. This hearing is about liberty, that property that we English love above all others. David Hart has taken away his mother's liberty.

"I beseech you, on behalf of Frances Hart"—James one by one pinned each of the twelve men with his gaze—"to give it back to her."

Slowly, heart pounding inside his chest, James sank back against hard wood.

Deliberately evoking the principle of English liberty was a double-edged sword: men all too often escaped punishment for abusing women, that they not be deprived of their liberty.

The county clerk called the witness for the plaintiff.

Face expressionless, James watched Frances stand in the witness box.

Emotion twisted inside him. James recognized it as pride.

Knowing the cost of losing, she still fought.

"Mrs. Hart." Gently he projected his voice. "Do you love your children?"

"I love my children very much."

Frances's voice was clear but stilted; she did not share her love.

Jurors two, five, six, eight and ten shifted back in their chairs, disappointed; the woman who dressed flamboyantly and graciously nodded when scrutinized, answered as any woman would answer.

James probed. "Do you love your son, David Hart?"

"Oh, yes." Warmth injected her voice; briefly she closed her eyes. "When he was born, I counted his toes and fingers and cried for the gift my husband had given me." Frances opened her eyes; they were luminous in the gaslight that revealed her every expression. "I did not come from a demonstrative family. Loving David, and being loved in return, was the most tremendous feeling I had ever experienced."

James allowed the love she obviously felt for her son to flow over the jurors before asking: "The madhouse doctors came into your home. Had it not been for your servants, they would have dragged you, literally, to an insane asylum. What was that like, Mrs. Hart?"

Wood groaned.

The jurors sat forward in their chairs. The audience sat forward on their benches.

Jack Lodoun sat forward on the counselors' bench, pen poised.

"I didn't understand . . ." Her bottom lip trembled, stilled. "I was preparing to leave the townhouse . . . to visit Kew Gardens; I've never seen them, you see . . . when someone knocked. Mr. Denton—he's my butler—opened the door. Two women swarmed around him and grabbed me by the arms." James felt the horror she had felt, being forcibly manhandled. "I was at first too shocked to be afraid. A man waved a paper about in front of Mr. Denton's face, and said he had a court order. I thought I was being arrested. I didn't know that women could be dragged off to an asylum because of a court order."

"When you discovered that your son had signed the papers for these people to drag you off to an asylum, what did you feel?" James asked as if it had not been he who had told her the news.

"I don't know if there are words to describe what I felt." She bowed her head for a long second before slowly bringing it back up. "I think it would have been less painful if my son would have stabbed me in the heart with a knife, because then the pain would have ended. I kept remembering how tiny he was as a baby. How trusting he was as a child. He used to climb up on chairs and cry, 'Catch me, Mama!' I would catch him, and he would throw his head back and laugh, and then he would wriggle out of my arms to do it again. And I would catch him again. I always caught him, because I loved him so much. I loved his laughter and his trust. When I discovered that my son had signed an order to have me sent to an asylum, I felt as if I had climbed onto a chair and jumped, only to have him turn his back to me."

She had not described her hurt to him; the hurt she described now ripped through his chest.

But he could not protect her as a man; forcefully James turned off his emotions. "You married David Hart Senior when you were fifteen; he was forty-four years old. Did you love him?"

James flinched at the affection that glowed in her eyes. "David was a gentle man. I don't believe that I loved him when we married." James tensed, seeing jurors three, nine and twelve stiffen. "I'm not certain a fifteen-year-old girl is capable of love. I was a child, and he wanted children. I was honored that he chose me to give him a family, but I didn't realize the meaning of love until I gave birth to my son. David cried when he held little Davie in his arms. I didn't know that men cried for happiness. I came to care for my husband very much, indeed. That feeling over the years grew. So, yes, I loved my husband."

She had shared her love and her pain, now it was time to share her happiness.

James glanced down at the notepad in front of him. "Were you happy in Kerring, Sussex, Mrs. Hart?"

"Yes."

"But you came to London after the death of your husband." Slowly he glanced up at her. "Why?"

"Dinosaurs."

Laughter spilled out of the gallery.

James's lips hitched upward in a smile. "Dinosaurs, Mrs. Hart?"

"When David died, a part of me died, too." Frances spoke to every widow and widower. "I had devoted my entire life to my husband, and to my children, and to my grandchildren, but suddenly my husband was dead, and I did not know how to respond to my family. My husband had always cared for me, but he was no longer there. I came to London to find . . . dinosaurs."

"Did you find them?"

The light that lit up her face almost blinded James. He had told her to give a slice of her life to the jurors: Frances gave each of them a slice. She made them smile when she told them about her discovery of electricity. She made them laugh when she told them about the dinosaur that spat at her.

She made them look at her as a person, rather than a woman.

James had accomplished everything he could do with her as a witness.

"Thank you, Mrs. Hart," he said neutrally. "I have no more questions, Your Honor."

Out of the corner of his eye, he glimpsed a slash of charcoal. On the morrow all of London would know Frances's face.

"Mrs. Hart." James's attention was snagged by Jack Lodoun. "You are suing your son for emancipation. Why?"

"I beg your pardon?" Frances asked, genuinely confused.

"Why are you suing your son? Our learned friend, Mr. Whitcox, claims that you have been profoundly affected by the act of David Hart signing a lunacy order. But in fact, Mrs. Hart, you did not go to an asylum. So how is it that you have been profoundly affected?"

James tensely waited for Frances to answer.

"A bond is created when a mother has a child, Mr. Lodoun," she said slowly. "A mother nurses that child, even when she herself is too tired to eat. She tends a child when he is ill, even though she herself might be ill. A child trusts his mother, but a mother trusts her child, also.

"I had to hide like a criminal for seven days. I could not inhabit my own home. I could not walk down a street, for fear that I might be apprehended. I still can not return to my home, for fear that David will sign another order to have me committed. I assure you, sir, fear has a very profound effect. I love my son, but I can no longer trust him with my welfare."

"You visited your son, did you not, Mrs. Hart, when you were 'hiding' from the madhouse doctors?"

"Yes."

"He could have collected the authorities and had you taken to this asylum, could he not?"

Frances visibly floundered. "I suppose so."

"But he didn't."

Frances recovered. "But he could have."

"So you are dragging your name—and the good name of your family—through the mud, simply on the basis of something that *could* happen?"

"Objection, Your Honor," James coldly interrupted. "It is clear that Mrs. Hart was in dire danger of losing her liberty."

"I will allow the question, Mr. Whitcox." The judge sat back in his chair, the chair in which James had aroused Frances. "Answer the question, Mrs. Hart."

"I visited my son in the hope . . . in the hope that there was a mistake. My son assured me that he had signed the order. Because he loved me, he said. He said that the doctor would make me like I was before my husband died."

"So you admit that your son has reason to fear for your sanity."

"I admit no such thing, sir," Frances swiftly rebounded.

"Did David Hart say that he would sign another lunacy order?" Jack Lodoun questioned.

"My son said that I was his responsibility."

"A simple yes or no, please, Mrs. Hart." Jack Lodoun was deliberately trying to discompose her. "Did David Hart say that he would sign another lunacy order, or imply in any way that he would further impose upon your liberty?"

"My son said he had sworn to his father that he would take care—"

"Your Honor," Jack Lodoun cut through Frances's response, "please direct Mrs. Hart to answer the question."

"You will answer the question, Mrs. Hart," the judge adjured.

Frances's gaze slammed into James. James nodded his head, the barest of movement.

"No, sir," Frances said in a stilted voice.

"So, again I ask you, Mrs. Hart, why are you suing your son?"

"Your Honor," James said bitingly, "Counsel is—"

"I withdraw my question, Your Honor," Jack Lodoun said. "I have no further questions for Mrs. Hart."

"You are excused, Mrs. Hart. This court will adjourn." The knock of wood on wood ricocheted through the courtroom. "We will convene after lunch."

Chapter
69

"Mrs. Hart." A warm hand closed over Frances's cold, stiff fingers. "Come with me. I have lunch waiting in Mr. Whitcox's chambers."

"Oh." Slowly Frances released the bannister she gripped like a lifeline. She didn't remember grabbing the wood. "I don't think we fared so well, Mr. Tristan."

"You did very well, indeed, Mrs. Hart." Comforting heat cupped her left elbow. "Come along, now."

Shadows writhed in the dim corridor.

Frances wondered if Eve had bitten into the forbidden apple, only to discover a core of rotten worms.

Warm fingers cupped her right elbow. Starting, Frances glanced up at James: he did not look down at her.

Silently the two men escorted her to the familiar chambers.

"Lunch is in the conference room," Avery Tristan said in a toneless voice, and disappeared through the arc.

Tears blurred Frances's vision. "I'm sorry."

Slinging his robe and wig into the black leather chair, James pulled her into his arms. "You were magnificent."

"Why *am* I suing my son, James?"

"Frances." His cheek was smooth, there against the side of her face. "Lodoun is doing his job. He's very good at his job. He will say anything to sway the jurors' opinion. That is what David is paying him to do. But you have the jurors. Didn't you feel them?"

Frances remembered the chuckles coming from below her.

"You said I should focus on you."

His arms tightened around her. "It went better than I anticipated."

The dread coiling inside her stomach tightened. "Then you must not have had very high expectations."

Warm lips feathered her temple. "Chin up."

Frances raised her face up to his.

Light illuminated James's face. "Let's get you comfortable."

The loss of the velvet coat chilled her.

"My children are in the gallery, James."

"Does that bother you?"

Yes.

"Shall I have Mr. Tristan remove them from the courtoom?" he asked.

"No." Frances had already spoken. "Thank you."

Warm fingers pressed her chin upward. "Trust me, Frances."

"I trusted my son."

Scalding moisture covered her lips. The heat of his tongue pushed aside the cold filling her body.

James pulled back slightly. His eyes beneath the sweat-darkened hair were solemn. His breath was almost as hot as his tongue. "I'm not your son, Frances."

"No." She looped her arms around his neck and brought his mouth back down to hers. "You certainly aren't."

Slowly the intimate heat filling her mouth withdrew. "You are a fickle woman, Mrs. Hart."

Frances blinked back tears. "Why?"

"Mr. Tristan said you asked him to give you a skating lesson."

A reluctant chuckle worked past the tight muscles inside her throat. "I would never have taken Mr. Tristan for a man who tattles."

James smiled. "But he has other redeeming qualities. Let's go and share lunch with him, shall we?"

Frances wished wholeheartedly that she had not eaten the soup and sandwich Avery Tristan had brought her.

She worked very hard not to regurgitate lunch when Jack Lodoun gave his opening speech:

"My learned colleague said that insanity is not the issue here, but I disagree. Frances Hart's state of mind is central to this trial. David

Hart, a loving son, in concern visited his mother in London, only to discover that she was not the mother who had left Kerring, Sussex, one and a half months earlier. Mr. Whitcox said that a responsible man does not commit his mother because he doesn't like her hair style, or because he doesn't like her clothes—and a responsible man would not—but David Hart was not acting irresponsibly when he signed a lunacy order for Frances Hart.

"Mrs. Hart abandoned her family three months after the death of her husband. I ask you, gentlemen: what would you do if your supposedly grieving mother suddenly dyed her hair? What would you do if your grieving mother cast off her mourning for—admittedly attractive, but totally inappropriate—clothing such as the costume Mrs. Hart now wears?

"David Hart promised his father that he would take care of his mother. David Hart is to be commended, not sued.

"Mr. Whitcox claims this trial is about a woman's liberty. I claim this trial is about a man's honor. David Hart has done what any honorable man would do: he is taking responsibility for his mother.

"I will reveal to you the types of associates Mrs. Hart has made in London: I assure you, gentlemen, you, too, would be concerned to learn that your mother is associating with these men and women.

"Mrs. Hart claims she has suffered irreparable damage by the son she loves, and that she cannot trust him. But what about the damage Mrs. Hart is doing to her son?

"This trial is a mockery, launched only because Mr. Hart has cut off the monthly stipend that his father requested in his will that he provide for Mrs. Hart. *Requested*, gentlemen. If Mr. Hart had trusted his wife, then he would have outright stipulated she receive the funds, and she would have them.

"But David Hart Senior discharged the responsibility to his son, so that his son could ensure his mother used the money wisely.

"She has not, honorable sirs.

"She abandoned her children when they needed her the most. She rented a townhouse in London, far away from the family she claims to love. She cast aside mourning—only three months after the death of her husband—and frivoled away her allowance on totally inappropriate clothing.

"Frances Hart needs a man to be responsible for her, because she clearly is not responsible for her own actions. To grant Mrs. Hart liberty from her son, would in fact be doing a great injury to her. I urge you to deny this suit posthaste."

Chapter
70

J ames felt the loss of Frances in his sleep: instantly he woke up. Pale pink crawled through the closed curtains.

Of Frances there was no sign.

A sweeping hand revealed that the sheets were cool where she had lain beside him.

Fear coursed through him. Frances had said very little after the court adjourned for the day. The expression on her face when Jack Lodoun had presented his opening statements had sliced through him like jagged glass. It had not eased his pain to see that David Hart's expression had matched that of Frances.

He sat up. And noticed the slash of light coming from the bathroom. Silently padding across the thick carpet, he eased open the door.

Frances sat on the toilet, lid down, staring at a book.

James knelt in front of her, grimacing slightly at the impact of bare knees and icy, ungiving marble.

"Mr. Harmon, in a presentation, said that many people don't believe dinosaurs are real." Frances traced a purple Megalosaurus with her forefinger; the shadow of her lashes gouged deep hollows underneath her eyes. "Do you?"

James's throat tightened. "Absolutely."

Frances had shown him many things that he had never thought to see.

"Why didn't Mr. Lodoun mention that I am sexually involved with a man?"

James was a private man, but Frances needed his honesty. "Because he was my wife's lover."

Frances's head snapped upward. "Mr. Lodoun was intimate with your wife?"

"Yes," James said.

"How long have you known?"

"A few days."

"How did you discover it?"

"He was confrontational in court during Mary Bartle's trial," James said. "He said that I wouldn't win 'this time.' One day, inside the courthouse, when I went to the toilet, he was standing at the urinal. He'd seen us in the restaurant that Sunday night. He asked if I'd found a woman who was more amusing than preparing for a trial. I turned the question around and asked if he had found such a woman. He said he had, but that she'd died."

Silently Frances waited for him to continue.

"Jack Lodoun has distinctly colored eyes," James said, the past so clear now. "Periwinkle eyes. I dreamed that we were in court together, and a curtain—the same periwinkle as the curtains in my wife's drawing room—was draped behind the bench. When I woke up, it dawned on me that my wife was the woman to whom Jack Lodoun had referred."

"It was the morning you woke me to"—a faint flush tinted her pale cheeks—"to kiss my clitoris."

James smiled, a half smile: he still had not broken her of blushing. He brushed her hair back from her face. "I kissed more than your clitoris."

Her gaze searched his. "Did you confront him?"

"Yes."

"Were you angry?"

James dropped his hands and cupped her hips. Her soft flesh was cold. "I am many things, Frances, but I am not a hypocrite."

"Would you have been angry"—she hesitated—"before?"

Before his wife had died, she implied. Before he had experienced Frances's passion.

"I don't know," he said truthfully.

He didn't know if he would have granted his wife a divorce. There was no point in questioning the past when he had so much in his future.

"When I saw Mr. Lodoun at Mrs. Bartle's trial, I thought he looked familiar, but I couldn't place his face until tonight." Frances glanced down at the purple Megalosaurus. "I saw him in the museum."

"Yes, he told me."

"I don't think he likes me."

"He's looked at the giraffe, too."

Her gaze jerked upward. "Have you?"

"I'm sure every boy who's ever been in the museum has sneaked a look."

"Girls, too, I imagine."

"I hope so," James said.

Frances traced the thigh of the spiked monster she had stood in front of while learning his sex. "I love you, James."

Love should not hurt, but it did.

"I know you do, Frances."

"Do you think it's a symptom of my illness?"

James took the book out of her hands and firmly closed it. Standing up, he laid it beside the basin. Leaning down, he grasped her underneath her arms and pulled until she stood before him and her nipples prodded his chest. "Let's get ready for court."

The shadows in her eyes were darker than the shadows that bruised her cheeks. "Is it too late to stop it?"

"Are you accepting defeat?"

"I hate sitting there."

James could not imagine sitting in the dock, a woman, while men bandied about his life. He tugged her toward the shower. "I'll give you something to help pass the time."

He could feel her watching him as he unscrewed the Rose Jet. "An orgasm?"

James turned on the water cocks. "Do you object?"

"My home is your home, James."

Water cocooned them; the Rose Jet fountained up between them.

"And there is no pain inside our home," James said.

He soaped her water-slickened skin . . . her gentle fingers that curled around his . . . her arms that held him; her neck that arched to give him access.

"They do love you, Frances."

Frances wrapped her arms around his waist. "Thank you for not disparaging my son."

James gently rubbed his cheek against hers, prickly stubble against velvet cream. "Did I tell you that I admire you?"

"No."

"I do." He turned her so that her back molded to his front. "Push your buttocks out."

She was moist enough to accept him without pain.

James knelt, holding himself high inside her. She straddled his thighs; he straddled the Rose Jet. Reaching around her, he inched forward until the water shooting up from the floor lapped her clitoris. She jerked inside his arms with her first orgasm, and everything in the world became their union.

"Good morning, Mrs. Hart." The butler held his hands behind his back. "Mr. Whitcox. Shall you be eating your breakfast now?"

"Yes, thank you, Mr. Peasebody."

The familiar warmth of James's fingers followed her through the morning room. An oak chair with a padded silk seat slid back from the table.

Wordlessly Frances sat down. A steaming cup of coffee appeared before her.

James sat down beside her. "What have you there, Peasebody?"

"It's Mrs. Hart, sir."

Frances froze, cup midway between the table and her mouth. "I'm in the paper?"

James had told her it would happen: she had hoped for once he would be wrong.

"Indeed you are, Mrs. Hart." A rare smile broke over the butler's face. "Right here."

The newspaper was folded back to a middle page.

At least she wasn't on the front, she thought with a small sigh of relief. The sigh caught in her lungs.

Her likeness stared up at her.

James leaned over the table and angled the paper so they could both read the headline: "Hart Versus Hart: A Sussex Woman In Search Of Dinosaurs Sues For Emancipation."

"Oh." Frances's eyes opened wide. "The artist was very kind."

"Why do you say that?" James asked.

She looked much younger than her forty-nine years. "I look rather nice."

"You do very well, Mrs. Hart," the butler said, peering over her shoulder.

Tears burned Frances's eyes at the butler's kindness. "Thank you, Mr. Peasebody."

"Read the article, Frances," James said.

Bracing herself, she read the first paragraph:

Frances Hart, a forty-nine-year-old widow from Kerring, Sussex, has taken her thirty-three-year-old son, David Hart, to court in order to gain emancipation. The son signed a lunacy order to have Mrs. Hart committed. One of the symptoms cited for her lunacy was Mrs. Hart's age. Mrs. Hart, who appeared quite lucid in her testimony, is represented by none other than James Whitcox, Q.C., who successfully represented Mary Bartle.

The article then detailed the lunacy law that allowed men to confine innocent women, and mentioned a woman who several years earlier had successfully sued the doctors who had declared her insane.

"I'm glad he gave information about the law." Frances pushed the paper away. "It's a bad law."

"Frances." Warm fingers cupped her cheek. "The reporter supports you."

"Yes." Warmth suffused her. She turned the paper over. "It's the same newspaper that printed that nasty article about you."

"Mr. Nickols writes for the *Pall Mall Gazette*," James said easily. "Ah, breakfast. Thank you, Peasebody."

Frances had learned her lesson the day before: she ate a slice of toast.

Chapter
71

The gallery was gorged with spectators. Ogling. Whispering.
Never still.

I don't think one ever really gets used to it.

John Nickols was the first member of the Men and Women's
Club to be called to the witness box.

"Mr. Nickols," Jack Lodoun asked, "are you a member of the
Men and Women's Club?"

The reporter, at least, had not needed to be carried to the witness
box; he sat in his chair. "Yes."

"You write for the *Pall Mall Gazette*."

"Yes."

"You write articles which many consider are unfit to be published."

"Many would consider anything other than scripture to be unfit
for publication, sir."

A small glow of pride formed in Frances's stomach: unlike herself, the reporter was not intimidated by Jack Lodoun.

"What do you discuss in the meetings, Mr. Nickols?"

"We discuss many things. In the past we've discussed Mr. Darwin and natural selection. We've discussed the Malthusian movement."

"So you discuss preventive checks."

A gasp swept over the gallery. Frances focused on the reporter.

"We have discussed preventive checks, yes."

"Did Mrs. Hart participate in this discussion?"

"Yes."

"Thank you, Mr. Nickols."

Inanely Frances remembered the madhouse doctor's comment that, given the opportunity, men and women could be democratic.

"Mr. Nickols." Frances instinctively glanced at James. "There are six women—other than Frances Hart—who belong to the Men and Women's Club. Is that correct?"

"Yes."

There was no recognition in the eyes of the two men, no sign of the intimate bonding Frances had witnessed when they had clung to one another while disembarking from the train.

"Do you think those six women are insane?" James asked.

John Nickols's eyes momentarily gleamed with amusement.

"Objection, Your Honor!" Jack Lodoun exclaimed.

"I withdraw the question, Your Honor," James said easily. "What is your impression of Mrs. Hart, Mr. Nickols?"

"Objection, Your Honor," Jack Lodoun protested.

"Your Honor, Mr. Lodoun summoned the members of the Men and Women's Club to discredit Mrs. Hart's character. Surely these men and women are allowed to share the reasons why they voted her into their club."

"I will allow the question, Mr. Whitcox," the judge said. "You may answer, Mr. Nickols."

"When I was first introduced to Mrs. Hart, I was angry at her because there was no pity inside her eyes. When I confronted her, she said there are those who think of a woman's age as being crippling. My impression of Mrs. Hart was—and is—that she is an extremely kindhearted woman who would go to great lengths to make others feel comfortable."

Frances swallowed; the lump in her throat did not disappear.

"Thank you, Mr. Nickols."

Frances watched as one by one the members were summoned.

Louis Stiles was strangely composed: he blushed, but he did not glance away when the two barristers questioned him. Jane Fredericks's anger simmered at a manageable rate. George Addimore managed to sneak in the fact that he had been shocked by the lunacy order. Dr. Sarah Burns knocked the air out of Frances's lungs.

"Dr. Burns," James said, "You are a doctor of medicine."

"Yes, sir."

"As a physician, you are licensed to sign a lunacy order, are you not?"

"Yes."

"Have you ever signed a lunacy order?"

"Yes."

"For what purpose?"

"A father wanted to teach his daughter obedience."

"And so you signed this order."

"I deeply regret my actions, sir."

"Why is that?"

"Because I signed an order to commit a girl who was not insane."

"But the girl was disobedient, you said."

"So the father said."

"Dr. Wedon yesterday testified that any woman who flaunts authority—or who shows eccentric qualities—is by nature insane. Do you agree with this, Dr. Burns?"

"No."

"Why not?"

"By Dr. Wedon's definition, sir, every person in this courtroom should be confined to an asylum."

Laughter broke out in the gallery.

"I object, Your Honor," Jack Lodoun said stridently.

"Your Honor, Dr. Burns is a qualified physician who has the same authority to sign a lunacy order as does Dr. Wedon. Unless, of course, Mr. Lodoun's objection stems from Dr. Burns's sex?"

"I will allow Dr. Burns's testimony, Mr. Lodoun," the judge said sharply.

James smiled. "Thank you, Dr. Burns, that will be all."

Hope filled Frances.

Joseph Manning was the last member to be called.

Frances tensely waited. Only to dissolve in disbelief when he vehemently defended the Men and Women's Club, and described Frances Hart as a woman of character.

". . . Mrs. Margaret Hart," echoed over the garbled whispers and boring eyes.

Frances stared down at James's impassive face. And knew that he was responsible for her daughter-in-law standing in the witness box.

Her assumption was proven correct when Jack Lodoun asked the pregnant woman a few summary questions only.

Hazel eyes met her gaze for long seconds before focusing on Margaret Hart.

"Mrs. Hart," James said gently. "Are you well?"

"Yes, sir." Margaret blushed. "Very well, thank you."

James glanced down at the notes he had scribbled over the course of the trial. "You have been married to David Hart for how long, ma'am?"

"Just over twelve years. This will be our fourth child."

"Have you had much contact with Frances Hart, your mother-in-law?"

"I have lived in the same house as Mother Hart for all my married life, sir."

"Would you describe her as a loving mother?"

"Oh, yes, sir."

"Would you describe her as a loving grandmother?"

"She loves her grandchildren dearly."

"How would you describe Frances Hart?"

"I would describe Mother Hart as a loving person, sir. As a woman who has through the years sacrificed her own happiness for the happiness of her family."

"Look at your mother-in-law."

Frances met the doe-brown gaze of her daughter-in-law. The shadows she had seen underneath the pregnant woman's eyes no longer existed.

"What do you see, Mrs. Hart?"

"I see a woman, sir, who glows with good health and happiness."

"Do you think Frances Hart is happy?"

"When she visited last time, her face became radiant when she spoke of London."

"You are referring to her visit after David Hart had signed the lunacy order."

Margaret's guilt vibrated inside the courtroom. "Yes, sir."

"You don't find Frances Hart's hair or her clothing inappropriate, Mrs. Hart?"

"No, sir," Margaret said earnestly. "I am, quite frankly, sir, envious."

"You do not see her appearance as being disrespectful of David Hart, Senior?"

"Father Hart was a good man, sir. He had been confined in his bed with a bad heart for two years before he died. Mother Hart took care of his every need. While his departure was sad, it was expected, and actually quite peaceful. Father Hart died as he had lived, surrounded by his family."

"Do you feel Mrs. Hart has neglected her family while she was in London?"

"I love Mother Hart." Margaret glanced down at her hands that gripped the dark oak of the bannister. "But truthfully, sir, it has been rather nice, having my family to myself for a while. Mother Hart would never interfere, of course—she's the most wonderful mother-in-law imaginable—but she has left a legacy that is difficult to fill."

"What is that, Mrs. Hart?"

"Mother Hart has been selfless in her devotion. I relied on her. We all relied on her. But sometimes, sir, when we rely extensively upon someone else, we become less than what we should. I think selflessness may sometimes lead to selfishness on the part of others. I think, to be a woman, one must be a little selfish. I think, when that occurs—a selfless woman who suddenly develops a sense of self—that those who are used to being the center of attention, may become insecure. I believe men sometimes do unreasonable things when they are insecure, and do not realize it, because they are used to having this undivided attention." Margaret glanced up. "Does that answer your question, sir?"

"Perfectly, Mrs. Hart." A sharp pang stabbed through Frances's chest, hearing the gentleness in James's voice. "Thank you. You may stand down now."

Frances fixedly stared at her hands. Her daughter-in-law had for years seen what Frances had only recently realized: by living through her family, she had hurt them, perhaps irreparably. Her son had not been able to see that she had individual needs, because she herself had never acted on her needs.

The legacy Frances had left was a legacy of selfishness.

Her fault. Not the fault of her son.

James's closing speech was a distant buzz. It was followed by the closing statements of Jack Lodoun.

"Mrs. Hart." Frances glanced up through a blur of tears. Avery Tristan stood beside her chair. "The judge has instructed the jurors. Come wait in Mr. Whitcox's chambers."

Chapter 72

"I'll see to Mrs. Hart now, Mr. Tristan." Familiar heat traveled up Frances's elbow. "Thank you."

James pushed open the door to his chambers.

Frances blindly walked into his arms. "Mr. Lodoun summoned Margaret on your behalf."

Moist heat kissed her ear. "Yes."

"She knew."

"Yes."

"But how did you?"

"She said you glowed."

Frances drew a shaky breath. "Will it be long, do you think?"

Chill air replaced the heat that enveloped her. "No, I don't think it'll be long at all."

James reached up to remove his wig.

"Leave it," Frances said impulsively.

James halted. "Why?"

"It reminds me of how you'll look someday."

"While you'll have your bright red hair."

"Yes." Her lips quivered. "My eldest granddaughter thinks it grew this color."

"And so it did."

"What do we do now, James?"

The long pin securing her hat slid free. "We wait in our home, Frances."

A small fire snapped inside the grate.

She relaxed her head against leather and closed her eyes at the familiar stretch of warm fingers. "Your wig smells."

"It should," James said, leaning his head back against hers. "It's been dead for over a hundred years."

Opening her eyes, Frances touched a gray curl. "You can't afford a new one?"

"I'll have you know, *madame*, that wigs that belonged to famous barristers are highly valued."

She studied his closed lashes and the fringe of shadow they created. "This wig belonged to a famous barrister?"

"To my grandfather twice removed."

Gently she touched the fan of darkness. "He was famous?"

James held still for her exploration. "Quite."

"Will you meet my family?"

He opened his eyes and turned his head to catch her gaze. The hazel eyes were cool. "Win or lose, Frances?"

Winning suddenly did not seem at all important. "Yes."

Liquid glistened inside his eyes. "I would be honored to meet your family."

"Will you introduce me to your family?" she asked over the knot inside her throat.

James closed his eyes and turned his head toward the fire. "Certainly."

"Was it illegal, what you and Mr. Lodoun did?"

"Some might think so."

"What will happen to Mr. Lodoun?"

"He will continue the law, as I do."

But he would not have a woman to love, as James did.

The soft knock shook Frances. Tension coiled inside her, tighter than a wire bustle. She secured her hat while James briefly conferred with his clerk.

"Ready, Frances?"

No.

"Yes."

Tensely she waited in the dock, fingers clutching her reticule, her entire being focused on James and her son. David's face was vulnerable, as it had been when he was a child. James's face was impassive, as she suspected it would always be, no matter that tears might glitter in his eyes.

Suddenly the hazel eyes staring up at her blazed in triumph.

Frances realized she had not heard the verdict. The look in James's eyes told her everything she needed to know.

Frenzied shouts and applause broke through the courtroom: there were no jeers.

Frances was abruptly riveted by the sight of six women and five men: the members of the Men and Women's Club—flanking John Nickols's chair on either side—stood in the back of the gallery, clapping.

"Mama?" Frances stared up at her son; tears streamed down his face, little Davie who liked his boats. Warm arms wrapped around her. "I love you, Mama."

Without warning, a bouquet of familiar scents surrounded her: David, her firstborn; Helen, her second born; Prudence, her third born, Abigail, her fourth born and Timothy, her baby.

A man stood in the white paneled doorway: Avery Tristan, his face alight with victory. Standing in front of him was a petite woman; she held back, uncertain.

It dawned on Frances that James had instructed the clerk to bring her family to her.

She held out her hand to Margaret, her first daughter-in-law, a wise woman.

Hazel eyes drew her gaze downward.

Win or lose, she had promised James.

Frances suddenly laughed out loud from sheer joy.

Winning was so much better than losing.